e7

LUCK BE A LADY

Also by Anna King

LIFE IS JUST A BOWL OF CHERRIES
RUBY CHADWICK
A HANDFUL OF SOVEREIGNS
BOW BELLES
PALACE OF TEARS
FRANKIE'S MANOR
FUR COAT, NO KNICKERS

LUCK BE
A LADY

Anna King

LITTLE, BROWN AND COMPANY

A *Little, Brown* Book

First published in Great Britain in 2001
by Little, Brown and Company

A CIP catalogue record for this book
is available from the British Library.

ISBN 0 316 85175 2

Typeset by Palimpsest Book Production Limited
Polmont, Stirlingshire
Printed and bound in Great Britain by
Clays Ltd, St Ives plc

Little, Brown and Company (UK)
Brettenham House
Lancaster Place
London WC2E 7EN

In loving memory of my sister,
Barbara Masterson.

I would like to thank the staff and carers at
Farmfield Hospital for the love and dedication
they showed towards Barbara; as do all the family.
We are all very grateful for the joy and affection
you brought into Barbara's life.

My thanks to a very special friend, Susan Bull, who nagged, pushed and threatened me with emotional blackmail if I didn't deliver a chapter to her every week. Thanks, Sue.

I'd also like to thank my children, Tony and Vicki, for creating the name of Rebecca Bradford. They would prefer money, but they will have to make do with my thanks.

CHAPTER ONE

Rebecca Bradford walked from the scullery into the front room carrying a steaming mug of tea and a small plate of digestive biscuits, then paused, her eyes looking longingly at the comfortable armchair drawn up by the fire, her body feeling the softness of the worn, sagging chair, then, sighing, she opted for one of the four hard-backed chairs tucked neatly under the dining table. Dunking one of the biscuits into the mug, she ate the softened digestive with relish, realising just how hungry she was. Immersing the last half of her biscuit, she muttered a soft 'damn' as the biscuit dropped into the tea. Scooping the soggy mess out of the mug with a spoon, she laid it on the side of the plate, wondering why it was that she couldn't eat a dry biscuit, yet couldn't eat it once it had been dropped into her tea.

Resisting the impulse to fetch another one, she removed the last remnants of the broken biscuit from her mug, drank the remainder of the tea, picked up the mug and plate, and was making her way back to the scullery when her eye once again caught sight of the armchair by the fire. Dithering with her conscience, she went over in her mind the work she had already done that day and the jobs that still needed doing. Being a Friday, the bulk of the weekly housework had been done, until Monday, when she would start all over again. There was a clothesline full of washing drying in the cold October wind out in the back yard, the house was sparkling, and the lamb stew for dinner was simmering away nicely on the stove, so why shouldn't she have ten minutes' rest? Her conscience eased somewhat, she was across the room and ensconced in her favourite armchair before she could change her mind. Raising her eyes to the carriage clock on the mantelpiece, she saw it was just on three o'clock; plenty of time for a bit of a rest before taking her cousin Maude her afternoon cup of tea in bed before bringing in the washing.

Easing off her slippers, she tucked her legs under her bottom, thinking that if she was going to have a rest, she might as well do it in comfort. Gazing into the glowing fire, Rebecca let her thoughts roam free, travelling down the years, glad that her memories could be recalled now without the heartbreak which had accompanied them for so many years.

Yesterday, 10 October 1912, had been the fifth anniversary of the death of her parents and two younger brothers – all four of them taken by an outbreak of smallpox in the small town of Frinton in

Essex that had been their home since birth. Why she, Rebecca, her elder brother Phil and her sister Amy, the youngest child, should have escaped the deadly disease remained a mystery. The priest who had resided over the funerals had solemnly announced it was God's will and not to be questioned by mere mortals. But Rebecca, then fourteen, had not only dared to question God's will, but had screamed her defiance against the Almighty's haphazard disregard for human life, shocking the parish priest into momentary silence, a state of shock that had been very brief. Rebecca smiled wanly into the fire as she recalled the red-faced priest's outrage as he had ordered her to get down on her knees and pray for forgiveness. But the young girl, instead of being brought low in the face of the priest's murderous countenance, had refused to be cowed in the presence of such revered authority, continuing her tirade until she was dragged away to her room by an embarrassed Phil, who now saw himself as head of his depleted family, and therefore accountable for his sister's outburst. Rebecca had never forgotten her brother's actions; even now, years later, she still harboured a small degree of resentment against him.

Being the eldest, Phil, to Rebecca's mind, should have stood by her, comforted her and protected her from the priest's wrath, but Phil, then seventeen, had been a weak youth, easily intimidated and terrified by any form of authority. Now, five years on, her brother was still the same – the weak youth had grown into a weak man. If Phil had been made of sterner stuff, they wouldn't have had to take the offer of help from Richard Fisher, a distant cousin of their late father. Feeling the old resentments stirring in her body, Rebecca forced herself to relax. It wasn't Phil's fault he was the way he was, nor could the past be changed, so it was no good rehashing past events, it was the future that counted – still . . . !

Shrugging her shoulders, she put her brother from her thoughts and let her mind return to the events that had transpired after the funerals. The turn-out had brought together family members none of them had seen for years. In fact there were a few the three children had never clapped eyes on in their lives. One of these relatives had been Richard Fisher, an overweight, over-familiar man Rebecca had disliked on sight. Not so her brother, who had remained in deep conversation with the pot-bellied man, both of whom had continually darted furtive glances in her direction. When the last of the mourners had departed, Phil, his face and bearing proclaiming his guilt and shame, but still desperately trying to appear the man of the house, had informed his younger sisters that their cousin Richard had kindly offered them all a home in the East End of London, miles away from their home and environment in Kent. Rebecca had listened in sheer horror at the unexpected turn of events. The thought of leaving their home had never occurred to her; not when she had an elder brother in a steady job at the local factory. She had assumed that Phil would take care of herself and Amy, and life would go on as before, as far as schooling and day-to-day

4

existence were concerned. Amy, at the tender age of ten, had been totally bewildered. The shock of losing both beloved parents and two brothers in such a short space of time had left her in a highly emotional state of mind. The small girl had loved both parents, but had utterly adored her father, William – a quiet, shy man whom Amy had always been able to twist around her little finger – and, like most children, had made full use of her power. Now, with her father gone, Amy had transferred her allegiance to her big brother, desperate to continue to keep a male figure at the centre of her crumpled world. But Phil was no William Bradford, whose outward shyness had hidden a strong character and sharp wit, attributes Phil had not inherited. Fortunately, Amy had been too young to notice her brother's inadequacies, needing only a man's presence to cling to.

Being of stronger character than her brother, Rebecca might have worn him down and shamed him into staying where they were and providing for them. But Richard Fisher had been a determined man, and Rebecca, as forceful as her personality was, had been swept along with his plans to rehouse them. In less than two weeks, Rebecca, Phil and Amy had been spirited away from their home and friends and ensconced in the comfortable three-bedroomed terraced house in Welbeck Road in Hackney.

On the journey to the East End, Phil had gone on and on about how lucky they were to be getting a house at a very reasonable rent, pointing out solemnly that he wouldn't have been able to keep up the mortgage on the house in Kent, and they should consider themselves fortunate that Richard Fisher had come along when he had, otherwise they would have been in dire straits before too long; and he had added that the job as assistant manager in Richard's warehouse business paid a lot more than he had been getting at the small factory in Kent. All in all, things had turned out rather well for Phil. Rebecca had listened without comment, knowing her brother's real reason for accepting Richard Fisher's offer had simply been a means of absolving himself from the responsibility of looking after his sisters single handed. She had also been highly suspicious of their newly acquainted cousin's seemingly generous offer, asking herself over and over why this man, who had never to her knowledge even visited her parents when they were alive, should be so concerned about their welfare. After all, they were strangers to him. When she had voiced her concern to Phil, he had simply shrugged her queries off, preferring, as always, to take the line of least resistance, and let others do the worrying for him.

Rebecca's mistrust had soon proved to be well founded. The house had been nice enough, and the rent half of what such property was normally leased at, but what their new benefactor hadn't mentioned was the fact that he had an invalid sister in residence; a sister who had to be looked after twenty-four hours a day. Oh, he had been clever, had Richard Fisher. For years he had been paying a fortune for two nurses to look after his bed-ridden sister around the clock, and when, at his distant cousin's funeral, he had set eyes on the strong, healthy Rebecca, his devious mind had sprung into action, for in the young girl he had found an unpaid nurse and housekeeper for his sister, leaving him free to set up residence in a smart flat in Stoke Newington and leave behind the sister he had come to despise.

Her eyes fixed absently on the fire, Rebecca gave a short, mirthless laugh. The death of her parents had been a godsend to Richard Fisher. If she had been older at the time, she would have walked out on the first day when she knew what was expected of her. But then, if she had been older, she would never have left her home in the first place. She might not have been able to keep up the mortgage on the house, but she would have found employment and somewhere for her and Amy to live in the same area. Instead fate had decreed that she should end up looking after an invalid relation, destroying all her early hopes and ambitions for her future, for she could see no end to her present life at this moment in time.

Shifting her gaze upwards, she visualised her cousin Maude lying in bed, her huge body comfortably buried under clean sheets, blankets and a thick eiderdown, her only concerns in life her food and comfort. The mental picture brought a tight grimace to Rebecca's generous mouth. Being of a kind nature, Rebecca wouldn't have minded looking after Maude, or anyone in similar difficulties. But Maude Fisher, like her brother, was a selfish, demanding individual, and had, from the very first moment of introduction, looked upon the pretty, golden-haired young girl as a servant, tolerated only to do her bidding without any thanks or appreciation for her efforts. And as the years passed, she had become more demanding, more truculent, and had even stopped making the effort to use the chamber pot by herself – a feat she was, Rebecca was sure, quite capable of. When Rebecca had first taken up the role of nursemaid, Maude had been able to walk to the indoor closet Richard had installed at considerable expense. But as she became used to Rebecca's ministrations, Maude had become lazier and lazier, until now, as Rebecca had angrily told Phil a few nights ago, Maude would have her wiping her backside for her if Rebecca had been willing – which she wasn't, and had told her cousin in no uncertain terms. The next day Maude had fouled the bed, leaving Rebecca no choice but to clean up the disgusting mess, a chore that had made her sick to her stomach for the rest of the day.

A stray piece of coal spat out of the fire onto the hearth, jerking Rebecca out of her reverie. Quickly picking up the glowing ember with the fire tongs, she threw it back into the blaze and shook her head in annoyance. Here she was, not five minutes ago, telling herself not to dwell on the past, and still she was doing just that. But she was only human, and sometimes she couldn't help herself. Sighing, she closed her eyes. She had sat down for a rest, so she might as well make the most of it. Just ten minutes and then she would get the washing in and take a cup of tea up to Maude. The next sound she heard was the patter of rain hitting the windows. With a cry of alarm, she jumped out of the chair and headed for the garden, the only thought in her mind to get in the washing she had so laboriously slaved over for most of the morning. As she almost skidded through the dining room, Maude's querulous voice floated down the stairs.

'Rebecca. Rebecca, get up here now. I need the chamber pot.'

Caught in mid-flight, Rebecca shouted back angrily, 'Well, you'll just have to hold on a bit longer. I've got to get the washing in before it gets soaked.'

'I can't wait. You get up here right now, madam, or else you'll have to clean up the mess afterwards. I'm a sick woman, I can't hold on . . .'

Her voice at screaming pitch now, Rebecca yelled back, 'Well, you'd better hold your backside together a bit longer, Maude, 'cos, I'm telling you now, you mess that bed again, and I'll leave you to lie in it until after dinner. And don't think I won't, 'cos I've just about had enough of it. Do you hear me?'

Without waiting for her cousin's reply, Rebecca rushed out into the darkening dusk of the small back garden, grabbing frantically at the piles of sheets and towels blowing in the strong October wind. The rain was coming down harder now, and Rebecca could have wept, seeing all her hard work ruined.

'Becky! Becky, you out there? Hang on, I'll give you a hand.'

Amy's young voice was like music to Rebecca's ears. Lifting her head over the bundle of washing in her arms, she saw her sister come flying through the back door and shouted, 'Careful, Amy, there's a patch of ice just . . .'

Her warning came too late. Amy, all arms and legs, had already run onto the treacherous sheet of muddy ice. The next minute she was skidding past Rebecca and down the garden path on her bottom, her high screams of laughter and fright filling the air.

The comical sight quickly restored Rebecca's natural humour, her own laughs mixing with her sister's wails. Five minutes later, wet and shivering with cold, they were both back inside the house, still laughing as they sorted through the washing.

Luckily it was only damp, and as Rebecca set up the ironing board and heated the flat iron to dry the sheets, she said jovially, 'You'd better get changed out of that dress, love, so I can put it in to soak. It's covered in mud, but, oh, you should have seen yourself sliding down the path. I haven't had such a good laugh in ages.'

As if on cue, Maude's peevish voice resounded down the stairs. 'When you two have both finished having a good laugh, maybe one of you'll help me get to me chamber pot. And a cup of tea would be nice. If it ain't too much trouble.'

Rebecca clapped a hand to her mouth. She had forgotten all about Maude. Well! So much for her desperate need for assistance earlier. Leaving the iron to heat up, she made for the stairs when Amy's hand stopped her.

'I'll see to her, Becky. I've got to go up and get changed anyway. Besides, she's always all right

with me. Must be my dazzling personality, eh!'
With a low girlish chuckle, Amy ran up the stairs,
calling out gaily, 'It's all right, Auntie Maude, I'm
coming.'

Rebecca watched Amy go, her mouth curling into
a soft smile. At fifteen, her sister was without doubt
the sweetest, most lovable person Rebecca had ever
known. She never lost her temper, was always amiable, and possessed a beautiful temperament which
Rebecca envied. Everyone loved Amy, even that old
battleaxe upstairs, and that was saying something.
The only flaw in Amy's personality was that she was
too trusting. She could never see any bad in anyone,
and although that in itself was an admirable trait,
it could also be a dangerous one, especially where
men like Richard Fisher were concerned.

Her mouth tightening, Rebecca began attacking
the mountain of washing piled on the kitchen table.
Although Amy liked everyone, it was the men in her
life that she gravitated to more than the women. It
was as if, even after all these years, Amy was still
looking for a father figure. Affectionate by nature,
Amy was always cuddling and hanging onto Phil
every chance she got, which was fine, he was her
brother after all. But Richard – Rebecca would never
call him Uncle, any more than she would call Maude
Auntie – was, to her mind, a slimy individual. But
as usual, Amy could see no wrong in him. Yet
every time Rebecca saw Amy sitting curled up on
the couch with him, or throwing her arms around
his neck in greeting, her stomach turned over. More
than once she had detected a look in the man's eyes

11

that was anything but fatherly. For that reason, she would never leave the two of them alone together. She had voiced her concerns to Phil, but of course it had been a waste of time. Phil had a cushy life now, thanks to his cousin, who had supplied him with a job and a roof over his head, and there was no way he was going to take the chance of rocking the boat, not even at the expense of his little sister's safety.

Banging the iron down, Rebecca folded a sheet, and placed the next one on the ironing board. Her brother was gutless, always had been and always would be. He hadn't an ounce of gumption in him, and though Rebecca loved him as a brother, she despised him as a man. If it were up to her, she would leave this house and find a job and somewhere to live for herself and Amy, but Amy was happy here. She had her job in a small café just ten minutes' walk away, where she worked different shifts, often, like today, finishing early if she worked her lunch break, and she was happy in her work. Amy was a creature of habit, as their mother had been. She hated change of any kind, and the one time Rebecca had suggested moving out and finding a place of their own, Amy had cried tears of bewilderment, asking a torrent of questions between each sob, until Rebecca had finally had to drop the idea. Of course, that had been a few years ago and, if Rebecca was truthful, she herself didn't like change much either. She just got so fed up sometimes.

'Auntie Maude wants to know why she can smell stew cooking on a Friday night, and it had better not be because Phil isn't bringing home fish and chips, 'cos she's been looking forward to a nice bit of haddock all day.' Amy came laughing into the room, her cheeks flushed as she gave a good imitation of her cousin's voice.

Putting the last of the washing to one side, Rebecca glanced at the clock, surprised to see it was already getting on for six o'clock, and smiled wanly. 'It's just a precaution, you know . . . Just in case . . .'

Amy's smile wavered as the implication of her sister's words sank in, remembering last week when Phil had come home late, all shame-faced apologies as to why he hadn't brought their supper home with him as he had promised. It hadn't been the first time he had let them down on their Friday treat, but he had promised her faithfully this morning, as they had set off for work together, that he wouldn't let it happen again, and this she tried to convey to her elder sister as she began to set the table, chattering all the while. 'Well, we'll have to have it reheated for tomorrow, Becky, 'cos Phil'll be bringing home the supper tonight, just like he normally does and—'

'Like he normally does if his horse wins, you mean, Amy.' The words were out before Rebecca could stop them, and when she saw the look of distress fill the blue eyes set in the lovely heart-shaped face, and the way Amy's long shiny blonde hair shook in denial before lowering her head, Rebecca felt a stab of shame tear through her body. Oh, she shouldn't have said that, it had been uncalled for. Amy knew only too well her brother's addiction to betting, yet still she never gave up her faith in him, no matter how many promises he broke.

13

But then, Amy had a nice nature. Unlike you, you miserable old cow! Rebecca reprimanded herself harshly. Briskly now, she helped Amy set the table, and was putting the large plate of bread and butter in the middle when the front door opened, the sound bringing a rush of apprehension to both girls' stomachs. Then they breathed freely as Phil bounced into the room, bringing with him the unmistakable aroma of freshly cooked fish and chips.

'Come on, girls, look lively. I've had to queue for nearly half an hour for this lot. We all thought old Fred had gone down the Thames to catch them himself, he was that long.' Taking a mug of piping hot tea from a grinning Amy, he took a deep gulp, then sniffed the air suspiciously, his smile swiftly replaced by a grimace of displeasure. 'I see the old stew was on standby. You don't have much faith in me, do you, Becks?'

Busily laying Maude's tray, Rebecca kept her face averted from her brother's accusing glance, warning herself to keep the peace for Amy's sake. She said lightly, 'Of course I do, Phil. As much faith as you have in your four-legged friends.' She smiled disarmingly at her brother. 'Now, I'd better get this upstairs before Maude starts yelling for her . . .'

The tension eased as they all grinned and said together, 'Nice bit of 'addock.'

With the united laughter ringing around the house, peace was once again restored. And when, after a pleasant evening of playing cards and chatting amiably, Rebecca retired for the night, her last drowsy thought was that if only every night

14

could be like this one, then life would be more bearable.

Downstairs, Phil Bradford sat sprawled in front of the dying fire, his blunt, attractive features set in lines of deep contemplation as he thought back over the events of the day. By Christ! That had been a close shave and no mistake. If that last nag hadn't romped home . . . A deep shudder coursed through his large-set frame. It didn't bear thinking about. Leaning forward, he ran his fingers through his thick, black hair in agitation, his dark brown eyes wide with undisguised relief that, once again, he had been lucky. But his luck couldn't hold out forever. Prodding at a glowing ember with the poker, his thoughts whirled round his head. As it was, he had been able to pay off what he owed at the bookies, and still had a few quid left over. Oh, and he mustn't forget about the poxy fish and chips, must he? Dear me, no. Not with Saint Rebecca waiting for him to come home empty handed, with her never-ending pot of blasted lamb stew simmering away in the background to remind him exactly what she expected of him. Well! He had spiked her guns tonight, hadn't he?

The satisfied smirk slipped from his face as he thought of his sister, his conscience digging at him sharply. He wasn't being fair, and he knew it. It was little enough that his sisters asked of him, and he knew, deep down, that without Rebecca's strength he would be lost – they all would. Throwing back the last of his drink, Phil stood up, then leant his arm on the mantelpiece and stared at his reflection in the oval mirror. His face seemed to leap and dance back at him as the last of the embers burnt down, and then the room plunged into total darkness. Shivering, Phil lit a candle and made his way to his room, promising himself that tomorrow would be different. Tomorrow he would be more sensible and only have a small bet. Just the one. And even as his mind formed the thoughts, he knew that the only person he was lying to was himself.

CHAPTER TWO

Saturday morning down any market in the East End was always busy, and Roman Road in Bow was no exception. Hemmed in on all sides, Rebecca and Amy strolled aimlessly among the stalls, stopping to look now and then when something on a particular stall caught their eye. The weekend shopping hung in wire bags by the girls' sides. That chore out of the way, they were now enjoying what Rebecca termed 'window shopping'.

'Here, look, Becky. What about this?' Amy had dropped her bags and stopped by a clothes stall, her mittened hands holding up a red woollen skirt. Shifting the heavy bags she also held, Rebecca stopped to look at the skirt warily. It had definitely seen better days, but Amy, bless her, never had had much dress sense.

'I don't think so, love,' she warned hesitantly, but Amy had already been pounced upon by the eager stall holder.

'Lovely bit of stuff, that, darlin'. Look a treat on yer, that would . . . 'Ere, 'ow abaht this ter go with it?' To Rebecca's horror, the grinning man delved into the mass of assorted clothing and pulled out a gaudy pink and gold lace blouse. Holding it up against the smiling Amy, he declared loudly. 'Well, will yer look at that. Goes wiv that skirt like they was made fer each other.' Giving Amy a sly nudge, he winked, 'Have all the boys chasing yer down the streets in those, yer will.'

'All the dogs, more likely – or worse still, the law,' Rebecca muttered beneath her breath. Out loud she said brightly, 'I don't think so, thanks all the same. Come on, Amy.' But Amy refused to budge.

'How much are they?' she asked, her eyes lovingly roaming over the hideous garments.

Sensing a potential buyer, the stall holder stepped back, scratched his head as if thinking, then declared, 'Aw, go on, then. Two bob fer the both of them, an' a bleedin' bargain yer gettin', an' all.'

Rebecca groaned inwardly. Up until Amy had started work, she had been able to select her sister's clothes, but now that Amy was earning, she had the right to spend her money as she saw fit. Now she waited with baited breath as Amy hesitated, pulling the garments this way then that, until she said, 'I'm not that keen on the blouse, but I'll have the skirt. How much will that be?'

Reluctantly giving up on the sale of the blouse, the stall holder said gruffly, 'Give us a tanner, an' it's yours.'

Amy delved into her purse happily, her eyes

18

straying back to the garish red skirt, then she frowned. 'Excuse me, but there's a hole in it. Look, just there.' She pointed to a tiny hole near the hem of the skirt.

The trader gaped at her in disbelief, then with a roar he snatched back the skirt, crying, 'Yer 'aving a laugh, ain't yer? What d'yer expect fer a tanner, somefink straight from 'Arrod's. Go on, piss orf, yer cheeky cow, wasting me time like that.'

Genuinely mystified by the trader's reaction, Amy began to argue, 'But I didn't mean any harm, only it isn't much good if it's got a hole in it, is it . . .'

Stifling a laugh, Rebecca pulled the protesting Amy away from the glowering trader. 'Come away, Amy. You're making a show of yourself.' Still chuckling, Rebecca dragged her sister along the packed market road, uttering apologies as they inadvertently shoved other shoppers aside.

Her arms aching, Rebecca stopped for a moment to lay her shopping bags on the pavement, her eyes looking out for the tram. Now that the morning's expedition was out of the way, she wanted to get home. Beside her, Amy was also looking tired and fed up, her mind still on the red skirt that had been denied her.

Seeing the woeful expression on her sister's face, Rebecca smiled fondly, 'Come on, love. Let's get this lot home. Maybe you can get something else next week.'

Amy smiled and shrugged her shoulders wistfully. 'I know, Becky. But I did like that skirt, and I could have mended the hole. If it's still there next

Saturday, I'll get it.' Cheered by the thought, Amy perked up, her face breaking into a wide smile.

It was as they were passing a three-storey house on the corner by the tram stop that a shabbily dressed man pushed himself from the doorway, directly into the girls' path. Startled, they both stopped dead in their tracks.

''Ello, girls. Need any 'elp wiv yer bags?' The man was grinning, his eyes raking over both girls, eyes that held a look of malevolence. Automatically, Rebecca stepped in front of Amy; the protective gesture was not lost on the dishevelled man. Baring blackened teeth, he grinned mockingly. 'It's all right, girls. I ain't gonna 'urt yer. I just wanna see what yer've got in them bags. I'm sure two nice girls like you could spare some grub fer a hungry man.'

Her heart beating faster, Rebecca stared back at the man, her face betraying no sign of any fear. Behind her Amy whispered fearfully, 'Becky . . .', the tremor in her young sister's voice giving Rebecca added strength.

Drawing her shoulders back, Rebecca looked at the menacing figure barring their path and said evenly, 'Get out of our way before I call for help. There are plenty of constables nearby, so do as I ask before you get yourself into trouble.' She stared hard at the man, her mind praying for a policeman to appear. They were usually in abundance on a Saturday morning, on the look-out for pickpockets, but, of course, when you wanted one they were nowhere to be seen. As if reading her mind, the man moved closer, his foul breath wafting in Rebecca's face.

'Now, that ain't nice, darlin'. Besides, I can't see any coppers, can you? An' if there was any, me mates would soon let me know.' His eyes shifted over Rebecca's head. Instinctively she looked over her shoulder, her heart leaping in fright as two more men appeared from a nearby alley. Following her stare, Amy gave a startled shriek of fright as the men moved forward, blocking any chance of escape. Dropping her bags, she grabbed hold of Rebecca's arm, her blue eyes filled with terror.

'Becky . . . Becky, give them the shopping, please . . . I'm frightened.'

Rebecca too was becoming increasingly alarmed. It seemed as if the busy street had suddenly emptied, leaving them at the mercy of these dangerous-looking men. The sensible thing to do would be to hand over their bags, but her inbred strength of character baulked at the thought of giving in to these thugs. However, she had Amy to think of. Her fear forgotten, she threw the bags at the man's feet, her body seething with rage at being bested. 'Here, you miserable little creature. Take them, and I hope the food chokes you and your friends.'

The contempt in Rebecca's voice brought a look of fury to the man's filthy face. Gathering the spittle in his mouth he spat at Rebecca's feet. 'Yer shouldn't 'ave said that, girlie. I don't like being spoken ter like a piece of dirt. Just fer that, I'll take yer purses as well . . . An' maybe 'ave a bit of fun wiv the pair of yer.'

Rebecca's face blanched as the full realisation of the man's words struck home. Before she could utter another word, the man called to his friends, 'Quick,

21

lads. Get 'em down the alley.' Like lightning, the other two men sprang forward and grabbed Amy around the waist, one of the men planting a filthy hand over the terrified girl's mouth before she could scream. Stung into life, Rebecca tried to go to Amy's rescue, but a vicious lock on her arm prevented her from moving. Then the man's breath was against her cheek, the smell making her gag.

'Turn yer nose up at me, would yer, yer stuck up bitch. Well yer won't be so high an' mighty once I've finished wiv yer.'

Almost fainting with fright, Rebecca tried to gather her wits about her. Her eyes darted up and down the street. This couldn't be happening, not in broad daylight. Where was everyone? But the three men had planned their attack well. It wasn't the first time they had accosted women coming from the market, and although to both girls the episode seemed to have been going on for hours, in fact it had been only a few minutes since they had been waylaid.

Struggling wildly, Rebecca opened her mouth to scream, a scream that was never uttered as a hard fist slammed into the side of her face. For a few seconds, her head seemed to explode from the brutal blow, then her mind cleared. Sick with fear and pain, she twisted in the man's grasp and with her free hand raked the side of his face with her nails. Caught by surprise, the man uttered a string of vile oaths and staggered back. Acting from sheer preservation, and fear for Amy, Rebecca picked up one of the heavy bags and, with a strength she didn't

22

know she possessed, she swung it wildly at the man's head, but the man was too quick for her. Ducking out of the way, the heavy bag missed its target, the force of the weight knocking Rebecca off balance. With a sickening thud she fell face down on the cobbled ground, the bag of groceries spilling out and scattering over the pavement. Barely conscious, she felt herself being dragged roughly along the hard cobbles. Then, as if from a great distance, she heard a man's voice shouting. The cruel arms that had encircled her fell away and dimly she heard the sounds of a scuffle, then more shouting and cursing as she closed her eyes and prayed. Suddenly the street was alive with people and when a strong arm came around her shoulders she flinched, her hands coming up to fight off the man who was holding her.

'It's all right. It's all right, you're safe now, you're safe.'

Ceasing her struggles, she looked up warily. Staring down at her were a pair of deep brown eyes filled with concern.

'Look, don't move for a minute. Get your breath back first.'

Disoriented, Rebecca nodded. Then, as if being snapped out of a bad dream, she cried out, 'My sister. Where's my sister? Is she all right?'

The strong arm helped her shakily to her feet and a calm, deep voice said soothingly, 'She's fine, don't worry, she's being taken care of, look.'

Still trembling, Rebecca turned to where the man was pointing and saw Amy sitting on the ground, wrapped in a blanket and being fussed over by two middle-aged women.

The relief at seeing Amy safe and well, and knowing their nightmare ordeal was over brought a feeling of faintness over Rebecca's bruised body. If it hadn't been for the support of the stranger's arms, she would have slid back onto the dirty ground. Running her tongue over her dry lips, she winced, then gingerly touched her mouth where the would-be thief had dealt her the savage blow that had nearly robbed her of her senses. A large white handkerchief was put into her hands. Shyly she glanced back at the man by her side and tried to smile, then winced again at the effort.

'Thank you, sir. You're very kind. I don't know what we'd have done if you hadn't come along when you did . . . I . . .' To her horror and shame she began to cry, and was immediately surrounded by a small group of women, all of them fussing and tutting over the dreadful episode that had just taken place.

'They oughta be strung up by the balls, the bastards.'

'Nah, that's too good fer the likes of that riff-raff,' shouted another. 'Cut their balls off, I say. They wouldn't be able to hurt any other woman then, would they?'

Still unable to take in what had happened, Rebecca looked around her, a sob intermixed with a smothered laugh escaping her bruised lips as she saw the three men who had attacked her and Amy now surrounded by another group of women armed with wooden rolling pins and heavy pans, the said objects raining

24

down blows on the men as they cursed while trying to escape the wrath of the East End women, not known for their gentleness at the best of times.

'Here, take my arm. I live in that building.' The well-dressed man pointed with his walking cane to the building where Rebecca and Amy had been accosted. 'Please, let me take you to my house-keeper. She's very good in a crisis, and I'm sure you and your sister could do with a strong cup of tea and a rest after what you've been through.'

Her mind clearing, Rebecca shook her head, ignoring the flash of pain that darted across her temples. Now that the awful ordeal was over she just wanted to get her and Amy safely home.

Through trembling lips she answered softly, 'Thank you once again, sir, for all your help, but I'd rather get my sister home. She's only fifteen and she's had a terrible shock.'

The rugged face staring down into hers smiled gently. 'I think your sister isn't the only one who's had a shock. Now, why don't you be sensible and let me help. There's no way I'm going to let you travel home the state you're in. When you've rested I'll drive you both home in my carriage.' When Rebecca still hesitated, the smiling man added, 'If not for your own sake then for your sister's.'

An old woman shambled up beside them, her thin lips parted into a toothless smile of concern. 'C'mon, love. Mr Jackson's right. Yer poor sister can hardly stand, an' yer don't look much better yerself.'

Knowing the man and woman were right, Rebecca nodded tiredly, but when she felt the tears again beginning to well up behind her eyes she quickly lowered her head. She couldn't remember crying since her parents' and brothers' deaths, and although she had good reason to shed a few tears now, she couldn't bear to let strangers see her cry, no matter how kind they were. But her efforts were in vain.

'That's it, love, you 'ave a good cry,' the old woman cooed maternally. 'It'll do yer the world of good. It's all very well trying ter be brave, but yer'll only do yerself more harm than good if yer try ter bottle it up.'

Devoid of all resistance now, Rebecca let herself be led away, thankful to have a strong body to lean against and grateful for the muscular arms holding her tight. Behind her, a crying, trembling Amy was also being helped along by two women, their arms wrapped protectively around her small body. At the entrance to the three-storey building, the man stopped and turned to the old woman. Vaguely Rebecca saw him dip his hand into his pocket and extract a shiny coin, placing it into the kindly woman's grubby hand.

'Oh, no, Mr Jackson. I can't take yer money, I ain't done nothing ter deserve it.' All the same, her hand had tightened around the coin, a look of profound relief crossing her wrinkled face.

'Take it, Flo, and buy yourself a hot dinner. Just don't let that no-good husband of yours get his hands on it, else he'll be straight down the pub and you won't see a penny of it. Promise me now.'

The woman pulled a tattered black shawl tighter across her scrawny chest and smiled ruefully. 'Don't worry, Mr Jackson. That old bastard ain't getting his 'ands on this.' Her voice, now holding a tremor, added softly, 'Gawd bless yer, Mr Jackson. I was at me wits' end just a few minutes ago. The rent man's due, there ain't a bit of food in the 'ouse, an' that old bastard of a 'usband of mine took me last few coppers from me purse while I was asleep an' . . .'

The man called Mr Jackson patted the old woman's shoulder, smiling sympathetically. 'You know where I live, Flo. If you're ever in trouble, come and see me – not that you will, you're too bloody proud. Look. I'll ask around and see if I can find you some part-time work. I've got a few people who owe me favours, I'll see what I can do.'

Dimly Rebecca listened, wishing they would conclude their conversation quickly. She was feeling hot and giddy, and was blinking her eyes and shaking her head in an effort to stay conscious. The ordeal she had suffered was finally taking its toll. Looking over her shoulder to where Amy was being supported by the two women, her pretty face blotched with tears, her tiny body still trembling with fear, Rebecca thought of what could have happened to her beloved sister if this kindly man and the women from the market hadn't come along when they had, and the prospect was so horrifying she felt sick. Her head began to swim alarmingly, then her vision blurred as darkness swept over her. She tried valiantly to shake off the unfamiliar sensation but it was no use. The last words she heard were Amy screaming her name, and the old woman crying out, 'Oh, the poor little cow, she's . . .' Then nothing but blissful, oblivious darkness.

CHAPTER THREE

'Well I've done all I can, Jimmy. What the two young women need now is to go home and let their parents take care of them. At the risk of stating the obvious, they've both had a severe shock. Nasty piece of business all round, poor little things. Anyway, I'll be off now, Jimmy. Like I said, there's nothing else I can do, so I'll leave them in your capable hands.' The tall, well-dressed man picked up his black Gladstone bag and top hat and moved towards the door. 'I've left a bottle of medicine on the sideboard. It's a mild sedative, just in case they need a little extra to what I've already given them. But I doubt if they'll need more than another dose tonight. The young are very resilient. Once they've got over the shock of being attacked, they'll probably be too angry to waste time brooding.'

The two men walked to the door and shook hands.

'Are we still on for the game tonight, Tom?'

The doctor smiled, then gave a small chuckle. 'You won't be happy until you've bankrupted me, will you, Jimmy? Eight o'clock all right?'

'That'll be fine, Tom. See you later . . . And, Tom, thanks.'

'You won't be thanking me when you get my bill, it's the only time I ever get any money out of you.'

Behind the two men, Rebecca lay motionless on the long, comfortable sofa. Her eyes were closed, but her mind was beginning to clear, and the event that had occurred only a short while ago replayed itself over in her mind. Her body gave an involuntary jerk as she recalled the awful experience, and for a brief moment she wondered if she had dreamt the whole sordid affair, so unreal did it seem now she and Amy were safely settled in this warm, comfortable house. With a great deal of effort, she struggled to open her eyes, then sighed with relief at the sight of Amy curled up on a matching sofa to the one she was lying on, apparently dead to the world. Rebecca closed her eyes again, wanting to remain in this blissful state of peace and tranquillity, but her inner strength wouldn't allow her to luxuriate in her present form of mind. Gathering all her willpower, she slowly opened her eyes again and tried to sit up, only to find herself being gently but firmly laid down once more. Blinking rapidly, she tried to focus on the face that leant over hers, and found herself looking into a pair of warm brown eyes filled with genuine concern.

'Now, now, young lady, you just rest a while longer. The medicine the doctor gave you will be wearing off soon, then I'll see about getting you and your sister home. Your parents must be getting worried by now. In the meantime I'll get my housekeeper to make some hot, strong tea and—'

'We don't have any parents . . . we live with . . . with our cousin and brother . . .' Rebecca's tongue seemed to be glued to the top of her mouth. Running a dry tongue over her parched lips, she tried to continue. 'We have to get . . . get home. My cousin is bed-ridden, and . . . and one of the neigh . . . neighbours is looking after her. She'll want paying extra if . . . if we're late home, and . . .'

Strong hands pushed her back down on the soft cushions. 'Don't you worry about your neighbour, I'll see to her . . . Ah, there comes the tea.' The man smiled as a small, elderly woman came into the room carrying a tray. 'Best medicine in the world for shock, or so I'm told.' Turning to the woman behind him he said softly, 'Pour out a cup of tea, will you, Bessie, and try and wake up the girl, will you?' As the woman laid down a cup of steaming tea on the table by Rebecca's side, the man added, 'And tell Charlie to get the carriage ready when you've seen to the girl.'

The housekeeper glanced at her master and grunted amicably, 'Yes, Mr Jackson. Of course, Mr Jackson. Anything else you'd like me ter do, Mr Jackson? Stick a broom up me arse and sweep the floor while I'm at it?'

The dark-haired man laughed fondly. 'Now that you mention it, Bessie, the carpets could do with a good clean. You're getting slip shod in your old age.'

The elderly woman shot her master a withering look, but her eyes were twinkling with mirth as she replied curtly, 'I ain't too old ter give you a clip round the ear, yer sarky git.'

Rebecca listened to the genial banter in bewilderment. She didn't know much about how the other half lived, but the woman certainly didn't seem to act like Rebecca imagined a housekeeper should towards her master. As if reading her mind, the man looked at Rebecca and winked broadly.

'Don't take any notice of Bessie. She's got a heart of gold. I've known her since I was a nipper with the ars – backside hanging out of my trousers. I honestly don't know what I'd do without her, she's—'

'If yer was gonna say arse, then say it. Backside . . . Huh!'

Rebecca looked over to where the woman was gently coaxing Amy awake, and despite the trauma she'd been through, she felt her lips curving into a smile. The woman called Bessie saw the tremulous smile and grinned back.

'Yer wouldn't think it ter 'ear 'im talk, but he was brought up in the back streets of Bow. Proper little tea leaf he was an' all. An' his language – Gawd Almighty, it'd 'ave made a sailor blush, an' 'im only nine at the time. Now he's gone up in the world, he finks he's Lord Muck. But yer should 'ear him when he's in a temper. There ain't no posh talking then, I can tell yer. Effing and blinding an'—'

'All right, Bessie, that's enough,' the soft voice had hardened. 'I'm sure our guests aren't interested in my background. Leave the girl, and tell Charlie to

31

bring the carriage round now.'

The smile dropped from the elderly woman's face, her demeanour changing as she realised she'd gone too far. Propping the still drowsy Amy up onto a pile of cushions, she said quietly, 'All right, Jimmy. I'll go and get Charlie straight away.'

As she walked from the room, the man rose swiftly to his feet calling out, 'Bessie, Bessie. Hang on a minute.' But the stiff-faced woman had already left the room. Swinging around, the man dropped into the armchair facing Rebecca and smiled ruefully. 'Sorry about that. There's times I could cheerfully strangle her. But she'll make me pay for talking to her like that. Oh yes! It'll be the silent reproachful looks and my meals slammed down in front of me for days now.' He spread his arms wide and grinned. 'Bloody cantankerous old cow.' Rolling his eyes upwards he laughed out loud. 'Now you know she was right about me. I always revert to my cockney upbringing when I get in a temper. But you know what?' He leant forward. 'I'm glad I've got Bessie around. Because if ever I start getting too big for my boots, she's always there to bring me back down to earth and, as you've noticed, she doesn't mince her words.'

As she listened to the man talking, something was niggling at the back of Rebecca's mind, something that wasn't quite right. Trying to concentrate she attempted to think what it was that was troubling her. Then it came to her, and the realisation of whose house she was in brought her bolt upright.

'You're Jimmy Jackson the bookmaker, aren't you?'

The man was about to answer the question with a cheerful retort, when something about the look in the young girl's eyes stopped him. His face straight now, he said, 'Yes, I'm Jimmy Jackson, the bookie, does that trouble you? You're not one of the Salvation Army mob, are you?'

Swinging her legs over the side of the sofa, Rebecca replied stiffly, 'No, I'm not. But I do have a brother who's addicted to gambling, to the extent that some weeks he doesn't come home because he's bet and lost his entire week's wages, which in turn means the rest of us have to live on whatever my sister earns. And ten shillings a week doesn't go far when there's four mouths to feed and the rent to be paid. And guess who the runners who take his bets work for?' Rebecca's head was up, her eyes challenging him, then her gaze faltered as she saw the look of anger beginning to burn in the dark eyes.

'I'm a businessman, Miss, not a thug. Nobody forces people to place bets with my runners. It's people like your brother who seek us out, not the other way round – at least, not the people who work for me. It would be more than their jobs were worth, and they know it.' Jimmy Jackson stared back hard at the young woman, wondering why he was wasting his breath. Women like this one, glaring up at him as if he were the devil's advocate, would always put the blame of their men's shortcomings down to men like himself.

Impatiently, he tutted and turned his broad back on Rebecca, saying sharply now, 'If you and your sister are ready, I'll go and see what's keeping the carriage.' Nodding brusquely, he turned swiftly and left the room, his sudden departure leaving Rebecca feeling as if she had just lost something dear to her, and these feelings in return had her stumbling to her feet in annoyance. Embarrassed and flustered, Rebecca looked over to where Amy seemed to have fallen back to sleep.

'Amy! Amy, wake up, love. We're going home. Come on now . . .' Rebecca added hastily, as her sister showed no signs of moving from the comfortable confines of the couch. 'Amy! I said we're going. Hurry up, for goodness' sake. I don't want to leave Mrs Gates with Maude too long.'

Amy, her eyes still filled with drowsiness from the sedative she had been given earlier, answered softly, 'I'm ready, Becky, I'm ready. I just feel a bit tired, that's all.' A wide yawn split her young face as if to give evidence to her words, then she grinned sheepishly. 'Sorry, Becks, I feel I could go to sleep on a clothesline at the minute.' Slipping her slim legs to the floor, Amy got unsteadily to her feet. Then, her eyes wary, she asked hesitantly, 'Are we walking home, Becky? Only I still feel a bit groggy and . . .'

Rebecca was quick to see the look of fear that crossed Amy's face and swiftly dropped the notion of refusing the offer of a lift home from Jimmy Jackson. Anyway, her own feelings concerning the man's business must be put aside so she could thank him properly for all his kindness. After all, he had saved her and Amy from a very unpleasant experience, an experience that could have ended in tragedy if he hadn't intervened when he had.

Helping Amy to the door, Rebecca reassured her sister quickly, 'No, it's all right, love. Mr Jackson has kindly offered us a lift home. Can you make it downstairs?' Rebecca's eyebrows furrowed in concern at the sight of Amy's pallid face.

Bravely attempting a smile, Amy answered, 'Of course I can. I told you, I'm just feeling a bit wobbly. I'll be fine once I get home.'

Their arms around each other, the two girls were about to leave the room when Bessie, her lined face creased further with concern, appeared out of nowhere, her strident voice filling the air. ''Ere, where you two off to? Hang on while I get some help.' Swirling around she looked at Rebecca and demanded, 'An' where's his nibs gorn ter? He was suppose ter be looking after the two of yer.'

Rebecca forced a smile to her face. 'It's all right, really, Mrs . . . um . . .'

'Bessie, love. Me name's Bessie. We don't stand on ceremony around 'ere.'

Finding herself at a disadvantage, Rebecca smiled back weakly. She wasn't very good at first names, at least not until she had known the person concerned for some time . . . Still . . .

'Thank you, Bessie, but like I said, we're fine. If you'd be good enough to show the way, we'd be very grateful. Also I, that is, we, would like to thank Mr Jackson for his kindness, if you could find him for us before we leave.'

The elderly woman stared at the young woman,

her quick eyes noting the high colour that was staining the pretty face and neck. Grinning knowingly, she nudged Rebecca in the side.

'Good-looking sod, ain't he? Got all the women round these parts falling over themselves to get at him. Can't blame 'em either. If I hadn't been like a mother ter him, and was thirty years younger, I'd 'ave a go meself.' She chuckled, a loud raucous laugh.

Rebecca's face tightened. 'Really, Mrs . . . I mean, Bessie. That thought had never occurred to me, I can assure you.'

But Bessie only laughed louder.

'C'mon, ducks. Let the starch outta yer drawers. There's no harm in admitting ter fancying a bloke, 'specially a bloke like my Jimmy. And don't yer worry about thanking him neither. He'd 'ave done the same for anyone. He's a good bloke, is Jimmy, one of the best.'

'He's also a bookmaker, and people like your Mr Jackson don't know the misery they can cause. Or if they do, then they don't care as long as their own pockets are kept lined by those less fortunate.'

The smile had dropped from the old woman's face, all laughter gone now as she faced this young madam who had just done the unforgivable in Bessie's book. She had slandered Jimmy's name, and nobody did that in front of Bessie Wilks. Glaring now, she poked a bony finger in a startled Rebecca's chest.

''E also 'appens ter be the man who saved you and yer sister from 'aving yer knickers pulled round yer ankles, you ungrateful little cow.'

Amy, now wide awake, started to tremble in the

face of this little woman's fury, and wondered why Becky had to go and say something like that. She was always upsetting somebody, was Becky. She didn't do it deliberately, Amy mused quietly, it was just a knack her elder sister seemed to have.

Any further altercation was stopped by the appearance of a young man, shabbily but cleanly dressed, who stuck his dark head around the door, asking cheerfully, 'You ladies ready ter go? Mr Jackson's waiting fer yer both downstairs . . . All right, Bessie?' he inclined his head at the still glowering woman.

'Yeah, I'm fine, Charlie. Our guests were just leaving.'

Sensing the atmosphere, the young man backed from the room, his eyes quickly raking the visitors appreciatively before leaving, his heavy boots making a loud thudding noise as he ran back downstairs.

Feeling awkward and a little guilty now, Rebecca said stiffly, 'I'm sorry if I offended you. I meant no harm and . . . and I'd like to thank you again for all you've done for us today. You've been very kind.'

For an answer the elderly woman sniffed loudly and turned to Amy. 'You look after yerself, ducks, an' if you're ever passing by, drop in fer a cuppa, eh.'

'I will,' promised Amy, who then impulsively threw her arms around the elderly woman. 'And thank you so much, Bessie.'

Somewhat embarrassed by the emotional show of affection by her sister, and still feeling flustered and guilty by her attitude concerning her saviour, Rebecca quickly bundled Amy out of the door and down the stairs to the waiting carriage.

''Ello, ladies, yer carriage awaits,' the young lad Bessie had called Charlie grinned at them. Opening the door wide, he assisted Amy into the coach first then turned to Rebecca, who gratefully took his arm as he helped her up the two steps. Flopping wearily onto the plush seat beside Amy, Rebecca was about to speak when she became aware of the other occupant of the carriage. There, sitting not a foot away, was Jimmy Jackson, his rugged face impassive as he regarded his two passengers. Once again Rebecca felt the heat rise in her face at the close proximity of the man.

Wetting her lips nervously she started to say, 'There's no need for you to accompany us, Mr Jackson, we . . .'

Jimmy Jackson turned to face her, his eyes – eyes that had only a short while ago twinkled with kindness – still dark with anger.

'Don't give me any more grief. I'm seeing the pair of you safely home. After all, I don't want either of you on my conscience if anything should happen to you, not with the burden of guilt I already have to bear doing the despicable work I do.'

Her colour rising further, Rebecca was about to retort when she decided against any further comment. The man sitting opposite wasn't the kind of man you argued with. Averting her gaze, she put her arm around Amy's shoulders and prayed for the journey to end so she could get away from this stranger who had stirred feelings in her she had never experienced before.

CHAPTER FOUR

'There yer are. Gawd 'elp us, I was just about ter call the police, I was that worried . . . Oh my Gawd, what's happened ter yer?' Ada Gates stepped back in horror as she saw the bedraggled state of both young women. Then she was being moved gently to one side as a tall, broad-shouldered man, dressed in the style of the gentry, followed Rebecca and Amy into the house.

'I'm afraid your friends have had a bit of a nasty fright, love. I'm sure they'll tell you all about it after I've gone, but apart from a bad shock, they're perfectly all right, so I'll leave them in your capable hands.'

Dipping his hat to the women, he turned sharply on his heel and was about to leave when a loud, querulous voice floated down the stairs, demanding angrily, 'Where the bleeding hell have you two been until now? Get up here this minute.'

Rebecca glanced up at the ceiling, tiredly, then turned to Mrs Gates, saying wearily, 'Could you go up to Maude please, Mrs Gates, and tell her I'll be up shortly.'

Shooting a pensive look at the trio standing in the hall, Mrs Gates nodded reluctantly. She was dying to know who the gentleman was and, more importantly, what had happened to the two young women, but she did as she was bid, though she took the stairs slowly hoping to catch some snippet of conversation that would enlighten her. But here she was disappointed, for the three people remained mute until she was out of earshot.

At the same time, the door to the scullery opened to admit a irate-looking Phil.

'Thank God you're home. I've only just got in myself and Maude has been driving me mad. Where've you been? I've got to go out and . . .' Phil stopped abruptly as he saw the man standing by the front door. Immediately his demeanour altered, and the change turned Rebecca's already quivering stomach to one of nausea.

His face magically broke into a wide beam of good-natured camaraderie as Phil stepped forward, his hand outstretched. 'Mr Jackson. Oh, please, don't stand there like a stranger. Come in, come in. Can I offer you a drink of some kind?'

Jimmy Jackson looked at the fawning man with distaste, wondering fleetingly how such a strong-willed young woman could have a brother, for Jimmy assumed it was the brother, such as this one. Ignoring the outstretched hand, Jimmy looked to the two women and, his voice softer now, said kindly, 'I hope you both recover quickly from your ordeal, ladies, and if I can be of any service in the future, please don't hesitate to call on me.'

The change in the man's voice startled Rebecca. All the way home he had hardly uttered a word, and then it had been directed at Amy, who had cheerfully given their names and told this virtual stranger most of their business, much to Rebecca's annoyance at the time. Swallowing loudly, Rebecca moved towards the door.

'Thank you, Mr Jackson, and . . . and I'd just like to say how sorry I am for my earlier behaviour. I have no excuse, it was very bad manners on my part,' she smiled weakly, 'as your housekeeper informed me in no uncertain terms.'

At the friendliness in Rebecca's tone, Jimmy visibly relaxed, his rugged face creasing into the familiar smile Rebecca had first witnessed before his identity had become known to her – and her subsequent reaction to the news.

Phil watched the scene, his mind racing furiously. Jimmy Jackson was renowned as a lady killer, and the way he was looking at Rebecca left Phil in no doubt that Jimmy Jackson had taken a shine to his sister. His fertile mind raced on, gathering momentum with each passing second. What if they got together! Lord, what a result that would be. Him, Phil Bradford, having the famous Jimmy Jackson as a brother-in-law. Desperate now to keep the well-known figure in his home, Phil bustled forward, all bonhomie and charm.

'Here, here, come in, please. Let me get you that drink I offered, it's the least I can do after you've gone to the trouble of bringing my sisters home.' Smiling widely, Phil pulled Rebecca and Amy to him, an arm around each of their shoulders, conveying an attitude of brotherly love and concern. 'I don't know what I'd do without my little sisters.'

Jimmy's eyes hardened. He could read Phil Bradford like a book, which wasn't difficult with a man such as the one standing in front of him. Oh, yes, he could imagine exactly what Bradford was thinking. He was obviously hoping to get his bookmaker off with his sister, and by doing so reap in family-connected favours. Well, if that was his intention then the man was going to be sorely disappointed. After a miserable childhood watching his parents rolling home drunk every night and beating seven bells out of each other, he had been put off marriage for life, until . . . Quickly shutting down on painful memories, Jimmy made to take his leave. Not that the golden-haired girl wasn't attractive enough – she was, and in different circumstances he would probably have been more than interested. But Jimmy preferred his women docile with not too much between their ears, and Rebecca Bradford certainly didn't come into that category.

The smile dropped from his face. His features set into hard lines, and his eyes steely he said curtly, 'I think you'd be better off offering your sisters a drink, they need it more than I do at the moment, or haven't you noticed the state they're both in? I'd've thought that the welfare of a man's younger sisters would take priority over everything else.' The look of contempt on Jimmy Jackson's face caused Phil's head to snap back on his shoulders. Then, for the first time since they'd walked in the door, Phil took a closer look at his sisters, noting their dishevelled clothing and pale faces, especially Becky, who had a livid bruise on the side of her cheek.

Crying out in sudden genuine alarm, Phil asked frantically, 'Bloody hell! What happened to you? Have you been attacked?'

Jimmy gave a low sardonic laugh. 'Well done, Mr Bradford, though it wouldn't have taken a genius to work that one out. Still, I suppose we all have our own set of priorities. But seeing as you ask, your sisters were set upon by three thugs. Luckily I happened to be in the right place at the right time and was able to frighten them off. I'm only sorry I couldn't have appeared sooner and saved your sisters from a very nasty ordeal.'

A stab of guilt and panic coursed through Phil's body as the full realisation of the danger his sisters had been in hit him hard. For though he was essentially a selfish and weak man, he genuinely loved his sisters and he felt a surge of rage towards the unknown men who had attacked Becky and Amy engulf him. But when he looked once more at the muscular man eyeing him with obvious distaste, his innate nature to protect himself rose to the surface. Eager to redeem himself in Jimmy Jackson's eyes, Phil pulled Rebecca and Amy closer to his body, his face red, his eyes bulging with rage.

'The filthy bastards. Just wait until I get my hands

on them . . . And I'll find them, don't you worry. And when I do, they'll wish they'd never been born. Nobody hurts my family and gets away with it – nobody!'

Rebecca heard Phil's words and sighed tiredly. He wouldn't do anything, it was all talk and bluster. The thought of Phil scouring the streets looking for their assailants and meting out due punishment brought a giggle to her lips, the sound bordering on hysteria and desperate fatigue. Pulling away from Phil's embrace, she muttered softly, 'I'm sorry, but I'm going to have to have a lie down, and Amy too.' Taking her sister's hand, Rebecca gently led her towards the stairs, all the while talking gently to the silent girl.

Rebecca was halfway up the stairs when she stopped, turned towards the hallway and, looking directly into Jimmy's eyes, said, 'Thank you once more, Mr Jackson, from myself and Amy. I can't even begin to think what would have happened if you hadn't come along when you did.' Then she continued up the stairs, hardly able to put one foot in front of the other. She was almost at the top when she halted again. This time she directed her gaze at her brother.

'You'll have to stay in and see to Maude, Phil. I just can't cope with her right now. So wherever you were thinking of going, you'd better cancel it – see you later.'

Phil hurried to the bottom of the stairs, calling after the retreating figures, 'Hang on, Becky, I can't look after Maude. I've got an important meeting to go to . . . Becky . . . Becky . . .' But there was no answer from his sister. Maude, however, had plenty to say.

'Here! What the hell's going on down there? Becky! Amy! One of you answer me, you little cows. I want me tea, and I need to go to the bathroom.' The softer voice of Mrs Gates could faintly be heard trying to pacify the irate woman, but still Maude continued to shout, her voice filling the entire house.

Caught up in his own little world, Phil temporarily forgot about their distinguished visitor and added his voice to Maude's.

'Becky! Becky! Look, come back down a minute. I told you, I have to go out. You're not leaving me with Maude all evening. I—'

'Leave it! If you haven't the decency to stay in, then I will.'

Startled, Phil spun around, his cheeks turning bright red at the contempt in Jimmy Jackson's voice.

Desperate to explain himself, he spluttered wildly, 'It's not like it sounds, Mr Jackson. I won't be long. I mean I wouldn't leave my sisters in the state they're in for long. What kind of man do you think I am?'

The look on Jimmy's face was answer enough. 'Go on, get out, you miserable piece of shit. How two lovely girls like your sisters could have a worthless, gutless bastard like you for a brother is a mystery to me . . . Go on, get out. The very sight of you sickens me.'

His head bowed, Phil scurried past the glowering figure. Hastily plucking his heavy coat from the back of the door, Phil hurried from the house. After the door had closed behind him, Jimmy thought long and hard, then sighed. What the hell was he supposed to do now? Footsteps on the stairs brought his head up eagerly, and he was surprised to find how disappointed he was when the elderly neighbour appeared.

Ada Gates shuffled nervously at the bottom of the stairs, her eyes darting back and forth from the smartly dressed man, up to the sound of Maude's shrill voice as she continued to call out for her absent cousin. Walking forward slowly, Ada, her eyes flickering uncertainly, said quietly, 'I'm sorry, sir, but I'll 'ave ter get back home. Me son'll be 'ome soon fer his dinner. I'm ever so sorry, sir. I don't like ter leave the girls in this state, but I'll pop back later an' see how they are.'

Ada Gates was sixty-two years old, married for thirty-eight of them and widowed these past two years, and glad of the peace she was too. Yet when her tired old eyes looked into the handsome face towering above her and saw the twinkling brown eyes and roguish lips curved into a smile she felt her legs go weak at the knees – a feeling she hadn't experienced for nearly forty years.

'It's all right, love. Don't you worry about the two girls. I'll stay and see to everything until their brother gets back. Now, you get yourself off home before your son comes in shouting for his dinner . . . Oh, and, here, thanks for stopping. I'm sure the girls will be very grateful to you.'

Ada looked down at the shiny sovereign resting in the palm of her hand and gulped loudly. She never got more than sixpence for looking after Maude when both girls were out of the house. Not that she was complaining. She didn't like taking any money off Becky, but then again she couldn't afford to be too charitable, not in her circumstances. And that old cow upstairs could be a right nasty piece of work sometimes. Still, it didn't seem right somehow. Stuttering slightly, Ada muttered awkwardly, 'Fanks, sir, but . . . but I can't take all . . . all this. Not . . . not just fer sitting wiv Maude fer a few hours, but . . . but, well, fanks anyway, sir. I'll see Becky later.'

Jimmy pushed the coin back into the woman's hand, a warm glow filling his chest at the woman's honesty, especially as it was painfully obvious that she, like so many others, genuinely needed the money just to survive. Mind you, this was the second sovereign he had given away today. If he carried on like this he'd end up broke himself.

Still smiling warmly, Jimmy said, 'Take it, love. You can see I'm not short of a few bob, and you've done me a favour, so you take the money with a clear conscience.'

Still reluctant, but feeling somewhat easier in her mind, Ada wrapped her shawl around her shoulders as she prepared to leave the house.

'Fanks again, sir. I can't say it won't come in handy, 'cos it will. But, sir . . .' Ada stopped, her eyes blinking rapidly as Maude's strident voice ranted above her. 'What yer gonna do about her?' Ada jerked her thumb upwards. 'I don't like ter speak ill of anyone, but she can be a right old . . .'

47

Jimmy put his hand up and laughed.

'Don't you worry about her, love. I'll see to her. Now you get off home and I'll see you later maybe.'

As Ada left the house, Jimmy called out to Charlie, telling him to come back in a few hours, then went back inside. Taking off his coat, Jimmy wandered around the front room for a few moments, wondering how the two girls could possibly sleep through such a racket. Taking a deep breath, and wishing he had some of the sedative mixture Dr Barker had prescribed for the two young women, Jimmy walked up the stairs towards the sound of the loud voice that was now verging on the edge of hysteria.

CHAPTER FIVE

The sound of laughter woke Rebecca from a deep sleep. Momentarily disoriented, she lay still for a few moments trying to gather her thoughts. Turning her head slightly, she peered in the darkness at the clock by her bed and saw that it was just after seven o'clock. Still half asleep, she threw the quilt off and realised she was fully clothed. It was then she remembered the events of the day and for a moment she panicked. Surely she hadn't slept the clock round. If so, then who had been looking after Maude; more importantly, who was causing the laughter that had woken her? Glancing over at the single bed beside her, Rebecca saw that Amy was still fast asleep. Quickly now, she leapt from the bed, searched round the floor for her slippers and hurried from the room.

As she approached Maude's room she could hear a man's voice, then her cousin's laughter, a sound that wasn't heard very often. Puzzled, Rebecca opened the door then stopped dead in her tracks. For there, sitting by the middle-aged woman's bed, sat Jimmy Jackson, his rugged face wreathed in smiles, as was Maude's, and that sight alone rendered Rebecca speechless. In all the years she had been in this house, she couldn't remember the woman cracking a smile, let alone indulging in a good laugh.

Sensing her presence, both heads turned in her direction. Then Rebecca had the second shock of the day, for her cousin, her fat face beaming with delight, said in a voice filled with affection, 'Come in, love, come in. Oh, you poor little mite. What a thing to have happened, and in broad daylight too. What's the world coming to when two young women can't walk the street without fear of being attacked? I was just saying to Jimmy here that the scoundrels should be publicly flogged.' At the sound of Maude using the man's first name as if they were old friends, Rebecca's eyebrows rose in wry amusement. And the way Maude was looking at her with such benevolent concern brought a short burst of stifled laughter to Rebecca's lips. She must still be dreaming. It was the only rational explanation Rebecca could think of to explain the extraordinary scene she was witnessing.

Jimmy's keen eyes watched Rebecca's face. By the look of bewilderment etched on the pretty features, mirrored also in the wide blue eyes, it was obvious the young woman wasn't used to being treated with such kindness by the bed-ridden woman. Then he turned his gaze back to the bed and saw the glimpse of hostility in the older woman's eyes as she surveyed her cousin. Then, aware that Jimmy had turned his eyes on her, Maude quickly adopted the persona of the concerned relative once more. But that brief glimpse of the hard, grey eyes was enough for Jimmy to realise that things were not all they had at first seemed to be between Rebecca and her patient. A feeling of pity for the young woman standing in the doorway rose in Jimmy's chest. No wonder she had been so short with him. With a brother who gambled all his wages, and the burden of looking after the woman in the bed day and night, he could well understand her animosity towards him when she had realised who he was.

Rising from the chair he walked over to Rebecca and, gently taking her arm, said softly, 'I think a strong cup of tea is in order, Miss Bradford. If you'll show me the way to the kitchen I'll make us all some.' Leading her from the room, Jimmy turned his head back towards the bed, adding cheerfully, 'And while I'm at it, I'll make you something to eat, Miss Fisher. Better still, how about if I pop round to the chippie? I'm feeling a bit peckish myself. What do you think?'

Maude's face creased into lines of greedy anticipation at the thought of her favourite food, but anxious not to appear to be too eager she simpered fawningly, 'Oh, no, Jimmy. I couldn't put you to that trouble, you've done enough for us already. Look, why don't you come back here and keep me company? Rebecca can go; I mean, she's had a good sleep, and I'm sure she wouldn't mind, would you, love?'

Although Jimmy's face remained amiable, a cold glint came into his eyes as he surveyed the obese figure lying propped up in the large bed. 'I don't think that would be wise, Miss Fisher. After what happened today, I'm sure the last thing your cousin needs is to have to go out on the streets at this time of night.'

Maude saw the look of dislike in Jimmy's eyes and swallowed nervously. Aware she had let her true colours show and eager to ingratiate herself into this striking man's good books, she replied with empty sincerity, 'Oh, dear. What must you think of me, Jimmy? Of course you're right. When I think of what could have happened to my Rebecca, and Amy . . . Well, it makes me go cold all over.'

'Don't distress yourself, Miss Fisher. I can see how fond you are of the girls, so you can rest easy knowing she'll be staying here where she'll be safe.' Nodding his head curtly, Jimmy, still holding Rebecca's arm, left the room.

Hitching herself further up in the bed, Maude called after them, 'Thanks, Jimmy, that's a weight off my mind. And, Jimmy, never mind all that Miss Fisher stuff, my name's Maude, you—' The door closed firmly behind the couple.

Her face settling into grim lines of frustration, Maude slumped back against the pillows, cursing herself for a fool. It was true she cared what happened to Rebecca, but only from a selfish point of view. If anything happened to her cousin, then who would there be to look after her? Certainly not her brother, who had left the house with indecent haste the moment their newly found family had been installed. And she doubted very much if Richard would be prepared to fork out for a live-in nurse again. There was still Phil and Amy, but she couldn't see that selfish young man giving up his life to care for her, which left only Amy to fall back on if anything happened to Rebecca. The worried frown left her face as she thought of her youngest cousin. Amy wouldn't leave her to fend for herself. She wasn't as capable as Rebecca, of course, but she was such a pretty young girl, she wouldn't stay unattached for long. No! Rebecca was her lifeline, and now she had befriended a man like Jimmy Jackson, life could become a lot easier for all of them, and, she, Maude, would have to watch herself when he was around in future, and he would be around. She'd seen how he had looked at Rebecca, and the protective way he had led her from the room. Oh, yes, Jimmy Jackson would be around for a while. A satisfied smile tugged at her lips as she lay down and waited for her supper to arrive.

Sitting at the kitchen table, her hands wrapped gratefully around a mug of steaming tea, Rebecca shyly said to the man sitting opposite her, 'Thanks. It was good of you to stay, especially after the way I spoke to you earlier. I feel very ashamed of the way I acted and—'

Jimmy held up a warning hand.

'Don't be daft. You'd just come through a terrify-ing ordeal, it was only natural you'd want to lash out at someone. Fortunately I've a strong back; I don't get offended easily.'

Rebecca shook her head, a wan smile pulling at her lips. 'I wish I could put my rudeness down to shock, but I would have acted just the same if we'd met at a dinner party; not that I've ever been to one.' The smile wavered a little as she saw the man's gaze fixed strongly on her face. Clearing her throat, she stumbled on quickly, 'It was nothing personal, believe me. It's just that . . . Well . . .' She shrugged her shoulders tiredly. 'When you're waiting on a Friday night for the bread-winner to come home, praying and hoping that he hasn't gambled all his wages and worrying yourself sick that there'll be no housekeeping money to get you through the week, I'm afraid it can make a person very bitter. But as you pointed out earlier, no one forces people to gamble, and if my brother didn't place his bets with your runners he'd only find somebody else to do business with. He's addicted, you see, he can't help himself, but . . . but it's very hard living with a gambler. Yet when all's said and done, Phil's my brother, and I know he doesn't hurt us deliberately, he's just weak, he always has been. It doesn't stop me loving him, even though I could cheerfully strangle him at times.'

As she spoke Rebecca kept her gaze firmly on the table, afraid that this man, this kind man, should see the tears beginning to well up behind her eyes. But when a strong hand gripped hers reassuringly it was nearly the undoing of her. As if stung, she quickly pulled her hand free, stammering, 'I'd better check on Amy, she'd sleep her life away if I let her.' Deeply conscious that she was gabbling but unable to get her emotions under control, she carried on, 'When I first woke up and saw the time, I thought it was morning. Then when I heard the laughter coming from Maude's room I thought I must still be dreaming; she doesn't laugh very often and—'

She broke off suddenly. What was the matter with her? Here she was practically on the verge of telling this virtual stranger all of the family's business. Her of all people. She had never been one to gossip, or confide her personal business to anyone, but there was something about this man that loosened her tongue. If she wasn't careful she'd be crying on his shoulder next. As she stood up, Jimmy rose from his chair too, and for one awful, heart-stopping moment Rebecca had the oddest desire to throw herself into his arms. She was saved from making a spectacle of herself by a loud knocking at the front door.

'It's all right, I'll get it,' said Jimmy, 'it'll be Charlie with your supper, you sit down and rest.'

Rebecca nodded, grateful for the welcome diversion, and the chance to sit down before she fell down.

The sound of men's voices carried through into the kitchen, and when Rebecca recognised the familiar voice talking to Jimmy Jackson she let out a soft groan. Then there were loud footsteps coming nearer and, composing herself, Rebecca pasted a smile on her face as Billy Gates entered the room.

'Becky! Oh Gawd. I got in late from work and me mum's only just told me what happened, I came straight round. You all right, love? . . . Bloody Hell! Look at yer poor face, it's all bruised an' swollen . . .'

Rebecca smiled up at the worried man standing in front of her. 'I'm fine, Billy, really. Amy and me had a nasty fright, but we're both all right now, thanks to this gentleman.' She nodded over to where Jimmy stood in the doorway, his penetrating eyes giving Billy the once over.

Jimmy saw a mountain of a man with a shock of unruly brown hair falling over a heavy-set face, the overall impression being one of immense strength, until you looked into the black eyes; then Jimmy was reminded of a puppy, a puppy who was at this moment looking at his mistress with unconditional concern and deep affection. Then there was another knock on the door. This time it was Charlie, his face beaming as he carried a large parcel from which was emanating a tantalising smell of freshly cooked fish and chips.

''Ere yer are, miss. Sorry I was so long, there was a bleeding great queue an'—'

'It's all right, Charlie,' Jimmy's voice spoke crisply. 'You're here now, so let's be on our way and leave Miss Bradford and her family to enjoy their supper in peace.'

Charlie's face fell in bewilderment. 'But, Guv, yer told me ter get enough fer us an' all, I—'

'Yes, well, there's been a change of plans. Miss Bradford has a visitor and, besides, I've just remembered I've got company coming around at eight.'

56

Rebecca started to rise, saying haltingly, 'Really, Mr Jackson, there's no need for you to go, at least not until you've had something to eat. You must be hungry after spending most of the day here looking after us. And as Charlie says, he's already bought enough for us all, it'd be a shame to waste good food.'

Charlie looked eagerly at his governor, his hopes falling at the set look on Jimmy's face.

'It won't be wasted, Miss Bradford. Charlie can take his portion with him; you can give mine to your friend.'

All eyes turned on the unexpected and uninvited visitor, causing the man in question to fidget uncomfortably for a few seconds. Then he straightened his back and moved behind Rebecca's chair, his hand coming out to rest protectively on her shoulder.

'Goodbye, Miss Bradford. Please give my regards to your sister, and your cousin of course.' Before Rebecca could make any further protest, Jimmy turned on his heel and, after hastily sorting out Charlie's portion of food, both men left the house.

As the front door closed behind them, Rebecca's body slumped in disappointment. She had almost forgotten about Billy's presence until he spoke, his voice cheerful now the two men had left. 'I'll give Amy a shout, shall I, Becky? And d'yer want me ter get some plates out, or shall we eat 'em outta the paper? I prefer me fish an' chips better that way. They never taste the same off a cold plate.'

Wearily Rebecca looked up into the broad, grinning face and sighed. 'I'm sorry, Billy, I don't mean to be rude, but would you mind leaving? Here . . .' She slowly took out one of the wrapped parcels and held it out to him. 'You take it home with you, and tell your mum thanks for staying with Maude today, it was good of her.'

His face betraying his disappointment, Billy took the offered parcel, muttering, 'All right, I know when I'm not wanted. If yer need me, yer know where I am.'

When the door slammed behind him, Rebecca let out a sigh of relief. Of all the times for Billy to show up . . . Oh! What the hell. It didn't make any difference. Jimmy Jackson would have left soon anyway. He'd only stayed to keep her company out of kindness. Blinking rapidly, she went out into the hall and called up the stairs to Amy, ignoring Maude's cries for her supper. She could bloody well wait for a change.

'I thought we was gonna stay and 'ave our tea wiv the girls.' Jimmy and Charlie were seated inside the carriage, the younger man busily shovelling the hot food into his mouth, his face crestfallen. He had been looking forward to spending some time with the young blonde girl, and he said as much to his governor. 'She's a right smasher, ain't she, Guv? The younger one, I mean. Not that the other one ain't good looking an' all, but I sort of took a shine ter Amy. She seems really nice.'

Jimmy glanced sideways at the young man. 'Forget it, Charlie, a girl like that's well out of your class,' he said curtly. 'And for goodness' sake, hurry up and finish that, I'd like to get home some time tonight.'

Charlie looked at his governor apprehensively. It wasn't like Jimmy to be so short with him. Then the penny dropped. It was that other bloke turning up that had put Jimmy in a bad mood. Stifling a knowing smile, Charlie quickly finished his supper and climbed up into the driver's seat. Well, well! This was a turn up for the books. In all the years he'd worked for Jimmy Jackson he'd never known him to get into a flap over a woman – and his governor had certainly had his fair share of them. Grinning broadly, Charlie directed the horse forward into the late-night traffic, his hopes rising. Maybe he would get the chance to see Amy again, because if Jimmy had taken a shine to her sister, then he wasn't the kind of man to let any opposition put him off. Whistling tunelessly, Charlie drove on.

CHAPTER SIX

'Well! Did he say he'd be back? I mean, he must have said something. A man like that don't go out of his way for just anyone. All right, so maybe he'd have done the same for anyone, like you keep telling me, but he didn't have to stay with me while you and Amy had a rest, did he? And he didn't have to pay Ada Gates extra for her trouble either. Oh, no! He took a shine to you, me girl, and if it hadn't been for that big oaf from next door barging in where he wasn't wanted, then Jimmy—'

'Oh, for goodness' sake, give it a rest, will you, Maude!' Rebecca snapped angrily. Her cousin's bed freshly made up, she added shortly, 'There, all done. Do you want any help getting back into bed, or do you think you can manage to move from the chair to here by yourself?' The open sarcasm wasn't lost on Maude, who, with a great deal of huffing and grumbling, heaved herself awkwardly from the high-backed armchair and clambered into the double bed, her large frame dropping onto the feather mattress as if just having accomplished a great ordeal. But if her body was tired, her mouth still had plenty of life left in it.

'Never mind telling me to give it a rest, madam. I don't know what's the matter with you. You get a chance of someone like Jimmy Jackson and you let him get away, then pretend like you couldn't care less, as if you had dozens of eligible men hammering the door down for a chance to take you out. You mark my words, girl, you won't get many chances to—'

Rebecca whirled on Maude angrily. 'No, you're right there, Maude, I'm not going to get many chances, not while I'm stuck here day in day out looking after you, am I? Then again, maybe I should get out more; in fact, I could even get my own place, and take Amy with me. I could easily get a job, I'm not fussy what doing. After all, I'm used to hard work; I've had plenty of practice, haven't I?'

Looking up into the hard, blue eyes, Maude's heart skipped a beat, a thread of panic stirring in her chest. This wasn't the first time Rebecca had threatened to walk out, and she could have at any time over the past few years. Maude knew that Rebecca had stayed this long only because of Amy and Phil, but for how much longer would her cousin tolerate her lifestyle? And as Maude continued to hold Rebecca's gaze, she realised, as if for the first time, that Rebecca was no longer a young girl, but a strong, independent woman;

and a lovely looking one at that. Then there was Amy, who was also growing up fast. What if she were to meet some young man, and, looking as she did, it could only be a matter of time before Amy brought a beau home; then where would that leave her, Maude? Because once Amy married, then there would be no further reason for Rebecca to stay. The feeling of panic continued to rise in the obese frame. She wouldn't be able to depend on her dear brother, not any more. As far as Richard was concerned he'd done his bit. Oh, no, if Rebecca were to leave, then Richard would shove his only sister into a home, and leave her there to rot.

Her mouth suddenly dry, Maude licked her lips nervously and tried to conjure up what she hoped to be a sincere smile as she said in a conciliatory tone, 'Now, now, love, I didn't mean any harm, I just want to see you happy, that's all, I—'

'Oh, don't give me that old rubbish, Maude,' Rebecca snapped back. 'You couldn't give a damn about me, you never have. The only reason you're so keen for me to get hooked up with someone like Jimmy Jackson is because he's got loads of money, and your crafty little mind is always thinking of ways to make your life easier. Huh! That's a laugh. I don't see how it could get any easier, because you don't have to lift a finger. You're waited on hand and foot, day and night, and don't think I don't know you could do a lot more for yourself than you let on, because I'm not that much of a fool.' Moving away from the bed, Rebecca paused at the door, a smile curving her lips. 'Maybe I will look up Mr Jackson,

Maude. Like you say, he's a good catch, and he has a beautiful home. Though if I were to become the future Mrs Jackson, then Richard would have to make other arrangements concerning you, because I certainly wouldn't take you with me.' As Rebecca witnessed the look of sheer horror that passed over Maude's face she gave a harsh laugh. 'I think that's what's termed "shooting yourself in the foot". I'll be up with your dinner at the usual time.'

When the door closed quietly behind Rebecca, Maude remained staring across the room, her heart pounding inside her chest like a sledge hammer, her mind whirling frantically as she visualised the future if Rebecca left her. Laying back on the plump pillows, she squeezed her eyes shut, her thoughts travelling back down the years to her youth.

Her parents had married late in life, her mother giving birth to Maude when she was thirty-nine. Edward and Matilda Fisher had been overjoyed at the arrival of their daughter, and had lavished all their love and devotion on the child they imagined would be their only one. It had come as a great shock when, at the age of forty-three, Matilda had found herself pregnant once more, for at that age Matilda Fisher had thought she was past her child-bearing years. When Richard was delivered safely, they had both thanked God for their good fortune, though the young, spoilt Maude hadn't shared in their enthusiasm, seeing the new-born baby as an unwelcome intrusion into her orderly, exclusive world. Her doting parents had quickly recognised their young daughter's resentment of her brother, but, like most parents, had imagined the years would alter Maude's animosity towards her younger sibling, and that in time their adored children would form a loving bond. That had never happened, for Richard, like his sister, had been born with a selfish nature, a fact that both parents had recognised, but refused to acknowledge openly. Those who knew the family had often speculated how two good-natured people like Edward and Matilda had produced such unlikable children, declaring that Maude and Richard, both as obnoxious as each other, must have inherited their unpleasant traits from long-dead ancestors.

When Maude was twenty-three, her father suffered a heart attack and died suddenly. Left alone with her quarrelsome son and daughter, Matilda Fisher, who had always been dependent on her husband, quickly deteriorated, and within a year, she too had died. Friends and family, who had paid their respects to the body in the open coffin, had commented afterwards that poor Matilda had looked happier dead than she had when alive. Left to fend for themselves, Maude and Richard had formed an uneasy alliance, each realising that, for the time being, they needed each other. Their parents, although not rich, had been comfortably off, and had left everything they owned to be shared among their offspring; except for the warehouse business Edward Fisher had founded, which had been left to his only son. But while Richard had kept the company going, and had other interests outside his home and working environment,

Maude had continued to languish at home, going out only to shop for new clothes, and any other luxuries that caught her eye.

The turning point in their lives had come about when Richard, then twenty-two, had met a young woman and fallen in love. When he had declared to his sister his intention of getting married, Maude had suddenly developed a mysterious ailment and taken to her bed. Despite the numerous doctors Richard had brought in to examine his older sister, no explanation could be found as to why Maude had abruptly become an invalid. Richard had his suspicions, for whatever other faults he had he wasn't a stupid man. Maude had always been in perfect health before the announcement of his forthcoming marriage. Things would have been different if Maude had formed other interests and acquaintances, as he had, but the truth was that his sister had never had the ability to make friends, and at the age of twenty-six, an age when most women were married with children, Maude, who was unattractive, both inside and out, was unlikely ever to achieve the married state. Knowing his sister as he did, Richard assumed she would soon get tired of lying in bed, for if there was one thing Maude loved, it was going out and spending money. So he bided his time, continued his courtship, paid a neighbour to drop in on Maude once a day, and carried on with his life.

A year passed, and still Maude remained bed-ridden, apart from the occasional excursion down to the kitchen to cook herself a meal, after which she would proclaim herself to be exhausted. By this time, Richard's fiancée was becoming increasingly impatient at the continuous delay in setting a date for their wedding. In desperation, Richard had suggested that they get married and move in with Maude until his sister was better; it was a suggestion that hadn't gone down well with the young woman in question. If it hadn't been for Richard's concern as to what people would think of him for deserting his ailing sister, he would have left Maude to fend for herself without a second's thought. But other people's opinion had always been important to Richard and, desperate to portray the impression of a decent, concerned brother, he had stayed, and lost his fiancée in the process – a fact he had never forgiven Maude for. If he had disliked his sister before, the hate he eventually built up towards her over the years became so intense he couldn't bear to go near her for fear of what he might do. Eventually he hired a nurse to come in every day, then it became necessary to engage another nurse to be in attendance during the night, for there was no way on God's earth he was going to go anywhere near the woman who, to Richard's mind, had ruined his life.

Maude stirred uneasily in the double bed, feeling tears of self-pity well up behind her eyes. She knew only too well Richard's intense dislike of her, for he had never tried to hide how he felt, at least when they were on their own, an occurrence that had become less and less over the years. Then had come the news of the deaths of their cousins. At first

Richard hadn't wanted to go, then he had decided that it might look bad if he was the only one of the family not to attend the funeral, even though he hadn't seen the Bradfords for years. And the rest, as they said, was history.

Blinking back the tears, Maude tossed fretfully from side to side. When Richard had first brought the remainder of the Bradford family home, she had been incensed at having her house invaded by strangers. But Richard had made it quite clear that he couldn't afford to carry on paying the exorbitant fees for the care she was receiving, and that either she accepted being looked after by the young Rebecca Bradford or she could go into a home. And it wouldn't be one of those posh homes either. Oh, no, Richard had spent enough money on his sister over the years. If she opted for a home, then it would be the cheapest one he could find; and Maude knew what she could expect from places like those. The arrangement had worked out better than Maude had thought, and up until today she had imagined herself set up for life. Now she wasn't so sure.

As the tears finally escaped from beneath her eyelids, Maude contemplated that, in the process of ruining Richard's life with her sudden affliction, she had also ruined her own. Maybe if she had made the effort years ago while she was still reasonably young, she might have made a life for herself, but now, at the age of forty-six, it was too late for her to start over. Beating at the quilt with her pudgy fists, she cried silently, 'I don't want to start over. I want things to stay as they are. It's not fair . . . It's not fair.' The tears

67

rained down her face as she thought of the life she had wasted, knowing that she had brought about her predicament of her own free will. She tasted the salty tears as they ran into her mouth – tears of anger and desperation, but mostly brought on by fear.

As Rebecca descended the stairs, her heart was also beating rapidly, but for very different reasons. It had been two weeks since she and Amy had been attacked, but it seemed like only yesterday. She was still badly shaken by what had happened, as too was Amy, who was at present curled up in the armchair reading one of her favourite novels, which supposedly reflected true life, but was, in Rebecca's mind, a load of old toffee. Peeping into the front room to make sure her sister was all right, Rebecca saw Amy, her nose engrossed in the well-thumbed paperback book, and crept silently into the kitchen where she began to prepare the Sunday dinner, her mind going over the events of the fortnight.

Deliberately skipping over the attack, Rebecca thought back to the evening after Jimmy Jackson had left the house, with a reluctant and sullen Billy Gates leaving soon afterwards. Upstairs, Maude had worked herself into a frenzy, shouting down the stairs, demanding to know what was going on, then Phil had arrived home at ten o'clock with Richard in tow. Both men had fussed over the two young women, declaring all sorts of retribution if ever they got their hands on the scum who had attacked their girls, words that had hung emptily in the air, for neither of them would ever have the gumption to face the kind of men who had waylaid their charges. It had also been obvious that Phil and Richard had been profoundly disappointed to find their esteemed guest had flown the coop, as was evident by their talk of wanting to meet with Jimmy Jackson and thank him personally, when what they both wanted was the chance to ingratiate themselves with the well-known bookmaker. Even this morning, Phil had come into her room asking if she wanted to send a letter or short note of thanks, which he would be only too glad to deliver, of course. His kindly countenance had soon dropped when Rebecca had replied stoutly that she had already thanked the man, and had no intention of dragging the sordid affair out any longer. Looking like a child who had just been refused a bag of sweets, Phil had flounced from her room muttering angrily under his breath, his bedroom door slamming behind him, where no doubt he still was, either asleep or sulking. Rebecca lifted her eyes and sighed heavily. If he started again when he finally dragged himself out of bed, she'd go for him with the nearest object to hand . . . Oh, yes, she would. Her head bounced on her shoulders as if adding emphasis to her silent words.

With the joint of meat in the oven and the potatoes peeled, Rebecca took off her apron and went into the front room, where Amy was just closing her book.

'Don't tell me, let me guess,' Rebecca said cheerfully. 'Their eyes met across a crowded room and it was love at first sight – or they hated each other at first sight, fought all the way through the book and ended up falling in love; which version was it this time?'

Amy looked up guiltily, then smiled shyly. 'Oh, Becky, you're such a cynic. It can happen, you know. I mean, no one would ever get married if it didn't, would they?'

Rebecca had to admit to a certain logic in what Amy said and answered back playfully, 'Yes, I suppose so, but not in the way those kind of books portray life. For instance, have you ever read a book where the hero is short, fat and bald, and the heroine has a face like a horse, no bust, and legs like drumsticks? Oh, no, in those kind of books, the hero is always tall, dark and handsome, with bulging thighs encased in tight trousers, and the heroine is blond and beautiful, with legs up to her armpits and a heaving bosom; why their bosoms are always heaving has always been a mystery to me. The nearest I've ever got to seeing a heaving bosom is when Maude's in one of her moods, and I don't think that sight would make any man's heart beat faster, do you?'

Amy looked at her sister and both girls started to giggle, imagining Maude's ponderous breasts rising and falling beneath the bedclothes. The giggles soon turned to loud laughter, and they continued to laugh even when Maude began banging on the floor above. Wiping her eyes, Amy sniffed, hiccuped and said, 'You seem to know a lot about these kind of books. I thought you never read any of them. Whenever I see you with a book, it's always by Dickens or

Thackeray.' A sly smile tugged at Amy's lips. 'You do read them, don't you, you crafty thing.'

A flush of guilt rose in Rebecca's cheeks, then, looking at Amy's gleeful face, she admitted sheepishly, 'Yes, all right, I've read some of them. But only when I need something I don't have to concentrate on. And you must admit, love, they are all the same stories. The writers just change the names and locations around a bit, but the end result is always the same. Anyway . . .' Rebecca stood up, her manner brisk. 'How about helping with the vegetables, young miss, or do you plan to copy our dear cousin and expect to be waited on?'

Amy uncurled her legs and rose from the confines of the armchair, then, with a mischievous glint in her eyes, she said, 'Jimmy Jackson's not bad looking, and you're not too bad yourself. It's a pity your bosom doesn't heave . . . Ooh . . . !' Amy ducked as Rebecca aimed a playful swipe at her blonde head.

It was after three. The Sunday roast had been consumed by a sullen Phil and a subdued Maude, the latter in her room, of course, and Rebecca and Amy were just finishing off the last of the washing-up when a loud knock sounded at the front door.

Rebecca and Amy exchanged glances.

'Oh, Lord, I hope it's not Billy again. He's hardly been off the doorstep this past fortnight, and while I appreciate his concern, I can't help feeling he's only using what happened to us as an excuse to visit more often.' Hanging up a tea towel, Rebecca looked to Amy, saying, 'Will you get it, love? And if it's Billy, tell him I'm lying down, or something. I really can't face another hour or so of stilted conversation. I mean, his heart's in the right place, but he's so boring. He could put a glass eye to sleep.'

Amy nodded sympathetically, then chuckled. 'I take it he's not your idea of the dashing hero from one of my books, eh?'

Suppressing a laugh, Rebecca playfully picked up the tea towel and flicked it at the disappearing rump of her sister, then sat down at the small wooden table, her ears listening out for the voice of their visitor, but unable to hear properly from the kitchen. Then she jumped as Amy, her eyes shining, her pretty face wreathed in smiles, came bounding into the room, her arms filled with the biggest bunch of flowers Rebecca had ever seen.

'It's that Charlie. You know, Jimmy Jackson's driver. He wants to know if I'd like to take a walk over the park with him. Can I, Becky? Ooh, please, can I go?'

Rebecca looked up at the pleading animated face, then to the flowers, and was ashamed to experience a pang of jealousy at her sister's evident pleasure. Summoning up a smile she said mischievously, 'As long as he isn't wearing skin-tight breeches encasing bulging thighs – among other parts of his body, I don't see why not. Anyway, since when did you need my permission to go out?'

Amy squealed with delight. Dropping the flowers onto the table she threw her arms around Rebecca's neck, crying, 'You know I always ask you before I go out anywhere, Becky.'

As her sister left the room at a run, Rebecca called after her, 'Hang on, aren't you going to put these flowers in water? I must say Mr Jackson must pay his employers well if they can afford to buy presents like this.'

Then Rebecca's stomach lurched as Amy swirled around, saying, 'Oh, Charlie didn't buy them, they're for you – from Jimmy. Sorry, Becky, I meant to say.' Still beaming with excitement, Amy added, 'What shall I wear, Becky? What about my yellow dress, or maybe the blue one; what do you think?'

Her heart still hammering, Rebecca said nonchalantly, 'Seeing as you're going to have to wear your coat, I don't see how it matters what you wear . . . Uum, Amy, did Charlie have any message, I mean . . .?' She felt herself blushing, then when she spoke again she was annoyed to find herself stammering. 'Well, not that I'm that bothered. It was very nice of Mr Jackson to send me the flowers . . . I just wondered, that's all,' her voice trailed off lamely.

'No, he didn't say anything. Just to give you the flowers with Mr Jackson's compliments.' Amy stopped in her mad dash, her eyes surveying her sisters flushed cheeks. 'Not that you're bothered, of course.' Then she let out a peal of laughter before scurrying from the room.

Rebecca sat looking at the bouquet of flowers, wondering where Jimmy Jackson could have obtained such a beautiful bunch at this time of the year. Slowly picking them up, she held them to her nose, breathing in the heady aroma, her eyes glowing with pleasure at the kind gesture. It would have been nicer if the man himself had brought them around in person. Still, as the saying went, it was the thought that counted. She was busily putting them into a large crystal vase when Phil, his face bearing no trace of the sullen features he had displayed throughout dinner, burst into the scullery, his entire being filled with excited agitation.

'Quick, Becks. Jimmy's waiting outside in his carriage. I'm just off upstairs to change . . . Oh, for Christ's sake, leave those . . .' He indicated the flowers Rebecca was carefully arranging. 'He might go if you don't show your face . . . Come on, get a move on!'

Rebecca turned to her brother, who was dressed in an old pair of trousers, his shirt unopened to the waist, with an equally decrepit pair of braces holding up the ill-fitting trousers. Fighting down the churning in her stomach, she curled her lips scornfully. 'Will you take a look at yourself, Phil. It's embarrassing the way you're behaving. Anyone would think King George himself was waiting outside the door instead of your bookie. And although I don't know Mr Jackson that well, having only met him the once, I don't imagine him to be the sort of man to be impressed by obsequious behaviour. In fact it's positively cloying. As for getting changed, unless Jimmy Jackson is another way inclined – which I very much doubt – I shouldn't think he'll be looking at how well dressed you are.'

Now it was Phil's turn to blush as Rebecca's harsh words hit home. But she wasn't finished yet. Slowly completing her task she added dryly, 'It's a pity Richard isn't here as well. You'd make a right pair.

One of you could lick Mr Jackson's boots while the other one polished them.'

His face angry now, Phil hissed spitefully, 'You can be a right bitch at times, Becky, you . . .'

Rebecca returned his malevolent glare with studied impunity. 'You may be right, Phil. Maybe it has something to do with the environment I've been living in these past five years. Being an unpaid dogsbody can sour a person's disposition, but you wouldn't know anything about that way of life, would you?'

Brother and sister locked eyes, but it was Phil who turned away first, and with an angry, muttered oath, he spun on his heel, and like Amy bounded up the stairs to make himself presentable.

Rebecca glanced down at her red dress, a dress she had had for many years, and which still had plenty of life left in it. A serviceable dress she wore when round the house or out shopping; but then where else did she ever go? She had other clothes – skirts and blouses and dresses she had made herself over the years, a task she enjoyed immensely when she had the time to indulge in her passion. She had always been adept with a needle and thread, a talent passed on to her by her late mother, and enjoyed nothing better than creating her own styles of dress. Yet she rarely had the opportunity to wear any of her creations, until today. Glancing towards the open door, Rebecca could see an awkward-looking Charlie standing just inside the front room – and outside, sitting in a waiting carriage, was Jimmy Jackson, probably waiting for an invite into the house. Once again Rebecca looked down at her old dress and sighed. How could she possibly change into something more presentable after what she had said to Phil? A wry smile hovered around her lips as she recalled her words to Maude earlier on. It looked like Maude wasn't the only one to have 'shot herself in the foot' today. Removing her apron, Rebecca took a quick look in the small mirror hanging on the far side of the kitchen wall. Her face was flushed, and wisps of her thick golden hair, pleated into a neat braid at the base of her neck, had escaped the tight pins and were lying in disarray around her forehead and cheeks. She started to tidy her hair, then let her hands fall by her side. If Jimmy Jackson wanted to see her, then he would see her as she was. Taking a deep breath she ventured forth to greet her visitor.

CHAPTER SEVEN

Jimmy Jackson sat patiently outside the terraced house in Welbeck Road waiting for Charlie to return from his errand. Being a Sunday, Jimmy was anxious to get to his club, a club whose hallowed doors he would never have been allowed to stand outside only ten years ago. But times had changed, or at least he had, in monetary terms that is. Beneath the affluent surface he, Jimmy Jackson, was still the same cockney lad he had always been – as Bessie was constantly reminding him. Taking another look at the front door Charlie had disappeared into, and seeing no sign of life, Jimmy sighed and leant his head back against the leather upholstery. He didn't often dwell on the past, thinking it a fool's pastime, but at moments like this, when there was nothing else to occupy his mind, he couldn't help but remember his childhood, and how far he had come since those early, harrowing days.

Born to parents who were both drunkards, Jimmy had learnt how to survive on his own. It was a lesson he'd had to learn fast, or perish on the back streets of the East End. His first memory was of being thrashed with a leather belt, and the constant ache of an empty belly. Both memories were painful, but if he had received even a modicum of love and affection from either of his parents, life would have been tolerable. In the dingy back street where he had been born, there were many families like his, poor and often starving. Yet even in families such as these, the majority of the parents did their best for their offspring, often going without, as long as their children were fed and clothed. Not so the Jacksons, who were looked down upon by their neighbours, and in a community such as the one in which Jimmy had been raised, that was something to be deeply ashamed of. Not that either of his parents cared. They were always too drunk to worry about what the neighbours thought of them. It was these same neighbours who, although desperately short of food themselves, would often give the small, hungry child a bite to eat, and offer him shelter when he had run from the hovel he called home out onto the filthy street for safety, terrified by the sight of his parents fighting and screaming abuse at each other.

By the time he was seven, Jimmy had learnt to take care of himself. He would scour the markets looking for a few hours' work in order to buy food, and if there was no work to be found, then he would resort to picking the occasional pocket. Jimmy felt no remorse for his past thieving. It had been done out of necessity. These times had been rare, but when he had been forced to steal he had done so without thinking twice. It was a case of survival, for without the odd wallet or purse he had lifted, he would have died; it was as simple as that.

At the age of eight he had been taken on as a runner for a local bookmaker. The work had been easy enough; it was keeping a sharp look-out for the law that had been the hardest part of his job. Betting was illegal then, just as it was now, but it was the runners who took all the risks. If caught, they faced imprisonment, and the penalties were harsh, while the actual bookmaker, the man behind the gambling enterprises, carefully covered his tracks, usually beneath the veneer of a respectable businessman. The law knew of these men, but to succeed as a bookmaker a man had to be smart, and with the money pouring in on a regular basis, these men could afford highly skilled bookkeepers to account for every penny that swelled their coffers.

Jimmy had been a runner for only a few weeks before he felt the strong arm of the law. It had been a month after his eighth birthday when the burly constable had caught the young boy taking a bet from an elderly woman outside the Hackney Town Hall. Screaming, kicking and punching, the terrified child had been dragged by the scruff of the neck down the busy thoroughfare of Mare Street. The officer had been just a few minutes away from the police station when Bessie Wilks, her scrawny arms laden down with cheap groceries, had collided with the struggling boy and irate policeman. Even in his terrified state, Jimmy had recognised Bessie immediately. She was one of the neighbours who had often fed and sheltered him during his childhood. He had gazed at her with anguished eyes, feeling the vice-like grip of the constable's hand around the back of his neck. For a few agonising moments, the woman and boy had locked eyes, then Bessie, her voice rising to a shrill scream of protest, had let go of her shopping, whereupon tins and other assorted goods had rolled and bounced noisily down the cobbled street. Jimmy's heart had soared as he'd quickly realised Bessie's intention of causing a diversion, but the streetwise constable had maintained his grip. Bessie had screamed louder, crying out for help to retrieve her week's shopping. A small crowd had formed, glad of the unexpected entertainment on a gloomy Saturday afternoon, and the constable's grasp had loosened as he attempted to pacify the distraught woman. It was all Jimmy had needed. With a strong, swift jerk, he had twisted from the policeman's hold, and like lightning was off down the streets, his strong young legs pumping frantically as he literally ran for his life.

Later that night he had returned to his old street under cover of darkness and knocked on Bessie's door. Bessie had opened the door warily, then, seeing the young boy, had quickly ushered him inside. But instead of the warm greeting Jimmy had envisaged, he'd received a hard clout around the head accompanied by the words, 'Yer stupid little git.' Still dazed, he had then been given a hot meal of beef broth and dumplings with two doorstop slices of bread to mop up the hastily reheated meal. Over his late supper, Bessie had told Jimmy his parents had done a flit over six months ago, no one had heard of them since. The news had come as a great relief to Jimmy, and when, later that night, he curled up on Bessie's wooden floor under threadbare blankets, he had slept soundly and without fear for the first time in his young life. From that day on Bessie Wilks had become his adopted mother.

Jimmy's life had altered from that day. With a safe home to return to, he had become more confident, and with careful saving and the shrewd mind he had been born with, he gradually began setting up his own betting empire. It had been a long, often perilous business, for local bookmakers didn't take kindly to opposition, but Jimmy had persevered. It had taken him over ten years to establish his own patch; now, at the age of twenty-eight, he was where he had always wanted to be – at the top, living in a home he had at one time only dared dream of, and with enough money tucked away to ensure he never went hungry again.

Yet although Jimmy didn't mind recalling his early days from time to time, there was one part of his past he refused to dwell on. Even as the thought entered his mind, Jimmy quickly shut down on the painful memory. That episode in his life was over and done with. It was the only part of his past that even Bessie wasn't allowed to mention. But despite his iron determination, a hazy vision of a face with bright green eyes and smiling full lips flashed across

81

his mind. Gritting his teeth, Jimmy shook his head impatiently and took out his gold fob watch. Seeing the time, he clenched his lips in angry frustration. He should have known better than to agree to let Charlie visit the young girl Amy, when it was obvious the poor young man was smitten with the lovely blonde, even though he had been in her company for only a short space of time. But the boy was young, and the young were susceptible to romance, as he knew only too well. It was as one got older that a person became more cynical; or maybe it was just him. But if it was, then he had good reason to feel the way he did. Taking another look at his watch, Jimmy clicked his tongue, his patience fast running out for his erstwhile employee. The bloody little sod, he was taking liberties now, and Jimmy wasn't the type of man you took liberties with, as Charlie should know by now.

When another five minutes passed, Jimmy leant forward on the leather seat and was about to alight from the carriage when he saw the front door opening wider and a slim form emerge from the house. At the sight of Rebecca Bradford, Jimmy experienced a stirring in his stomach that he hadn't felt for many years, and inwardly cursed himself for coming here today. He could just as easily have got another of his men to drive him to his club, after all, it was Charlie's day off – so why hadn't he? To make matters worse, he'd had Charlie stop to pick up a large bouquet of flowers for the woman approaching the carriage. As soon as the flowers had been laid carefully on the opposite carriage seat, Jimmy had berated himself for the gesture. After all, he had already helped the two young women, and stayed to look after the old trout in the upstairs bedroom while the girls rested, and he wouldn't have offered his services if that miserable excuse for a man, namely Phil Bradford, their supposedly loving brother, hadn't made a quick exit. But, as he'd been telling himself for the last fortnight, he would have done the same for anyone, and after the elder sister had dropped her hostile demeanour towards him, and thanked him for his kindness, that should have been an end to the matter, especially as there was obviously another man in the picture. It was true that Rebecca hadn't been that pleased to see the heavily built man from next door; it had been equally obvious that the man in question imagined himself to be an important part of the young woman's life. All right, he grudgingly admitted to himself as the woman drew nearer, Rebecca Bradford was a very attractive woman; she was also evidently a very moral one to boot. And as Jimmy wasn't looking for any long-term commitment, there seemed little point in continuing the brief association.

'Mr Jackson, how nice to see you again.' Rebecca was standing in front of the carriage, her face only inches from his. 'And thank you so much for the flowers. You really shouldn't have gone to the trouble, but I'm very grateful, they're lovely.'

Jimmy shuffled uncomfortably on the seat. 'It was my pleasure, Miss Bradford, and I'm glad to see you looking so well after your recent ordeal. I hope you didn't mind Charlie calling on your sister, he's hardly spoken of anything else since he met her. I'm afraid your sister has acquired an admirer, but if Charlie's not welcome, you only have to say the word, and I'll soon have him out of your home.'

'Oh, no, that won't be necessary; in fact, I'm glad he called. I haven't seen Amy this happy since . . .' Rebecca shrugged her shoulders uneasily, thinking that maybe she shouldn't have revealed Amy's feelings to this man.

An awkwardness descended over the two people until Jimmy, clearing his throat said, 'The police tell me that the men who attacked you are due in court on Tuesday. I've been asked to appear as a witness. Will your brother be coming with you and your sister to court? If not, then maybe you'd allow me to accompany you both.' The moment the words were out of his mouth Jimmy cursed himself for a gormless fool. Not five minutes ago he'd been telling himself to stay away from this woman; now he was offering to spend the day with her.

Rebecca's face lit up at his words. She had been dreading the court case, as had Amy, but with a man like Jimmy Jackson by their side, the ordeal wouldn't be so bad. 'That would be wonderful, Mr Jackson, although you've already done so much for us, I don't want to put you to any more trouble. My brother and uncle have said they'll come with us, but . . .'

She didn't have to explain further, not to Jimmy, who had quickly summed up the brother, and the uncle couldn't be much better, otherwise Rebecca Bradford wouldn't be looking so relieved at his offer.

Doubtless, she would be able to attend court without a male presence, unlike most women who couldn't seem to do anything without a man's arm to lean on. But Rebecca Bradford wasn't the type of woman Jimmy was used to associating with; she had courage and character, plus that undefinable trait that spelt class. And that was something you couldn't acquire, it was a quality one was born with, and this woman looking at him with open gratitude had it in abundance. As Jimmy held her gaze he couldn't help thinking what a terrible waste it was of such qualities, squandered and stifled by her living standards, looking after a bed-ridden harridan, and having a stupid, gutless brother to contend with as well.

Feeling a flush spreading over her face, Rebecca coughed quietly before asking hesitantly, 'Would you like to come inside for a drink, Mr Jackson? It's very cold out here.'

Jimmy jumped guiltily as he looked at the shivering figure. What was he thinking of, sitting in the warm cab, while this young woman stood freezing on the cobbled pavement? He had his hand on the handle of the carriage when Charlie and Amy emerged laughing from the house, and immediately Rebecca stepped back, her arms hugging her slim body to ward off the cold October wind.

'Sorry I took so long, Mr Jackson,' Charlie grinned in at his employer. 'I'll drop you off at the club then I'm going over the park with Amy . . . If that's all right with you. I'll pick you up about six, all right, Guv?'

85

Tearing his eyes away from Rebecca, Jimmy nodded. 'Yeah, all right,' then, his attention back on Rebecca, he added kindly, 'I'll pick you and Amy up on Tuesday, Miss Bradford . . .'

'My name's Rebecca, Mr Jackson, and thank you.'

Jimmy smiled broadly. 'And mine's Jimmy. Until Tuesday then, Rebecca.'

Rebecca smiled back then waved as the carriage drove off. As she turned to enter the house, Phil, looking very dapper in his best suit, came bounding towards her. Rebecca smiled wryly. 'Sorry, Phil, looks like you've missed the boat again. Better luck next time.'

Hurrying into the warmth of the house, Rebecca scurried towards the blazing fire, while a stiff-faced Phil remained on the pavement, his bleak eyes fixed on the disappearing carriage.

CHAPTER EIGHT

'There, that wasn't so bad, was it?' Richard Fisher, his fat face wreathed in smiles of paternal benevolence, beamed down on his cousins as the small group left the Old Bailey. 'That judge didn't waste time, did he. Ten years a piece for the two accomplices, and fifteen years for the ringleader, and they got off lightly if you ask me. If I'd had my way, the whole lot of them would be dangling from the end of a rope. Still! That's another three ruffians off the streets, and thanks to our friend Jimmy taking the stand as the main witness, you two girls didn't even have to go through the added ordeal of testifying. Thanks, Jimmy, mate.'

Jimmy looked at the proffered hand with thinly veiled contempt. This was the first time he'd met the portly man, yet already he was calling him by his first name and acting as if they'd been close friends for years. The brother was just as bad. How two lovely, independent young women like the Bradford sisters could have such weaklings as menfolk was a mystery to him. So much for the theory of the weaker sex. Though Jimmy had never agreed with that old adage. He'd known women who could chew nails and wipe their arses with sandpaper without turning a hair; not that he would put Rebecca and Amy in that category, but . . . ! Conscious of the girls' anxious glances, Jimmy took the offered hand reluctantly, and when the sweaty, pudgy hand tried to keep the grip for longer than necessary, Jimmy disentangled his grasp roughly, then quickly turned his back as he saw the hovering Phil nervously moving forward, his hopeful smile dropping at the deliberate snub.

Turning his attention to the two girls, Jimmy doffed his hat and asked cheerfully, 'Can I give you girls a lift home, or maybe you'd like to have a drink to celebrate? I know I could do with one after sitting in that place for the last four hours. Just our luck that our case was on last, but you never know with these things . . .' Jimmy was amazed to hear himself babbling like an awkward youth. Spreading his legs wide, he clasped his hands firmly behind his back and said in a firmer voice, 'Of course if you'd rather go straight home, I'll drop you off first. Your aunt must be worried.'

At the mention of Maude, Rebecca's back stiffened. Of course her cousin would be worried. Worried she would be left alone to fend for herself if Mrs Gates decided to get off to her own home. Maude would also be dying of curiosity by now –

well, she'd just have to wait a little longer, wouldn't she?

'Thank you, Mr Jack— I mean, Jimmy.' Rebecca smiled warmly, unaware of the effect she was having on the rugged man. 'Actually, Maude and Richard are our cousins, we only refer to them as Aunt and Uncle out of courtesy. But, yes, we'd love to go for a drink, wouldn't we, Amy?' She turned to where Amy was excitedly nodding.

'Oh, yes, please, Jimmy,' the younger girl answered breathlessly, before adding shyly, 'We've never been in a pub before, have we, Becky?'

Rebecca's face coloured slightly. Lord, but Jimmy must think she was a complete drudge. To have lived in the East End for as long as she had, and at her age to have to admit she'd never been in a pub was somehow shaming, as if she didn't have a life. Then again, she didn't, did she? A deep feeling of determination began to burgeon through her body. She'd been meaning to do something about her sorry state of affairs for a long time, and now seemed as good a time as any to make good her resolve. Tilting her chin up proudly she replied, 'No, we haven't. In fact, I'm afraid we've both led very dull lives. I think it's about time we changed that, don't you, Amy?'

Hearing the on-going conversation, both Richard and Phil moved nearer the trio, anxious not to be shut out. 'That sounds like a great idea, Jimmy.' Richard slapped Jimmy on the back, a gesture that brought a tight, grim line to Jimmy's mouth. If there was one type of person he couldn't stand it was a sycophant. As the words formed in his mind, Jimmy silently laughed at the use of the word. Sycophant, huh! Crawler sounded much better, it had more bite to it. The English language was a wonderful thing, and Jimmy had struggled to educate himself over the long, hard years, spending every spare hour in the public library in a bid to learn all the things he had missed out on through his lack of schooling during his formative years; but you couldn't beat the good old-fashioned words when describing people such as these two men.

Helping the girls into the carriage, where a grinning Charlie was perched up in the driver's seat, Jimmy said quietly, 'I won't be a minute,' then turned to the still-hovering men. Lowering his voice, he hissed harshly, 'Listen, you two ponces, the only reason I'm here is because of the girls, so piss off and stop trying to pretend we're old mates, because we ain't, and never will be. I just feel sorry for those two poor cows for having two miserable, gutless excuses for men in their drab lives. And you . . .' he scowled at Phil, who fell back a pace in fright. 'I ain't gonna tell you to stop gambling, 'cos you can't. It's in your blood and you'll never change, more's the pity, so I'll keep taking your bets, 'cos at least that way, you won't have to worry about getting your legs broken if you can't pay up. But you'd better not let those girls go short because of your habit, or you'll have me to answer to. D'yer understand me, Bradford?'

Phil gulped noisily then nodded. 'Yeah, all right, Jim— I mean, Mr Jackson,' he amended hastily at the look of pure venom etched on the face glaring at him. Then, with a sudden burst of strength, he blurted out, 'I know I'm not the best brother in the world, but I do love my sisters and—'

Already walking away, Jimmy rounded on the hapless Phil. 'Well then, bleeding well show it, and look after them. They deserve better, and if you were any sort of a man, you'd know it.'

Phil's eyes dropped under the accusing stare, and Jimmy, recognising the genuine shame the other man was feeling, relented. 'Look, if you can't stop gambling . . . Well then you might as well do it where I can keep an eye on you. Come and see me on Monday and I'll see if there's anything going by way of a job. That's if you're interested.'

Phil's eyes lit up, his shoulders straightening, as a new feeling of worth surged through him.

'Oh, I'm interested all right, Mr Jackson, and, thanks.'

Jimmy looked hard at Phil. 'Don't thank me yet, 'cos if I do give you a job, I'll be making sure half your wages goes straight to your sister.'

Phil held the penetrating gaze. 'I understand. And I'll be at your place first thing Monday morning.'

With a curt nod of his head, Jimmy strode away and climbed into the waiting carriage. Behind him, Richard, his face almost purple with indignation at the slight he had suffered, turned on his cousin. 'In case you've forgotten, young man, you work for me, and a bloody good job it is too, considering your lack of qualifications to do anything better. You'd—'

'It's a rubbish job, and you know it,' Phil shot back angrily. 'All right, so I was grateful for it when we first moved down here, but it's been five years now, and I'm still doing the same old boring job. Oh, you might have given me the title of assistant manager, but it's an empty title, as you well know. I've got no responsibilities, no job satisfaction, and I certainly don't get assistant managerial wages. Why, I'm only getting a few bob more a week than I did when I first started working for you.' Gathering courage, Phil added, 'No, I've had it with your poxy job. I'm going to work for Mr Jackson, if he'll have me, and—'

Richard's eyebrows rose in disdain. 'Well, well. So it's Mr Jackson now, is it? What about all that talk about coming here today to meet your friend Jimmy? Huh! That's a laugh. It's about as funny as actually meeting the almighty Jimmy Jackson.' Turning up the fur collar of his Afghan coat, the stout man glared at Phil. 'I don't know why I bothered, and the way you were sucking up to him was embarrassing. The man's obviously just a well-dressed ruffian. Why, he's as common as muck. You go and work for him, if that's the way you want it, I won't have any trouble filling your position. But one thing I will say is, you'd do well to keep the girls away from his influence.'

Phil's eyes flickered to the fat, outraged face. Then with a rare show of character he replied tersely, 'Then you'd better tell Mr Jackson that yourself, because I'm certainly not going to. As for my sucking up . . . Well, I've had a good teacher, haven't I . . . Uncle?' The men's eyes locked for a brief few moments before Phil, his back straight, and feeling lighter and prouder in himself than he had in a long time, walked away.

*   *   *

Richard Fisher glared after the retreating figure, his fleshy features contorted in rage at being so humiliated.

After all he had done for that family, this was the thanks he got. Well! He wasn't going to take this kind of treatment lying down, oh, no. Almost bursting with self-righteous indignation Richard hurried towards the nearest pub, his cunning mind feverishly searching for a way to get back at the Bradford family.

An hour later, and with a liberal helping of whisky warming his system, Richard suddenly thought of Ivy Harris. A crafty smile spread over his thick lips as he conjured up a picture of his former fiancée. It had been twenty years since his engagement had been broken off, and he hadn't seen hide nor hair of Ivy until six months ago.

Settling back in his chair, Richard remembered his shock at meeting the woman he had once promised to marry coming out of Harrods one Saturday afternoon in the late spring. He hadn't recognised her at first, but she'd certainly remembered him. After a lot of awkward smalltalk, they had gone for a drink, whereupon Ivy had informed him that she had been twice widowed, neither of the marriages producing any offspring, much to her regret. They had, however, left Ivy comfortably off. It had been obvious to Richard that Ivy was on the look-out for husband number three. Not wanting to renew their former relationship, Richard had skillfully managed to ward off the hopeful woman's coy advances. He hadn't been adverse to seeing her again, in fact he had been pleasantly surprised to find she hadn't altered much over the years. She had put on some weight, but at their age, who hadn't? Richard's thoughts paused as he glanced down at his bulging stomach, then shrugged; Ivy hadn't seemed bothered by his appearance. Apart from the added pounds she had gained, Ivy was still an attractive woman; better still, she obviously wasn't short of a few bob.

Since that first unexpected meeting, Richard had seen Ivy on several occasions. At first he had imagined it to be coincidence, then he had realised that Ivy was deliberately arranging the chance encounters. He couldn't pretend that he wasn't flattered, but after so many years living the uncomplicated life of a bachelor he was reluctant to change his pleasant lifestyle – until now! Downing the last sip of the amber liquid, Richard rose unsteadily to his feet. Perhaps it was about time he thought of settling down. After all, he wasn't getting any younger, and with the warm glow of the imbibed whisky filling his body, Richard wondered what it would be like to be a father.

Leaving the warmth of the pub, Richard hailed a passing cab. On the journey home, his mind conjured up images of himself, Ivy and a child, the perfect family scenario growing on him mile by mile, minute by minute. Then he frowned. How old would Ivy be now? Quickly counting up the years, he suddenly relaxed. By his calculations, Ivy must be thirty-eight, maybe a year older. Not the ideal age for bearing children, but then his own mother had given birth to him at the grand old age of forty-three. Nodding his head in satisfaction, Richard made up his mind. He would see Ivy as soon as possible. There wouldn't be any need for a long courtship, they had done that twenty years ago. Of course the flat he was living in at present would be too small for the family he was planning – but he had another home, hadn't he? The crafty smile was back in evidence as he thought about what he was planning to do. Oh, he couldn't wait to see the look on Rebecca's face when he told her he was planning on moving back in with his new wife. For years, the wilful young girl had openly defied him, showing not the smallest modicum of respect or gratitude. When she did deign to speak to him, she had never made any pretence of her feelings towards him. But he had put up with her behaviour because it suited him. It had also suited him to have Phil working for him for a pittance. Now that arrangement had also changed. As for Maude . . . ! His shoulders lifted involuntarily. He had supported his sister for long enough, and if Ivy hadn't been prepared to live with Maude twenty years ago, she certainly wouldn't contemplate it now. Still! There were homes to care for people such as his sister, and he'd make sure it didn't cost him too much. Maude had lived a life of luxury for years, but now her days of comfort were numbered.

As his mind raced on, Richard felt not the slightest compunction for his older sister. They had never liked each other. The only reason he had looked after her as long as he had was to keep face with the neighbours and his business associates; now that didn't seem to be important to him any more. Besides, he could always maintain that Maude was safely ensconced in a reputable nursing home; who would know the difference?

In the darkness of the cab, Richard's mind shifted to the only person who had ever offered him any happiness. As a picture of Amy floated in front of his mind, Richard felt a stirring in the lower half of his body. Shifting uncomfortably on the leather seat, the portly man experienced a moment's shame, then quickly thrust it aside. He was a man, wasn't he? And what man could fail to be aroused by such a lovely girl as Amy? His youngest charge had no inkling of his feelings concerning her, for Amy was an innocent, and Richard had hoped to use that innocence for his own gains. But Rebecca had seen through him from the start. Whenever he and Amy were in the house, Rebecca always made sure they were never left alone together for long. But Amy, bless her, always gave the man she called uncle a kiss and a cuddle whenever he visited. And right behind her would be Rebecca, her face stony as she watched the affectionate scene being played out. Richard sighed. He would be genuinely sorry to see Amy go out of his life, but he certainly wouldn't be sorry to see the back of the rest of them. Bloody ingrates!

With Amy still at the forefront of his mind, Richard remembered that she would be sixteen in February. He had planned to give a party to mark the occasion, thus furthering the impression of the kind, generous man he purported to be. His eyes lit up with excitement. Of course, that was the perfect answer. He would keep quiet about Ivy for now and go ahead with the proposed surprise party. What better time and place to inform all those concerned about his forth-coming marriage? Rubbing his hands together with barely suppressed glee, Richard visualised the shock and astonishment his announcement would cause.

The cab drove on into the growing darkness while Richard continued to ponder on his plans for the future. Yet while his mind envisaged heady images of a son or daughter, or perhaps both, to call him father, he forgot that his intended bride had already been married twice without producing a single child.

CHAPTER NINE

Seated on hard chairs in the snug of the Flying Horse public house, Rebecca and Amy kept glancing around their new environment nervously. The noise coming from the public bar was deafening. Neither girl had ever seen so many people packed into such a small space. And what people! It seemed to the inexperienced girls' eyes as if every shape and form of life had crammed themselves into the crowded pub, and over the hubbub of shouts and raucous laughter an old piano was gamely trying to make itself heard above the almighty din. Yet through their nervousness there was also a stomach-churning sensation of excitement. But while Rebecca strove to maintain a calm exterior, Amy, her youthful exuberance bubbling over, cried loudly, 'Oh, Becky, isn't it wonderful? I've often wondered what a pub was like, but I never imagined it would be as exciting as this.'

Rebecca shot a warning look at her sister. 'Shush! Don't draw attention to us, Amy. I'm not sure you're old enough to be in a pub, and I don't want to take the chance of us being thrown out, so just try and look inconspicuous.' Even though they were seated in the comparative safety of the snug, Rebecca could see the admiring glances of the crowd of men milling around the public bar directed at them.

A look of fright crossed over Amy's face. 'I never thought of that. How old have you got to be to go into a pub?'

Rebecca, her eyes fixed firmly on the wobbly table, answered softly, 'How should I know, love? I've as much experience of pubs as you have; which is absolutely nothing.'

Lifting her eyes, Rebecca looked around the public bar trying to locate Jimmy or Charlie, praying desperately that one of them would appear. She was becoming increasingly uncomfortable in the alien surrounding, and it was taking all of her strength not to get up and run out of the frightening environment she had been placed in. Yet if she succumbed to her fear, she would look foolish; not only to herself, but also to Jimmy Jackson. Her head rose sharply. What did it matter what Jimmy Jackson thought of her? Then her inbred integrity rose to the surface and mocked her. Of course Jimmy's opinion of her mattered. If it didn't, if she had no feelings for the man whatsoever, then she wouldn't be here in this pub, striving to appear as if she was accustomed to sitting in pubs daily, when in fact she was almost scared out of her wits.

For something to do, Rebecca began rifling through her bag, while at the same time keeping up a running patter of smalltalk with Amy; anything to pass the time until the men returned – anything to keep her mind off the charismatic Jimmy Jackson. Though Lord knows he wasn't just what she would call good-looking, he possessed far greater and more powerful attributes, and those attributes were causing alarming sensations in Rebecca's mind and body that she was unable and too inexperienced to deal with.

She was saved from further mental turmoil as Charlie strode through the snug door carrying a tray of drinks. 'Here yer are, ladies. Sorry I took so long, it's always crowded at this time of the day, 'cos of all the people coming in from the Old Bailey. It's like a day out fer some people. I can't say as I can see the attraction meself, I mean sitting fer hours in a smelly court, packed in like sardines, but there yer go, it takes all sorts, don't it?'

Rebecca looked up into the grinning face gratefully. If she'd had to wait here much longer she would have made a run for the door, and to hell with what Jimmy thought of her. Thinking of the man in question, Rebecca glanced at the snug door, her face falling as she realised that Charlie was on his own.

Carefully laying the tray of drinks on the table, Charlie saw the disappointment on Rebecca's face and smiled inwardly. Jimmy had done it again, though this time Charlie didn't think the young lady would be as easy to get as her predecessors.

Picking up the glass in front of her, Rebecca looked warily at the clear-coloured liquid and asked hesitantly, 'Thanks, Charlie. Um, what is it?'

Charlie gave a loud chuckle. 'Well, we didn't know what yer drunk, so the guv'nor ordered a gin an' tonic fer you, and a lemonade fer Amy . . . He'll be 'ere in a minute,' he added impishly as he saw Rebecca's eyes stray once more to the closed door.

Turning back to Charlie, Rebecca was quick to notice the amused look on the young man's face and, feeling awkward and determined to appear sophisticated, she took a swallow of the drink nonchalantly, then gasped as the unfamiliar taste caught in the back of her throat causing her to cough loudly. Mortified, she tried to stem the bout of coughing but only succeeded in spluttering and coughing louder, much to the amusement of the elderly men and women occupying the snug.

'You all right, Becky?' Amy was on her feet in concern. Then to Rebecca's everlasting shame Jimmy appeared, took in the situation at a glance and began slapping her on the back, while at the same time offering her a large white handkerchief to mop up the trickle of drink that was running down Rebecca's chin. Her face scarlet, both from the bout of coughing and the excruciating embarrassment, Rebecca tried to stand, her only thought to get away from this awful place and the grinning faces surrounding her.

She was halfway out of her chair when a firm hand

clasped her shoulder, preventing her from rising any further.

'I'm sorry, Rebecca. It's my fault. I'm so used to ordering gin for my lady fr— What I mean is, most women prefer gin, I just didn't think. Will you forgive me for my thoughtlessness . . . please?'

Rebecca gazed up into the warm, brown eyes and was glad for the excuse to sit down, for the strength had suddenly drained from her legs.

'Jimmy, is it all right me being in a pub?' Amy, sensing her sister's feelings, attempted to draw attention away from Rebecca and give her time to compose herself. 'Only Becky and me aren't sure how old you have to be to come in a public house. Becky said to try and act inconspicuously, so nobody would notice us.'

Jimmy looked first at the anxious young girl, then shifted his gaze to Rebecca, his keen eyes taking in every detail. Rebecca was wearing a royal blue coat, the design of which he had never seen before, and a plain, wide-brimmed hat of the same shade of blue. Beneath the hat, Rebecca had fashioned her dark blond hair into an elegant plait held in place by unseen pins, with tendrils of the glossy hair falling in wisps at the base of her neck and face. His eyes shifted to Amy. The younger girl was dressed in a dark red coat and hat of similar design, but where her elder sister had opted for the sophisticated look, Amy had left her shiny, bright blond hair loosely spilling over her shoulders, and reaching to the middle of her slender back. Taking in the appearances of these two striking young women,

Jimmy thought of what Amy had just said about trying to act inconspicuously, and tried to stifle a laugh. But it was no good. Throwing back his head, Jimmy emitted a loud roar of laughter, and once he'd started he couldn't stop.

Startled, Rebecca and Amy looked at each other in bewilderment, wondering what could have caused such unmitigated amusement.

His bout of mirth subsiding, Jimmy wiped his eyes and grinned. 'Sorry, I couldn't help it. I mean, the thought of you two trying to look inconspicuous, especially in a place like this, well . . . !' Rebecca and Amy exchanged glances again, then looked around them at the shabbily dressed men and women, the majority of whom were grubby and unkempt, then took stock of each other, a smile forming on their lips as they realised the incongruity of Amy's statement. Then Jimmy began chuckling again, and the sound was so infectious that both girls found themselves joining in the merriment. Soon the entire snug was ringing with laughter, though the majority of the people gathered didn't know what they were laughing at. Then Jimmy ordered drinks all round, and soon the small room took on the atmosphere and conviviality of a family party.

During this time Rebecca had tried the gin again, this time, however, she took a small sip, grimaced, then took another tentative swallow until much to her relief the glass was empty. Proud that she had managed to finish the unappetising liquid, Rebecca was feeling quite smug when, to her utmost dismay and horror, another, larger drink was placed before her. Staring down at the filled glass with rising panic, Rebecca wondered frantically what she was going to do. It wasn't like trying to get rid of a piece of unwanted food when dining out. There was no obliging dog beneath the table ready to help out in a situation like this. Forcing a smile to her face, Rebecca gamely lifted the glass to her lips, but it was no use. She simply couldn't drink another drop of the revolting stuff.

'Is your drink all right, Rebecca? I can always get you a lemonade if you'd prefer.' Jimmy was staring into her bemused face, his eyes filled with undisguised amusement.

Straightening her back, Rebecca replied firmly, 'It's quite all right, thank you. I'm sure I'll get used to the taste eventually.'

Jimmy had to turn his head away from the flushed face for fear he would start laughing again. Lord, but she was a stubborn mare. It was obvious she hated the taste of the gin, but she'd probably persevere even if it choked her, rather than admit defeat. A feeling of guilt suddenly attacked Jimmy's conscience. He shouldn't have ordered Rebecca another gin, especially when it was evident that the girl had never drunk spirits before today. He had wanted to see how she could be with a few drinks inside her, now he realised he'd been cruel to bait the naive girl, particularly after her ordeal at the Old Bailey. The sense of guilt quickly changed to one of anger. What the hell was he playing at anyway? There were a dozen other places he could be right now, so why was he sitting here with this gauche young woman, wasting both his time and hers? Yet she had seemed so pleased when he'd invited her and Amy for a drink, and even though Rebecca wasn't enjoying the drink itself, she was displaying a certain element of suppressed excitement at being taken out of her usual drab existence. And Amy was definitely having a good time, partly due no doubt to the undivided attention Charlie was bestowing upon her. Well! This would be the last time he would see either of the girls again, so he might as well make sure they had a day to remember. Tapping Rebecca's arm, he winked broadly, 'You don't have to drink that if you don't want to, love. I'll get you something else.'

'Oh, no, it's fine, really,' Rebecca protested lamely, but Jimmy had already gone to the bar. Feeling miserable and unbearably stupid, Rebecca gazed around the small room, thinking as she did so that the place was beginning to grow on her. Everyone seemed so happy and at ease and here she was with a face as long as a wet weekend in August. Taking a deep breath she picked up her drink and was about to brace herself for another sip when it was taken from her hand. Startled she glanced up into Charlie's face.

'Give it 'ere, girl, I ain't fussy what I drink.' With one single gulp the glass was miraculously empty. Rebecca could only marvel at the young man's digestive system and silently thanked him for his sensitivity and kindness in coming to her aid. When Jimmy reappeared with a glass of lemonade and two pints of ale, his eyes immediately went to the empty glass, then lifted suspiciously to his employee, but Charlie was engrossed in conversation with the captivated Amy, seemingly unaware of his governor's presence.

Nodding towards the empty glass, Jimmy commented wryly, 'I see you've finished your drink, and in one go by the look of it. How on earth did you manage that – unless you had some help!'

Rebecca shrugged, then said airily, 'Oh, it's not too bad once you get the hang of it. I quite enjoyed it actually.'

Jimmy grinned mischievously. 'In that case, I'll get you another.'

Immediately Rebecca amended hastily, 'No! . . . I mean, no thank you. I've had enough, really, and besides, I don't want to arrive home drunk. Now that would give Maude something to moan about. I'd never hear the end of it.'

Hitching his chair nearer, Jimmy paused for a moment, then asked quietly, 'Tell me about yourself, Rebecca.'

And much to Rebecca's surprise she did just that. Normally reticent about her personal life, Rebecca found herself telling this man her life story. Because of the noise surrounding them it was necessary to move closer together, or shout her business to all and sundry. When she had finished, their faces were almost touching and somehow her thigh was now resting comfortably against Jimmy's. Throughout her sheltered life, Rebecca had never been in such close proximity with a man before, or so intimate, and the heady feeling that was coursing through her body was

106

equivalent to the way she would have felt if she had indeed drank all that gin.

'You mean to tell me that you have to look after Maude day and night without recompense; and pay rent into the bargain? That's bloody scandalous, especially as the house is owned by that fat bastard . . . Sorry!' Jimmy smiled sheepishly as Rebecca flinched at the sound of the word that so aptly described the odious Richard Fisher. Spreading his hands wide, Jimmy added, 'You see now what Bessie meant when she said how I reverted to type when I'm angry, but I'm not apologising for that. People take me as they find me, I don't pretend to be anything other than what I am.' Taking hold of the slender fingers, Jimmy ignored the warning voices in his head and asked, 'And how do you find me, Rebecca Bradford? Villain or hero?' Leaning even closer, he smiled tenderly. 'Or hopefully a bit of both.'

The touch of his hand, and the warmth of his breath that smelt pleasantly of ale was intoxicating, making Rebecca doubly glad she hadn't drank the remainder of her gin, else she'd be falling at this man's feet by now. Then, out of nowhere, her mind conjured up a picture of Maude, and with the unpleasant thought Rebecca was reminded sharply of her obligations at home. Reluctant to break the enchanting spell that was gripping her, yet unable to ignore the fact that she was needed elsewhere, Rebecca drew her hand away from the warm, comforting grasp. As she relinquished contact with Jimmy's touch, the public house suddenly jumped back into focus. For a short while Rebecca had felt as if she and Jimmy were the only people in the room, now the loud talk and high-pitched laughter once again filled the smoky atmosphere.

Smiling shyly she murmured, 'I think you're a very kind man . . . despite your occupation.' The lines of her mouth turned up impishly. 'And I'll always be grateful for what you've done for Amy and me, but now I'm afraid I'll have to get back home. Like it or not, I can't leave Maude with Mrs Gates any longer.' Her eyes sparkling with laughter, she added, 'I like Ada too much to subject her to that ordeal for any longer than necessary.' Pushing back her chair, Rebecca rose to her feet and called to Amy that they had to go. The young girl looked at her sister in dismay.

'Oh, Becky, must we? I'm having such a nice time, can't we stay a bit longer, please?'

Gathering up her bag and gloves, Rebecca replied firmly, 'I'm sorry, love. I don't want to go either, but we have to get back home. Mrs Gates and Maude will be worrying about us.'

At the mention of the woman Amy called aunt, the young girl sighed, but she didn't offer any further argument. Like Rebecca, Amy had been transported into a different world this past hour, but now it was time to go back to the real one.

The journey home in Jimmy's carriage was a much pleasanter one than the original. This time the three people aboard chattered and laughed like old friends, and when Charlie shouted down cheerfully, ''Ere we are, girls, 'ome sweet 'ome,' Amy's face fell and Rebecca's stomach tightened as she realised that her time with the engaging Jimmy Jackson was now over.

As Charlie helped her down from the cab, Rebecca bravely pasted a watery smile to her lips as she thanked him, while inside, the knowledge that she would probably never see Jimmy again was creating a sensation of disappointment so keen it was physically painful. She put her hand to her stomach absentmindedly, a gesture that was not lost on the watching Jimmy.

'Are you all right, Rebecca?' he asked in concern, fearing the unaccustomed gin had upset the young woman's system.

Aware she was holding her stomach, Rebecca quickly removed her hand saying brightly, 'Yes, just hungry that's all. I haven't had anything to eat since last night. I was too nervous to have any breakfast.'

Jimmy leant forward to say his goodbyes. Apart from the court hearing, the day had turned out very pleasurable, much better than he had anticipated. But all good things . . . as the saying went. There really was no point in continuing the short acquaintance any further. His mind formed the words, 'Goodbye, ladies, it was nice meeting you.' Instead, when he opened his mouth to speak he heard himself saying, 'I'm sorry, I didn't think, or I would have taken you both for a meal.' Now that he thought of it, he was suddenly reminded of how hungry he himself was. With the thought of food came the image of *Fontaines*, a French restaurant in the West End he frequented on special occasions.

As the notion entered his mind, he dismissed it hurriedly. Oh, no! He wasn't going down that road. Besides, it wouldn't be fair on Rebecca to let her think he was interested in her. Even if he was, nothing could ever come of it, and she was too decent a person to toy with. Still, it wouldn't hurt to take both girls out for a meal nearby, just to sort of round off the day. After that he would bid them goodbye, and that would be an end to it. Leaning further out of the carriage window, he said, 'If you can get someone to stay with Maude, maybe you'd let me make amends and take you both out to dinner tonight. Nothing fancy, just a bite to eat at a restaurant round here.'

Rebecca stood stock still on the cold pavement, a ripple of excitement gripping her body. She should say no, she really should. A man like Jimmy Jackson was out of her league. She wasn't so naive as not to know the type of women a man like Jimmy normally cavorted with, but Amy would be with them, and it would be lovely to be taken out to a restaurant. It would also be very selfish of her to deny Amy the unexpected treat. *Hypocrite!* her inner voice shouted back at her. Swallowing hard, and conscious of Amy's imploring look, Rebecca answered, 'Thank you, Jimmy, that would be lovely.'

As Charlie clambered up into the driver's seat, Jimmy called out, 'I'll call around eight.'

After waving off the carriage, the two girls walked sedately into the house. Once inside, however, Amy let out a squeal of joy. 'He's taking us out to dinner,

Becky, and to a restaurant . . . Ooh, Becky, isn't it wonderful?' Jumping around the room, Amy continued to chatter away happily, and Rebecca, for once, didn't try to dampen her younger sister's mood. How could she, when she herself felt fit to burst?

'There you both are. I was beginning to think Jimmy had kidnapped the pair of you and sold you into slavery.' Phil appeared at the bottom of the stairs. 'I sent Ada off over an hour ago, and that one upstairs is nearly out of her mind with curiosity.'

Rebecca looked at her brother suspiciously. It wasn't like Phil to be so amenable when he had been left with Maude.

'We've been to a pub, Phil, and Jimmy's taking Becky and me out . . .' Amy, her face aglow, was holding onto Phil's arm.

Before she could say anything else, Rebecca quickly cut in saying, 'Go up to Maude, please, Amy, there's a love. Tell her I'll be up to see her in a minute.'

Amy seemed to fly up the stairs, her excited voice heard long after she disappeared from view.

Phil followed Rebecca into the kitchen, his countenance and demeanour maintaining a happy front. Bracing herself for the inquisition that was sure to start at any moment, Rebecca put the kettle on the hob then turned to face her brother.

'All right, Phil, let's get it over with. I'm sorry I was so long, but I've as much right to stay out now and then as you have . . . No! Hang on, I'm not sorry at all. It's about time you took some responsibility for Maude and—'

111

Phil stepped back a pace, his hands held high. 'Whoa, just a minute, did I say anything? Well, did I?'

Rebecca studied him with suspicious eyes. 'No, you didn't, but you normally do. In fact you always moan if I stay out longer than an hour, and seeing as shopping is the only break I get away from this place, then I think I'm entitled to a bit of fun now and then.'

Lounging on the hard kitchen chair, Phil averted his eyes from Rebecca's angry glare, his fingers reaching out to tap a nervous tattoo on the wooden table.

'You're right, Becks. I have been a selfish sod, but things are going to change, I promise.'

Rebecca turned away, sighing heavily.

'I've heard that one before, Phil. If I had a sovereign for every time you've said that, I'd be a millionairess by now.'

Jumping out of his chair, Phil, his voice bearing an element of desperation, appealed to the stiff back. 'It's different this time, Becks. I've already told Richard to stuff his job . . . I've had a better offer.'

Rebecca whirled around, her eyes wary. Phil saw the look of disbelief and smiled. Strutting around the table he stuffed both hands into his pockets and said airily, 'As from Monday, I'm going to work for Jimmy Jackson, so what d'yer think of that, eh?' He was about to add that Jimmy would be making sure half his wages went directly to Rebecca, but decided against it. He was feeling immeasurably proud of himself at this minute, and to inform his sister that his wages were going to be docked in her favour would somehow take away his feeling of importance.

'When did this happen?' Rebecca had left the stove and was now gripping the edges of the table.

'Oh, when Jimmy came back from seeing you and Amy into his cab. We had a bit of a talk, and he offered me a job.' He broke off and chuckled. 'You should have seen Richard's face, Becks. I thought he was going to have a heart attack.' His mind carefully skirting over the true account of the heated conversation, Phil continued, 'Anyway, I start Monday. I don't know what I'll be doing yet, but anything's got to be better than working for Richard . . . By the way, did I hear Amy say Jimmy's taking you both out tonight?'

Rebecca returned to the stove and lifted the boiling kettle from the hob. Then, adopting her brother's attitude, she replied casually, 'That's right, but only if I can get Mrs Gates to look after Maude.'

Strutting around the small room, Phil waved his hands loftily. 'Don't worry about Maude. I'll stay in tonight and keep her company. You and Amy go out and enjoy yourselves.'

Rebecca could only shake her head in bemusement at the sudden turn of events; not least the change in Phil. But how long would that last? And what about Richard? He wasn't going to be too pleased at having one of his employees snatched out from under his nose.

'Things are beginning to look up, aren't they, Becks?' Phil was hovering by her side, his sombre gaze, like that of a small child, seeming to beg for reassurance. And Rebecca, feeling a rare sense of affection towards her brother, reached out and patted his hand.

'Yes, it certainly looks like it, Phil.' After all, Rebecca mused silently, considering their present position, things could hardly get worse.

CHAPTER TEN

The Black Hat restaurant was situated in a quiet street off the busy thoroughfare of Bow. Although not up to West End standards, the small, family-run restaurant nevertheless attracted a more affluent class of customer than those of its contemporaries. Yet to Rebecca and Amy, who had never been anywhere posher than the local Lyons tea house, it seemed as if they had walked into Heaven; and the difference to the pub they had frequented earlier that day was markedly apparent.

Surrounded by women dressed in expensive clothing and men attired in morning dress, Rebecca sent up a fervent prayer of thanks that she had been blessed with the art of needlework, for without her skills, she and Amy would have looked sorely out of place amongst such finery. Displaying the air of someone who was used to being in such a place, Rebecca cast a covert eye at her sister. Amy

115

was wearing a lilac two-piece, the bodice of which was adorned with tiny pearl buttons. At Rebecca's insistence, Amy had fashioned her long hair into a neat bun, the effect of which had added a look of maturity to the heart-shaped face. Rebecca had chosen a dark green outfit she had only recently finished, wondering at the time if she would ever get the chance to wear it. Staring at the starched, white lace tablecloth, she reflected wryly that it was just as well this would probably be their last excursion into the outside world, for she and Amy had only two decent outfits each; and they had already worn the other ones to attend the Old Bailey hearing.

The table they had been allocated was for four people. Rebecca and Amy had been seated opposite each other, with Jimmy and a spruce-looking Charlie, wearing one of Jimmy's old suits, on either side. Unlike the atmosphere of the pub, the restaurant was filled with the muted sounds of conversation and the tinkling of cutlery against china and glass. The choice of menu had been left to Jimmy, who had ordered roast beef dinners for them all. Conscious of her table manners, Rebecca had deftly managed the various items of cutlery without any difficulty, as had Amy. Both girls had been taught the etiquette of eating at an early age by their late mother, and although it was an art they hadn't had to practise for many years, the early training had not been forgotten.

Their meal was delicious, and was enlivened by pleasant conversation. The four people finally laid down their spoons after finishing their dessert of chocolate gateau and cream.

'Cor, that was 'andsome. Thanks, Guv'nor.' Charlie gave a sigh of appreciation while patting his flat stomach, well aware of the disapproving glances that met his exuberant statement. Jimmy smiled at his young employee and shook his head in silent amusement. Trust Charlie to bring the tone of the evening down. He'd better be sure never to take the uncompromising young man anywhere up West. Yet Jimmy wasn't put out by Charlie's behaviour, for he too treated all people alike. Be they king or commoner, men such as Jimmy and Charlie would always be themselves; there wasn't a fawning or ingratiating bone in either of them, which was why Jimmy liked Charlie so much – he reminded him of himself when younger. Yet there was only nine years between the two men, though sometimes Jimmy felt old enough to be Charlie's father.

Taking hold of a bottle of champagne from a silver ice bucket, Jimmy winked at Rebecca, saying, 'I think this will be more to your liking.'

Taking a tentative sip, Rebecca relaxed. This was lovely, much better than that awful gin.

'Oh, yes. This is much better. In fact I could get quite used to it.' *Given half the chance*, she added silently.

'Could I have some, Becky?' Amy was looking longingly at the sparkling wine. 'Please! Just a little taste.'

Rebecca smiled fondly. 'All right, but just a drop. You've got work tomorrow, don't forget. I don't want to have to drag you out of bed with a sore head.'

Aware of her surroundings, Amy managed to contain her excitement as Jimmy poured a small helping of the champagne into her glass. But as she lifted it, and the bubbles of the champagne tickled her nose, Amy couldn't suppress a giggle.

'Ooh, that went right up my nose,' she squealed with delight, her words and laughter drawing more attention to their table.

Biting her lip, Rebecca lowered her eyes. No wonder Amy and Charlie got on so well, they made a right pair. *And who do you think you are?* her inner voice mocked. *The Queen of Sheba?* Then Amy spoke again, and this time her words brought Rebecca's head snapping back in fright.

'Look, Becky, there's Uncle Richard with some woman. I wonder who she is.'

Before she could stop herself, Rebecca's head had swivelled around to look in the direction of Amy's gaze. True enough, there was Richard, sitting at the far end of the restaurant, in the company of an attractive woman Rebecca had never seen before. The thought of the odious Richard having a lady friend had never entered Rebecca's mind; the image was too revolting to contemplate. Yet at his age it was only natural he would seek female companionship. The question was, how had he managed to acquire it? In a few, brief seconds Rebecca had quickly taken in Richard's companion, and though she was loath to admit it, the lady in question looked very presentable.

Jimmy too had quickly taken stock of Richard's lady

118

friend. Like Rebecca, he was surprised at the lady's, appearance. If he'd had to imagine a woman who would choose to be seen in Richard Fisher's company, he would have conjured up a rather different picture to the one he was witnessing.

'Don't stare, Amy,' Rebecca muttered. 'He might come over. Don't give him any encouragement, please.' The last thing she wanted was for Richard to join them, and ruin a lovely evening. The thought was so appalling that Rebecca lifted her glass involuntarily, downing the champagne in one swift gulp.

Jimmy's eyebrows rose in surprised amusement. Refilling the empty glass, he bent over the table and remarked archly, 'I don't think you need worry. After our brief meeting today, I very much doubt your uncle will be attempting to join us.'

As he spoke, Jimmy glanced over at Richard's table and saw the portly man begin to rise from his chair, a hovering smile on his thick lips. Jimmy's face darkened. Leaning back in his chair, he directed a warning look across the room and immediately Richard dropped back onto his seat, his fat face flushing in awkward confusion. Conscious of the silence that had fallen, Jimmy's eyes flickered around his table. The girls looked flustered and uncertain, and even Amy had stopped chattering. Charlie, on the other hand, used to seeing his governor in a temper, was keeping a low profile.

Mindful that his abrupt change in behaviour was causing the sudden embarrassing atmosphere, Jimmy quickly lightened the mood. Pouring out more drinks, he launched into a hilarious anecdote that soon had the occupants laughing and at ease once more; Amy in particular, who, taking advantage of Rebecca's distracted state, was now drinking her second glass of champagne.

When, at ten-thirty, Jimmy called for the bill, all four of the party were in a relaxed and merry mood.

Stopping off at the cloakroom before their journey home, Rebecca and Amy anxiously studied their faces in the long, gilded mirror that hung over a small line of washbasins adorned with gold-plated taps.

'I hate eating vegetables if I ever go out anywhere,' Amy was busily examining her open mouth. 'I'm always afraid I'll get a bit of cabbage stuck in my teeth, and everyone will be too polite to tell me. Do you remember that time I had to arrange the flowers in the café, and I got all that horrible brown stuff from the stalks all over my face? Nobody said a word, the rotten sods! I was walking around all day like it, and I didn't have a clue until I got home and you told me. Do you remember, Becky?'

Rebecca chuckled at the memory. 'Oh, yes, I remember. You looked as though you hadn't seen a bar of soap for a week, and you were so happy because people had been smiling at you all day. Looking back, it was quite funny at the time.'

Amy made a face in the mirror, her lips twitching with laughter. 'It might have been funny for you, but I . . . Oh, sorry, am I in your way?'

Amy stepped to one side as a tall red-haired

woman emerged from a small cubicle behind them and approached the washbasins.

'That's all right, it isn't very big in here, is it?' The woman smiled graciously and turned on the taps. 'I always try and get in here before eleven if I can. After that time, I prefer to wait until I get home. It's a lot quicker.'

Both Amy and Rebecca made a smile of agreement, as if they too were familiar with the restaurant's washroom facilities.

Carefully arranging her hat over her thick, plaited hair, Rebecca was about to secure it with three hatpins when she paused, uncomfortably aware that the red-haired woman was deliberately scrutinising her from head to foot. Her face and neck colouring under the woman's watchful eyes, Rebecca cleared her throat and asked tersely, 'Have we met before. I don't seem to recall your face, though I'm sure you'll know mine again if we meet in the future.'

The woman looked up at Rebecca with cold, green eyes, a mocking smile touching her full, painted lips. 'I'm sorry. I didn't mean to be rude. I was admiring your costume. Did you buy it from one of the big department stores, or was it made for you?'

The colour on Rebecca's face deepened. The woman, for some reason, was openly taunting her. Drawing herself up straighter, Rebecca replied sharply, 'I made it myself. Why! Are you looking for a seamstress?'

Listening to the conversation, Amy silently groaned. *Not again, Becky,* she pleaded mutely, her generous nature not recognising the spite behind the stranger's words.

The woman finished washing her hands and raised her eyebrows in feigned surprise. 'Dear me, have I offended you in some way? If so, then I apologise. I meant no harm.'

Rebecca looked at the beautiful face staring at her and found her own gaze faltering. Maybe she had been mistaken and had taken slight where none was intended. Yet she was usually very astute in judging people's moods and character. Then again, it had been a very long day, and a very unusual one, so she was prepared, for Amy's sake, to give the woman the benefit of the doubt. After all, she told herself, what was the point in making a fuss, especially now, when they'd had such a wonderful evening? Then again, there was no need to fall at the woman's feet in grovelling apology either. The last hatpin in place, Rebecca stepped back from the mirror to make sure her hat was straight, turned slightly to where the woman was drying her hands on a soft, white towel, then stopped. The woman was still watching her, the large, green eyes calculating Rebecca's every move, like a bird of prey studying its victim before pouncing. Bewildered by the stranger's hostility, Rebecca mentally shrugged tiredly. Some women were just born spiteful and Rebecca, suddenly feeling the strain of the day beginning to take its toll, refused to be goaded any further; the woman, whoever she was, wasn't worth the effort.

'Come along, Amy, we've wasted enough time in here.'

Only too glad to leave, Amy glided to the door, followed a few moments later by Rebecca. As she

122

made to leave the cloakroom, the woman's husky voice floated after her.

'Oh, will you give my regards to Jimmy? Tell him Heather was asking after him . . . Goodnight!' The door slammed shut in her face. Still smiling, the woman studied herself in the mirror, nodding at the reflection in approval. Humming a popular tune under her breath, she remained where she was long after the cloakroom door had closed.

Joining the waiting men, Rebecca and Amy let themselves be helped into their coats, all the while chattering away happily. But beneath her happy façade, Rebecca's stomach was churning. So that was the reason behind the woman's hostility. She was obviously one of Jimmy's old lady friends. No wonder she had acted as she had. Jealousy! That's what that unpleasant scene had been about. Pure jealousy. For some reason that thought gave Rebecca enormous satisfaction. As for the woman's message . . . Well, it was late, wasn't it, and her memory often played tricks after a long day.

As it was Charlie's night off, Jimmy hailed a passing cab, and within minutes they were heading back in the direction of Hackney, the red-haired stranger and her message, like Richard and his lady friend, pushed to the back of Rebecca's mind.

'I thought you were going to introduce me to your wards and their companions, Richard. After all, seeing as we're going to be family soon, I would have liked to meet the girls. And Mr Jackson. I've never met the man personally, well, I wouldn't, would I? But I've heard of him. Though I must confess I'm surprised that you and he are such good friends. He's not the sort of man I would have associated you with, but I keep forgetting you're a man of the world now and have a wide variety of friends to match your status. I wonder why Mr Jackson didn't come over to say·hello. Maybe he was being thoughtful, and didn't want to interrupt our meal. I'm sure I'll get another opportunity to meet him. After all, he's bound to want to meet the future wife of his closest friend, isn't he, Richard dear?'

Ivy Harris looked intently across the table at the squirming, red-faced man opposite, her skilfully made-up face disguising the sarcasm behind her words. She knew only too well that a man such as Jimmy Jackson would have no time for the likes of Richard. Taking a sip of her red wine, Ivy continued her silent perusal of her future husband. She had left him high and dry twenty years ago to marry a man old enough to be her father, with a thriving business and a three-storey house in Stoke Newington. Widowed six years later, Ivy had married her late husband's partner, Albert Harris. Her second marriage had lasted almost twelve years, which had been eleven years and ten months too long to Ivy's mind. Now here she was, back where she'd started, engaged to Richard Fisher; well, maybe not officially, but that would soon be remedied. Ivy thought of the man Richard purported to be his best friend, then took a closer look at the overweight man with receding hair and heavy jowls that would soon be husband number three, and sighed inwardly. Oh for the chance of marrying someone like Jimmy Jackson, or even bedding him for that matter. Twenty years ago Ivy would have stood a chance of the latter, but she had been too eager to get a ring on her finger and the security that it entailed to waste time looking for someone she could truly love and respect.

Looking back, Ivy realised her mistakes. At eighteen she'd had plenty of time, and as pretty as she had been, she could have had her pick of men. Maybe if she had waited, she might have ended up with someone like Jimmy Jackson, but it was too late for regrets now. Again Ivy sighed. Whoever said youth was wasted on the young had been right, and it would always be so. For the young never imagine themselves old, and therefore would never heed the warnings or advice of their elders, until they too aged and tried to pass on their life's experience only to have it ignored. And so life would always be, with youth never to be appreciated until it was too late. That fact, to Ivy's mind was one of the biggest tragedies of life.

Now she was nearing forty and still without a child to call her own. Richard Fisher was her last chance of becoming a mother. Ivy had always laid the blame of her inability to conceive at the door of her late husbands, telling herself that they had been too old, while knowing that a man is never too old to father a child. But it was more of a comfort than to confront the possibility that the fault might lie within herself. And Richard wasn't a bad sort when all was said and done. He was certainly the best she was going to get at her time of life, and Ivy was determined Richard wasn't going to get away a second time. With this thought uppermost in her mind, Ivy swiftly skirted over the topic of Jimmy Jackson, a subject that was obviously disconcerting to Richard. Reaching out, she took hold of the pudgy hand and tenderly stroked the fat fingers with as much affection as she could muster.

'Why don't you call for the bill, Richard, dear,' she murmured seductively. 'I feel like an early night . . . Don't you?'

Gazing into the adoring eyes, Richard's chest visibly swelled with importance, his manhood restored once more. Settling the bill, he escorted Ivy from the restaurant, his hand tightly gripping her arm. Richard had been a long time between women, and he was anxious to get Ivy home before she changed her mind. His mind clear of everything but the urge to get Ivy into bed, Richard forgot about his cousins and Jimmy Jackson and concentrated instead on the delights to come.

CHAPTER ELEVEN

Hidden from sight of the street behind the thick bedroom curtain, Maude sat in the darkness, her anxious eyes peering out every now and then into the night, her ears alert in case Phil should take it into his head to visit her. Though that was highly unlikely. He had brought her up a cup of tea over two hours ago, and that, to Phil, was what he termed looking after her. No, Phil wouldn't be back up unless she called for him and she had no intention of doing that. Normally she would have had him running up and down the stairs all evening, but after her last run-in with Rebecca, Maude was desperate to be on her best behaviour. Yet after a lifetime of being waited on hand and foot, and having someone at her beck and call at any hour of the day or night, Maude was finding the task she had set herself increasingly difficult; and it had only been a few hours.

At the sound of an approaching carriage, Maude shrank back from the window, hiding her massive frame behind the heavy curtain as she listened intently to the voices coming from the street. Her heart was beating so fast, Maude was afraid the people below would hear it. Berating herself for her stupidity, she nevertheless scurried as fast as her swollen legs would carry her back to the warmth and safety of her bed. Once propped up on the mountain of pillows, she assumed an expression of what she hoped portrayed patient resignation, and waited. One of them would be up soon. Either Rebecca or Amy always came straight to her room whenever they had been out of the house for any length of time. The minutes ticked by slowly, and her door remained closed. Shuffling about in the double bed Maude endeavoured to make enough noise to remind her young cousins of her presence, but the bed, although old, was a good one and no satisfying squeaks or groaning springs were forthcoming. Changing tack, Maude knocked over the stool resting by the bed, exclaiming loudly, 'Oh, dear, what have I done now?' in what she hoped was a genuine voice of regret, quickly assumed the look of martyrdom once more and waited. The door remained closed.

The high, laughing voices of the people down below rose, and Maude's thin lips tightened angrily. The bloody bitches. They were deliberately ignoring her and she was helpless to do anything about it. Maude had never worried what Richard or the Bradfords thought of her, or that silly, simpering

128

cow Ada Gates from next door; their opinions didn't matter. But she had always been desperately afraid of showing her true colours to anyone she deemed important; and Jimmy Jackson was just such a person. Those few hours he had spent with her on the day the girls had been attacked had been the highlight of Maude's sad and wasted life. That was why she had been so enthusiastic about Rebecca seeing him again. Maude had envisaged a life in the company of a man she could look up to and respect. A man she could spend the rest of her life with, without the contention of marriage. But Rebecca had soon put Maude right on that eventuality. Maude's black eyes narrowed as she thought back to that particular encounter, then her mind shifted to the sealed box hidden in the framework of the bed she rarely left. A satisfied smirk touched her lips as she conjured up a vision of the contents of the hidden box.

She had managed to put away quite a bit over the years. Rebecca had never asked if Richard contributed to the household, instead she had managed on whatever money Phil and then Amy brought into the house. Rebecca was also unaware that the rent money she paid Richard every week was duly handed over to her bed-ridden cousin in an effort by Richard to assuage his conscience regarding his sister; but if Richard ever found out about the money she had stashed away Maude knew his conscience would trouble him no further. Clasping her hands over the mountain of bedclothes, Maude peered at the closed door. Well, then. It was just as well she'd taken the precaution of looking out for herself, 'cos it was looking like no other bugger was going to. A feeling of deep resentment and self-pity flooded Maude's body. Two fat tears rolled down the plump face and Maude made no effort to wipe them away. They would serve to strengthen the unassuming and pitiful role she hoped to portray.

'I'll have to go up in a minute, the suspense is killing me. Normally she would be shouting the house down by now. She's obviously being on her best behaviour because you're here, but it can't last.' Rebecca smiled shyly at Jimmy then glanced upwards.

The five of them were seated in the sitting room around a blazing fire, enjoying each others' company. To Rebecca's mind the scene was idyllic. Even Phil was talking amiably with no trace of subservience in the face of their visitor. As for Amy . . . Rebecca's eyes flickered over to the battered, comfortable armchair where Amy was curled up, the ever-grinning Charlie at her feet, her young face beaming with happiness and contentment. If it wasn't for that one upstairs . . . Rebecca sighed and got to her feet. 'It's no good, I can't ignore her any more.' Stifling a laugh, Rebecca looked at Phil and said, 'You didn't smother her while we were out, did you, Phil?'

Her brother grinned back. 'No, worse luck. Though if I'd thought about it, I might have been tempted.'

Moving to the foot of the stairs, Rebecca paused, a hint of suspicion crossing her face.

'You have been up to see her, haven't you, Phil?'

Phil waved his arm airily. 'Of course I have. I brought her up a cup of tea earlier on.'

'How long ago is earlier on?'

Phil shrugged. 'I don't know. A couple of hours ago maybe, but I was listening out for her,' Phil hurried on as he saw the look of concern flash over Rebecca's face.

'You're hopeless, Phil. A person could be lying dead for days before you noticed. Oh . . . Never mind, I'll go and check.'

Jimmy stirred lazily in his chair. 'I doubt if your cousin would be so obliging as to die without making some kind of fuss. She didn't strike me as that type.'

Heartened by what he saw as Jimmy's support, Phil added, 'Jimmy's right, Becks. If Maude was ill, she would soon have let me know about it.'

Hurrying up the stairway, Rebecca stopped outside Maude's door. Reaching out, she grasped the door handle and paused. What if Maude had really taken bad and she, Rebecca, hadn't been here to care for her? Taking a deep breath, Rebecca turned the handle.

Maude was lying on the pillows, her hand resting across her heart, her face tear-streaked. Rebecca watched as the beady eyes opened warily and smiled grimly. How often had she witnessed such a scene when Maude, in a fit of pique, had tried to milk some sympathy. Hand on heart, the obligatory tears – no change here then. Her manner brisk, Rebecca said, 'We'll be coming up to bed shortly, as soon as our guests have gone. Is there anything you need before I go back down?'

Maude squeezed her eyes tightly closed. 'No, I'm fine,' she muttered in a weak, brave voice.

'That's all right then. I'll pop in before I retire for the night.'

And before Maude could protest, Rebecca had left the room.

'Goodnight, Jimmy, and thanks again for being with us today. And for the experience of East End pub life, it was quite an education, but the meal more than made up for it.' Aware she was babbling, Rebecca concentrated on staring at Amy and Charlie, who were standing only a few feet away, their heads bent together as they said their goodnights. An icy gust of wind swept over the figures on the doorstep and Rebecca wrapped her arms around her waist for warmth, grateful for something to do with her hands.

When the strong arms enfolded her, Rebecca flinched involuntarily, then bit down on her bottom lip in confusion. She had no idea of what to do next and was mortified when her entire body began trembling; and it had nothing to do with the cold.

Jimmy smiled tenderly as he sensed Rebecca's discomfort. The poor cow doesn't have a clue, he thought wryly, and was immediately ashamed of himself. It was a feeling new to Jimmy, yet this girl seemed able to evoke his conscience, even when he'd done nothing wrong, but he didn't loosen his hold. Instead he gently pulled her body into his and bent down to kiss the soft, cold cheek. 'You'd better get inside before you freeze,' he murmured softly, his breath fanning her face.

Grateful for the comparative darkness of the street, Rebecca didn't try to pull away from the comforting warmth of Jimmy's arms, neither did she respond in any way. She simply didn't know how to. Her mind was screaming at her to say something, anything, rather than remain silent, like an imbecile. She tried to think of something witty, or amusing; instead she blurted out lamely, 'Oh! I meant to tell you earlier – I met a friend of yours in the . . . the ladies' room . . . She said to tell you Heather was asking after you . . . Or something like that . . .'

Immediately Jimmy's hold loosened and in the quietness of the night, Rebecca heard him draw in a deep breath. Then, as if remembering she was there, he gave her a swift hug and stepped back, leaving Rebecca suddenly cold and bereft.

Jimmy too was experiencing a sense of loss, but it had nothing to do with Rebecca. Dragging his mind back to the young woman standing at arm's length, he repeated gently, 'Go on, get in the warmth.'

Rebecca nodded dumbly. 'Yes, I think I will. Goodbye, Jimmy . . . and thanks again.' Rebecca stepped into the house, glad to be out of sight before Jimmy saw the tears that had welled up behind her eyes. She was half hoping that he would call her back, but this time it seemed as if Jimmy Jackson wouldn't be returning; and it was all her own fault. Things had been going fine until she'd opened her big mouth and mentioned that ghastly woman from the restaurant. And by Jimmy's reaction to her name, it was obvious that the woman meant something to him, else why would he have gone so cold towards her? Her shoulders slumped, she walked slowly towards the fire and dropped into the armchair. Phil had already gone to bed, Maude was supposedly sleeping, so until Amy returned Rebecca had the house to herself.

The sound of the door opening brought Rebecca's head up in hope, a hope that quickly died as Amy bounded into the room.

'Coo, it's freezing out there . . . Lord, is that the time? I'd better get some sleep. Are you coming up, Becky?'

Rebecca shook her head. 'No, not just yet, love, but you go ahead. I . . . I won't be too long.'

Amy gazed down at the bent head then turned away. Slowly mounting the stairs, she looked back to where her sister sat, her eyes staring unseeingly into the dying flames, and felt a spasm of pity for the girl by the fire. This wasn't the time to tell Becky that Charlie had asked to see her again on Sunday, because, by the look of it, Jimmy hadn't asked to see Becky again. A spurt of anger, rare to Amy, rippled through her slender body. Who did that Jimmy Jackson think he was anyway? Her Becky was worth twice of his sort any day of the week, but she had thought he was genuinely fond of Becky. It looked as if she was wrong. She hated seeing Becky so miserable, and after such a lovely evening as well. The shine taken off her day, Amy continued her journey to the bedroom she shared with her elder sister.

Down below, Rebecca sat before the fire until the last spark of heat had been extinguished, her tortured mind going over and over the past few weeks. It was impossible to believe that she had only known Jimmy such a short while, yet in that time, Rebecca had felt more alive than she had ever felt in her entire life. An image of the red-haired woman swam before her eyes, and Rebecca shook her head savagely. 'You stupid, stupid, cow,' she muttered to the empty room. 'How could you have thought you had a chance with Jimmy, when there's women like that one ready to fall at his feet, and more if asked.' Yet would she, if asked? Wearily she shook her head. No! As much as she wanted Jimmy back in her life, she wasn't like those other women, and never could be.

When at last, her bone-weary body crying out for sleep, she dragged herself from the armchair, and with tears almost blinding her vision, she followed the path Amy had taken earlier.

CHAPTER TWELVE

'Bessie! Bessie! Where are you, woman?' Letting the heavy door slam behind him, Jimmy strode into the dimly lit room as if the devil himself was on his heels. Throwing his overcoat carelessly onto the nearest armchair, he went straight to the walnut cabinet in the corner and took out a bottle of brandy. Pouring out a large measure, Jimmy quickly downed the liquid in one gulp, the drink hardly wetting his throat before he was pouring another.

'Bessie! God damn it, woman. You died while I was out, or what!'

The door at the far corner of the room opened to emit a sleepy-eyed Bessie, her grey hair bound up in tortuous steel clips. Hugging a grey woollen dressing gown around her sparse body, the elderly woman shouted back, 'No, I ain't dead. But you will be if yer talk ter me like that again, yer loud-mouthed bugger. What's up with yer anyway?'

Jimmy glanced briefly at the bristling figure before saying tersely, 'Heather's back.'

Just two words, but they had the power to drain the strength from Bessie's limbs and voice. All fight gone from her, the aggression sifted from the lined face to be replaced by deep anxiety and fear.

Clutching at her throat, she reached out with her spare hand to find the armchair behind her and sank down in a crumpled heap. 'Oh my Gawd!' she breathed through dry lips.

Jimmy glanced at the small figure and laughed grimly. 'Yeah! And don't ask me how I'm taking the news, 'cos you look like I feel right now.' Seeing the dismayed face staring at him, Jimmy quickly poured another glass of brandy. Handing the balloon-shaped glass to the trembling form, he said, 'Here, get that down your throat, you look like you could do with it.'

Bessie grabbed the glass wordlessly and downed it in one go, then held it out for a refill. When the glass was replenished and the colour restored to her sunken cheeks, she said, 'So she's back, then. I've been expecting her to show her face fer years, but I was beginning ter think she'd gone for good. No such luck, eh!' Shifting in the chair, she looked up at the towering figure and asked, 'How d'yer know she's back, lad? Have yer seen her yerself?'

Jimmy shook his head, then, in a few terse words he told Bessie what had transpired.

'So, yer ain't actually seen her yerself then. Maybe that young girl got it wrong,' Bessie stirred

137

hopefully. 'I mean ter say, it might have been another Heather an'—'

'Oh, don't talk rubbish, Bessie,' Jimmy cut in sharply. 'How many Heathers do you know? No! It was her all right. And now she's made herself known, I should be expecting a visit any day.'

A silence fell upon the room as both occupants dwelt on the enormity of how this could change their lives. Finally Bessie stirred.

'Heather Mills back in the East End. Well! Well! And after all she said about never coming back. I suppose 'er fancy man dumped 'er an' now she's back looking fer a hand out. What yer gonna do, Jimmy?' Without waiting for an answer she carried on. 'Bloody hell! Heather Mills, she's—'

Jimmy swung round suddenly. 'Or Heather Jackson. Don't forget that, Bessie. She might just be Mrs Heather Jackson.'

Bessie struggled upright in the large chair, her fighting spirit once more to the fore. 'Now don't start that lark again, lad. You ain't married ter that trollop, an' nothin' she can say will make me believe it. An' yer can huff an' puff all yer like . . .' she said, her voice rising as Jimmy made a dismissive gesture with his hands. 'All that business happened a long time ago, an' there was never any proof yer was married. An' even if yer was, she's been gone for so long, yer could easily get a divorce. I don't know that much about divorces, but I'm sure yer can get one if yer other half goes missing fer eight years without a bleeding word.'

But Jimmy wasn't listening; he was back, ten years ago, to the time he had first met Heather Mills. Dimly he heard Bessie leaving the room and wished he hadn't woken her, but he had always gone to Bessie in times of trouble; it had become a comforting habit. Pouring another brandy, Jimmy paced the room, his mind whirling back in time.

He was eighteen, and just beginning to make a name for himself on the rough streets of the East End. On a Saturday morning in late September, when the sun was still warm and the air crisp, he had been collecting bets on a corner of Mare Street when the young, red-haired girl had come into his view. She was just emerging from the local dressmakers, her arms laden with parcels, when a crowd of youths had accosted her. Jimmy had immediately gone to her rescue, the crowing youths scattering rapidly when they saw Jimmy Jackson flying towards them, his fists clenched ready for trouble. The girl had been full of gratitude for his timely intervention, thanking him over and over, her pretty face animated with hero worship. It was heady stuff for a young man, and Jimmy, like any youth of his age, had been eager to establish himself as a man. After helping her with the parcels, he had taken the girl for a light lunch. Over piping hot cups of tea and an assortment of cakes, the two of them had talked and laughed like old friends, and by the time he had seen her into a waiting carriage Jimmy had already fallen in love.

For the next few months they had rarely been out of each other's company, much to Bessie's horror, for she had taken an instant dislike to her beloved Jimmy's new girl, not least because Heather had rapidly begun to eat into Jimmy's hard-earned savings. But the youthful Jimmy was besotted, and Bessie, seeing the way the land lay, had reluctantly kept her counsel.

In the dimly lit room, Jimmy stirred. If only he had listened to Bessie. But when had the young ever listened to their elders, especially when they were in love? Leaning his head back against the soft cushions, Jimmy smiled wryly as his mind took him back to that fateful weekend in August 1903.

He had been seeing Heather for almost a year when he suggested they go away together for the weekend. To his surprise and delight, Heather had agreed without a murmur. It had been easy enough to arrange. Heather had lost her parents when she was two and had been brought up by an elderly uncle, who was only too pleased to have his wayward niece taken off his hands for a while. Telling a disbelieving Bessie that he was staying with an old friend for the weekend, Jimmy had taken Heather to a small hotel on the outskirts of Kent, hopeful of a good time, but Heather had disappointed him, insisting they sleep apart until they were married. Bursting with adolescent love and unconsummated passion, Jimmy had proposed straight away, but Heather had laughed, saying that it wasn't that easy to get married. His hopes for a passionate weekend crushed, Jimmy had drowned his sorrows in drink. He still couldn't remember that Saturday night, but he did remember vividly that Sunday morning, when he had awoken to find Heather in his bed telling him they were now married.

A door banged somewhere in the house, jerking Jimmy from his reverie. For a moment he stiffened, then relaxed as he realised it was only Bessie bustling around in the kitchen. Instinctively his eyes had darted to the hidden safe in the far corner of the room, then he relaxed. No intruder would ever find it behind the false panel of wood Jimmy had made himself. Looking down at his empty glass, Jimmy pondered on getting another drink, but couldn't be bothered to get out of his chair. Impatient at how his thoughts were running amok, Jimmy forced himself to think back to the matter in hand.

According to Heather at that time, they had been married on the Saturday night by a Justice of the Peace. In his youth and inexperience, Jimmy had never queried Heather's claims. In truth he had been delighted at the unexpected turn of events. But all hell had been let loose when he'd returned home with his new bride to the small, one-bedroomed house he'd shared with Bessie. The following months had been hell on earth as Jimmy had striven to please both the women in his life; women who had hated each other on sight. Every night when he arrived home, tired and weary, Heather would be on at him to get rid of Bessie, while the older woman had kept a grim, reproachful silence that had torn at Jimmy's heart more than Heather's constant nagging. Their first Christmas together had been a disaster, and by the New Year, Jimmy had already tired of married life. So too, it appeared, had Heather, because barely into their fifth month of marriage, Jimmy had come home to find a jubilant Bessie and no wife.

The letter had been very short and to the point. Heather, it seemed, had met someone who could give her a better life, and had swiftly taken it. There had been no mention of a divorce, no mention of the hasty wedding that Jimmy still couldn't remember, and with Bessie constantly telling him there probably never had been a wedding, Jimmy had put Heather Mills down to experience and tried to forget about her.

It had been easy enough the first few years, as Jimmy concentrated all his thoughts and efforts into making something of himself. And if, at times, his mind had touched on that episode in his life, Jimmy had quickly pushed the images to one side. The notion that he might be a married man had never troubled him, for he'd had no intention of making the same mistake twice.

His throat dry, Jimmy stirred himself from the chair to get another drink, then began pacing the room. For the first time in many a long year, Jimmy was at a loss what to do next. If only Rebecca hadn't . . . !

He came to an abrupt stop in his pacing. Rebecca! Good Lord, he'd nearly forgotten all about her. Then he jumped as the strident voice hit his back, seeming to echo his thoughts.

'An' what about that Rebecca, then, eh? Yer seemed ter be getting on all right with her. What yer gonna tell her, or ain't yer gonna bother?'

Bessie, fully recovered from her earlier shock, came bustling into the room carrying a tray with two steaming mugs of cocoa.

Jimmy grinned. That was more like it. With Bessie shouting and hollering, life was back to normal. Hiding his amusement, he said wryly, 'I thought you didn't like Rebecca either.'

Bessie sniffed. 'I don't much. Stuck-up little madam, if yer ask me. But at least she's a decent sort, not a trollop like some I could mention.'

Taking the tray from her hands, Jimmy nodded towards the armchair. 'Sit down, you old trout, and we'll talk and try and sort this mess out, all right?'

And Bessie, after a moment's hesitation, gladly did as she was bid, thanking God that at least some good had come of Heather Mills's unwelcome return into their lives. It had been a long time since Jimmy had asked for her help, and for someone like Bessie, who thrived on being useful and needed, Jimmy's latter independence had become a source of discontentment.

Now, seated together around the fire, the two of them united against the world, Bessie felt her confidence returning. It was just like old times. Raising her head, she looked at the rugged, handsome face lit up by the fire and felt a lump come to her throat. He still needed her; her Jimmy needed her. And she suddenly realised that he always would. A stab of alarm clutched at her chest as she felt tears prick behind her heavy eyelids. Sitting bolt upright she shook her head. Bleeding Hell! What was the matter with her? She never cried, never! *You're getting old, girl*, she rebuked herself silently, before giving all her attention to the man sitting opposite.

'Come back to bed, darling, me backside's getting cold.' The plaintive voice of the sleepy-eyed man wheedled from the rumpled double bed. Propping himself up on one elbow, he patted the empty space by his side, pleading, 'Come on, love, I'm waiting,' but the red-haired woman seemed oblivious of his presence. Grunting with displeasure, the man rolled himself up in the heavy blankets with much huffing and bouncing on the well-oiled springs, yet still the woman remained staring out into the night. Realising his efforts were futile, the man gave one last punch to the feather pillow then settled down to wait for what he felt was owed him.

Heather Mills sat curled up in a padded wicker chair, her slender arms hugging her knees. She made an arresting sight, clad as she was in a long, shimmering white nightgown, her luxurious flame-coloured hair tumbling over her neck and shoulders, yet if the man, so eager for her company, had seen the coldness in the hard, glittering eyes, he would have been repelled.

A movement from the bed caught Heather's attention for a brief moment, then she returned to her thoughts. Up until six months ago she had been living a life of luxury in the company of Sean Finnegan, the wealthy middle-aged man she had left Jimmy for. She had met him one day, when, desperate to escape from her new, depressing environment, she had taken herself up to the West End in search of a day's solace from the contemptuous glare and scathing remarks of Bessie Wilks.

She had been sitting on a bench in Regent's Park, looking a picture of dejection, when the well-dressed man had passed by. Moments later he had returned to enquire if she was in need of assistance. Heather had swiftly noted the man's expensive attire and within seconds her fertile imagination had sprung into action.

Never one to let the grass grow under her feet, Heather had taken immediate advantage of the situation. Her hands had been hidden inside a cheap fur-lined muff, a Christmas present from Jimmy, which had made it easy for her to remove the thin brass wedding ring she had always hated. With a deception that came easily to her, Heather had sorrowfully spun a tale of being turned out of her home by an unscrupulous landlord, and was now helpless and alone and at her wits' end as to what to do next. She had portrayed the image of a helpless, frightened young woman to perfection, her performance rivalling that of the great Sarah Bernhardt.

An hour later she had found herself in the restaurant of the Savoy Hotel in the company of a smitten Sean Finnegan. He had offered to pay for a room for her in the hotel, clumsily adding that his offer was purely platonic and that he expected nothing in return. But Heather had seen the look in his eyes. She had always been aware of the effect she had on men and had known in that instant that she had made another conquest. Still playing the part of a breathless, innocent girl, full of gratitude for the kind gesture being offered her, Heather had made the pretence of returning to her lodgings to collect her belongings. Knowing Bessie's routine, she had returned to the house, secure in the knowledge that her hated adversary would be out down the market. Within half an hour she had packed everything she owned, stopping only to write a short note to Jimmy telling him she had met someone else and wouldn't be coming back. She'd had no compunction about leaving Jimmy, she was too shallow to have the capacity for true love and commitment.

Less than two weeks later she was sharing Sean's bed, and when the besotted man asked her to go back with him to his home in Ireland she had readily accepted. Sean Finnegan's home was a country estate in Cork, and for the next eight years Heather had enjoyed the life she had always dreamt of.

But her life of luxury had come to an abrupt end when Sean had suffered a massive heart attack. Heather had imagined she would stay on in the stately mansion to the end of her days, but she hadn't reckoned on Sean's relations. The close-knit Irish family had lost no time in ousting the woman whom they had seen as a unscrupulous gold digger. Now she was back where she had started, determined to rekindle her past association with Jimmy Jackson, especially now he had come up in the world; but it seemed it wasn't going to be as easy as she'd first imagined.

It had been quite a shock to see Jimmy in the

146

restaurant, even though she had been planning such a meeting for the past six months. During that time she had made discreet enquiries about the man she had left so hurriedly over eight years earlier. What she had discovered had been a source of delight to her. She had always known Jimmy had the drive and determination to make something of himself, and she hadn't been wrong in her earlier judgment. What she hadn't bargained on was the effect Jimmy Jackson still had on her, though it would seem he hadn't been wasting his time pining over her.

Her lips tightened as she brought to mind the young girl Jimmy had escorted to the restaurant. How old was she? Eighteen, nineteen at the most! The same age she herself had been when she'd first met Jimmy. Heather felt a reluctant stab of admiration towards the girl, admitting to herself that her attempts to intimidate the younger woman had failed miserably. Twirling a strand of thick hair around her finger, Heather idly wondered if the girl had passed on her message. If she had, then no doubt, at this very minute, Jimmy would be huddled in conference with that old witch Bessie, both of them deciding what to do about her. Heather uttered a mirthless laugh. Let them do their worst, she held all the cards. Her gaze flickered towards a door leading off the main room, her lips curving into a cruel smile of satisfaction.

The coldness of the room finally stirred Heather into life, and with a long, sinuous stretch of her arms and legs, she rose languidly and strolled over to the door. Opening it, she peered into the gloom, barely able to make out the small outline huddled under a thin blanket on top of a pallet bed. Carefully closing the door so as not to disturb the occupant, Heather walked slowly back to the bed.

The man heard her coming and smiled smugly. Throwing back the covers he eagerly waited for the voluptuous woman to join him under the blankets. By the bedside lamp, Heather saw the man's spindly legs and pigeon chest and felt her skin crawl. Hugging the flimsy nightgown around her body she said harshly, 'Get out. Go on, get out. I've had enough of your company for one night.'

The man jerked in the bed, his surprise quickly turning to anger. 'Now hang on, Heather. Don't you come all high and mighty with me. I've spent good money on you these past few months, I'm entitled to stay here as long as I like, especially as I'm paying the rent.'

Heather's lips curled in open disgust. 'You've been well paid. In fact looking back at what I've had to do for the privilege of your company, I'd say you owed me a rebate. You won't be getting your slimy hands on me again, Bert Underwood, so sling your hook before I start screaming.'

The man's face was almost comic in his disbelief at the sudden change in the woman he had imagined was enamoured of him. Then his features contorted into ugly lines of rage. 'Why you common little whore. I've supported you and your brat for months, so don't think you can get rid of me as if I was some common labourer. I'm a man of standing in the community, and I could make life very difficult for you if I wanted. Now, get your arse back into bed before I really lose my temper.'

Heather threw back her head and said sneeringly. 'Oh, please. You're really frightening me – don't make me laugh!' Walking slowly towards the man now clutching the bedcovers to his thin chest, Heather growled viciously, 'You pathetic little bastard. Do you really think you can frighten me into letting you slobber all over me? And as for all that talk about you being a man of standing, you seem to forget you're also a married man. What do you think your dear wife would say if she knew where you'd been spending your nights, when you're supposed to be away on business?'

The man's eyes widened in horror as Heather's words sank in.

She saw the alarm on the man's ashen face and moved in for the kill. 'You're not the only one who can make threats, Bert. Now get your skinny carcass out of my bed and out of my life . . . Move!'

As the man scrambled into his clothes, Heather watched with veiled amusement. When he was at the door she halted him in his hurried tracks.

'Just a minute, Bert. Before you go, I'll take whatever you have left in your wallet. Let's say it's for services rendered – and for keeping my mouth shut and your wife blissfully ignorant of her dear husband's activities.'

His slight body almost bursting with rage at being bested, the man drew out his wallet. Extracting three five-pound notes, he threw them contemptuously at Heather's feet. 'Here, take it, you fucking slag. But don't think you've got the better of me. I'll see you pay for this, don't—'

'Oh, piss off, you miserable apology for a man.' Heather had already turned away, and with one last murderous glance in her direction, the man hurriedly left.

When the front door slammed, Heather climbed into bed, careful to avoid the side Bert had previously vacated. Pulling the covers up around her neck, she closed her eyes, feeling suddenly weary. There would be no more men like Bert Underwood. After seeing Jimmy, no other man would do for her now. It would take time and a lot of planning, but she was determined to get Jimmy back. And if he wouldn't take her, then she would produce her trump card. Not many men would be capable of disowning their son, and Jimmy Jackson was no exception. He may have come up in the world, but people don't change. Jimmy had always been a man of principle, despite his profession. He might not be able to forgive her for what she had done to him, but he would never let his child suffer for her actions; and any money coming to his son would also benefit the child's mother. Content in that knowledge, Heather slept.

CHAPTER THIRTEEN

It was three weeks to Christmas and Rebecca was sitting at the dining table writing out a list of preparations for the coming festive event. In the past she had enjoyed the weeks leading up to Christmas, seeing it as a welcome break in her boring, drudge-filled life. This year, however, she was finding no joy in the previously diverting task.

It had been five weeks since she had last seen Jimmy, and his absence had left a painful void in her life. Amy was still going out with Charlie, but she rarely spoke to Rebecca about her growing attachment to the affable young man. Rebecca was aware that Amy's reticence at confiding in her was solely to spare her feelings, yet Amy's kind thoughtfulness only added to Rebecca's misery. It wasn't fair that Amy should have to curtail her happiness for fear of upsetting her elder sister. Laying down her pen, Rebecca ran a tired hand over her face. Poor Amy.

It must be killing the young girl trying to keep her natural outgoing exuberance damped down. Phil too was careful not to divulge too much about his new position working for Jimmy, for the same reason Amy was keeping quiet; and it couldn't go on.

The episode with Jimmy had been a revelation to Rebecca, and for a brief, wonderful time she had been lifted from her mundane life, but now that time was over. Jimmy wasn't coming back. The knowledge was painful but she had to accept it and put the past behind her. Yet Jimmy had shown her another side of life, and because of that short, exciting moment, Rebecca would never feel the same again.

She was about to resume her list when the front door opened to emit a red-faced Richard.

'Brr, it's bloody freezing out. I wouldn't mind a hot cup of tea, Rebecca, love.'

Without looking up, Rebecca replied shortly, 'Help yourself, you know where the kitchen is, and the rent's on the table by the door.'

Stamping his feet on the doormat, Richard glowered at the bent head. By God, but that little madam had a shock coming to her. Striding past his young cousin, who was studiously ignoring his presence, Richard went into the kitchen and put the kettle on to boil. Taking off his thick overcoat and gloves he busied himself making the tea, inwardly seething at Rebecca's high-handedness. If he'd had any qualms regarding what he was about to do, then that surly piece had quickly soothed his conscience.

The tea made, Richard sat in the kitchen, marking

time until he would be forced to go upstairs and visit his sister. Gradually his temper abated, to be replaced by one of nervous excitement. His earlier plans of waiting until Amy's birthday to break the news of his forthcoming marriage had been thwarted by Ivy. She had made it quite clear that after all these years she wasn't prepared to wait any longer. Reminiscent of twenty years earlier, she had given Richard an ultimatum. Either they got married straight away or the engagement was off. This time, however, Richard had no intention of letting anything, or anyone, stand in his way. He would make his announcement on Christmas Eve, and the following week he and Ivy would be married. It was all arranged. All he had to do now was set the scene, and he had it all worked out as to how he would drop his bombshell. Rather than have to inform each member of the household of his intentions, Richard wanted them all gathered in one room, and what better excuse than to throw a party? There was only one fly in the ointment. Ivy wasn't that keen on leaving her comfortable house to move into Richard's former home. But he had assured her the move would be temporary. As soon as he was rid of the Bradfords and his detested sister, Richard planned to sell the house and move to a more salubrious location. This new idea had been enforced by the knowledge of Ivy's considerable nest egg. Of course he would never have considered marrying her if she had been penniless.

Rubbing his hands together in barely suppressed glee, Richard took a last swallow of his tea and returned to where Rebecca was still perusing the list of items she needed to buy in time for Christmas.

Adopting a cheerful manner he said heartily, 'Well, Christmas is nearly on us again. It seems to come around quicker every year. I suppose that's a sign of getting older.'

Rebecca glanced idly up at him then turned her attention back to her list. Normally this slight would have incensed Richard, but, knowing what was to come, he remained cheerful. Rocking back on his heels, he continued jovially. 'I was thinking we could have a small party on Christmas Eve. Just for the family and a few friends.' When Rebecca made no sign of answering, a cruel glint came into Richard's beady eyes. Maude had kept him informed of the goings-on at the house, and he now used that knowledge to his advantage. 'Maybe you could invite Mr Jackson. I'm sure he'd be delighted to attend, seeing as you've become so close.'

The malicious jibe wasn't wasted on Rebecca. Richard felt a moment's satisfaction as he saw Rebecca's face redden and her hand suddenly tremble. Blinking furiously, Rebecca took a deep breath. The cruel remark had hit home with a jarring force, but not for the world would she let Richard see how much he had hurt her. Keeping her eyes firmly on the piece of paper in front of her Rebecca replied airily, 'It's still your home, *Dick*. You can do whatever you wish, and I'll certainly ask Jimmy if he'd like to come, but he's a busy man, so I wouldn't hold your breath at the chance of renewing your brief acquaintance with him.

154

Though from what he told me, you didn't exactly hit it off at your first and only meeting. You're not the type of man Jimmy normally associates himself with. You're a bit ineffectual for his tastes.'

Now it was Richard's turn to feel uncomfortable. He still squirmed when he recalled his disastrous meeting with Jimmy Jackson, and the subsequent snub he had suffered at the restaurant, humiliating him in Ivy's eyes; and this little bitch knew it. But not content with reminding him of Jimmy's feelings towards him, she had added insult to injury by calling him by that hated name. The very sound of the word conjured up connotations that were both crude and offensive, and Richard had no doubt that was exactly what Rebecca had intended. Trying to assume a commanding figure, Richard clasped his hands tightly behind his back, stretched his neck from side to side and opened his mouth to make a suitable retort, but found none forthcoming. From years of experience Richard knew he was no match for Rebecca when it came to verbal sparring. To save face he made what he hoped was a dignified exit and went to see Maude. And for once the impending visit offered him a welcome diversion.

When Richard had disappeared upstairs, Rebecca laid down the pen and swallowed loudly. The spiteful bugger. Oh, how she hated him, and never more so than at this minute. A determined look came over her face. One thing was for certain. If Amy's relationship with Charlie resulted in marriage, then she, Rebecca, would be out of this house the day after the wedding. Not that she wanted her little sister to get married at such a young age, but Amy would be sixteen in a couple of months. Give her another year and she would be ready for marriage. Amy was the type of woman who was born to be a wife and mother. That being the case, Rebecca couldn't think of anyone more suitable as a husband for Amy than Charlie.

Glancing round at the clock on the mantelpiece, Rebecca saw that it was nearly eleven, and tutted impatiently. Amy had gone out early this morning to meet Charlie and had promised faithfully to be back at eleven in order to do the Saturday morning shopping with Rebecca. No sooner had the thought crossed Rebecca's mind than the door burst open and a smiling, rosy-faced Amy came running into the house.

'Sorry, Becky. Am I late? Oh good, it's not eleven yet, I was worried I'd be late back.'

Ashamed at her uncharitable thoughts, Rebecca smiled warmly. 'Don't rush, love, we've plenty of time yet. In fact the longer we leave it the better chance we have of picking up some bargains.' Picking up her list, Rebecca added, 'I promise myself every year that I'll leave the shopping to the last minute, it's what most women do. Ada always goes down the market late on Christmas Eve when the stall holders are desperate to get rid of their stock. She managed to get a turkey last year for sixpence. Granted it looked like it had died of old age and had just enough meat on it to feed her and Billy, but still, there's plenty of bargains to be had if you're prepared to take a chance. Then again, you could come back empty-handed and have to have sausages and mash for Christmas dinner, and I'm not brave enough to take that chance.' Rebecca knew she was babbling, but after that unpleasant encounter with Richard she couldn't help herself. Also she was cursing herself for saying she would invite Jimmy to the house for Christmas Eve when she had no intention of making herself look like a besotted fool to a man who obviously had forgotten all about her.

Amy stared worriedly at her sister. Something had happened in her short absence, that much was obvious. It was the only explanation she could think of to explain Rebecca's highly charged state of mind.

'Is anything wrong, Becky? You look upset.'

Rebecca gave a watery smile. 'Richard's here.'

'Oh!' There was no need for further explanation. Amy knew how much her sister disliked Richard. It was something Amy had never been able to understand. She herself had always been fond of her uncle Richard, seeing only the outward, kindly benevolent persona he portrayed in her company. Knowing it was no good to try and extol Richard's virtues, Amy said brightly, 'Shall we go then? I want to be back by three, Charlie's taking me out shopping for my Christmas present . . . Oh, sorry, Becky, I didn't mean to . . .'

Rebecca turned away impatiently. 'For goodness' sake, Amy. There's no need to keep tiptoeing around my feelings. I'm glad you're getting on so well with Charlie, he's a nice young man. Just

157

because things didn't work out for me and Jimmy there's no call for you to keep apologising for you being happy.'

An awkward feeling settled over the sisters until Rebecca, her good humour returning, cried, 'Oh, heavens. Let's get out of here before Richard comes down and starts fawning all over you. I know you don't mind his attentions, but it turns my stomach and I don't want to be put off my lunch. I thought we could eat out for a change, sort of an early Christmas treat. What do you think? And don't worry, we'll be back in plenty of time for you to go out with Charlie – again!'

Amy grinned happily. 'Oh, that'll be lovely, Becky. It's been ages since we had something to eat out. But what about Auntie Maude?'

Rebecca snorted. 'She'll be all right. I took her up a tray twenty minutes ago, I'm sure she'll be able to last for a few hours. Besides, like I've been telling you for years, I'm sure Maude's not as helpless as she makes out. From today I'm not paying Mrs Gates sixpence to come in and sit with Maude; I can think of much better things to do with the money. For instance, it can go towards paying for our lunch.'

At the concerned expression on Amy's face, Rebecca shook her head. It was no good. Unless Ada Gates was looking after Maude, Amy wouldn't be able to relax. Reluctantly Rebecca said in a resigned voice, 'All right, we'll stop at Mrs Gates' on the way out and ask her to come in.'

Immediately Amy brightened. 'Thanks, Becky. I know you think I'm a silly fool, but I can't help worrying about Maude. She really is ill, you know, she's not putting it on. No one would pretend to be so ill and spend all their life in bed if they could help it, would they?'

Rebecca sighed heavily. Amy would never change. She would always see the good in people, and what was wrong in that?

Not bothering to call up the stairs to tell Richard they were going out, Rebecca donned her winter coat ready to leave but Amy, as usual, wouldn't leave until she'd seen Richard and reassured Maude they wouldn't be too long. While she was waiting for Amy, Rebecca went to ask Ada if she would stay with Maude, and was dismayed when Billy answered the door.

His large, fleshy face broke into a huge grin when he saw Rebecca standing on the doorstep. 'Becky! What a lovely surprise, come in, come in.' Standing back, he gestured for her to enter.

Pasting a smile to her stiff face, Rebecca replied quickly, 'I'm sorry, Billy, I can't stop. I just wanted to ask your mum if she'd sit with Maude while me and Amy go shopping.'

Billy's face fell in disappointment. 'You're out of luck, Becky. Mum's got a cleaning job at one of the big houses in Carlton Avenue. She won't be back until four.' A sudden idea came to him. 'Hang on, I'll come in if you're stuck. I usually work on Saturdays, but it's my day off.'

Groaning inwardly, Rebecca's heart sank. She could see the reasoning behind Billy's kind gesture. Once he was in the house, he would spin out his stay

159

for as long as possible. Still, she had no choice but to take him up on his offer.

'Thanks, Billy, I'd appreciate that. We won't be long.'

Leaving the delighted Billy, Rebecca was thankful to see Amy waiting for her.

Two hours later, their bags full to bursting, the two girls stopped at the pie and mash shop for lunch. On the way home Rebecca was startled when Amy suddenly headed in the direction they would normally have taken before the attack.

'Hang on, Amy, where're you going?'

A sheepish look crossed Amy's face.

'I thought we might stop off and see Bessie before going home. She did say to pop in if ever we were passing.'

Stunned amazement gripped Rebecca before she croaked wildly, 'Are you mad? We don't even know the woman. We only met her once, and if I remember rightly, we didn't part on the best of terms; at least I didn't.'

The colour deepened in Amy's face. 'Actually, I've seen quite a lot of Bessie recently. Charlie often takes me to Jimmy's house to visit.' Seeing the anger and hurt etched on Rebecca's face, Amy hurried on, 'Oh, please, Becky, don't look at me like that. She's really nice when you get to know her. And it was your fault you got off on the wrong foot . . .' Amy's voice trailed off lamely, frightened she had gone too far.

Her face grim, Rebecca muttered tersely, 'If you

want to visit that house then you go ahead, I'll meet you at home.'

Close to tears, Amy pleaded, 'Please, Becky, come with me. I promise if Bessie says anything remotely nasty to you then I'll come straight home with you . . . Please, Becky, won't you just try, for my sake.'

Rebecca's emotions were running riot. The thought of seeing Jimmy again was overwhelming, but what if he made it plain he didn't want to see her? The humiliation would be unbearable. But what if . . . ? Realising that all she had to lose was her pride, Rebecca swallowed loudly.

'All right. But I warn you, Amy. If that woman so much as looks at me sideways, I'm off.'

Amy's face lit up with relief. 'Oh, she won't, Becky, honest. Only last week she asked me to bring you with me next time I visited.'

Still doubtful, Rebecca allowed Amy to persuade her, telling herself she was only doing it for Amy's sake. Still she couldn't stop her heart from hammering with excitement at the thought of the chance of seeing Jimmy again. That is, if he was at home. Gathering all her inner strength, Rebecca took a deep breath and followed her excited sister.

Bessie was in the hallway trying to master the new carpet cleaner Jimmy had bought for her, but was quickly discovering the blasted thing was throwing out more dirt than it was sucking up. In disgust she put the new contraption away and was about to revert to her old and trusted method of brushing the carpet by hand when there was a loud knocking at

161

the front door. Glad of the diversion, Bessie hurried to answer the summons. Throwing the door open the smile froze on her lips when she saw who her visitor was.

'Hello, Bessie, long time no see.'

Although Bessie had been expecting her, nevertheless her heart leapt in shock. At the same time she was relieved the waiting was over. She had been hoping that Heather might have aged, losing the good looks she'd had when Bessie had last seen her, but she looked exactly the same as she had eight years ago. If anything Heather appeared even more beautiful. The flame-coloured hair was still evident beneath a wide, velvet hat, her vivid colouring enhanced by the royal blue outfit she was wearing.

Her face set, Bessie barred the doorway, saying in a clipped voice, 'We've been expecting yer. But yer ain't welcome, so why don't yer sling yer hook.'

Heather smiled lazily. 'Now then, Bessie, what kind of welcome is that to give family? And I am family, you know, as much as you'd like to think otherwise.'

'Now look 'ere, Heather Mills. Yer might 'ave fooled Jimmy wiv that old cobblers, but I never believed yer cock an' bull story. Now sling yer hook, yer—' Bessie staggered back as Heather pushed past her.

'Shut your mouth, you vicious old hag. If anyone's going to tell me to go, it'll be Jimmy. Where is he?'

Recovering her balance, Bessie glared at the hateful figure. 'He ain't 'ere. And even if he was, he wouldn't want ter see you, yer old trollop.'

Loud footsteps sounded above their heads, and with a smile of satisfaction Heather laughed triumphantly.

'Nice try, Bessie. Now if you'll get out of my way, I'll go and have a word with my husband.'

The footsteps became louder, then a well-known voice shouted down the stairs, 'What the hell's going on down there? I'm trying to do some work.'

Bravely Bessie tried once again to bar Heather's path but she was no match for the younger woman's strength.

Heather was halfway up the stairs when Jimmy appeared, his features contorted in anger at being disturbed. He froze in his tracks as he saw Heather coming towards him. For what seemed an age the two people stood staring at each other, then Heather laughed.

'Hello, Jimmy. Like I just said to Bessie, long time no see.'

Jimmy's lips tightened. 'Not long enough, Heather. But now you're here you'd better come up. We have some issues that need to be cleared up.'

With an air of one familiar to the house, Heather climbed the stairs.

In the spacious living room Heather's keen eyes took in every detail. Judging by the expensive furniture and decor, Jimmy was worth a lot more than she had first imagined. Her bearing oozing confidence, she was about to sit down in one of the high-backed leather chairs when Jimmy's voice stopped her.

'Don't get comfortable. What I have to say won't take long.'

Heather's eyebrows rose mockingly.

'My, my. I see you've come up in the world, and not only in monetary terms. When I knew you, you spoke like a gutter brat. Now you could almost pass for a gentleman. I'm impressed.'

Standing by the fireplace, Jimmy leant his arm on the ornate mantelpiece, his eyes raking over the woman. She was still as striking as ever, and he was relieved beyond measure to discover that she no longer had any power over him.

'Let's cut the chit-chat, Heather. You haven't come to engage in idle gossip, and I'm a busy man. So let's get down to details. How much do you want? Or should I say, how much are you hoping to get out of me?'

Still confident she had the upper hand, Heather smiled. 'Why, Jimmy, what sort of welcome is that to give your wife? As for money, well . . .' Her eyes flickering around the room, she drawled, 'Judging by what I've seen I think a weekly allowance would be in order. On the other hand I'd be quite prepared to come back and take up my wifely duties.' Her voice dropping to a more intimate tone, Heather added softly, 'I know I did you a terrible wrong, Jimmy. But I was young and impressionable, we both were. Neither of us were ready for marriage. I realise a lot of water has passed under the bridge and I don't expect you to welcome me back with open arms, not after what I did. But can't we start again? We had something special once, surely . . .'

The contrite expression vanished as Jimmy's face creased into a wide grin. Then Heather jerked back as he began to laugh, slowly at first, then rising to a loud crescendo of unmitigated mirth.

The first signs of alarm began to grip Heather's body. She hadn't expected things to go smoothly, and had been prepared for a fight. What she hadn't been prepared for was the complete lack of regard Jimmy was displaying.

His laughter finally abating, Jimmy wiped his eyes and called out. 'Come in, Bessie. You might as well hear what I have to say. It'll save me having to repeat myself later.'

From behind the closed door, Bessie appeared, her lined face showing no sign of shame at being caught eavesdropping. Casting a malevolent glare at the still-standing Heather, she made her way to Jimmy's side.

'What is it, lad? Yer ain't gonna take 'er back, are yer?' Her voice filled with fearful uncertainty, Bessie looked beseechingly up at the beloved figure.

For an answer Jimmy opened the walnut bureau and drew out a long white envelope.

'This arrived this morning. I was going to tell you at supper, Bessie, but it seems as if I'll have to tell you now.' Under the watchful, apprehensive gaze of both women, Jimmy slowly drew out a sheet of headed paper. 'This, ladies, is a letter from Somerset House, and guess what? It seems there is no record of any marriage taking place between a

James Jackson and a Miss Heather Mills. So, what have you to say to that, Mrs Jackson?'

Beside him, Bessie slumped against his side in relief. But her moment of weakness was short lived. Spinning round to face the stricken Heather, Bessie shrilled, 'I knew it, I bleeding well knew it. Yer conniving little baggage. Thought yer could come back 'ere and sponge off my Jimmy, did yer? Well, I 'ope yer've got another fancy man lined up, 'cos you're getting sod all here. Now piss off!'

Heather didn't move. Of all things she had been anticipating, she hadn't bargained on this. But she still had an ace up her sleeve, and now was the time to play it. Determined not to let either of them have the satisfaction of seeing her brought low, Heather inclined her head in gracious defeat.

'It seems I've been found out. But you can't blame a girl for trying. I've never begged in my life and I'm not going to start now. But before I go, there's something I have for you, Jimmy, sort of an early Christmas present. If you'll wait a few minutes I'll go and fetch it. I won't be long.'

When she had gone, Jimmy and Bessie exchanged bemused glances. Bessie was the first to break the silence. 'What's she up ter now? It'll be no good, yer mark me words, lad.' Gazing up at him, Bessie murmured fretfully, 'Yer ain't gonna weaken, are yer, lad. 'Cos if yer do, she'll never leave yer in peace.'

Laughing grimly, Jimmy patted Bessie's arm. 'Don't you worry, old girl. That young, gullible boy who fell for Heather is long gone. And I'll tell you something else while I'm at it. Now the uncertainty about being married has been lifted, I'm going to call on Rebecca. I haven't been back to see her since the night Heather made her reappearance. I didn't think it would be fair on the girl. But now I know I'm a free man, I can start making plans for the future.'

Bessie's eyes widened. 'Gawd help us. Yer ain't saying what I think yer saying, are yer, Jimmy?'

Jimmy smiled at Bessie affectionately. 'Hold your horses, old girl. For all I know Rebecca might have forgotten all about me by now. Still, I'm going to go round to visit her later on today and see how the land lies; and I'll take it from there.' The geniality dropped from his voice and in a more sombre tone he added, 'To tell the truth, Bessie, I tried my damnedest to stay away from Rebecca, but somehow she got under my skin, and I haven't been able to stop thinking about her since. But don't go buying a wedding outfit yet. If she does agree to see me, I'll be taking things slowly. After all that business with Heather I'm not about to rush into marriage, not until I'm absolutely sure.' He uttered a nervous snort of derision. 'Listen to me. I'm talking as if Rebecca's going to fall into my arms the minute she sees me. For all I know she might have found someone else since I last saw her. I wouldn't be surprised. She's a lovely-looking girl, and a decent one to boot.'

Now it was Bessie's turn to snort. 'Don't give me that, lad. She won't 'ave forgotten yer. Bleeding hell! It's only been a few weeks. Nah! She'll still be interested. 'Cos, I'll tell yer this, Jimmy. That young piece fancied yer from the moment yer brought 'er into this 'ouse. Not that she would admit it. But I

167

know women, so yer can rest easy. I know I wasn't that keen on 'er at first, but after seeing that old tart again, your Rebecca seems like the Blessed Virgin in comparison.'

Squeezing the frail shoulders, Jimmy grinned. 'Thanks, Bessie.' Jimmy looked at the open door and tutted impatiently. 'She's taking her time. Maybe her talk about a Christmas present was just an excuse to make a dignified exit. Look, I'm not hanging around here all day waiting for her. Let's go down and see if there's any sign of her. With a bit of luck she's gone for good. I hope so. Then we can get on with our lives without the worry of her turning up on the doorstep when we least expect it.'

His arm still draped protectively around Bessie's shoulders, they descended the stairs to find Heather framed in the open doorway, her expression showing no sign of any disappointment at being bested.

'Bleeding hell! We was hoping you'd cleared off.'

Jimmy squeezed Bessie's shoulders, the gesture warning her to keep quiet. 'Well, Heather. If there's anything more, then be quick about it. Like I said before, I'm a busy man, I haven't got all day to waste playing games.'

'Oh, I'm not playing any games, Jimmy. I said I had a present for you. It just took me a bit longer to fetch it than I first thought.' Turning towards the blind side of the door, Heather said, 'Come here, son. I want you to meet your father.'

A young boy appeared by Heather's side, his small face filled with apprehension and fear.

Struck dumb, Bessie and Jimmy stared at the small figure, unable to utter a word at the unexpected turn of events.

Pushing the boy into the hallway, Heather crowed triumphantly, 'Seeing as you're not going to support me and I can't afford to look after a child, I'm handing him over to his father. His name is James. I was going to call him Jimmy, but I thought that was a bit common. Merry Christmas, Jimmy, and to you, Bessie, you old witch. I would say goodbye, but obviously I'll be popping back now and then to see my son. After all, I am his mother and I'll want to make sure he's being well cared for.'

Before either Jimmy or Bessie could move Heather had gone, shutting the door behind her. The small boy looked at the two strangers in bewilderment then began banging on the closed door, his face running with terrified tears.

'Mummy! Mummy! Come back. Mummy! Mummy! Don't leave me.'

'Jesus!' Jimmy breathed in stupefied horror. Then he was running towards the terrified boy. Scooping the struggling frame up into his arms Jimmy yanked opened the door, shouting, 'Heather! Heather, come back here . . . Heather!'

A carriage rolled by. Heather looked out of the window and gave a mocking smile. 'I'll see you soon, Jimmy. Get acquainted with your son in the meantime. I'll be back in time for Christmas. Bye.' Then she was gone, leaving Jimmy holding the squirming, screaming boy.

*   *   *

169

'Look, I'm not sure about this, Amy. Why don't you go in while I wait outside? If Bessie really doesn't mind seeing me, then you can come out and tell me . . . Goodness, what's that racket?'

The girls stopped on the corner. Then Rebecca's eyes widened in shock as she saw the woman she'd last encountered in the restaurant coming away from Jimmy's house and getting into a hansom cab. Moments later, Jimmy came running out holding a screaming young boy in his arms, his strong voice clearly heard above the child's cries.

Dimly Rebecca heard the loud exchange between Jimmy and the woman. Stunned beyond belief, she stood rooted to the pavement, her tortured mind whirling. So Jimmy was married. And not only married, he also had a son. Beside her, Amy too was struck dumb. All her hopes and scheming of getting Jimmy and Rebecca back together wiped out in a few, heart-wrenching seconds.

Jimmy was still staring after the carriage, his face a picture of bewilderment. It was as he turned to enter the house that something made him glance up the road. And there were Rebecca and Amy. But his tormented eyes registered only Rebecca.

He opened his mouth to call her name, but then, like Heather, she was gone.

CHAPTER FOURTEEN

The child wouldn't stop crying and pining for his mother, and Bessie and Jimmy were at their wits' end as to what to do with the young boy who had been unceremoniously dropped in their laps. As much as they both wanted to have seen the back of Heather, by the end of the second week, even Bessie would have given anything to open the door and see the hated painted face smirking at her. Coupled with the child's evident distress, he was causing even more worry by his refusal to eat more than a few scraps of toast and the odd biscuit. Every day Bessie would painstakingly prepare food in a desperate effort to tempt his appetite, but apart from picking at the meals set in front of him, young James was barely eating enough to keep a bird alive, and the weight was dropping off his small frame at an alarming rate.

Desperate to do something before the boy starved

to death in front of their eyes, Jimmy called in his old friend Tom Barker, but the doctor told the anxious Bessie and Jimmy there was nothing he could do, and the best medicine he could recommend was to reunite the boy with his mother. This diagnosis was met with a storm of derision, with Bessie shouting that if it was that easy, then they would have done so before now. The truth was that, despite Jimmy's best efforts, Heather was nowhere to be found. He had called in favours from every acquaintance known to him, and put the word out on the streets, offering a reward to anyone who could locate Heather Mills. This had resulted in dozens of filthy, unsavoury characters knocking at Jimmy's door declaring they had seen the red-headed woman in various parts of London. Jimmy had followed up every lead, even though his heart told him that the mass of vagrants had invented this information to extract money from him. In frantic desperation Jimmy had hired private detectives to try to discover where Heather was holed up, but the elusive woman had covered her tracks well.

It was now only a week to Christmas, but the house was far from feeling festive. For the first time since they had known each other, Jimmy and Bessie were at each other's throats with a vengeance. Jimmy was complaining he couldn't cope with a child and manage to run his business, and Bessie, worn to a frazzle, kept reminding Jimmy that she was too old to cope with any child, let alone one who wouldn't eat and cried day and night. She also kept reminding Jimmy that, like the non-existent marriage, there was no proof that the child was even his.

Things finally came to a head one morning when Bessie, almost dead on her feet from sitting up with the fractious, terrified child all night, told Jimmy that she couldn't cope any more and that if he didn't sort something out, and pretty damn quick, then he would be arranging a funeral very soon – hers! Packing the exhausted woman off to bed, Jimmy went in to the small boxroom that had been converted into a bedroom for the child and sat quietly by the bedside. The boy had fallen into an exhausted state of inertia, yet even in sleep his soft, childish mouth was tight and firm, as if, even in the throes of slumber, he was still maintaining a wall of resistance against the strangers he had been abandoned with.

Jimmy sat by the boy's bedside, his keen eyes searching for any resemblance to himself, yet he could find none. But what could he do? It wasn't the child's fault he had been landed in an alien environment with people he'd never clapped eyes on before, and Jimmy could hardly turn the child out onto the streets. Deep in thought, Jimmy tried to find a way out of the impossible situation he now found himself in. His thoughts turned to Rebecca, wondering if he may be able to elicit her help with the child, then he quickly dismissed the idea. He would more than likely receive a clout around the head with a heavy frying pan the moment he showed his face; and who could blame her? He'd already been to the house in Welbeck Road three times in the past fortnight, but Rebecca refused outright to see him. Then he had a flash of inspiration – Amy! Now there was a thought. If anyone could coax the child out of his shell, that person was Amy. With her beautiful face and sweet nature, surely she would win the boy's trust. Even Bessie, who wasn't lavish with her praise, had taken an instant liking to the young girl. And of course it would give him a reason to visit the house once more, this time with a valid excuse. Spurred into action, Jimmy took one last look at the sleeping form then bounded down to the kitchen.

Charlie was seated at the large, scrubbed wooden table, looking very much at home as he laughed and flirted with the maid Jimmy had recently employed, much to Bessie's outrage. Jimmy had had his work cut out for him to explain that the maid's position was only temporary. As he had forcefully pointed out to the irate woman, what with looking after the child day and night, she couldn't be expected to run the house as well. He had been going to add, 'Not at your age', but had wisely thought better of it. Although Bessie had ranted for days at what she perceived as having her position in the house usurped, Jimmy had seen the relief behind the elderly woman's anger. In truth Bessie was gratified beyond measure that the bulk of her workload was to be temporarily lifted. Yet not a day went by without her reminding Jimmy that the moment the business with the child was sorted out, then that young miss down in the kitchen would be shown the door.

'Morning, Guv'nor,' Charlie greeted Jimmy cheerfully. 'We off out?'

'If you can drag yourself away,' Jimmy replied crisply.

The asperity in Jimmy's voice didn't faze Charlie one bit, though the new maid's face turned crimson.

Donning his coat Charlie called out to the maid cheekily, 'See yer later, darlin'. Don't do anything I wouldn't do while I'm gone.'

The colour in the girl's face heightened, and she quickly busied herself taking a batch of scones out of the oven range.

Despite his urgency to get to his location, the smell of the freshly cooked scones reminded Jimmy he'd had no breakfast. 'Could you wrap me up a couple of those scones, Cissie? I'll eat them in the carriage.'

Flustered and eager to ingratiate herself with the rugged, immaculately dressed man who was her new master, Cissie Banks hurried to do Jimmy's bidding.

Taking the piping hot parcel, Jimmy turned to leave then stopped. Judging by the high colour in the girl's cheeks, and the scene he had walked in on, it was obvious that the new maid imagined she was in with a chance with Charlie. It wasn't the young man's fault, in fact he would have been horrified if he knew the effect he was having on the plain girl. The truth was that Charlie was one of those young men who laughed and flirted with any woman, whatever her age. There was no deviousness or mockery in his actions, it was just his nature to be friendly and affectionate to any woman. Not wanting any further disruptions in the already

175

fraught household, Jimmy turned to where Charlie was waiting by the back door and said, 'Go on, get the horses saddled. I want to get to Welbeck Road before Amy leaves for work.'

Instantly Charlie's face lit up in pure delight. 'Righto, Guv'nor. I'll have 'em ready in two shakes of a lamb's tail,' then he was gone, as eager as Jimmy to get to his destination.

Jimmy smiled wryly at the hovering girl. 'That's the quickest I've seen him move in months, lazy devil. Still, I can't say as I blame him. His young lady friend is a lovely girl. I wouldn't be at all surprised if there were wedding bells announced shortly. Anyway, I must be off. Bessie's sleeping at last, so would you keep an ear out for the boy, just in case he wakes? I don't want Bessie disturbed. I shouldn't be more than an hour at the most.' Jimmy turned away in discomfort as a look of shock and hurt passed over the girl's face.

As he climbed into the carriage, he justified his actions by telling himself that it was better to let the girl know where she stood, rather than see her suffer further humiliation and hurt when she found out Charlie already had a sweetheart.

After the men had left, Cissie Banks sank down onto a hard chair, her face a picture of misery at the knowledge that Charlie was already spoken for. A soft knock sounded at the tradesman's entrance and, sighing loudly in disappointment, Cissie rose to answer the door.

'Mornin', Cissie. Sorry I'm a bit late, I've had extra

deliveries to make, what with Christmas coming up.'

Cissie motioned for the delivery man to enter. Laying his basket on the table, the shy man uncovered his wares and waited while Cissie sorted through the assortment of meat. Picking out two large quantities of sausages and bacon, half a dozen pork chops plus a good sized cut of beef for the Sunday dinner, Cissie wrapped the meat up in a thick covering of soft mesh fabric and deposited the items into the larder.

The butcher watched her every movement, shuffling his feet awkwardly as he tried to start a conversation. But it was obvious by Cissie's silent indifference to his presence that she was in no mood to indulge in idle talk this morning. Normally she would offer him a mug of tea, and, if he was lucky and she'd been baking, a plate of freshly cooked scones or tea cakes would also be on offer. And on a freezing December morning like today, he had been looking forward to having something hot and filling to warm his shivering body before he set off out into the cold to finish his rounds. Masking his acute disappointment, the man prepared to leave.

'I'll pop the bill round Saturday morning . . . Oh, by the way, how's old Bessie? Not too bad, I hope. I know she's got a tongue on her, but she's got a heart of gold when you get to know her.'

Cissie made a deprecating clucking sound with her tongue. She certainly hadn't seen any evidence of the latter, though she'd certainly encountered the former side of the master's housekeeper.

When Cissie continued to bustle around the kitchen, the man gave up all hope of being offered any form of refreshment and hoped he would have better luck at his next port of call.

As he opened the back door, Cissie's voice stopped him.

'Just a minute, Cedric. Ain't yer gonna wait fer your morning cuppa?'

The man's face creased into a relieved smile. Placing his basket back on the table, he made himself at home while Cissie busied herself in making the tea, her mind working furiously.

Being possessed of a lazy nature, Cissie Banks had been on the look-out for a husband since the age of twelve. She had hoped Charlie would be that man, but now that avenue was obviously closed she would have to look elsewhere. On the pretext of checking two apple tarts cooking slowly in the oven, Cissie studied the butcher covertly. He must be thirty if he was a day, and she was only nineteen. Still, beggars couldn't be choosers, and Cedric North wasn't short of a few bob. Better yet, he was obviously a very lonely man since his wife had died, and seemed to have taken a liking to her in the short time she had been working in the house. There was also the fact to contend with that her time here was limited, and then she would have to start looking for another post; a prospect she was dreading. Apart from that old bag of a housekeeper, Cissie was enjoying her work in the spacious, well-furnished house, and wished she could be kept on; but that notion had been well and truly squashed. If, however, she played her cards right, she may never have to work again.

Pasting an inviting smile to her lips, Cissie laid a mug of piping hot tea and a plate of scones in front of the delighted man. 'There you go, Cedric, get stuck into those. Fresh outta the oven they are, I made 'em meself.'

Smacking his lips, the man looked up at the smiling face and said, 'By, they smell good, Cissie. You'll make some lucky man a good wife one of these days.'

Cissie turned away, her lips curving into a crafty smile. She had every intention of becoming a wife, but the moment the ring was placed on her finger she had no intention of ever doing a day's work again. Pulling up a chair she joined the man tucking into his breakfast.

Standing outside the door of number 17 Welbeck Road, Jimmy hesitated, his normally implacable reserve momentarily deserting him. Cursing himself for his cowardice, he took a firm hold of the brass knocker and banged twice, then braced himself for his welcome. He had anticipated either Rebecca or Amy answering the door; what he hadn't bargained for was the burly figure of Billy Gates filling the doorway.

Billy had been on his way out to work when the loud knocking had resounded through the house, but the intimidating figure of the local bookmaker was the last person he had expected to see. The genial smile dropping from his fleshy features, Billy glowered at the visitor.

'What d'yer want? Yer ain't welcome 'ere, so why

don't yer go away and leave the girls in peace. You've done enough damage already.'

His initial surprise fading, Jimmy moved forward impatiently. 'Unless you've taken up residence, I'll wait until one of the occupants of the house tells me I'm not welcome.'

Even though his heart was hammering wildly in his large chest, Billy stood his ground. 'Look, I've already told yer, yer ain't welcome 'ere, so why don't yer—'

His patience snapping, Jimmy reverted to his cockney upbringing and growled, 'Get outta my way, you great lump of lard. I ain't got time to piss about with the likes of you. If you ain't moved by the time I count five, you'll be picking your teeth up off the floor; d'yer understand?'

Billy swallowed nervously. Although he was about two stone heavier than the other man, Billy knew that his build was mainly fat, whereas Jimmy Jackson's solid frame was all muscle; he also had a reputation of dealing harshly with anyone who crossed him.

Soft footsteps sounded in the hallway, and it was with immense relief that Billy heard Amy's voice.

'Who is it, Billy?'

Confident that the man wouldn't resort to physical violence in front of Amy, Billy Gates regained his composure. Swelling out his massive chest, he answered, 'It's Jimmy Jackson again, Amy, love. Just say the word an' I'll soon get rid of 'im.'

Amy hurried forward, firmly pushing Billy out into the street. 'It's all right, Billy. I'll deal with this. You get off to work, or else you'll be late. And thanks for coming in, I'll let you know if we need anything.'

Carefully sliding past the grim-faced man, Billy drew his shoulders back, gave what he hoped was a threatening glance in Jimmy's direction, then swiftly scurried down the street.

'What do you want, Jimmy? I thought we'd made it quite clear last time you visited that Becky doesn't want to see you.' Her tiny face pale and drawn, Amy showed no signs of letting Jimmy into the house. Looking over his shoulder to where Charlie was sitting atop the carriage, his face and neck swathed in a large woollen scarf, she gave a tremulous smile. Taking advantage of her distraction, Jimmy gently moved her aside and entered the house.

He hadn't taken more than a few steps when he felt a shove in the middle of his back. The assault on his person carried little weight to a man of his strength, but it was unexpected, causing him to lose his balance for a few moments. Then Amy was standing directly in front of him, hands on hips, her normally smiling face creased in anger. It was a side to Amy that Jimmy had never encountered. Indeed, he would never have imagined her to be capable of such rage.

'I told you Becky doesn't want to see you, Jimmy. Come to that, neither do I, not after the way you've treated her. Taking her out and making a fuss of her, pretending you cared, when all you were doing was filling in time when you had nothing better to do. What happened? Was your wife out of town at the time?'

Caught off guard, Jimmy found himself tongue-tied, but not for long. Pulling at the buttons of his heavy overcoat in an attempt to cover his uneasiness in the hostile atmosphere, Jimmy answered gruffly, 'I don't blame you for hating me, Amy. But believe me, things aren't what they appear to be. If Becky will only give me a few minutes of her time, I can explain . . .'

'Well, you can't.' Amy stared him down, her face defiant. 'Even if she was willing to see you, she couldn't. She's not well. She's been in bed for the last three days, and for Becky to stay in bed it must mean she's really ill. So if you think I'm going to let you disturb her, you've another think coming.'

Jimmy's stomach lurched in alarm, his eyes raising to the ceiling. 'Becky's ill! Well, why the hell didn't somebody tell me?'

'Why should they? It's nothing to do with you.' Tilting up her chin, Amy added scornfully, 'It's a pity you didn't show such concern before now, but then I don't suppose your wife would be too happy to find you'd been seeing another woman behind her back.'

Jimmy winced at the contempt in Amy's voice while marvelling at the sudden change in her character. But he wasn't going to be put off his task by a slip of a girl. Moving towards the stairs, he said firmly, 'Like I've already said, it's not what you think, but I haven't time to explain now. I must see Becky, so if—'

With a swiftness that startled Jimmy, Amy sprang to the foot of the stairs. 'If you take so much as .

another step, I swear I'll find the nearest heavy object and smash you over the head with it. You've hurt my sister enough, I'm not going to let you hurt her any more.'

It would have been easy simply to move the furious girl to one side, but Jimmy hadn't the heart. Also he believed her threat, and he didn't relish the idea of being bashed over the back of the head. Stepping back, he held out his hands entreatingly. 'Look, Amy. I never intended to hurt Becky, I still don't. The reason I came here today was to ask for your help.'

Still on her guard, Amy eyed him warily. 'I can't imagine how I could help a man in your position. You must have a dozen flunkies only too pleased to help out the great Jimmy Jackson. Unless you want me to put a good word in for you with Becky. If that's what you've come for, then you've had a wasted journey. My sister's worth more than becoming a married man's mistress, and she'd spit in your face if you so much as suggested it.'

A deep sigh rippled through Jimmy's body. Lord! Of all the receptions he had tried to prepare himself for, not for a moment had he imagined that Amy, of all people, would treat him with such antagonism. He hadn't expected his task to be easy, but he certainly hadn't banked on being greeted with such venomous hostility.

Running his hand over his face he said tiredly, 'All right, Amy, you've made your feelings quite clear, so I'll come straight to the point. For a start I'm not married and never have been. That woman you saw me with was someone I knew many years ago. I'm not going to bore you with all the sordid details, but the crux of the matter is, she's left me with a child she claims is mine. To be perfectly truthful, I don't know if he is or not, but that's beside the point. Since Heather dumped him at my door, the poor little sod hasn't stopped crying for his mother. He's hardly eaten a thing since he arrived and he won't let either me or Bessie near him. Even the sight of us sends him into a state of hysteria. I've had the doctor in to him but there's nothing he can do. The best advice he could offer was to find the boy's mother . . . Huh!' A snort of tired derision escaped Jimmy's tight lips. 'As if I haven't tried. She said she'd be back before Christmas, I truly hope so, for the child's sake, because if she doesn't, then by the time she does show her face, it might be too late for the boy. When she does decide to come back, she'll be wanting money. She sees the child as a bargaining stick, and God blast her to hell, she's got the upper hand over me. When she does finally reappear I'll give her anything she wants, I don't have any other choice. In the meantime I still have the child to contend with; and that's why I've come round.'

He stopped to wet his lips, hoping Amy would speak, but she remained steadfastly mute. Running his hand distractedly through his thick hair, Jimmy continued, 'I was hoping you might come and try and talk to him. You've a way with people that's very rare. If the child doesn't take to you, then he won't take to anyone. Please, Amy, I'm begging you.

You're my last chance. I'm truly afraid the child will die if he carries on the way he is. Whatever his mother's done, he shouldn't have to suffer. Will you come? . . . Please, Amy. I don't know what else to do. I'm at my wits' end.'

Amy had listened silently to Jimmy's story. If he had just come to try and talk her into letting him see Becky she would have remained firm. But this was different. The thought of a small child wasting away, terrified at being abandoned with strangers, tugged at her tender heart. Her body relaxing for the first time since Jimmy had entered the house, Amy murmured, 'All right, Jimmy, I'll try. But not to salve your conscience. I'm only agreeing to do what I can for the child's sake.'

Letting out a loud sigh of relief Jimmy said gratefully, 'Thanks, Amy. You don't know how much this means to me. I'll wait while you get your coat.'

'Just a minute,' Amy shot back angrily, her hackles raised once again. 'In case you've forgotten, Becky's ill in bed. I can't just walk out and leave her. Then there's my aunt to consider, she can't be left either. Or are you so wrapped up in your own problems you can't think of anyone else but yourself?'

Jimmy's head snapped back, his face reddening, his anger now matching Amy's. 'Of course I haven't forgotten. If you'd given me a minute, I was going to suggest asking your neighbour in while we were out. Furthermore, I fully intend to send Charlie to fetch Dr Barker to attend Becky as soon as he's dropped us off home . . . By the way, what did your doctor say was wrong with Becky?'

The anger seeping from Amy's face, her gaze dropped to the floor. 'I haven't had the doctor in. Becky said not to and that she'd be fine after a good rest. She's only got a cold. Besides . . . I've had to have time off work to look after Becky and Auntie Maude, and . . . and the truth of it is, we . . . well, we just can't afford to pay for a doctor.'

'Can't afford to pay for a doctor's visit?' Jimmy's voice rose incredulously. 'What are you saying, girl? Even if you've lost a couple of days' wages – and I'll soon sort that out – I pay Phil good money, and send half his wages through the post to Becky each week. So unless you require the services of a brain surgeon, you should have ample money to pay for . . .' Jimmy halted in his tirade as he saw the startled look spring to Amy's eyes.

In that moment the truth was clear. Neither girl had seen a penny of the money he had been sending to this address since Phil had begun working for him. Somehow, the devious bastard had managed to waylay the postman and pocket the money intended for Becky's use. A red mist descended over Jimmy's eyes. Through gritted teeth he ground out, 'Where is he? Where's that thieving, conniving brother of yours? By God he's got some explaining to do. That's if I don't wring his miserable neck first.'

Her hand clutching at her throat, her mind in turmoil, Amy whispered, 'He left for work just before you arrived, he . . .' Her voice broke. Oh, he wouldn't. Phil wouldn't do that to them. He'd been so good lately. There had only been one week when he hadn't been able to give Becky her full housekeeping money, but he'd made it up to her the following week, giving Becky an extra ten shillings. Yet if what Jimmy was saying was true, then Phil had been stealing from them every week since he'd started working for Jimmy.

A wave of dizziness swept over Amy. Sinking down onto the bottom stair, she buried her face in her hands. She didn't want to believe what Jimmy had said, but why would he lie? Deep down, Amy knew he was telling the truth; she also admitted to herself for the first time that her brother was not only an inveterate gambler, but now it seemed he had stooped to the level of a common thief. Even knowing how ill Becky was, he still hadn't offered to pay for the doctor to call, protesting that he didn't have the money to spare. And all the time he was gambling his wages away while his own sister lay ill upstairs. The very thought made Amy sick to her stomach. She thought back down the years to the times when Becky would have a go at Phil for coming home empty-handed, knowing there was barely any food in the house and the rent to be paid to Uncle Richard. Her uncle would have forgone the rent money if Becky had told him they were in difficulties, but her elder sister would rather have gone on the streets than be beholden to Richard; and Phil knew it. During all those unpleasant times, Amy had always stood up for Phil, begging Becky not to be so hard on him. But no more!

When she finally lifted her head, Jimmy's heart lurched in pity at the devastating effect the news he'd imparted had had on her. In those few, awful moments, Amy seemed to have aged. The open, trusting eyes Jimmy had come to admire and hold in deep affection were now dimmed in sorrow.

In a dignified voice Amy said softly, 'I'll go and tell Becky what's happened; about the child I mean,' she added hastily. There was no way she could tell Becky what Phil had done, not in her present state. 'Could you go next door and ask Mrs Gates to come in? I'm afraid I don't have the sixpence we normally give her, but unlike my sister I'm not too proud to ask if you'll pay her.'

Unable to look into the stricken face any longer, Jimmy turned away, his insides churning with a mixture of rage at Phil and a sadness that Amy had appeared to have lost some of her childlike innocence. She had been blessed with a rare quality that Jimmy had never encountered before. He only hoped that special gift hadn't been destroyed for ever.

Lying among sweat-drenched sheets, Rebecca stirred at the sound of loud voices coming from below. Through her fevered brain she dimly registered Jimmy's voice, but was too ill to wonder at the significance of his visit. Then all went quiet. Tossing fitfully, Rebecca wondered what was wrong with her. Apart from the odd cold, and her monthly pains, she'd never had a day's illness in her life, until a week ago. But what had started as a mild cold had quickly developed into a raging fever, leaving her as weak as a new-born kitten. When she had no longer been able to fight off the illness that was racking every bone in her body, she had taken herself off to bed, thinking that a good, long sleep would soon have her back on her feet again. That day had turned into three, and if anything she felt worse now than she had at the first onset of what she had assumed was merely a common cold.

Minutes later Rebecca heard her door open and Ada Gates's timid voice call her name, but she hadn't the strength or will to answer. Before the door closed, Rebecca had already fallen back into a deep, feverish sleep.

CHAPTER FIFTEEN

True to his word, Jimmy sent Charlie off the moment they alighted from the carriage, with strict instructions not to return until he'd located Dr Barker and taken him to attend Becky, after which he was to come back immediately to inform Jimmy and Amy of Becky's condition.

Jimmy had barely ushered Amy into the house when an almighty din greeted them. 'What in tarnation is going on?' Jimmy exclaimed before striding towards the sounds of the disturbance that was coming from the kitchen, with Amy following warily behind. The sight that greeted them stopped them in their tracks.

There was Bessie, bundled up in her dressing gown, her grey hair falling in scraggly strands around her face and shoulders, and huddled up in the farthest corner of the spacious kitchen stood a shaking, crying Cissie. Beside the distraught girl stood a man who was vaguely familiar to Jimmy, his face crimson at being caught up in the catfight between the two women and looking as if he was about to make a bolt for the door at any moment.

'What the bloody hell's going on here? I've been gone less than an hour and come back to a bloody battlefield.'

Bessie spun around, her skinny arms wrapping the dressing gown tighter around her quivering body.

'I'll tell yer what's going on, mate. I come down ter make meself a cuppa and what do I find, eh?' Pointing a shaking finger at the terrified girl, she screeched, 'That little trollop canoodling with the bleeding butcher. All over each other they were, like a bleeding couple of dogs. Another minute an' they'd 'ave been 'aving it off on the floor . . . On my floor. The dirty little hussy, an' with him an' all. Why, he's old enough ter be her father. And you, yer randy bugger . . .' She advanced on the wide-eyed man, her finger wagging accusingly in his startled face. 'Yer should be ashamed of yerself. Mucking about with a girl half yer age, an' yer poor wife hardly cold in her grave. But then that's men fer yer. Get their leg over a dead cat if there was nothing else available.'

Jimmy stood dumbfounded, unable to believe the scene being played out before his eyes, while Amy, cringing with embarrassment, silently backed from the room. She had hardly stepped back into the hallway when Jimmy's voice, sounding like the wrath of God, thundered, 'I couldn't give a damn if

191

they were having it off on the bleeding table, as long as they gave it a good scrub down afterwards. Now get yourself back to bed where I left you, Bessie, or by God, I'll . . .'

'You'll what, Jimmy, lad?' Bessie glared at him defiantly. 'Yer gonna sack me if I don't do as I'm told. Well, yer won't 'ave to. 'Cos if that little baggage ain't outta this house by the time I'm dressed, then I'm off.' Her voice suddenly wavering, Bessie said, 'I've 'ad enough, Jimmy. What with the boy and worrying what's going on, with that loose piece prying into every room in the 'ouse, I can't take any more. It don't seem like it's me 'ome any more . . . an' . . . an' I'm tired, lad. I'm so tired.'

His anger evaporating in the face of Bessie's distress, Jimmy gently put his arms around her trembling shoulders and turned her around, leading her out to where Amy was nervously waiting outside the door.

'Look after her for a minute, Amy, love, will you, while I try and sort this mess out.' Running his hand distractedly through his hair, he gave Amy a wry smile. 'Lord, what a day, and it's not even ten o'clock yet.'

'It's all right, Jimmy, I'll see Bessie gets back to bed and rests before I go and see the child.'

Flashing Amy a grateful look, Jimmy returned to the kitchen.

'I must apologise for my housekeeper,' he directed his remark to the still snivelling Cissie. 'She's been under a lot of strain lately. It was nothing personal against you, Cissie. Bessie has always run this house without any assistance, despite my repeated offers to hire help. To her way of thinking, having you here makes her feel useless, and to a proud woman like Bessie, that's a bitter pill to swallow.'

Wiping the free-falling tears from her reddened eyes, Cissie sniffed loudly. 'We wasn't doing anything, sir. Just 'avin' a bit of a laugh and muckin' about. Then I told Cedric about how worried I was about me position here being only temporary like, an' he was just giving me a bit of a cuddle ter cheer me up when that old . . . I mean, Mrs Wilks came in and started shoutin' and swearin' at us . . . Ooh, an' she said some terrible, nasty things, sir. An' like I said, we weren't even doing anything wrong.'

Jimmy was at a loss as to what to do for the best. He desperately needed help in the house, unless he was prepared to learn how to run a home, do the housework, cook the meals, run his business, and look after a fractious child. And as dexterous as he was, he was still a man, and men didn't run households, that was women's work. But after this little fracas today, there was no way Bessie and Cissie could remain under the same roof without murder being done. Sighing deeply, Jimmy took out his wallet. Extracting a five-pound note he laid it on the table.

'I'm sorry, Cissie, but I'm going to have to let you go. I realise it's unfair, and I know it might be a while before you find another position, but this compensation money should keep you going until you find work.'

Cissie's eyes lit up greedily at the sight of the crisp,

white note lying on the table. That was more than two months' wages to her. She'd be able to have at least a month off before she started looking for another position. Careful to hide her glee, Cissie picked up the note and said timidly. 'Thank you, sir, you've been very kind. I was worried sick I'd be thrown out on the streets if I didn't find work straight away. Me landlord's a right old skinflint. Now I can take me time lookin' fer another job without worryin' about being homeless, especially out in weather like this.'

Jimmy held up his hand to stop the flow of gratitude, impatient now to have the sordid, embarrassing business over and done with. 'It's no more than you're entitled to, Cissie. Now if you'll excuse me, I have to see how Mrs Wilks is . . . Oh, and if you need a reference, please feel free to come to me, I'll be more than happy to oblige. It would be the least I could do in the circumstances.'

When the tall, impressive figure had gone, Cedric Smith let out a gust of relieved breath.

'Bleedin' hell, Cissie, girl, you've done well out of this business. Five pounds, phew! I bet you think it was worth all the unpleasantness now, don't yer. I know I would, if I'd just been given a fiver fer being called a few names, even if it was a bit nasty at the time.'

Cissie was thinking along the same lines. Never in a hundred years would she have expected such a generous offer from the master, but being the greedy girl she was, her mind was busily trying to find a way to cash in further on her unpleasant experience. Her face doleful, she uttered a soft sigh.

'I know, it was very good of Mr Jackson to give me such a large amount of money, especially as he didn't 'ave to. But I still 'ave to find another job, and somewhere else to live. I had been hoping I might be offered a live-in position, 'cos to be honest, Cedric, I hate that place where I live. The landlord's always making a pass at me, he's a horrible old man, and all the rooms are crawling with cockroaches. I try and keep mine clean, but the whole house is so old and run down, it's impossible. I even saw a rat the other night. It frightened the life outta me, I hate the bloody things. To make matters worse, I don't even have a lock on me door. I'm afraid to close me eyes most nights in case I wake up and find the landlord in me room with his dirty hands all over me. I know I can afford ter get a better place now, but I don't want ter spend the money Mr Jackson gave me until I can get set on in another post. I mean, five pounds is a lot of money, but it won't last for ever.' Giving vent to another sorrowful sigh, Cissie added wistfully, 'I suppose I'll just 'ave to put up with where I'm living until I get another job.'

Cissie Banks made a pathetic, forlorn picture, and Cedric Smith, his kind heart going out in pity for the girl's obvious distress, thought furiously, a germ of an idea entering his mind.

Clearing his throat loudly, he felt the colour rise in his face as he said hesitantly, 'Now look, Cissie, don't take this the wrong way, but . . . but, well, like you know, since me wife died I've been living alone.

Now, it's not a big house like this one, but there's plenty of empty rooms lying idle.' The colour in his face deepened as Cissie stared at him wide-eyed, her expression a picture of fearful apprehension. 'Now hang on, Cissie, love, it's not what yer think. All I'm suggesting is that if yer want ter come and stay with me . . . in your own room, of course, then you're more than welcome . . . Just till yer find another job and a decent place ter live.'

When the tears began to well up in Cissie's eyes once more, a look of alarm crossed the anxious butcher's face. For one awful moment he was afraid she was going to start howling again, then she fluttered her eyes and laid a warm hand on his arm.

'Oh, Cedric, you're so kind. I don't deserve a friend like you. I was dreading going back ter me lodgings early. It's bad enough 'aving ter live there at night, without spending the day there as well.'

The big man's features lit up in delight. 'Then you'll come and stay with me? . . . Just temporary, of course, until you're more settled,' he amended hastily. 'And I'll even put a lock on your door so you can sleep easy,' he laughed heartily at his own wit.

Ten minutes later Cissie was ready to leave, but not until she'd put several items of silver cutlery into her bag. As she closed the door for the last time she looked upwards and grinned. 'You've just done me the biggest favour of me life, yer old bat. I only wish I could tell yer so an' see the look on that sour, wrinkled face of yours, but I'd better not push me luck.'

Climbing into Cedric's delivery cart, Cissie snuggled

up close to the grinning man. Just let her get her foot inside his house, and she'd be set for life. Lock on the door, huh! Her door would be firmly open from now on. Cedric Smith was a kind, decent man and would never take advantage of any woman, but he was a man, and all men, no matter how high and mighty or clever they may be, each and every one of them kept their brains in their trousers when it came to women. Sighing with contentment, Cissie looked forward to her new life – a life of luxury and idleness.

'Please, Bessie, try and get some rest. Jimmy's worried sick about you, and so am I.' Amy tried once more to cover Bessie up, but the recalcitrant woman wasn't to be appeased.

'How can I rest, when I don't know what's going on in me own 'ouse? I never thought I'd see the day when I was kicked outta me own kitchen. Well! If Jimmy prefers to keep that little madam on, then I'm off.'

'Now you're being silly,' Amy shot back. 'Jimmy thinks the world of you, and you know it. He'd be lost without you, and you also know very well he'd never choose some stranger over you, so why are you being so hard on him?'

Bessie turned her face sideways into the pillow, and when she spoke, her voice was so muffled Amy had to strain to hear the old woman's words.

'It's 'cos I'm scared, that's why. I never thought the time would come when I couldn't cope, but since the boy arrived I've begun to realise I'm getting old,

197

and it scares me, Amy, love. It scares me half to death.'

Amy's eyes, misted over at the fear and sadness in Bessie's muffled voice. Lowering herself onto the side of the bed, Amy took hold of the gnarled hand lying outside the bedclothes and whispered tenderly, 'Bessie, anyone would be worn out with what you've had to put up with these last two weeks. I know I would. You're being too hard on yourself, you're not super-human, no one is. All you need is a bit of help to get you over this bad period and you'll be as right as ninepence in no time.'

Bessie turned her reddened eyes on the pretty girl. If only someone like Amy could come and help out in the house. Oh! What a blessing that would be. Just being in the lovely girl's company always lifted Bessie's spirits. If Amy was here, Bessie would be able to rest and recover her strength, her mind easy in the knowledge that the house and Jimmy and the boy were in good hands.

A sudden surge of strength flowed through Bessie's body. Lifting herself up onto her elbow, she looked beseechingly at the young girl and whispered hopefully, 'You wouldn't consider coming to work here, would yer, love? You'd be well paid, an' I'd be able to rest easy knowin' yer was lookin' after things. 'Cos even when I feel better, I've gotta admit it, I could use some help round the house. It's been gettin' harder and harder these past few years, but I just didn't want ter admit it, even ter meself. But after these past weeks, I can't ignore it any more. I'm getting on, love, an' I just can't manage by meself any more. Jimmy's been on at me fer years ter let him hire a maid, but I wouldn't have any of it. Pride yer see, Amy, love. I wouldn't admit I needed any help, but I can say it to you. And I can't bear the thought of any more Cissies in me 'ome, but that's what I'll have to do, if you don't want the job. I don't expect yer ter make yer mind up straight away, but will yer think about it, love . . . Please? It'd mean so much ter me.'

In the face of such an anguished appeal, what else could Amy do but agree; but as kind-hearted as she was, there was one stipulation she had to make clear. 'I'll help all I can, Bessie. We stopped off at my place of work on the way here while Jimmy had a word with my employer. I don't know what Jimmy said to him, but it seems I've got the rest of the week off, and with full pay. So I'll be able to come in every day, providing Becky's all right, of course. She's got a very bad cold, and it must be bad, because she's been in bed for the past couple of days, and Becky never lies about in bed.' An impish grin curving her lips, she added, 'I would, given half the chance, I love my bed. Anyway, Jimmy's sent Charlie to fetch Dr Barker to see Becky, just to be on the safe side. I'm sure the doctor will be able to give her something to make her feel better; though I don't know if Becky will be very pleased when the doctor turns up out of the blue. She'll probably tear me off a strip for letting Jimmy know she's been poorly. Anyway, like I said, providing Becky's all right, I'll be able to come in every morning and stay until the evening for the rest of the week. After that, I'll come round every morning before work, and after I finish for a few hours, until you're on your feet again, and the problem with the child is settled.'

At the look of disappointment etched on Bessie's face, Amy said softly, 'I'm sorry I can't take you up on the offer of working here permanently, Bessie. But you see, I love my job. Oh, I know it's not very glamorous, and the pay's not too good, but I enjoy working with lots of people, and I've made some very good friends there. The work may be hard, and when we're very busy I sometimes don't get the chance to sit down all day, but I have a laugh, and I'm always so busy, the time just seems to fly by.' As the older woman began to display further signs of distress, Amy squeezed the small hand tightly. 'Like I said, I'm going to help all I can during the week, and I'll spend most of the weekends here.' A wistful look clouded her eyes. 'If only Becky didn't have the responsibility of looking after Auntie Maude, I know she'd be only too happy to help out. Even the way things ended with her and Jimmy, Becky wouldn't see anyone in trouble if she could possibly help. But as things stand, I'm afraid that's out of the question.'

Bessie's eyes began to droop, then her head fell sideways onto the pillow, the hand that had been gripping Amy's suddenly limp.

Gently placing the hand under the bedclothes, Amy crept from the room, wondering if Bessie had heard her remarks concerning Becky. Perhaps it would be better if she hadn't. For despite Amy's assurance that Becky would be willing to help out in the house if she could, Amy seriously doubted if

200

her sister would ever set foot inside Jimmy Jackson's home again, at least not while there was a chance she might bump into the man himself.

Letting herself out of the room, Amy stood on the landing wondering what to do next. The house was deathly quiet, which was a welcome relief after the initial chaos she had walked in on.

She was about to go downstairs in search of Jimmy when the sound of a child's frightened cry shattered the quietness. Following the direction of the distressed sound, Amy stopped outside a door tucked away around the side of the large landing. Stopping only to take a deep breath, Amy turned the handle and entered the room.

CHAPTER SIXTEEN

The child heard the door open and instinctively scrambled up in the small, single bed until his back was pressed hard against the wooden bedpost, preventing any further movement he might have made to escape whoever was about to enter his unfamiliar room.

His eyes stretched as wide as they could go, he waited fearfully, then his small body relaxed slightly as a pretty, blonde girl stuck her head around the door.

'Hello, there. My name's Amy, may I come in?'

His initial fear subsiding, but still keeping alert, he nodded silently.

Careful not to alarm the child, Amy cautiously entered the room, her movements slow, her face smiling and friendly.

'So, you're the little James I've been hearing so much about. It's nice to meet you, I hope we can become friends. But that's up to you, of course.'

The boy's eyes flickered over Amy's head to see if the strange man and frightening old woman were behind the pretty girl. Seeing the landing was clear, his small frame relaxed further, though his eyes remained wary.

'Have you come to take me home to my mother?'

The hope in the boy's tremulous voice brought a lump to Amy's throat, but on no account could she allow her emotions to show. Advancing towards the bed slowly, she shook her head ruefully. 'I'm afraid not, love . . . At least, not right now,' she added quickly, as the boy's face began to crumble in disappointment. 'Is it all right if I sit on your bed, James?'

The child's head drooped onto his chest, but he made no sign of rejecting Amy's proposal.

Careful not to make any sudden movement that could startle the child, Amy gently eased her slender frame onto the edge of the bed. Painstakingly choosing her words, Amy said quietly, 'I know you must be missing your mummy, and I know exactly how you feel. You see I lost my mum when I was about your age, and even now I'm grown up, I still miss her dreadfully. But you're a lot luckier than I am. You see, James, I know you're not happy here, but you'll be seeing your mummy very soon when she comes to take you back home, but I'll never see my mum again because she's in Heaven now with the angels. And no matter how much I used to pray and cry and hope that she wasn't really dead, I knew deep down that I would never see her again. But your mummy is very much alive and well, and probably can't wait to come and fetch you. Now how do you think she'll feel if she comes back and finds you've starved yourself to death, eh? She'll be very sad if she loses her little boy, and you wouldn't want to cause her any pain, would you?'

The boy shrugged his tiny shoulders despondently. 'No, I don't want to make my mummy sad; but why did she leave me here? I didn't do anything wrong a'tall. I'm a good boy, so I am.'

As the boy spoke, Amy's forehead creased in an expression of perplexity. There was an inflection in the boy's voice that, if she didn't know better, she would swear was an Irish accent. Distracted for the moment, Amy quickly put her curiosity on hold for the time being.

'Oh, James . . . You don't mind if I call you James, do you?'

Again the small shoulders lifted listlessly. 'No, I don't mind.'

'I'm glad, and you can call me Amy if you want to. Now then, you mustn't think your mummy left you here because she didn't love you, or because you were naughty. The reason she left you here for a little while was because . . .' Amy stopped mid-sentence. What on earth could she give by way of explanation as to why that cruel-hearted woman had dumped her only child without any warning, or reassurance to the bewildered, terrified boy? Fortunately, Amy had always been possessed of a good imagination, and she now put this talent to good use. 'The reason your mummy left you here was so that you'd be well looked after while she went around all the shops to look at all the toys and games, so she could write down a list of Christmas presents to send to Father Christmas for you, and she couldn't take you with her, could she? Otherwise you'd have known what you were getting for Chris— Oh!' Amy clapped her hand over her mouth in mock horror. 'Oh, Lord! I've spoilt the surprise now. I was supposed to keep it a secret. Your mum's going to be so cross with me when she finds out. Me and my big mouth. I'm going to get into such a lot of trouble.'

Almost afraid to look at the child to see his reaction, Amy bent her head in a gesture of trepidation. Then she felt a tiny, warm hand wrap itself around her fingers. Lifting her head, she looked into a bright pair of huge green eyes, and although a tremor of nervousness was still evident on the small lips, the boy looked as though a great burden had been lifted from his young mind. 'Don't you be worrying now, Amy, d'ye hear me? I won't tell, honest I won't.'

Mindful to maintain her worried demeanour, Amy whispered, 'Are you sure you won't let it slip, James? After all, you are just a little boy, and . . .'

The boy pulled himself onto his knees, his head held high. Placing his right hand over his heart, he said solemnly, 'I swear on the soul of St Patrick, I'll not say a word.'

Again Amy bent her head, but this time it was to hide the laughter bubbling to the surface at the solemnity in the child's tone. Also his words were a good excuse to satisfy Amy's burning curiosity.

Clasping the hand gratefully, she said, 'Thanks,

205

James. I believe you.' Bending her head closer to the dark-haired child, she murmured. 'I'll tell you another secret, shall I? Not only can't I keep a secret, I'm also very nosy, and I can't help noticing your accent.'

'My what?' The little face screwed up in confusion.

'I mean, the way you speak. If I didn't know better, I'd swear you were Irish, but you can't be, can you?'

'A shy smile crept over the elfin face. 'Not really. But I was born in Ireland, so I was. Me and my mum lived with Uncle Sean in a great big house – much bigger than this one.' His small arms stretched wide as if to demonstrate his words. 'It had huge gardens, and a big fountain. It was lovely. I was very sad when Uncle Sean died and we had to leave.' The brightness in the boy's manner dimmed at the recent memories. 'I loved Uncle Sean, he was a grand man. I wanted to call him Daddy, but my mum wouldn't let me. And when I started school, the other children made fun of me at first because I had no dad. So I told Uncle Sean, and he came to pick me up one day and told me that when I saw him, I was to call him Dad, so the children wouldn't tease me any more; and they didn't after that day. Uncle Sean said we had to keep it secret from Mummy in case she got cross, but whenever we were on our own, I always called him Dad, so I did, and he called me son.' A single tear rolled down his face. 'I wish Uncle Sean had been my dad, then we could have stayed in our house in Ireland, but my aunties and uncles said we

206

had to leave, 'cos my mummy wasn't Uncle Sean's wife . . . Amy . . . !' His voice dropped to a whisper. 'Mummy said that man who lives here is my real dad . . . Is he, Amy? Is that man called Jimmy my daddy?'

Stumped at the unexpected turn the conversation had taken, Amy sat silent, at a loss as to how to answer. Swallowing nervously, she replied, 'I'll be honest, James, I don't know for sure, but this I will say. Jimmy is a wonderful, kind man, and a very brave one. He'd make any child a wonderful father. In fact, it's because he's so brave that's how my sister and me first met him. He saved us from being murdered in the street.' As the words spilt out, Amy justified her account of the incident by telling herself that it wasn't far from the truth. She and Becky could well have been murdered if Jimmy hadn't come along that day. Seeing as she now had the child's full attention, and thinking it wouldn't do Jimmy's cause any harm if she were to elaborate a little, she launched into the story of the attack by the gang of thugs. The more she continued with the story, the more embellished it became. As she talked the child edged nearer, his beautiful green eyes wide with awe.

'Is that really true, Amy? It's not some tale you're telling me, so as I'll like that man.'

By this time Amy had convinced herself that her account of the unpleasant incident was true. 'Every word, cross my heart.' She made the sign of the cross on her breast.

The boy let out a deep sigh of admiration. 'He

must be very strong, to be sure, and brave to be able to fight ten men on his own, and beat them all. And you say they had knives and big sticks, and Jimmy beat them all with his bare hands?'

A small thread of shame stole over Amy, but she quickly thrust it aside. It didn't hurt to exaggerate a bit now and then, especially in this instance. Already the boy had called Jimmy by name, instead of refer-ring to him as 'that man'. Maybe she should add that Bessie too had been involved in the rescue, but thought that, even for a child of James's tender years, that might be pushing the grounds in credibility too far. A dry chuckle escaped her lips. Maybe she had a touch of the Irish in her, for they were renowned for telling a tale. And even if she did say so herself, the yarn she'd just spun would be worthy of any true-blooded Irish woman.

'Is your sister like you?'

The sudden shift in conversation caught Amy off guard. Poor Becky! She hadn't given her sister a moment's thought since she'd entered the house. How could she have been so thoughtless? It was true she'd had a lot to occupy her mind during the past couple of hours, but that was no excuse. And surely Dr Barker should have been back by now. A feeling of consternation rose in her chest, and it was with a great effort she managed to quell her rising panic. She had managed to get on with the boy much better than she had hoped, and she didn't want anything to spoil their new, tenuous friendship.

Keeping her voice calm, she answered, 'I'm afraid my sister's not very well at the moment. She has

a very bad cold. I would have called the doctor
in to see her, but my sister's very stubborn and
wouldn't let me.' Dropping her voice to a con-
spiratorial whisper, she confided to the boy, 'To
tell the truth, we didn't have any money to pay
for the doctor to come, and when Jimmy found
out, he sent Charlie . . . That's his driver, and my
young man,' she added shyly, 'to fetch the doctor
who looked after me and my sister after we were
attacked. He's one of the best doctors in London, so
I'm sure he'll be able to make my sister better. It's
lucky for us we have a friend like Jimmy, because
we would never be able to pay for a doctor as good
as Dr Barker.'

'Is that the old man who came to see me?' The
child asked curiously.

'Yes, that was Dr Barker. He's a lovely man, and
a very good doctor, but I suppose any doctor can
be a bit frightening if you've never seen him before.
Especially when they open that horrible black bag
they always carry with them. All those strange
objects and bottles of pills and medicines would
frighten anyone.' She made a face at James and
was rewarded by a light chuckle of amusement.
Delighted at the progress she had made in such a
short time, Amy decided now was the right moment
to get to the real reason as to why Jimmy had asked
her here.

'Now then, young man. I don't know about you,
but I'm starving. Seeing as the new maid's gone and
poor Bessie is fast asleep, I suppose I'll have to cook
us all something. What would you like?'

Ignoring Amy's question, James asked tentatively, 'Will I have to eat with them?'

Amy's heart sank. Obviously it was going to take a long time before the child felt comfortable with the other occupants of the house. Still! He wouldn't be here for much longer. His mother would be back any day now, if for no other reason than to extort as much money as she could out of Jimmy. She certainly wouldn't be returning out of any concern for her child.

'No, you won't have to eat with Jimmy and Bessie, not today anyway. Jimmy will probably have his lunch downstairs, and poor Bessie's fast asleep in bed; she hasn't had a proper night's sleep in days, poor soul.'

'Is the old woman ill?'

Patting down his bedcovers Amy replied briskly, 'No, not exactly. She's just very tired and very worried about you. She's also quite elderly, and she's just plain worn out. That's why I've come around to help until she gets better.'

A look of consternation came over the boy's features. 'Why would she be worried about me? Sure, and she doesn't even know me.'

'Yes, well, that may be so, but Bessie is a dear, kind soul who wouldn't see anyone in trouble if she could help in any way. I know she can be a bit scary when you first meet her; in fact she and my sister didn't get on very well when they first met – but they're very good friends now.' As yet another lie slipped off her tongue effortlessly, Amy reflected that she must get a firm grip on reality. Yet life could be so boring at times. What harm could it do to be a little economical with the truth now and then? Especially if it harmed no one and made people happier, like young James, who now bore no trace of the frightened child she had first encountered.

'And don't try to change the subject. I asked you what you wanted to eat. What's your favourite food?'

Amy watched in pity as the hungry boy struggled with his conscience. She could read his mind like a book. To his childish way of thinking, to give in now would be tantamount to letting the strange man and old woman think they had won him over. On the other hand, his belly was crying out for proper nourishment.

In a brave attempt to save face, the boy answered casually, 'All right, I'll have something to eat . . . But just because I like you, not because of them.'

Amy kept a straight face as the boy began to reel off his favourite foods, her face falling in dismay as the list continued to grow. 'I like beef and baked potatoes and puddings, and I like pork chops and mashed potatoes, and I like mince and onions with fluffy potatoes, and I like Irish stew, but only if it has dumplings in it, and I like—'

'Whoa, whoa! Hang on a minute. I asked what you liked, not a blooming menu. For a start, roast beef and potatoes will take hours to cook, and I'm hungry now. I don't know if there're any mince or chops in the house, and as for Irish stew, I haven't a clue how to make that.'

Two dimples appeared in the child's cheeks. 'It's

211

easy, Amy. All you do is put some bacon and sausages and onions and carrots and potatoes into a big pot of water and let it cook. Then you put the dumplings in when it's nearly ready; sure an' it's dead easy, so it is.'

Amy looked at the boy in astonishment. 'And how on earth would a young boy like you know how to cook?'

The childish lips curved into a secret smile of triumph. 'I used to sit in the kitchen and watch Bridie cook. It was always lovely and warm in the kitchen, and Bridie used to give me hot chocolate and biscuits when my mummy wasn't looking.'

Amy was beginning to wonder what the child had been allowed to do when his mother was around; not a lot by the sound of it. The more she learnt about Heather Mills, the less Amy liked the woman; and there weren't many people Amy didn't like – though in Heather Mills's case, Amy was quite prepared to make an exception, if only because the woman had abandoned her child in such callous circumstances. There was something else that had been nagging at Amy's mind as she'd listened to him talking about his life in Ireland. If this Sean fellow was so well off, and according to the boy the Irishman had loved him like a son, then why on earth hadn't a woman like Heather Mills married the man? It didn't make sense. She must have known that if anything happened to her lover she would be evicted from the house they had shared for eight years, having no legal claim over the dead man's estate. Unfortunately, as much as she would have liked to know more about the affair, it wasn't the kind of subject one could bring up with a young child. Even if she had, Amy doubted if James would have been able to supply any answers.

Jerking her mind back to the matter in hand, Amy said briskly, 'Look, like I said, I'm hungry now, so how about I go and get some fish and chips? Tomorrow I'll come back and cook one of your favourite dinners, but for today you'll have to have something quick; you do like fish and chips, don't you?'

The little face lit up in delight. 'Oh, yes, please. Mummy says fish and chips are only eaten by common people. Me and Uncle Sean used to sneak out and get some from the town and eat them out of the paper when Mummy wasn't at home. I always had to have a bath afterwards though, in case Mummy smelt it on my clothes and hands.'

Amy had to turn away for fear the boy would see the look of loathing displayed on her face. The poor little mite! And yet despite all she'd heard about the child's upbringing, it was obvious he adored his mother. Amy shook her head in wonderment. Maybe there was a kind side to Heather Mills's character that no one else had seen; but Amy very much doubted it. Adopting a brisk tone she declared,

'Right then, fish and chips it is. I'll just pop downstairs and ask Jimmy if he wants anything, then I'll get straight off to the fried fish shop.'

She had barely touched the door handle when the boy shot out of bed and ran to her side. 'You are coming back, aren't you, Amy? You won't leave me, will you?'

Looking down into the apprehensive eyes, Amy felt her own begin to prickle. 'Of course I'm coming back, silly. Now get into bed and keep warm. I won't be long, I promise.'

She waited until the boy was back in bed before she turned to leave, only to be stopped once more by a small plaintive voice. 'Amy!'

'Yes, love?'

The boy made a sound in his throat, while at the same time his chin began to wobble. 'Will you . . . I mean, can I ha . . . have a cudd . . . cuddle before you go?'

In three strides, Amy was across the room holding the small, trembling frame as tight as she dared. Afraid she was about to cry, she hastily relinquished her hold and said as firmly as her emotions would allow, 'I'll be back as soon as I can. Be a good boy while I'm gone.'

Once outside the room, Amy leant against the door, unable to hold back the flow of tears any longer. It was some minutes before she was able to pull herself together, and, conscious of the time slipping away and knowing the child would be counting every minute until her return, she hurried down the stairs in search of Jimmy.

In the kitchen, Jimmy was in danger of wearing a hole in the linoleum-covered floor as he paced the room in angry frustration. Every fibre in his body yearned to go straight to his office in Bow to confront that thieving, miserable little bastard he had employed only in order that the girls wouldn't go short of money. Jimmy could have set Phil on as a runner, it was all he was fit for, but no, he had to go and offer him the post of collecting the bets brought in by his army of street employees. Not that Jimmy was that much of a sentimentalist. He had always done his own accounts, and since employing Phil Bradford he had been extra diligent in making sure every penny was accounted for. So far, he had found no discrepancies in his books. But that didn't mean the deceitful bleeder hadn't found another way to line his pockets at Jimmy's expense. By God! When he got his hands on him . . . !

He stopped his pacing as the aroma of the wrapped parcel laid on the kitchen table wafted up his nostrils. Food was the last thing on his mind at the moment, but he knew how disappointed Amy would be if she came down and found he hadn't touched his impromptu lunch. Not bothering to fetch a plate, Jimmy ate the tasty food out of the grease-soaked newspaper, but although he finished the meal down to the last chip, he didn't taste a morsel – his mind was too preoccupied, not least with his concern about Becky's health. Where the bloody hell was Tom? He'd sent Charlie to find him over three hours ago; Jimmy knew that his friend was a very busy man and much in demand, and with this thought, he tried to curb his impatience. But patience had never been one of Jimmy's strong points. With an exclamation of frustration, he threw the empty wrapping in the bin and continued to pace the room, his hands clasped tightly behind his back.

It was another twenty minutes before he heard the carriage approaching the house, and he was at the front door before Charlie had pulled the horses to a stop.

'Well! How is she? Is it serious? What's wrong with her?'

Tom Barker shot the harassed Jimmy a withering look.

'If you'll let me get a foot inside the door and get a word in edgewise, I'll tell you. And a strong drink wouldn't go amiss either, I've had a hell of a morning, and I've still another three house calls to make.'

Knowing his old friend was a man not to be intimidated or rushed, Jimmy gritted his teeth and followed the doctor into the house. Taking him up to the sumptuous lounge, Jimmy poured out two large brandys, then had to wait until the doctor had made himself comfortable in one of the high-backed leather chairs.

Unable to control his impatience any longer, Jimmy exploded, 'For God's sake, man. Get on with it. I've been waiting hours for you to get here.'

Tom raised a derisory eyebrow and calmly took a swallow of his brandy. 'In case it's escaped your notice, Jimmy, I'm not your personal physician, expected to come running at your beck and call, but I'll let it slide this time.' Resting further back in the chair he looked over his glass and said mildly,

'I've seen the young lady in question, and although her condition isn't life threatening, she is however suffering from a severe bout of influenza. Furthermore, if I hadn't been called when I was, it could very easily have turned into pneumonia. Luckily I was called to her – or should I say commanded!' Both his eyebrows rose in mock derision this time. 'I've given her something to reduce the fever and, with proper care, she should be up and about in time for Christmas, but only if she has good nursing. I left the medication with the neighbour, plus instructions as to the importance of the young lady getting plenty of rest, but to be honest, the woman looked terrified out of her wits at being landed with such responsibilities. I doubt very much whether she'll be able to cope; the poor woman doesn't strike me as capable of looking after herself, let alone someone as sick as Rebecca. Then of course there's the aunt to take into consideration. The blasted woman never stopped calling for me the whole time I was in the house. Not to enquire about her niece, or is it cousin? Well, whatever the relationship, after a cursory enquiry as to how Rebecca was, her main concern was to tell me all about her own ailments. I tell you, Jimmy, in my profession we doctors meet some difficult patients, but we always have to try and maintain a kindly disposition – but that woman would try the patience of a saint. I'm afraid my allegiance to the Hippocratic Oath went flying out of the window within two minutes in her company. Another thing I have to say, and it may sound uncharitable, but I think the

217

woman's nowhere near as disabled as she makes out. True, I've never examined her, nor have I any intention of doing so, but after nearly thirty years of attending the sick, any doctor worth his salt can spot a malingerer a mile off.'

He stopped briefly to take another sip of his drink, and Jimmy, as if seeing his friend properly for the first time, noticed how tired the man looked and was instantly ashamed at his earlier outburst. Tom Barker was wealthy enough to retire, and at the age of fifty-five, he would be well in his rights to do so, but the thought had never occurred to him. Tom cared too much about the sick and needy simply to opt out of medical practice and put his own health first. Maybe if his wife had still been alive he might have thought differently, but that dear, sweet lady had died ten years earlier. Now there was nothing else to fill Tom's days except his work, and he wouldn't give that up until his own health eventually failed him. Jimmy prayed fervently that that day was a long way off.

Downing the last of his drink, Tom got to his feet. 'I'm afraid I'll have to get on, Jimmy. Like I said, I've still another three house calls to make. Now, as to young Rebecca – and Charlie here has filled me in on the news regarding Amy coming in to help with the boy – I've taken the liberty of stopping off at the hospital and hiring a nurse to stay with her, because at the risk of repeating myself, that neighbour, as kindly a soul as she appears, just isn't capable of looking after a sick person. In fact, if your purse will run to the expense, I'd suggest you allow me to hire an extra nurse so that Rebecca will have twenty-four-hour care.'

Jimmy shook his head impatiently. 'Of course I can afford it. As you're constantly reminding me, Tom, I'm rolling in it, so to speak. Hire as many nurses as you deem fit and hang the expense.'

Seeing his friend to the front door where Charlie was waiting to drive the doctor to his next port of call, Jimmy asked anxiously, 'She will be all right, won't she, Tom?'

Tom Barker looked at his friend affectionately. In all the years he had known Jimmy Jackson, he had never known the man to show such concern over a woman. Donning his black, high hat, Tom grinned. 'I'm not in the habit of lying, Jimmy, especially where my patients' health is concerned. It could have been very serious, but you got me there in time to halt any further complications, and with constant nursing, and Rebecca's young, strong constitution, she'll be up and about in time for Christmas.' He stopped, a puzzled look clouding his tired eyes. 'I've already said that, haven't I? Lord! I'm either working too hard or going senile. Given the choice, I think I'd prefer the latter. At least then I wouldn't be aware of how irritating I'm becoming. Anyway, I'll be off now, but I'll have those nurses at the house within the hour, and I'll call in myself tomorrow morning just to check that everything's going all right. See you, Jimmy . . . Oh, by the way, how's the boy coming along?' Before Jimmy could answer, a childish laugh floated down the stairs, causing both men to exchange startled glances.

'It seems my question was superfluous. It's a pity Amy didn't decide to take up medicine. She would have made a wonderful nurse, especially with children.' With a last wave of his hand, Tom climbed into the carriage ready to attend his next patient.

In the child's room, Amy was beginning to fret. It had been over three hours now since Charlie had gone for Dr Barker. Then she tried to calm her nerves by reminding herself that the doctor probably had other patients to see first, and as Becky only had a bad cold, then obviously he would leave his visit to her sister until his rounds had ended.

'Look, Amy, I've finished all my dinner, aren't I a good boy?'

Absently Amy patted the small head. 'Yes, you are a good boy, James.'

The smile of happiness dropped from the child's excited face. 'Don't you like me any more, Amy?' he asked wistfully, his childish mind recognising that he no longer had the undivided attention of the young girl he had so quickly taken to.

Immediately Amy put her worries to the back of her mind and gave the boy a ferocious hug. 'Don't be daft. Who couldn't like a lovely little boy like you? To tell the truth, I'm just a bit worried about my sister. You remember I told you she was a bit poorly? Well, I'm waiting for the doctor to come back and tell me how she is, that's all. I'm sorry if I was ignoring you. Now then, let me take these greasy papers down to the kitchen, else the whole room will stink of fish and chips. I've also got to

220

look in on Bessie and see how she is. She was still fast asleep when I brought the dinner home, so I let her rest and put hers in the oven to keep warm. I'm sure I'll know when she does wake up, 'cos she'll be out of bed and wandering around the house, afraid something terrible might have happened while she was asleep.' Kissing the boy's forehead, Amy gathered up the cold, greasy newspapers and, with a reassuring wave, and blowing a kiss to the little boy, she slipped out of the room. Stopping to check on Bessie and finding her still asleep, Amy made her way to the kitchen where she found Jimmy donning his overcoat and gloves.

'Where are you going, Jimmy?' she asked in alarm. 'I thought you were going to wait until Dr Barker had returned.'

So absorbed in his thoughts had he been, Jimmy hadn't heard Amy enter the room. Spinning round, he clapped his hand to his forehead, a look of guilt crossing his face. 'Lord, Amy, I'm so sorry. Tom's already been. In fact he's just left. Now, it's all right, don't panic . . .' He moved forwards quickly as Amy's face turned white with fear. 'Becky's going to be just fine. And to be on the safe side, I've asked Tom to hire two nurses to look after her around the clock. But she's going to be fine, I promise you. Tom says she'll be out of bed within the next few days, so you see you've nothing to worry about.'

The colour returning to her face, Amy stared back at Jimmy, her eyes filled with accusation. 'Didn't you think to come up and tell me the minute the doctor arrived? I've been nearly going out of my mind with worry. You can be a right selfish sod at times, Jimmy Jackson.'

Although Jimmy had already witnessed the strong character Amy possessed, nevertheless he was still taken aback at the anger in her tone, especially as she had sworn at him. That in itself shocked him more than her fury.

'Look! I've said I'm sorry, and I am. You're right, I can be a selfish sod at times, and I apologise, but I can't change my ways at my time of life . . . Hang on, Amy, where are you going . . . ?'

Hurrying out into the hall, Jimmy saw Amy donning her coat and hat, her mouth set in grim lines of determination.

'If you think I'm staying here when my sister's so ill she needs two nurses to watch over her day and night, you've got another think coming. Now get out of my way.'

For the second time that day Jimmy felt the full force of Amy's temper as she knocked his restraining arm out of her way.

'Please, Amy. Will you just wait a minute? Don't you think I'm just as worried? I haven't left the house all morning in case I missed Tom. Now I know Becky's going to be all right, there's some urgent business I have to attend to. If you'll just stay an hour longer, I swear I'll get you back home the minute I return. Please, Amy . . . Just another hour, that's all I ask.'

The mulish look remained fixed on Amy's face, and Jimmy's heart sank. If she and Charlie did end up marrying, then that amiable young man had a few shocks coming to him if he ever inadvertently upset his young wife.

Just as he was about to admit defeat, a loud wail resounded through the house. 'Amy! Amy! Come quick, I don't feel well.'

At the sound of the child's voice, both Amy and Jimmy jumped, startled at the distressed sound. In the heat of the moment they had both forgotten about young James. Her expression losing none of its grim determination, Amy took off her coat and hat.

'An hour, Jimmy, no more, or I swear you won't be seeing me back here tomorrow, or any other day for that matter.'

Grateful for the diversion, Jimmy lost no time in leaving the house, his eyes on the look-out for a passing hansom cab. He was in luck. Within five minutes he was on his way to Bow.

'Oh, James. Oh, you poor little love. Here, get out of bed while I clean you up and get some fresh sheets.'

The child made a pathetic figure, covered in sick and shaking with fear that he would be scolded for making such a mess. 'I'm so . . . sorry, Amy. I . . . I couldn't help it,' he sobbed uncontrollably until Amy had him washed and tucked back into his freshly made bed. Luckily, Amy's frequent visits to the house to see Bessie had enabled her to locate the linen cupboard without having to disturb the old woman from her much-needed sleep.

Holding him close she murmured soothingly, 'It's

not your fault, love, it's mine. I should never have
let you eat so much, especially such greasy food
like fish and chips. Your poor tummy just isn't
strong enough to take a lot of food in one go right
now. We'll have to start building you up slowly, so
your stomach can get used to proper food again.'
Smoothing back the dark hair from the boy's sweating forehead, Amy said softly, 'You try and get some
sleep, love. You'll feel better when you wake up.'

The boy nodded and closed his eyes. 'Will you be
here when I wake up, Amy?'

Amy stopped, her teeth biting down hard on her
bottom lip. She was desperate to see Becky, yet how
could she refuse the child's request? He would be
devastated if he woke up and found her gone. Sighing
she replied tenderly, 'I'll be here, James. Now go to
sleep, there's a good boy.'

His trust in the young girl unconditional, the child
immediately fell into an exhausted sleep.

It was only when Amy was drinking a mug of tea
in the kitchen that she wondered where Jimmy had
been so keen to get to in such a hurry, then her jaw
dropped as realisation set in. He'd gone to confront
Phil. As the knowledge of what Jimmy was capable
of doing to her brother sank in, Amy was surprised
to find she couldn't summon up any sympathy for
him. After what Phil had done to her and Becky, he
deserved everything that was coming to him. And
as she realised the harshness of the thoughts that
were so alien to her, Amy realised that she was no
longer a child. No more would she be so gullible,

or trusting. Yet even as this realisation echoed around her mind she whispered sadly, 'But I don't want to feel like this. I want to be the way I was before today. Please, God! Don't let me become hard and unfeeling, it's not the way you've made me, and I don't want to feel this way.' Yet her anger was mainly fuelled by a feeling of betrayal. Ever since her father had died, Amy had always looked upon Phil as a substitute parent. She had trusted him without question and loved him unconditionally, even at those times when they'd all had to suffer because of his gambling addiction. Never in all that time had her love or trust in her big brother wavered – until today.

Dropping her face in her hands, Amy wept. She cried for Becky, she cried for the frightened child upstairs, and finally she cried for Phil. Her brief paroxysm of tears subsiding, Amy sniffed and wiped her eyes, then stared out of the window, her gaze fixed on the street. If Jimmy wasn't back within the hour as he had promised, then she was going home. She didn't like leaving the child, but there was no way she was prepared to wait longer than an hour before she returned to her own home – and her sister.

Easier in her mind now that she had decided on a definite course of action, Amy let her body relax. Hopefully, Jimmy would only give Phil a verbal warning, but she very much doubted it. Whatever the outcome, one thing was certain, Phil would be out of a job by the end of the day, and where would that leave her and Becky?

An idea sprang into her mind. Of course – Uncle Richard! As soon as he learnt of their dilemma, he would help. He might even give Phil his old job back. Despite what Becky thought of Richard, he had always been kind and thoughtful to Amy; furthermore, unlike Phil, her uncle Richard had never betrayed her trust.

Confident that she had solved their immediate problems regarding money worries, Amy stretched out her arms on the table, laid her head on the makeshift pillow and indulged her tired and fretful mind in a much-earned rest.

CHAPTER SEVENTEEN

Phil Bradford sat behind a shabby desk inside an equally shabby room studying a cheap ledger splayed out on the worn surface. Alongside the ledger was a pile of betting slips, beside which rested piles of coppers and silver coins. On his right-hand side was a small pile of banknotes, most of them ten-shilling notes, with a few pound notes adding a splash of colour to their drab brown contemporaries.

Phil had just finished entering the slips pertaining to the coins, and was about to embark on the more lucrative bets, when the door of the room was flung open. Taken by surprise, Phil jumped, then let out a sigh of relief. 'Blooming Hell, Jimm— I mean, Mr Jackson! I thought it was the coppers come to raid the place. You nearly gave me a heart attack.'

Jimmy strolled casually into the gloomy room. 'Oh, I think that's the least of your worries, Phil. I pay my men well to keep a good look-out for the law, besides which, some of my best customers are coppers.'

Still keeping an amiable façade, Jimmy strolled around the room, his actions denoting that of a man with time on his hands and nothing to fill it with. There was nothing about Jimmy's manner to betray the deep rage that was burning through him. He had been angry enough when he'd left the house to come here, but after sitting in a traffic snarl-up for over forty minutes, then having to walk the rest of the way here, conscious of the time slipping away and the promise he had made to Amy, Jimmy's anger was now at boiling point. Warning himself to remain calm, Jimmy remarked affably, 'Aren't you going to ask me what I'm doing here, Phil?'

Phil glanced up in surprise. 'No, Mr Jackson, why should I? It's your business, you can come and go whenever you want, it's nothing to do with me.'

Jimmy walked slowly over to the grimy window that overlooked the blacking factory, his face inscrutable. 'Actually, my visit is something to do with you, Phil. In fact, my being here is very much your business.'

Alarm bells began to sound inside Phil's head, and he felt a tremor of fear begin to tingle at the base of his spine. Clearing his throat, he took out a handkerchief and made a great pretext of blowing his nose. 'Excuse me, Mr Jackson. It's all this dust, especially at this time of year. It plays havoc with my chest.'

His voice deceptively mild, Jimmy looked at his employee with feigned concern. 'I'm sorry to hear that, Phil. I had no idea you suffered so much with your health. Maybe you should consult a doctor.'

Giving a watery smile, Phil said dolefully, 'Oh, I don't think there's much point in doing that. There's not much a doctor can do. Besides, I can't be throwing my money about on doctors when I've got a family to support.'

Jimmy stared down at the smiling face in utter amazement. Was the man really that stupid? Hadn't he realised where this conversation was leading? Again Jimmy stared deep into the other man's eyes, and saw the sudden leap of fear enter them.

At last! Apprehension was finally dawning; or so Jimmy thought until he remarked, 'I've just been to see Becky. Amy told me she wasn't feeling very well, so I thought I'd just pop round to see you and ask if there was anything I could do to help.'

The fear slipped from Phil's eyes, his body slumping in relief. Thank God! For a minute there he'd thought Jimmy had . . . Recovering his wits, Phil was immediately all brotherly concern. 'That was good of you, Mr Jackson. But it's nothing serious. Becky's as strong as a horse, she's just got a bit of a cold, that's all. I did offer to call out a doctor, but Becks—'

Every muscle and fibre in Phil's body jerked as a heavy fist came crashing down on the desk, scattering the coins and paper that littered the surface.

'You two-faced, lying, deceitful bastard,' Jimmy roared, his rugged face almost white with anger. 'For your information, Bradford, your sister is very ill. Tom Barker has just come back from seeing

Becky and, according to him, that little cold was on the verge of turning into pneumonia. Luckily Tom got to see Rebecca before that happened, and I've engaged two nurses to look after her around the clock. But if I hadn't called around this morning, and got help when I did, Becky might have died – and what would you have done then, eh? 'Cos you're fuck all good to anyone on your own.'

Finding himself trapped against the wall, Phil tried to shift his chair, but Jimmy had jammed the desk up tight against Phil's middle, leaving him powerless.

'It's funny you should mention calling in a doctor to see Becky, 'cos that's the first thing I asked Amy. And guess what, Bradford? She told me they hadn't enough money for a doctor's visit. Now then, that can't be true, can it? Not with the pound note I take out of your wages each week and send to Rebecca. Not that you're worth the money I pay you, but that's beside the point. There's something else that's puzzling me – when I mentioned the money to Amy, she didn't seem to know anything about it. No, that's not quite true. She definitely didn't know anything about it. Now that can mean only one of two things. Either Rebecca hasn't told Amy about the money, and I can't see any reason for her not to, or . . .' His voice dropped to a growl. 'Or someone's been waylaying the postman every Saturday morning and stealing that money.' Spreading his hands over the desk, Jimmy leant forward until his face was only inches away from the terrified younger man. 'Now who d'yer think would be low enough to steal

230

from his own sisters, eh? Especially when one of those sisters could have died for want of half a crown to call out the doctor.'

Like a cornered rat, Phil pressed his back hard against the unyielding chair, his eyes wild and staring. 'It's not what you think, Mr Jackson . . . I've been putting the money away for . . . for a sort of surprise for the girls . . . I . . . I was going to use it to buy something special for them for Christmas.'

'*Liar!*' Jimmy's hands shot out and grabbed Phil around the throat. 'What sort of a mug d'yer take me for, you snivelling little bastard! I know where the money's been going – straight on some nag's back. Or is it the dogs you fancy? Probably a bit of both. Anything for a bet, eh, Bradford?'

Phil's mouth opened and closed like a floundering fish suddenly deprived of oxygen, while Jimmy showed no trace of compassion for the man's mortal fear; his contempt for Phil was too great to allow him to feel any emotion for the other man's predicament. The urge to smash his fist between the glistening eyes was overwhelming and, afraid that if he hit the man he might not be able to stop, Jimmy released his stranglehold on Phil's neck with a snort of disgust.

'Get out! Get out of my sight while you can still walk. Go on, piss off, before I beat the shit out of you, you worthless, thieving apology for a man. I feel sick to my stomach just being in the same room as you.'

As quickly as his shaken limbs would allow, Phil

231

scrambled from behind the desk and bolted for the door.

Phil didn't stop running until he was sure there was no chance of Jimmy coming after him. Gasping for breath, the sweat pouring in rivulets down his face despite the biting December air, Phil staggered into the nearest pub and ordered himself a large whisky; but he didn't stop shaking until two thirds of the liquid had entered his trembling system.

Not trusting himself to stand, Phil called to the potman for another drink, his tortured mind churning this way and that for a way out of his predicament.

That first Saturday morning, on his way out to work, when the postman had handed Phil the letter addressed to Becky, Phil had put the envelope in his pocket with every intention of giving it to Becky when he got home. He had already given her the housekeeping money the night before, so he knew she had enough to get the weekend shopping. All that week, Phil had experienced a sense of pride each morning as he had set off to work, and that sense of pride had reflected on Becky, who had begun treating him with more respect than she had done in years. She had been against Phil working for Jimmy at first, mainly due to the fact that gaming was illegal, and those found in the employment of any form of gambling faced imprisonment. Which was a bit of a farce, since it was well known that the late King Edward had been notorious for his love of gambling, much to his mother's despair, and much of the so-called nobility had a passion for betting.

Phil had been quick to assure Becky that he would be working in an office, dealing in legitimate work, and Rebecca, her eyes sceptical and knowing, had let the matter drop. Phil knew his sister was no fool, but he was a grown man, so there was nothing she could do about where or for whom he worked. Phil also had a sneaking suspicion that the only reason Rebecca hadn't made more of a fuss was because she was sweet on Jimmy, though she would rather walk on hot coals than admit it. But the new-found respect she had been showing her brother was due to the fact that he had stood up to Richard for the first time in his life, and by doing so had shown himself to be a man she could be proud of.

But, that morning, seeing the envelope addressed to Becky and knowing who it was from and what it contained, Phil had felt a moment's shame. He hadn't told Becky that Jimmy had given him a job only on the condition that Phil agreed to have his wages docked and half of his pay sent directly to Rebecca. All that day Phil had struggled with his emotions. The thought of having to admit to Becky the true reason behind his new line of work would be, to Phil's mind, the utmost humiliation on his part. And if he told Becky the truth, he would see that look come back into her eyes, that look of mild contempt that had been levied at him for years. He had honestly intended to give the money to his sister, in fact he had formulated a plan in which he would tell Rebecca that he had been given a raise in salary, thus accounting for the extra pound, and hoped that Jimmy wouldn't bring the matter up in Becky's company.

233

Then Jimmy had stopped coming to the house, and the extra pound in his pocket, coupled with the gambling addiction that had plagued him since coming to London, had proved too great a temptation for Phil to ignore. He was wise enough not to place any bets with Jimmy's runners. Instead, Phil had started giving his custom to one of Jimmy's rivals, a man by the name of Big George, and that decision was the worst gamble he'd ever taken in his life. What had started off as a run of good luck had quickly turned sour, and now he was in debt to the tune of sixty pounds.

Finding himself getting deeper and deeper into debt, Phil had considered the possibility of fiddling the books, but that idea had been squashed as soon as it had entered his head. Jimmy always checked the books himself, accounting for every penny, so there was no way Phil could hope to steal from his new employer. Yet even up until an hour ago, Phil had imagined he could find a way out of the mess he'd landed himself in. Just one good bet, that's all he had needed, just one sure-fire certainty and his worries would have been over. He'd been in tight spots before, but then he'd always had a job before, and the money to bet with. Now he had no job, no money, and owed sixty pounds to Big George; and nobody welshed on a bet with Big George and lived to boast about it.

His nerves calmed by the whisky, Phil stared moodily into his rapidly emptying glass, his fear turning into bitterness. It was all right for some people. There was Becky – Miss Goody Two Shoes

Becky. She gets a bit of a cold and suddenly she's being nursed around the clock, and being treated by one of the best doctors in London – and that sort of treatment didn't come cheap. Phil uttered a mirthless laugh. He should know. It was because of that old skinflint Richard not wanting to pay out for nursing for Maude that had landed them all in London in the first place.

Briefly Phil considered going to his cousin for help, then shrugged defeatedly. There was nothing Richard would like better than to have Phil crawling back to him for help; but what other choice did Phil have? Jobs weren't that easy to come by if you had no particular trade or profession, and the bulk of the labouring work was had by those bloody Irish coming over to London in droves.

Besides – Phil drew himself upright – he might not have any fancy qualifications, but he was no bloody skivvy either. He wasn't going to sweat his guts out for a few poxy quid a week, like that gormless lump of lard Billy Gates. Phil's fingers tightened around the glass. There must be a way out of this mess. There must be.

If only Jimmy and Becky's relationship had developed further, then there might have been a chance of Phil asking his sister to put in a good word for him. But any chance of a romance flourishing had been shattered by the arrival of Jimmy's bastard.

Sighing heavily, Phil got to his feet. First off, he'd better get home, at least there he'd be safe from Jimmy Jackson and Big George. But he couldn't lie low forever. Praying for a miracle, Phil reluctantly downed the last dregs of his drink and headed for home.

Yet not once in his self-pitying frame of mind did Phil give a thought to Rebecca's state of health.

'Thanks, Wilf. Now you know what you've got to do, don't you? Just take the betting slips and money from the boys, and put it all into a bag, then bring it round to my place about sevenish, OK?'

'Yeah, yer can trust me, Guv'nor. I won't let yer down.' *I wouldn't bleeding well dare.* The middle-aged man looked at the retreating back of his employer. He'd worked for Jimmy Jackson for nearly six years now, and as governors went, Jimmy was one of the good ones. You played fair by him, and he'd play fair by you. The man seated himself behind the recently vacated desk and rubbed his hands happily. He would be here for only a few hours at most, but at least it was better than being out on the streets freezing his balls off while keeping an eye out for the law. Tomorrow he'd be back out on the streets as a runner, but for a short while he had been put in an important position and he was determined to savour every minute of it.

Hearing footsteps on the stairs, the man called Wilf pulled his shabby jacket together, assumed an expression of importance, and waited for the approaching runner to bring in the takings.

A loud wail brought Bessie out of her deep slumber. For a moment she thought she was dreaming, then, with an alertness of mind that would put many a younger woman to shame, she leapt out of bed and headed down the landing.

The boy was huddled up in the middle of the bed holding his stomach, and as Bessie entered, her nostrils picked up the strong smell of vomit pervading the small room.

At first the boy had imagined it was Amy, his little face dropping in fear at the sight of the elderly woman standing in the doorway. Immediately his howls increased. 'Amy! I want Amy. I don't want you, go away. Amy! Amy!'

Fully awake now, Bessie's eyes screwed up against the deafening wails. 'Yeah, an' yer ain't the only one, either, mate,' she snapped irritably. For the past two weeks she'd coaxed, pleaded, bribed and cajoled this child to get him to at least be civil to her, but it seemed all her efforts had been in vain. Not the best tempered person, Bessie, her nerves stretched almost to breaking point, was about to let out a yell that would have frightened the devil himself, when she looked more closely at the child, saw the genuine fear etched on his tear-stained face and relented. It wasn't the poor sod's fault he had a bitch for a mother, but by God, she couldn't take much more of this malarkey. For days now, her hands had been itching to give the boy a good clout round the ears, but somehow she hadn't been able to do it.

Leaving the door wide open, she called over the banister, 'Amy! Amy! Where are yer, girl?'

The house remained silent. Bessie's forehead wrinkled in confusion. Amy wouldn't just go off for no reason. She wasn't the type of person to

leave someone in the lurch without any explanation. It just wasn't in the girl's nature. Worried
now, Bessie went back to her room, and, turning
up the gas lamp, she saw the hastily scrawled note
propped up against the base of the lamp.

Dear Bessie,
Sorry I've had to go out, but my sister is
ill. Jimmy said he'd be back ages ago, and
I can't wait any longer to see how Becky is.
I'll be back as soon as I can. If James wakes
up before I get back, tell him I won't be long,
  Love, Amy.

Groaning, Bessie slumped down on her bed. Peering at the bedside clock, she saw it was nearly
six o'clock. The trouble was she had no idea how
long ago the note had been written. Amy might
be back any minute, or she might have just left.
If that was the case, then she, Bessie, would have
to contend with the child herself. As another cry
floated down the landing, Bessie's chin jutted out
firmly. She'd never let anyone get the better of
her in all her life, and she wasn't about to let
that alter, at least not by a snotty eight-year-old
child. Pulling on her dressing gown, she marched
back to the small room and, without any preamble,
said briskly, 'Well now, lad. It seems Amy's had ter
go out fer a while, and Gawd knows where Jimmy's
gone off to, so it's just the two of us. And believe
me, mate, I ain't that thrilled at the idea neither.'
  The child had stopped crying, whether out of

sullenness or because he knew it would do him no good Bessie wasn't sure, nor did she care. At least he'd stopped that infernal racket. Bustling into the room, she turned up the lamp and looked closer at the boy, trying, as she had been since the day he'd arrived, to see if she could spot any resemblance to her Jimmy. But apart from the dark hair, she could see no characteristics that would prove he was indeed Jimmy's son. What he was though was a child in distress, and he had to be cleaned up and sorted out for the evening until Amy returned.

Stating the obvious she remarked, 'You've been sick then?' Dumbly the child nodded, his face bent over his bunched-up knees. 'Yeah, well, that was a stupid question, wasn't it? Hang on, an' I'll get some clean sheets.' Within minutes she was back. Without a word she scooped the child off the bed and deposited him none too gently on the floor.

'You stay put while I make the bed, then I'll run yer a warm bath, it'll help ease yer tummy. What's made yer sick, then? It can't be anything yer've eaten, 'cos yer ain't eaten anything, an'—'

'I had some fish and chips with Amy . . . the pretty girl. She bought them for me, but I was sick afterwards . . . And I was scared I'd get told off, but Amy was kind, and said it wasn't my fault, and . . . and that she shouldn't have made me eat greasy food after I hadn't eaten in such a long time.'

Bessie continued making the bed, her face, hidden from the child, a mask of astonishment. This was the first time she'd ever heard him talk properly. She wasn't aware she was holding her breath until the

239

child resumed talking, then she let out a large puff of air; but still she kept quiet, fearful of setting the boy off again if she spoke. The room remained silent except for Bessie's movements.

It was as she was putting the thick eiderdown back on the bed that the boy muttered, 'Are you going to tell me off, lady? Sure, and I didn't do it on purpose, I swear I didn't.'

Turning to face him, Bessie replied briskly, 'Well, of course yer didn't get sick on purpose. Nobody gets sick on purpose, it's bloody 'orrible, being sick.' The boy's nightshirt was covered in vomit and he was shivering with a mixture of apprehension and cold. Rolling up her sleeves, she advanced on the pathetic-looking bundle. As always when she came near him, the child flinched. But this time Bessie wasn't standing for any nonsense. Scooping him up in her arms, she carried him to the bathroom. While the hot water was running, Bessie swiftly divested the boy of his soiled garment and wrapped him in a large towel.

'Right then, lad. We'll 'ave ter wait a few minutes fer the bath to fill, but it won't take much water fer a little 'un like you.' Wrapped up in the enormous bath towel, the child looked lost and vulnerable, and despite her bad mood, Bessie's kind heart went out to him. Kneeling in front of him she chuckled, 'Gawd! Yer remind me of the time when that Jimmy of mine stuffed his greedy little face so much, he was throwing up all night, silly little sod. Now that was his own fault.' She leant back on her heels, a smile touching her lips as her mind went back down the

240

years to when Jimmy was the same age as the young boy eyeing her so warily. 'He must've been about yer age at the time. I remember it like it was yesterday. Thought he was gonna die, he did. Like I said, he was about seven or eight, an' I 'ad ter go and help out a neighbour who'd taken ill. Anyway, while I was out, Jimmy decided ter go down the market ter see if there was any odd jobs wanting doing. Yeah! I remember it all now. It was just about this time of year an' all, maybe a bit nearer Christmas. Anyhow, the markets was extra busy an' Jimmy was able ter get a few jobs running errands and 'elping out on the stalls. Worked nearly all day he did, poor little sod, but he earned a few bob. And what does he do? Instead of coming straight 'ome with the money, he decides ter treat me ter some pie an' mash, with a few jellied eels thrown into the bargain. Well, that was all well and good, I mean, some little boys would've spent all the money on themselves. But not my Jimmy. Always 'ad a kind 'art, did my Jimmy; still has, though he don't show it very often. Well, the upshot of it was that when he finally gets home I've gone out looking fer 'im, worried outta me mind I was that something had happened ter 'im. And all the time 'e was sitting at 'ome stuffing his face with pies and mash and jellied eels. Then, when I didn't come back, he only went an' ate most of mine an' all. So I arrives back 'ome, nearly in tears 'cos I thought I'd lost him fer good, an' there he was, large as life, a big grin on his dirty little face and 'e said ter me, "I got yer a treat fer yer tea, Bessie, look!" Then he pointed

241

ter what was left of me supper. He was so proud of 'imself that I didn't 'ave the 'art ter scold him. Ter tell the truth, lad, I was that pleased ter see his cheeky, grubby face, I could've kissed him. But I ain't one fer all that kissing and cuddling lark . . . Oops! Here's me gabbing away, an' nearly forgetting about the bath. Hang on while I pour some cold into it. Yer don't wanna be scalded on top of being sick, now do yer?'

The boy gave a tremulous smile. 'No, that wouldn't be very good, a'tall.'

Testing the water with her elbow, Bessie whipped the towel from the skinny body and lowered him into the warm water. Lathering up a bar of Pears soap, Bessie began washing the silent boy. ''Ave a splash about, if yer want, lad. I know my Jimmy used ter love a splash around, when I could get the little devil into a bath, that was. Mind yer, back then, we didn't 'ave a posh bath like this one. I kept an old tin bath out in the back yard, and 'ad ter fill it up by boiling the water on an old stove. Took me hours sometimes, it did, 'cos I didn't 'ave many pans to boil the water in. But yer should 'ave seen the state of the water once Jimmy 'ad got out. Black it used ter be. Looked like he'd been down the coal mines for a week.' A softness stole over Bessie's wrinkled face as she remembered back to those days. They had been hard and, at times, even desperate. But she and Jimmy had pulled together, and stayed together.

Realising she was becoming maudlin, Bessie jerked her head back, saying crisply, 'Right then, you're all washed. D'yer wanna get out and back ter bed?'

The elfin face peeped up at her. 'What happened to the man called Jimmy . . . I mean, when he was sick, like me?'

Bessie threw back her head. 'Oh, that. Gawd! I'd forgotten about that tale. Well! Like I said, he'd stuffed so much grub down his throat that an hour later he was chucking up and screaming. Gawd! What a night that was. Coming out both ends it was. I 'ad me hands full that night, I can tell yer. In more ways than one!'

At the look of bewilderment mirrored on the child's face, Bessie grinned. 'Take no notice of me, lad. I'd explain it ter yer, but I don't think yer'd wanna know . . . Upsadaisy.' Scooping him out of the bath, Bessie wrapped the boy in a clean towel and carried him back to his room. Taking a flannel nightshirt – one of six that Jimmy had sent her to buy – out of the top drawer of the tallboy, Bessie soon had the child dressed for bed and tucked up warmly under the covers.

Picking up the soiled bedding, Bessie stood up and, catching a glimpse of herself in the mirror that hung over the tallboy, let out a startled shriek. 'Bleeding hell, mate. No wonder you're so scared of me, I nearly gave meself an 'art attack seeing meself in that mirror. I look like a bleedin' witch.'

A sound came from the bed that sounded like a stifled sob, and Bessie shook her head in defeat. And she had thought they'd been getting on so well too. Saddened, she turned to leave the room when the noise became louder. Bessie's face dropped in astonishment as she realised the child was actually laughing. Her spirits rising, she placed one hand on a scrawny hip and demanded jocularly, 'An' what's tickling you, me laddo?'

Chuckling louder, the boy peered over the covers and smiled, the first smile Bessie had seen on the elfin face. Heartened by the boy's merriment she added, 'Are yer laughing at me, yer little scally-wag?'

A pair of green eyes sparkled up at her. 'You're funny, lady. You make me laugh. And . . . and I'm not scared of you any more. I'm sorry I was rude to you before.'

Like Amy, Bessie noted the trace of an Irish brogue, and, like Amy, Bessie wondered where the boy could have picked it up. Certainly not from around these parts. Then her heart almost turned a somersault, and with two quick strides she was at the boy's side. 'Do that again, lad?'

Still smiling, the boy asked, 'Do what, lady . . . I mean, Bessie,' he added shyly. And there it was. That cheeky smile. The dimples that pitted his cheeks, but most of all the way he raised his eyebrows in childish devilment.

Her heart hammering against her ribcage, Bessie sat down on the side of the bed. 'That cheeky look you just gave me, yer little rascal.'

'What, like this, d'ye mean?' Again the grin was back in place, along with the rising of the sparse eyebrows. And Bessie was thrown back into the past with a force that almost knocked the wind out

244

of her. For there, grinning up at her, was her Jimmy at the same age. The same impish grin and gestures of the eyebrows and shoulders were Jimmy's characteristics to a tee. Except for the green eyes, she was looking at a replica of her Jimmy. With a stifled cry, she grabbed the startled boy into her arms, hugging him fiercely.

Not expecting such a show of affection from the old woman, who up until a very short time ago had always been careful to keep her distance, James's initial reaction was to pull away. But until Amy had appeared on the scene, the child had been starved of any sign of true affection since Sean Finnegan's untimely death. A feeling of warmth and security crept through his small frame, then he was hugging Bessie back, his small arms wrapped tightly around her neck.

And that was how Jimmy found them when he arrived home.

Standing in the doorway, his face a picture of bemusement, Jimmy tried to take in the scene before him. Then Bessie, sensing his presence, turned, and with a catch in her voice said joyously, 'Come and say hello to yer son, lad.'

CHAPTER EIGHTEEN

'I'll have to go soon, Becky. Jimmy asked me to take James to the shops for a new pair of shoes. Nobody noticed he had a whacking big hole in one of his shoes until yesterday, when I took him over the park for some fresh air. Poor little mite! That woman left him without so much as a clean set of underwear. Bessie had to go and buy him some new clothes and nightshirts, and judge what size to get, 'cos she had to go out on her own to get them. He wouldn't let her anywhere near him at first, but he's much better with her now. The other night, there was only Bessie in the house to look after him, and they had to get on with it. You could say it was a sort of Baptism of Fire for them both, but James is still a bit wary of Jimmy. Bessie's told him that Jimmy is his dad, but James clams up whenever the subject is mentioned. It must have been hell for the poor thing those first two weeks. But in a way, it was a blessing in disguise for us, because if James had taken to either Bessie or Jimmy, then Jimmy wouldn't have come round to ask me for help, and you might have died.'

Becky shifted her body further up the bed, until she was sitting bolt upright, her mind only half digesting what Amy was saying. Lord, but she felt tired and washed out, like she'd been dragged through the mangle on wash day. As if her physical ailment wasn't bad enough, she had also had to come to terms with what Phil had done, and that knowledge had hurt her much more than any illness could ever have done. She had always known Phil to be a weak man, both in character and in his gambling addiction, but to steal from her and Amy . . . ! When she thought of the Friday nights Phil would arrive home with their fish and chip supper, then grandly hand over the housekeeping money with the air of the man of the house supporting his family, and all the time . . . She felt her eyelids begin to droop and shook her head vigorously to stay awake.

'Becky! Are you feeling bad? Shall I call for the nurse?'

Instantly Becky was wide awake. 'God! No. The bloody woman's driving me to distraction. It's always, "And how are we today?" Or, "Have we been to the toilet yet? Shall we have some more medicine?" Honestly, Amy, I'll go mad if she stays here much longer. Thank God I've only got one nurse now. The other one was even worse. Her favourite was to wake me up so I could take a sleeping pill. Still, Dr Barker's coming at ten. I'm going to ask him if I can go downstairs . . . Well! What I mean is,

247

I am going downstairs, but it would be better if he suggested it. He's a lovely man, and I don't want to fall out with him, but I can't stay cooped up here in bed for another day.' She looked up at Amy wistfully. 'I wish I could come with you, love. It feels like I've been lying here for months instead of a few days, and at this time of the year as well. It's Christmas Eve tomorrow and there's no preparations been made. Then there's the worry of this blooming party Richard's determined to hold here. He was here this morning at eight, pretending to call in to see if I was any better; as if he cares about my well-being. The only reason he's concerned is because he wants me up and about to organise the party. Well, he's had that! If he's so keen on having a knees-up, then he'll have to organise it himself. Because between you and me, Amy, I wouldn't do it even if I was feeling well enough . . .' A bout of sneezing cut her conversation in mid-flow.

The spasm over, Becky lay back on the pillows. 'Goodness! If a bout of sneezing can almost knock me out, then I think it's safe to say there won't be any Christmas festivities held here tomorrow night.' Wiping her streaming eyes with another clean handkerchief, Becky added, 'He's up to something, Amy. He must be. In all the years we've lived here, he's never once suggested we celebrate Christmas together, let alone hold a party. When I told him earlier that if he wanted a party, then he'd have to hold it at his place, he got all agitated, insisting we had it here. No! He's up to something, you mark my words. Anyway, you'd better get going. I'm sorry I couldn't meet James, but I don't want to risk him catching my cold.'

At the door, Amy, keeping her head averted, said quietly, 'Jimmy asked after you. He said he hopes you're feeling better soon, and . . . and, maybe he can come and visit, when you're up and around again . . .'

Becky shook her head sorrowfully. 'There's no point, love. I admit I did have hopes that . . .' She lifted her shoulders dispiritedly, then managed a faint grin. 'You know, like one of the stories you like to read so much. But that's never going to happen now, not with that woman coming back and latching onto him . . . I know, I know . . .' she said weakly, as Amy started to interrupt. 'She's not his wife, like she claimed to be, but she is the mother of his child, and nothing is ever going to change that fact. Neither is she ever going to go away, not while she can hold the child as a bargaining stick. And if Jimmy was in love with her once, who's to say those feelings won't come back. No! I've got to face facts. This Heather Mills is a beautiful woman, she can also take the boy away whenever it suits her; and she knows it. What chance do I have against those odds?'

Amy gazed at her sister helplessly. In Becky's shoes she would probably feel the same. Nodding, she mumbled, 'I'll be home about eight. Bye, Becky.'

'Bye, love.'

Before the door closed, Becky heard Maude's shrewish voice rising, and that of the nurse trying to pacify the irate woman. Idly, Becky wondered what had set Maude off this time. When first Dr Barker and then the nurses had come to tend for Becky, Maude had been beside herself with jealousy at the attention her cousin was receiving. She had tried in vain to coax Dr Barker into her room, but the wily old doctor was steering clear of Maude. The nurses, however, seemed to think they had no authority to ignore the cantankerous woman; and Maude had quickly sensed their confusion and played on it shamefully. Becky glanced at the bell on the bedside table, then decided against summoning the nurse. She didn't really want anything, she just wanted to annoy Maude.

She also wanted something to take her mind off Jimmy, but it was no good. Every waking moment she thought of him, and when asleep, she dreamt about him. He was in her blood, like an illness. But illnesses could be cured – there was no cure against love. Her eyes welled up with hot tears, and she made no effort to stop them. She was bound to feel weepy, she'd been very ill. And once again Jimmy had come to her rescue.

She heard footsteps on the stairs and froze as they stopped outside her door. For what seemed an age, the person on the other side of the door made no sound or attempt to enter the room. Then the footsteps moved on, and Rebecca expelled a long, loud breath of relief. She hadn't seen Phil since she'd become ill, and in light of what he had done, she didn't want to. Every day he would stand outside her door, trying to summon up the courage to talk to her, and each time she would hold her breath until he went away. Her mouth tightened in grim determination. She must get better soon, she must. With Phil out of work, and only Amy's small wage to rely on, they would soon be in desperate straits.

No doubt Richard would still expect his rent money. As it was, the repugnant man was full of himself at the news of Phil losing his job. To his further delight, Phil had gone crawling to him for his old job back. Angrily Rebecca beat her fists against the eiderdown in frustration. Not only was her brother weak, cowardly, addicted to gambling and a thief, he was also bloody stupid. Surely he must have known Richard would be crowing over Phil's dismissal, and just waiting for the chance to get his revenge. Not only had Phil swallowed his pride, he had also gone to the factory to ask for his old job back, instead of waiting to see Richard alone. Richard had not only denied Phil a job, he had done so publicly, making certain all those in the factory – the same men Phil had once had charge over – had been witness to their former manager's shameful humiliation.

If Phil had lost his job for any other reason, Rebecca could have found it in her heart to feel sorry for him, but by his deceitful actions, he had killed the last shred of respect she had for him. Her eyelids drooping once more, Rebecca tried to think of a way to ease their financial worries, but she felt so tired.

Across the hall, Maude's voice continued to reverberate through the house. Her lips tight, Rebecca reached out for her bell.

*   *   *

In his room, Phil paced the floor like a caged animal. All he had in his pockets were a few pennies, and with each day that passed, his debt to Big George was accumulating interest. A deep shudder of shame ripped through his body as he recalled, for the umpteenth time, the memory of himself going cap in hand to Richard, and that smug bastard taking no time in bringing Phil to his knees. He could have just said no. But that wasn't enough for Richard. Instead, he had thrown open his office door and bellowed his business all over the factory floor. Another shudder tore through Phil's body, the awful memory making him cringe with embarrassment.

By God! He'd get Richard back for the way he had treated him. His fat cousin might be laughing now, but one day Phil would wipe that smug look off of the red, fleshy face.

Feeling suddenly drained, Phil slumped onto the edge of his bed, knowing his silent protestations and threats were as empty as his pockets. Groaning, he dropped his face into his hands. Unless a miracle happened, he was in deep trouble, and miracles didn't come along that often – even at Christmas.

Jimmy was seated at the bureau going over the day's takings. As usual at this time of year, the number of bets had increased considerably. There were numerous people who never placed a bet throughout the year, then, come Christmas, they felt in a festive mood, and parted with sixpence, or a shilling in the hope they would win and give their families a Christmas to remember. Then there were those who scrapped together every penny they had to place a small wager, hoping and praying their chosen horse would enable them to provide a turkey for their Christmas dinner, or even just enough to buy their children a small present. Jimmy always recognised these kind of bets from his normal punters, and always, without fail, experienced a twinge of guilt when the horse in question lost, knowing that the children of the family would wake up to empty stockings on Christmas morning, and stale bread and cold dripping for their Christmas dinner. Then he would remind himself that nobody forced these people to part with money they could ill afford, and he was fairer than most of the bookies around the East End. Jimmy had never used bully boy tactics in collecting his money, simply because he had decided at the start not to let anyone run up a tab. All bets placed had to be paid up front. If the punter couldn't afford to bet, then Jimmy refused to take it. Putting his pen down, Jimmy leant back against the leather chair, his face a study of concentration.

Despite Bessie's assurances that the boy was his, Jimmy still wasn't sure. He certainly hadn't seen any resemblance to himself, but as Bessie had pointed out, people rarely noticed their own characteristics in others. What if the boy was his? More to the point, did he want to be a father?

Since the night when Amy had left the boy alone with Bessie, the two of them had become the best of friends. Yet try as he might, Jimmy couldn't get the boy to open up to him. The child seemed quite at ease in Jimmy's presence, but he never attempted to talk unless Jimmy spoke first. When the child did address him, he called Jimmy either sir or mister, even though Bessie had told the boy Jimmy was his father. But James was only eight years old, and probably confused or too shy to bring up the matter in Jimmy's presence. A part of Jimmy wanted Bessie to be wrong, because if he was the boy's father, then he would have Heather to contend with until the boy grew to adulthood; and that was a good ten years in the future. Yet another part of Jimmy yearned to acknowledge the child as his.

Now that he was no longer fearful of them, James had become quite amenable. In fact, Jimmy wouldn't have recognised him from the shrieking, terrified boy who had lashed out at him and Bessie at every opportunity. Now he felt safer and more at ease, the child was showing his true nature. He was good-tempered and easy-going, forever asking questions of Bessie. But the most asked question was, 'When is my mummy coming to get me?' Maybe the boy was more relaxed now because he knew it was Christmas Eve tomorrow, and his mother had said she would come for him at Christmas.

A sudden thought struck Jimmy. What if Heather didn't come back? What if she had met some other mug with plenty of money, like that poor fool Sean Finnegan, whom Amy had told him about; would she still come back for her child, or would she simply vanish again? If so, the child would be devastated. Whatever other faults Heather had, she obviously had engendered a strong sense of love in the child for her. Yet didn't all children love their mothers, regardless of the way they were treated? Jimmy thought back to his own mother and gave a derisive grunt. She was a drunken bitch who beat him whenever she got the chance. He had never known what it was like to be cuddled until Bessie had taken him under her wing. Not that Bessie was one for being over demonstrative, but she had shown him love, and given him peace of mind and security. But that didn't alter the fact that Jimmy had loved his mother. As cruel and unfeeling towards him as she had been, Jimmy remembered trying to get some affection from the slatternly woman who had borne him, and receiving only abuse instead. Still, he had persevered, until that day, on the run from the police, he had left home and gone straight into Bessie's comforting arms.

An unfamiliar sensation stole over Jimmy, and with a start, he realised that tears were pricking his eyes. Angry with himself, he jumped from the chair and poured himself a drink. Bleeding hell! What was up with him? Imagine him, Jimmy Jackson, getting all sentimental over a mother that hadn't given a damn about him. Knocking back the drink in one go, Jimmy twirled the empty glass around in his fingers, his eyes sombre. He had just given himself the answer to his own question. No matter how cruelly his own mother had treated him, Jimmy had still craved her attention. Maybe James was the same, because any woman who could callously dump her child on strangers, just to get money, was no kind of mother in his eyes.

The doorbell chimed downstairs, then childish

laughter brought Jimmy's eyes towards the door, his features softening at the delightful sound. He could hear Bessie's strident tone and Amy's happy banter, then his stomach lurched as he heard the boy, his voice high with excitement, ask, 'Can I show Jimmy my new shoes?'

A sudden silence greeted this unexpected request, then Bessie and Amy began talking at once, both anxious to appear normal, for fear the boy might sense their feelings and change his mind.

Swiftly, Jimmy resumed his seat at the bureau, and had just picked up his pen when there was a knock at the door. Clearing his throat he called out, 'Come in.'

James came bounding into the room, his innocent face lit up with uncontrolled excitement. 'Hello, Mister. I've been to the shops with Amy. We went on a tram, and all the shops were so pretty. They had loads of coloured lights in the windows, and lots of Christmas trees with silver and red tinsels and bright balls hanging from the branches . . . Ooh, you should have seen them, Mister. Sure and it was the prettiest thing I've seen in me life, so it was.'

Laying down his pen, Jimmy looked first at Amy's smiling face, then dropped his gaze to the boy. 'I'm glad you enjoyed your trip, James, but you must have seen the same kind of shops in Ireland at Christmas, or are the London shops better than the Irish ones?'

Jimmy's voice was warm, as was his smile, then his expression changed as the boy dropped his head and muttered, 'I don't know, Mister. We lived in the country, and . . . and my mummy said it was boring and there was nothing to do. She . . . I mean, my mummy doesn't like Christmas very much. Uncle Sean did promise to take me shopping to Dublin one Christmas, he said it was a wondrous sight to behold . . .' James's face lit up at the memory of the man he had loved so dearly, then his eyes clouded over. 'Mummy said it was too far to travel, but she used to go there with Uncle Sean, sometimes for a long time. Bridie looked after me when they weren't at home. But . . . but, Uncle Sean promised me he would take me this year, and he would have too . . . but he died, and so I never got to see Dublin a'tall.'

Gazing down at the bent head, Jimmy felt an overwhelming surge of pity for the child, coupled with a feeling of outrage towards Heather. So, she hadn't changed. Still putting herself first, as she always had and always would. Jimmy saw Amy move towards the boy and held a hand up to stop her. Nodding towards the door, he motioned for her to leave, and Amy, her pretty face troubled, did as she was bid.

James heard the door close and turned towards the sound, but before he could make any protest, or call out for Amy, Jimmy said jovially, 'Well, now, let's have a look at these new shoes of yours, young man. Then you can tell me more about the shops, 'cos I'll tell you a secret . . .' He leant nearer the child. 'To be honest, it's a long time since I went to the shops at Christmas, I'm always too busy. But if they're as wonderful as you say they are, then maybe

I'll go and have a look for myself. Here, sit yourself down and show me your new shoes.'

James obediently scrambled onto the settee, holding his new footwear out for inspection, his lips smiling shyly as he waited for Jimmy's approval.

Making a great show of admiring James's new acquisition, Jimmy crouched down, and, looking up at the child, said, 'Well, they're a smashing pair of shoes and no mistake. Amy must have taken you to a lot of shops before you picked out the best pair.'

'Oh, no, Mister. I picked out the first pair I saw,' James protested vigorously, a sudden spark of fear entering his eyes. 'I didn't waste time, honest I didn't. I wouldn't be a bother to Amy, sir.'

Again Jimmy felt his stomach lurch. Apparently Heather didn't much like taking her son shopping either. He was beginning to wonder if there was anything his former lover liked to do with her son.

'Here, move over, James. I'm getting cramp in my legs in this position.'

James shuffled his bottom along the settee, his eyes darting to the door, hoping Amy wouldn't be long. Apprehensive at being alone with Jimmy for too long, the boy began to tap his fingers on the arm of the settee.

Jimmy noticed the nervous reflex and felt a tingle of excitement at the base of his spine. He himself had the same habit of tapping his fingers on the nearest object whenever he was distracted. It used to drive Bessie mad when he was younger and they were living in the one room. He could still hear her yelling, 'For Gawd's sake, Jimmy, stop that blasted tapping.' He would look up in surprise, not realising he was doing it, then a few minutes later, he would start tapping the nearest thing to hand. It was a habit he still had, and now he was seeing it in the boy. Of course, it was a common habit, nothing spectacular, but still . . . What he needed was to spend some time alone with the boy, and with this thought in mind he asked, 'How would you like to see some real Christmas decorations?'

James's eyes widened in childish amazement. 'You mean, better than the ones I saw today?'

Jimmy nodded. 'Oh, yes. Much better than the ones you saw today. How about you and me taking a tram and going up West!' At the look of puzzlement that crossed James's face, Jimmy laughed. 'This is the East End, and up West means the West End. I haven't been up West at Christmas for a couple of years now, but I imagine it's still as breathtaking as it always was at this time of year. What d'yer say, James? Would you like to come out with me for the afternoon? Just the two of us.' When the boy continued to hesitate, Jimmy lowered his voice and asked simply, 'Please, James. Will you let me take you out for a while? I think we should get to know each other . . . What d'yer say?'

The small fingers continued to tap the wood carving on the arm of the settee in agitation. Then, as if gathering courage, he asked, 'Will this place be as grand as Sean said Dublin is at Christmas?'

Jimmy gave a relieved laugh. Bending nearer the boy's face he mimicked, 'Sure, and it's a wondrous sight to behold, so it is.'

A loud peal of shrill laughter greeted the remark. 'You sounded just like Uncle Sean, Mister.'

A spark of hope lit up Jimmy's face. 'You'll come then? Just the two of us?'

James remined silent for a few moments, his forehead crumpled up in lines of thoughtfulness; then he nodded. 'All right, Mister. Shall I go and tell Bessie and Amy we're going out?'

Relieved beyond measure, Jimmy nodded. 'You do that, James. I'll get my hat and coat and follow you downstairs in a minute.'

Scrambling off the settee, the boy made for the door. Reaching up to the brass handle, he looked over his shoulder at Jimmy and asked innocently, 'Are you really my dad, Mister?'

The question, so unexpected, caused Jimmy's head to jolt back painfully. Swallowing hard, he looked into the green eyes that were gazing across at him, eyes that held a trace of fearful apprehension, and answered quietly, 'Yes, I am.'

The boy's gaze held Jimmy's for what seemed an eternity, and during that time, the fear fell from his eyes. His young voice high with childish emotion, he cried, 'All right. See you downstairs.'

Dumbly Jimmy nodded. He had been dreading this moment, now it seemed he needn't have worried, for with the simplistic nature of a child, his son had accepted the truth without question. Jimmy stood stock still for a few seconds until the sound of the boy's shrill voice calling for Amy brought him roughly out of his momentary shocked state.

With a few short strides he was out on the landing,

looking down on the small figure who was now halfway down the staircase excitedly attempting to negotiate the steep stairs as fast as his short legs would allow.

Leaning over the banister, Jimmy called out anxiously, 'Slow down, son, I don't want you breaking your neck.'

James looked upwards, his angelic face spreading into a wide grin. 'Don't worry, Mister, I'll be all right.'

And he was. Jimmy stayed on the landing until the child was safely at the bottom of the stairs, then turned slowly and returned to the living room where he poured himself a large brandy. The glass was almost empty before Jimmy recalled himself calling the child son. It had been an unconscious slip of the tongue on his part, yet he had liked using the affectionate term. But for how long would he be able to indulge in his new-found happiness? His expression pensive, Jimmy wandered over to the fireplace and leant his arm on the mantelpeice, his gaze centred on the blazing fire in the hearth. Up until a few weeks ago he hadn't even known he had a son, and even when Heather had dumped the child on him, he had secretly resented the intrusion into his ordered life. Yet within those few, heart-stopping moments his life, as he knew it, had changed for ever.

He had a son – and nobody, least of all that heartless bitch Heather Mills, who was a disgrace to all decent, loving mothers, was going to take his child away from him.

His face grim and determined, Jimmy began to make plans.

CHAPTER NINETEEN

Rebecca couldn't sleep, which wasn't surprising since she had slept most of the day, as she had done most days since the onslaught of the influenza that had rendered her as weak as a new-born baby. Now she was feeling a good deal better, but wide awake. Staring into the gloomy room, lit only by a low burning gas lamp, Rebecca impatiently drummed the bedcovers with her fingers while trying to ignore the need to visit the bathroom. Lying flat on her back, she tried to decide which was most urgent: the need to use the toilet, or the craving for a cup of tea.

Leaning up on her elbow, she looked to the bottom of her bed, and there was the nurse, fast asleep, her mouth hanging open, seemingly dead to the world. But Rebecca knew from experience that the slightest move on her part would instantly awaken the middle-aged woman, and Rebecca didn't have the heart to disturb her. The poor woman was exhausted, not from looking after the patient she had been hired to nurse back to health, but from running around after that truculent, whining old battleaxe across the landing. Sighing, Rebecca lay back down and tried to ignore her bodily needs, but it was no use. Hardly daring to breathe, she moved the bedclothes off of her and gingerly swung her legs over the side of the bed. As her bare feet touched the icy linoleum she shivered involuntarily then grimaced, fearful that the nurse would sense her movement and wake up, but the exhausted woman slept on.

Looking over to where Amy lay in the single bed adjacent to hers, Rebecca saw that her sister, like the nurse, was in a deep sleep. Carefully picking up her dressing gown from the bottom of the bed, Rebecca crept out onto the landing, her silent progress halted abruptly as she heard the chain flush in the bathroom. Her heart beating fast, Rebecca retreated back into the open doorway of her room. The only person who could be up and about in the middle of the night was Phil, and she had no desire to come face to face with her brother. The resentment she harboured towards him regarding his underhand, deceitful actions was still fresh in her mind, as was the overwhelming sense of betrayal at the knowledge that he could have stooped so low in order to feed his gambling habit. Rebecca knew she would have to face him sooner or later, but that ordeal would have to wait until she was completely well. Even then she wasn't looking forward to the confrontation. Conscious of the rapid beating of her heart, she waited, then, as the bathroom door opened, her jaw dropped in shocked astonishment. For it wasn't Phil who emerged from the bathroom, but Maude. Stunned beyond belief, Rebecca watched as her cousin scurried across the landing and into her room, the agile figure bearing no resemblance to the invalid creature who professed to be incapable of managing more than a few steps, and that feat possible only when assisted.

Rebecca's shock soon turned to anger, and that initial anger gradually developed into a slow, burning resentment towards her elderly cousin. Slowly descending the stairs, Rebecca made her way to the kitchen, her mind so preoccupied she no longer noticed the bitter cold that pervaded the house. While waiting for the kettle to boil, she sat down heavily on the hard kitchen chair, her thoughts whirling as she recalled the scene she had just witnessed. Then she thought back over the years and the times she'd had to change Maude's disgusting, fouled sheets and then wash down the obese, disagreeable woman. And the years of fetching and carrying she'd been subjected to. And the more she recalled those wasted years, the angrier she became, until it took all of her willpower not to go back upstairs and physically pummel the hateful old cow until she screamed for mercy. This idea was immensely satisfying, though her common sense told her that in her weakened condition she was in no fit state to swat a fly. But she was well on the way to recovery, and once her body was restored to full strength she would be out of here. The days of her being a skivvy were over.

264

The shrill whistle of the kettle brought her to her feet, her eyes darting upwards, fearful that the sound would wake the nurse, but the house remained silent. After her second cup of tea she gradually began to calm down. She was still angry with the way she had been taken for a mug all these years, but grateful she had discovered the truth while she was still young enough to make a new life for herself and Amy.

Suddenly she shivered as the coldness of the room seeped into her body, and with a reluctant shrug of her shoulders she made her way back to her bedroom. After visiting the bathroom Rebecca paused on the landing; her baleful eyes directed at Maude's room, she felt her anger returning. She had always guessed that Maude was capable of doing a lot more for herself than she made out, but never in her wildest imaginings had Rebecca envisaged just how active her cousin really was. But Maude's comeuppance could wait a while longer. Now that Rebecca knew the truth she held the upper hand, and she was going to make good use of her new-found knowledge.

Turning towards her bedroom, she stopped as she heard a strange sound coming from across the hall. Her curiosity getting the better of her, she resisted the temptation of the warmth and security of her bed a little longer and tiptoed silently along the carpeted landing. Outside Maude's room Rebecca pressed her ear against the door, her forehead furrowing in confusion. Pressing her lips tightly shut to avoid any sound she might make inadvertently, she gently turned the handle and peeped inside. The sight that met her eyes caused her lips to spring apart, and it was only with a supreme effort that she prevented herself from crying out. For there, with her enormous back to her, was Maude, engrossed in counting a mountain of coins heaped high in the middle of the double bed.

As Rebecca watched through the crack in the door, Maude gave a satisfactory grunt, before putting the money back into a long, flat box, then, dropping to her knees, she placed the heavy box into a hidden panel in the base of the bed before climbing back under the quilted bedspread. Stunned and shaken beyond belief, Rebecca gently closed the door. Her mind numb, she returned to her own room and quickly got into bed, but she didn't sleep. Instead she let her mind wander down the years once more, but now she remembered the times she had gone hungry in order that Maude could enjoy nourishing meals; and all the time Maude had been lying on top of a virtual fortune.

Rebecca was still awake when the dawn broke and the nurse finally awoke. Making a pretence of sleep, Rebecca lay motionless as the nurse bent over her still form. She remained in the same state when the alarm clock woke Amy, wanting and needing to be alone with her thoughts. The time wasn't yet right to disclose Maude's unforgivable deceptions, but soon – very soon, because the way Rebecca was feeling, she wouldn't be able to keep quiet for long. Her eyes heavy, Rebecca fought to stay awake, then let sleep overtake her troubled thoughts. And when she slept, she had a tight smile on her lips, knowing that her days of servitude were numbered. But before she left this house she would tell that dirty, deceitful old cow exactly what she thought of her. That was one confrontation she was looking forward to.

A few miles away, Jimmy had also experienced the frustration of a sleepless night. Unlike Rebecca, however, Jimmy didn't waste time lying in bed. At five o'clock he was up and dressed, his agile mind busily putting the final touches to his plans of the previous day.

When he entered the living room he was momentarily taken aback by the icy coldness of the room. He hadn't noticed the cold while he was getting washed, he'd been too busy thinking about the day ahead, and the imminent arrival of Heather. Now his thoughts were more in order, the freezing temperature hit him like an icy spray of water. Normally by the time he arose Bessie was already up and about and had the fire going. Rubbing his hands for warmth, Jimmy allowed himself a slow chuckle.

'You're getting soft, Jimmy lad,' he admonished himself out loud as he set to the task of lighting the fire. The cold hearth had already been prepared by Bessie the night before and within minutes Jimmy had a blazing fire going. Pulling the armchair nearer the warmth, Jimmy again went over what he planned to do when Heather arrived – if she arrived! Knowing that his former lover's only real love in life was money, Jimmy was prepared to offer her whatever she requested in exchange for keeping

267

James with him. In return Jimmy was determined to make Heather sign an agreement to the effect that once paid she would never bother him again. That stipulation was essential, for Heather would bleed him dry if presented with the opportunity. And as desperate as Jimmy was to keep his son, he was no fool. The only problem that Jimmy could see was the child himself. The poor lad would be devastated once he knew his mother had abandoned him for good, but Jimmy comforted himself with the knowledge that children were resilient, and with Amy and Bessie's help he hoped it wouldn't be too long before his son accepted Jimmy as his father, and acclimatised himself to his new life. And when he had finally got rid of Heather, he would be free to renew his acquaintance with Rebecca. As the image of her sweet face floated across his mind's eye, Jimmy smiled tenderly. Knowing women as he did, he was confident that once he had made sure Rebecca knew his intentions were honourable, she would welcome him with open arms. Well! Maybe not with open arms, but Jimmy was sure she wouldn't be averse to his calling on her.

A loud growl from Jimmy's stomach reminded him how hungry he was after lying awake most of the night. Glancing over at the grandfather clock, he saw it was just coming up to six o'clock, which meant that Bessie would be up quite soon. It also meant he didn't have to stir himself to make his own breakfast. Settling himself more comfortably in the chair, Jimmy fixed his gaze on the far door, waiting for Bessie to appear. His lips curved into a smile as the door handle turned, then dropped in surprise when, instead of the grey-haired woman, James – his dark hair standing on end, and dressed in a white nightgown that reached his ankles – tentatively poked his head around the door.

'Morning, Mister. Has . . . has my mum come yet?'

His hunger forgotten, Jimmy felt a lump rise in his throat. Hot on the heels of the unfamiliar emotion came the sinking realisation that his earlier thoughts about keeping the child weren't going to be as simple as he'd imagined.

Clearing his throat to hide his awkwardness, Jimmy said kindly, 'I shouldn't think your mum's even awake yet, mate, it's only six o'clock. Still, now you're up, you'd better come over here and get yourself warm. Come on, I won't bite,' he added self-consciously as the boy hesitated. Then the inviting sight of the roaring fire got the better of James's wariness and slowly, his eyes flickering over the room, he came to stand by Jimmy's chair.

Seeing the shivering, tiny figure, Jimmy reached out and plucked the boy up into his arms, cuddling the cold form into his body, at the same time steeling himself for rejection. But none came. Instead the child nestled deeper into Jimmy's strong arms, his tousled head resting comfortably against Jimmy's broad chest. His body relaxing, Jimmy absently stroked the dark hair.

'I expect you're hungry, I know I am. Here, listen to that.' Jimmy let out a roar of laughter as another loud growl rippled through his stomach.

The boy lifted his head to look into Jimmy's face, his childish lips crinkling into a shy smile. 'My tummy does that when I'm hungry. It happened once when we were in a shop, and my mummy said I embarrassed her.' James's voice lost some of his merriment as he recalled the incident, then his face brightened. 'But sure you can't help it if your tummy makes a noise, can you, Mister?'

Jimmy looked down into the large, beguiling eyes and smiled tenderly. 'No, you can't help it, mate.' Holding the boy's thin shoulders, Jimmy held him at arm's length so he could see him better and asked quietly, 'Have you often been hungry, James?'

The boy swallowed nervously as he avoided Jimmy's gaze. 'Not very often, Mister, only since we had to leave Ireland, and sometimes when I haven't got an uncle to look after me and Mummy. But I've got plenty of uncles, but . . . but they don't stay with us for long . . .' His low-pitched voice trailed off guiltily as if suddenly aware he had said too much, and in doing so was being disloyal to his mother.

Guessing what was going through the boy's mind, Jimmy hugged him tighter, mainly to keep the child warm, but most of all so that James couldn't see the rage that was suffusing his face. He had already made up his mind to keep the child, but even if James wasn't his son, Jimmy would still have been outraged at the way he had been treated. Gradually Jimmy relaxed, taking comfort from the child's proximity. James too was content to stay where he was, feeling secure in the arms of the man who was his father, even though to James's young mind the word father was just that, merely a word. Still, it was comforting to sit like this in front of a blazing fire. The child hadn't felt so wanted and secure since before Sean Finnegan had died. The warmth of the fire, added to the closeness of their bodies, caused a feeling of drowsiness to settle on them, and when Bessie stuck her head around the door some twenty minutes later, she found them fast asleep. Smiling broadly, she wisely left them in peace.

Richard Fisher let himself into the house he still regarded as his home and immediately set about making a nuisance of himself. The first person he encountered was the nurse, who was indulging in a much-needed mug of strong tea together with a substantial fried breakfast. Even though Richard had already eaten a similar meal cooked by Ivy's housekeeper, the sight and smell of the food set his lips watering. Greedy by nature, he eyed the fried eggs, bacon and sausages with undisguised relish.

'I see you're making yourself at home, nurse,' he said heartily, in what he thought to be a condescending manner. If the cutting remark was meant to intimidate the middle-aged woman, he was sadly disappointed. Gladys Hook had been nursing for over thirty years, and during that time she had dealt with a variety of people. It came as no surprise to her that this fat, overbearing man was the brother of the equally fat, obnoxious woman upstairs. They were two of a kind. She was only grateful that this was her last day. Though if the young, pleasant woman she had been hired to look after had been her only

271

patient then she would have been more than happy to stay on.

When the night nurse had been discharged Gladys Hook had imagined her time would only be required from eight in the morning until eight at night. But she was a kindly soul, and although Rebecca had assured her that she and her sister could manage without her, Gladys had been loath to leave the two young women at the mercy of the cantankerous old bag who professed to be helpless. And of course the extra money came in useful, especially at this time of year, though sleeping in a chair instead of her own soft bed had been very uncomfortable. But at least she'd only had to endure the inconvenience for two nights, and tonight she would be back in her own bed. She hadn't met the mystery man who was footing the bill for her services, and she would have been less than human if she hadn't wondered about the unusual set-up, but she was kept too busy to dwell on the subject for long.

Swallowing a large chunk of sausage, she replied scathingly, 'Miss Rebecca told me to treat the house as my own while I'm here, and seeing as how you're not paying for my time, I don't see as how it's any of your business what I do.'

Stupefied at the woman's cheek, Richard stared down at the uniformed figure, his fleshy jowls quivering. To Richard, any person in service was supposed to be just that, servile. Pulling himself up to his full height, he was about to reprimand the woman for her lack of respect when she looked up, and the contempt and studious disregard mirrored

272

in the steely grey eyes stopped him in his tracks.

The prospect of another breakfast denied him, he mustered up his courage and said in what he hoped was an authoritative voice, 'I'll thank you to keep a civil tongue in your head, woman, else you may find yourself out of a job.'

Without looking up the nurse answered, 'As a matter of fact, this is my last day. Miss Rebecca has told me she no longer requires my services, though I have to say she's had precious little benefit of them, seeing as I've spent most of my time running around after your sister. Now if you'll excuse me, I'm trying to eat my breakfast in peace.'

Like all bullies, Richard was no match for anyone with a stronger personality than his own, and had to content himself with a loud grunt of disapproval before flouncing upstairs.

Rebecca was getting dressed when Richard burst into her room, and with a loud cry she snatched her clothes to her breast and shouted angrily, 'How dare you burst in here without knocking, you horrible little man. Get out of my room . . . NOW!'

Taken aback by the ferocity in Rebecca's voice, Richard hurriedly backed from the room, his fleshy face sweating profusely, his mind filled with the image of Rebecca standing in her underclothes. He had never seen his cousin so scantily dressed, and the experience had been a revelation. Mopping his brow with a large handkerchief, he walked quickly to his sister's room, hoping that he wouldn't encounter a similar scene. The thought of witnessing Maude in her underwear was too nauseating for words, though that unappealing prospect was hardly likely. Maude hadn't dressed herself for over twenty years, and Richard didn't think that habit of a lifetime was likely to change now.

As with Rebecca, he didn't bother knocking, though his reception was just as welcoming. 'Oh, it's you,' Maude snapped in disappointment as she saw her visitor. 'I thought it was the nurse. I've been awake for a good twenty minutes and I need seeing to.' She glowered up at him, and she made such an awful sight first thing in the morning that Richard had to avert his gaze to the floor. 'Anyway, what are you doing here at this time in the morning? You haven't come to start on about that wretched party you were planning, I hope. We haven't had people in this house since Mother and Father died, and I certainly don't want to start entertaining now.'

Walking over to the window, Richard made a pretence of looking out on to the street below, and with a malicious tone in his voice he answered gleefully, 'As a matter of fact, that's exactly why I've come around. But don't distress yourself, Maude, you don't have to participate if you don't want to,' knowing full well that his sister would never be able to lie up here while there was a party going on down below her room.

'Now you see here, Richard, I forbid you to—'

As if she hadn't spoken, Richard, his hands clasped tightly behind his back, turned to face her. Rocking back on his heels, he carried on, 'As

274

for the nurse . . . Well, I'm afraid you're going to have to wait a long time for her, she's just informed me she's leaving today. It seems our dear Rebecca no longer has need of her services.'

He had the pleasure of seeing Maude's face drop in abject disappointment, then, recovering her aplomb, she screeched, 'Never mind about Rebecca. What about me? I still have need of a nurse. Rebecca can't look after me the state she's in, and Amy's hardly here these days. As for Phil . . . Pah,' she spat out contemptuously. 'He's neither use nor ornament, and even if he was, it wouldn't be fitting for a man to attend to my needs.' Glaring at her brother through slitted eyes, she said resentfully, 'If you weren't so tight-fisted, you'd have a nurse in attendance regularly. You don't know what I've had to put up with all these years since that young slut arrived. She's barely civil these days. Oh, she does the essentials, but it's not the same as having a proper nurse looking after me.' Leaning forwards in the vast bed, she wagged a finger at Richard. 'Now look here, Richard. You get back downstairs and tell that nurse that she's stopping on and . . .'

Richard laughed unpleasantly. 'I'm not doing any such thing. In case you've forgotten, Maude, I'm not paying for her services, as you've so forcefully pointed out, and that being the case, I have no authority to tell her anything.' A crafty smile crossed his face. 'Of course you could send a message to Mr Jackson and tell him that you need the nurse to stay on, but somehow I don't think he'd be too happy to meet your request . . . Do you, Maude?'

275

Maude slumped back on her pillows, knowing she was defeated. Quickly taking advantage of her temporary dumb state, Richard seized his opportunity to escape, but he couldn't resist a parting shot.

'My guests will be arriving at eight. I estimate there'll be around twenty people present. As you don't want to join in the Christmas festivities, I suggest you ask the nurse for a sleeping tablet before she leaves. That way you won't be disturbed. Good day, Maude . . . Oh, and if I don't see you later . . . Merry Christmas.'

Feeling very pleased with himself, Richard banged the door after him, but his victory was short-lived.

'Well! What are you doing here at this time in the morning, *Dick*?' Rebecca barred his way, her face crumpled with distaste.

Normally Richard would have been cowed under such open hostility, but having been made to look a fool in front of the nurse, his back was up. With a forcefulness that stemmed from sheer vindictiveness, he shot back loudly, 'I came to tell you that the party is going ahead. I'm aware you have no intention of helping, so I've arranged to have caterers in. They'll be arriving at five, so I'd appreciate it if the kitchen was left free so as they can do their work.' Brushing past Rebecca, Richard swivelled his head to glare at her. Jerking his thumb towards Maude's bedroom he snapped, 'I'll tell you what I've just told Maude. The party's going ahead whether you like it or not. I don't have to remind you that this is still my house, and I don't need permission from you to use it as I see fit. Now, if you want to stay in your room all night, so

276

be it, it's no skin off my nose. I'd like you to attend, seeing as you're family. But like I say, it's entirely up to you.'

When Rebecca continued to stare at him with hate-filled eyes, Richard gulped nervously, then, with as much dignity as he could muster, he made his exit.

Out in the street he bit down on his lip anxiously. What if Maude and Rebecca made good their threat and boycotted the party? If they did, it would ruin his carefully laid plans. He had been looking forward to making his announcement ever since he had first thought of the idea. Every waking moment he had visualised the look of astonishment on Maude and Rebecca's faces when he told them he was getting married, and there would no longer be any place for them in the house.

Even Ivy had fallen in with his plans, which was strange since she had been dead against it when he'd first suggested selling her house in Barking and moving, albeit temporarily, into his former home. But ten days ago, she had suddenly changed her mind, indeed she was now positively anxious to make the move. Richard's eyebrows drew together, his suspicious mind wondering what had happened to account for Ivy's change of heart, then he shrugged. Ivy was an astute business woman. She was probably planning to sell her house for a tidy sum and keep a lump of the profits for herself. Even so, there would still be a decent amount left over. Everything had been going so smoothly until Rebecca had fallen ill.

His face set in mulish lines of determination, Richard drew back his shoulders, jutted his fat neck forward and climbed into the waiting cab. This party was costing him a small fortune, and despite Rebecca and Maude's protests, he couldn't see either of them sitting in their rooms all evening without making an appearance. He was confident that he could count on Amy's help in coaxing them from their rooms. Feeling enormously pleased with himself, Richard ordered the cabbie to drive him to his place of business.

Ten minutes after Richard had departed, Dr Barker showed up, his face falling into deep creases of surprise and disapproval when Rebecca opened the door.

Entering the house, he laid down his Gladstone bag, removed his high hat and stared at Rebecca reproachfully.

'Now then, young miss, I thought we'd agreed you were to stay in bed for at least another day.'

Rebecca smiled weakly. 'Don't scold me, doctor, please. I was going mad lying in bed, and I feel much better, honestly.' Feeling nervous, but knowing the best way to impart unwelcome news was to come straight out with it, she murmured hesitantly. 'You'd better know now, I've discharged the nurse.' Seeing Tom Barker's eyebrows rise in worried consternation, she hurried on. 'Now look, I'm not being silly. I really don't need a nurse any longer. Amy will be at home all over Christmas, so I won't be on my own, and besides . . .' She lowered her gaze, nervously pulling at her fingers. 'You know I'm very grateful to Jimmy for paying for my care, but I've never been comfortable in accepting charity, no matter how well meaning it is, and I also know private nursing doesn't come cheap. It was all right when I was really ill, but now I'm up and about, I simply can't in all conscience go on accepting Jimmy's money.' A trembling smile touched her lips. 'Besides, Maude was getting more benefit from the nurse than I was, so I've told Nurse Hook she can go today. She was only too pleased to get her marching orders. Maude has had her run off her feet, poor woman . . . The nurse, I mean, not Maude.'

At the mention of her name, Gladys Hook appeared. 'Good morning, Dr Barker. I've been waiting for you to arrive. I didn't want to leave before your visit.'

Taking off his heavy overcoat, Tom Barker fixed the nurse with a steely glance. 'Don't be in too much of a hurry to leave, nurse. I've been up most of the night delivering a child who was reluctant to enter the world and I could do with some hot food and drink. Would you fix me something while I have a word with this stubborn young woman?'

Nurse Hook bridled at the tone in the doctor's voice.

'Actually, doctor, I had no intention of leaving until Miss Amy arrived home. Miss Rebecca may think she's fully recovered, but she'll soon have a relapse if she's left alone to cope with her cousin. The dratted woman has nearly incapacitated me, and I'm as strong as a horse. Now, if you'll excuse me I'll fix some breakfast for you both.' Raising her eyes heavenward she added, 'And for Maude, of course. We don't want the poor dear wasting away.'

Rebecca looked at Tom Barker, a soft laugh bubbling on her lips. 'No, nurse, that would never do.'

When Gladys had left the room, Tom said dryly, 'Well, are you going to invite me to sit down, or do you intend to keep me standing during my visit?'

Instantly contrite, Rebecca cried, 'Oh, I'm sorry, doctor, please have a seat.' Leading him over to the two armchairs drawn up by the fire, they sat down facing each other.

Tom Barker studied the pallid face of the woman sitting opposite him and sighed. He was a good judge of character and knew it would be fruitless to try and persuade Rebecca to change her mind about discharging the nurse. Along with his concern for his patient – a woman he had grown very fond of and admired immensely – he was loath to sever all ties with her and that delightful sister of hers. It was a great pity that things hadn't worked out between Rebecca and Jimmy, for in his view this young woman would be the making of his dear friend. Jimmy hadn't said anything to him regarding Rebecca, but Tom had known Jimmy for many years and could read him like an open book. What he didn't know was how Rebecca felt about Jimmy. She wasn't the type of woman to tell her business to all and sundry and he admired her all the more for that. In his line of work the majority of his patients saw him as a doctor and priest combined. Being of a kindly and sympathetic nature, Tom Barker was normally only too happy to help his patients with their problems, knowing that a good deal of illnesses stemmed from worry. It was therefore very galling that the one person he would like to confide in him happened to be a very independent, proud woman who would rather walk barefoot on hot coals than burden someone with her own problems. Now if it had been Maude . . . !

He wasn't aware he had sighed heavily until Rebecca asked anxiously, 'Are you all right, doctor?'

Tom smiled reassuringly. 'Yes, my dear, I'm fine . . . Here, here, what am I thinking of? I'm the doctor and you're still my patient, at least for the rest of the day. Now then, let's have a look at you.' So saying, he took hold of Rebecca's wrist then listened to her chest. 'Hmm. Well now, your pulse is still a bit high, but that's only to be expected after a bout of influenza. The main thing is your chest sounds clear. What you need now is plenty of rest, though I don't suppose you'll get much of that once the nurse has gone . . . I don't suppose you'll reconsider. Jimmy won't mind. The man's a walking goldmine and . . .'

Rebecca lifted her chin high, her cheeks reddening. 'Jimmy may be very well off, in fact he could be a millionaire; it wouldn't make any difference. Any money he has he's worked hard for. Even if I don't approve of his line of work, the fact remains it's his money, and I've no right to expect any of his hard-earned money to be spent on me. No, doctor, the nurse is going. Like I've already told you, Amy will be here to look after me. She'll make me rest, don't you worry. She may appear to be scatter-brained, but beneath that childish demeanour there lurks a very strong character.'

Tom Barker bent his head to hide his amusement as he recalled Jimmy's account of the way Amy had practically attacked him the day he had tried to see Rebecca. Throwing his hands up in defeat he chuckled, 'All right, my dear, you've made your point, so what say we change the subject . . . Ahh, here comes our breakfast,' he added as Nurse Hook approached them carrying a heavily laden tray, from which rose a heavenly aroma of cooked food.

Smacking his lips, Tom rose and held his hand out to Rebecca. 'Shall we sit at the table, or maybe you'd rather take your breakfast with your cousin.'

Rebecca hurriedly got to her feet. 'Good God, no!' she exclaimed quickly, then saw the twinkle in the doctor's eyes and laughed. 'You're a very wicked man, Dr Barker. Maybe I'll call you out to attend my cousin. You can't refuse. After all, you are a doctor and as such you're bound to tend the sick and needy.'

Now it was Tom's turn to protest hurriedly. 'Pshaw. I don't have any such scruples. I may be a doctor, but I'm no saint. And as you've just pointed out my job is to attend the sick and needy, and at the risk of offending you, my dear, I don't believe your cousin is as helpless as she makes out.'

The laughter dropped from Rebecca's lips as she remembered the scene she had witnessed in the early hours of the morning. For a split second she considered sharing her secret with the doctor, then pushed aside the impulse. She had her own plan of how to deal with Maude.

Linking arms with the smiling man, she patted his hand. 'What say we forget about Maude and enjoy our meal.'

No sooner had the words left her lips when Maude's voice shrilled from above, causing all three people present to screw up their eyes with ill-disguised annoyance.

Setting the hot meal on the dining table, Nurse Hook, her lips tight with barely suppressed impatience, muttered, 'If you'll excuse me, I believe I'm being summoned,' and as she went to answer Maude's loud cries, Gladys thanked the good Lord that this would be the last time she would be called on to lay eyes on the loathsome creature.

'I expect you'll be having time off over the holidays, doctor.'

Tom Barker, his mouth full of crispy bacon, chewed quickly before answering, 'I sincerely hope so. But one never knows in my profession. People don't stop being ill just because it's Christmas. On the contrary, it's this time of year that most people become ill. Normally brought on by worry and hard work, or simply despair at being on their own at a time when most people have their families around them. Oh, yes, Christmas can be a very sad time for a lot of people.'

Rebecca thought quickly. She had no doubt that Jimmy would invite the doctor to spend Christmas with him and Bessie, but what if . . . ?

Carefully choosing her words, she asked tentatively, 'If you're not doing anything tonight, Richard is having a party here. I've told him I'm not prepared to help in the preparations, but he's going along with it anyway. He's even hired caterers to organise the event. You . . . you'd be more than welcome to come. In fact, I'd really like you to. I doubt if I'll know any of Richard's friends . . . Actually I didn't know he had any, but I expect his guests will be made up of business associates. So it would be nice for me, and Amy of course, if we had someone here we knew.'

Keeping his eyes on his plate, Tom replied slowly, 'Well now, that's very kind of you. I'd love to come . . . On one condition.' He waved a fork in the air. 'On no account must you tell anyone I'm a doctor, else I'll have every Tom, Dick and Harry queuing up to show me their boils and bunions or whatever else ails them.'

Rebecca let out a tinkling laugh that warmed the man's heart. 'I promise, doctor . . . Oops! I'd better not call you that this evening. I know, I'll call you Mr Barker, how about that?'

Studiously keeping his attention fixed firmly on his plate, Tom said casually, 'Thank you, my dear. I wonder if I might take the liberty of bringing a friend along with me. Would that be all right with you?'

Now it was Rebecca's turn to lower her gaze. She felt the colour rise in her cheeks and inwardly cursed herself for a gormless fool. It was painfully obvious that the friend Dr Barker was referring to was Jimmy; even the sound of his name in her mind caused her heart to thump wildly. She had only been in the man's company for a few days, yet in that short space of time she had fallen in love. Her mind mocked her silently as she recalled her scathing remarks about the love stories Amy was so fond of reading, and yet here she was, she who had been so superior, acting just like one of those insipid heroines in the cheap novels.

Swallowing her pride she started to speak, and was mortified to hear the tremor in her voice. 'Of course, doctor, you . . . !' Tears welled in her eyes and with a muffled cry, Rebecca ran from the table and buried herself in the shabby armchair by the fire.

Moments later she felt a strong hand on her shoulder and looked up into pale blue eyes – eyes that were filled with kindly concern.

'Don't be embarrassed, my dear. The influenza has left you very vulnerable despite your feeling of well-being. There's no shame in crying . . . Or of being in love.'

Shaking uncontrollably, Rebecca grasped the hand tightly.

'I feel so stupid. I mean . . . Well, I hardly know Jimmy, yet . . . yet from the first moment I saw him, even though we didn't get off . . . off to a good start, I . . . I haven't been able to stop thin . . . thinking about him. I . . . I thought there might be a cha . . . chance for me, but then that woman turned up, and . . . and now I know there's no hope.'

Tom Barker pulled the armchair up closer to the distressed woman. 'Now listen to me, my dear. I've known Jimmy for many years, and I know too that he feels the same way. As for this Heather Mills person, you needn't worry. Jimmy has no feelings for her whatsoever. His only concern is for his son, and that, and that only, is the only reason he'll be having any contact with that blasted, trouble-making woman.'

Rebecca lifted reddened eyes to his. 'But, it's so . . . so silly. You can't fall in love with someone you hardly know . . . Can you?'

The doctor smiled gently. 'Speaking from personal experience, I would say yes. I fell in love with my late wife the moment I clapped eyes on her. Unfortunately she didn't feel the same, and I had to chase her for nearly a year before she would even agree to go out with me. But we had over twenty glorious years together, and even though she's been gone for some time, I still miss her dreadfully. So you hang on to your dreams, Rebecca. This business with Jimmy's former lover will soon blow over, and when it does you make sure you're there for him, because he needs you, my dear. He might not realise it, but he does need you. He's also smitten with you. Every conversation we have always turns to you, and believe me, Jimmy's not the type of man to give his affections lightly.'

A sudden burst of hope surged through Rebecca's quivering body. 'Do you really mean it, doctor? I . . . I mean, you're not just saying it to make me feel b. . . better.'

'I'm not accustomed to making idle observations. I firmly believe in telling the truth, no matter how much it may hurt the person involved. Now then, you dry your eyes, and if you don't mind, I'll finish my breakfast before leaving. But I'll be back tonight, with my friend.'

Yet he made no effort to move. The sight of the lovely young woman in such distress tugged at his heart strings, and with an uncharacteristic gesture, he reached forward and took her in his arms and waited patiently until Rebecca had cried herself out.

CHAPTER TWENTY

'What time is my mummy coming, Bessie?'

Bessie, her head submerged in the black-leaded range, checking on the enormous turkey that had been in the oven since seven that morning, didn't answer at once. The boy had been asking the same question since six o'clock. He was already dressed in his beige winter coat, long black socks and the new shoes he was so proud of. By his feet was a small suitcase he had packed the night before, so he would be all ready to leave as soon as his mother arrived. His handsome little face was alight with nervous excitement; and the sight of him sitting so quietly, trying so hard to hide his apprehension, nearly broke Bessie's heart. It was now nearly nine-thirty and still there was no sign of Heather. In her heart of hearts she prayed the woman wouldn't show. James would be devastated, but Bessie was a firm believer in time being a great healer, especially in the case of children. Using the pretext of basting the turkey to hide her feelings, Bessie answered cheerfully, 'Now don't you go getting yourself in a state, lad. Your mummy will be here soon enough. Or are you in that great a hurry to see the back of us all?'

Instantly the boy was all contrition. 'Oh, no, Bessie. I like it here now, and I like you and Jimmy, and especially Amy. But I'll come back and see you, honest I will.'

Bessie's face, still averted, bore a mask of sadness. She, like Jimmy, hadn't wanted the child, but now neither of them could imagine life without him. As for his innocent declaration that he would see them often, that would be in the hands of Heather Mills. And if Bessie knew the woman, which she did only too well, then Heather would keep the child away from them out of spite, until she wanted more money.

In the living room above, Jimmy was pacing the floor impatiently. He was anxious for Heather to arrive so that he could get the business regarding the child resolved. One thing he was determined on was that when Heather left this house she would leave alone. There was no way on God's earth he was going to let her take his son with her. If she had been a good mother then things would have been different, but as things stood, he wasn't going to let his son be passed around from one so-called uncle to another.

When the doorbell pealed, Jimmy froze, then, squaring his shoulders, he prepared for battle.

Bessie heard the bell, but before she could move,

James was off the chair and running towards the front door as fast as his short legs would allow him.

'Mummy! Mummy!' His childish cries of delight echoed around the large house, the sound causing the two people who had grown to love and care for him enormous pain, knowing that the child's delight was going to be short-lived.

Looking over the banister, Jimmy saw Heather, resplendent in a maroon velvet coat and matching hat, enter the house and scoop the small body up into her arms.

'Oh, sweetheart,' she cooed. 'I've missed you so much. Have you missed me?'

His face glowing with happiness, and his voice quivering with suppressed tears of relief and joy, James answered fervently, 'Oh, yes, Mummy. I've prayed every night that you'd come back.' His voice broke. 'You . . . you won't leave me again, will you, Mummy?'

Laughing gaily, Heather hugged the tiny form close to her voluptuous body. 'Of course I won't, silly. I'm back now and as soon as I've had a word with Jimmy, we'll be on our way. We don't want Father Christmas coming tonight and finding you not with me, do we?'

'Oh, no, Mummy, 'cos he won't know where I am, will he? Have you sent him a letter telling him where I'll be tonight?'

Heather let out another peal of laughter. 'Of course I have, darling. Now you go and sit with Bessie until I've finished talking with Jimmy, there's a good boy.'

But the child hung on to his mother, terrified to let her go.

Seeing the situation, Bessie quickly took charge. Briskly taking hold of James she said gruffly, 'You come and 'ave yer breakfast first, me lad. You don't want ter pass out in the street from lack of food.' Darting a malevolent glance over the young head, she looked directly into Heather's eyes, mouthing silently, 'Though I don't suppose it'd be the first time, would it?'

The geniality dropped from Heather's face as she returned the look of hate that flowed between her and her old adversary.

Afraid that in a minute the two women would be at each other's throats, Jimmy swiftly intervened. Leaning over the banister, he called out, 'If you'd like to come upstairs, Heather, I believe we have some business to discuss.'

The coldness in his voice sent a momentary qualm through Heather's body, then she shrugged. Jimmy and that old cow could hate her as much as they liked, it made no difference to her. Judging by the way Bessie had acted towards James, it was evident the child had wormed his way into the elderly woman's affections. Hopefully he'd had the same effect on Jimmy.

Climbing the stairs in a slow, maddening, superior manner, Heather entered the sumptuous living room and proceeded to make herself at home. Sitting down on the plush settee, she looked up at Jimmy and drawled confidently, 'Well, Jimmy, how do you like your son? He's a nice little chap, isn't he?' She gave a tinkling laugh. 'I was almost afraid he might have forgotten me. After all, children do forget quite easily, but it seems I needn't have worried. I see you've bought him new clothes, that was very thoughtful of you.'

'Cut the crap, Heather, and let's get down to business.' Jimmy's voice and eyes were like stone, but it was the loathing etched on his rugged face that chilled Heather to the bone. She hadn't expected to be welcomed with open arms, but never had she imagined her reception would be this bad.

'I'll get straight to the point, Heather. How much do you want for the child? Because that's what this is all about, isn't it? To get as much money out of me as you can. But before I part with one penny, I want proof James is really my son.'

At the mention of money, Heather's spirits rose. Delving into her handbag, she pulled out a long document and handed it to Jimmy. 'I think you'll find this is proof enough, Jimmy. It's James's birth certificate, and as you can see, you're named as his father. And as his father you're obligated to support him. What have you to say now, Jimmy?' Her lips curved into a gloating smile, Heather watched as Jimmy scanned the birth certificate. Then her smile faltered as Jimmy let out a loud, triumphant laugh.

'You're right, Heather. As his father I have a duty to support him. I also have the right to keep him here with me. And that's exactly what I intend to do. I don't, however, have any obligation to support you, but I'm a fair man, so I've decided to give you a hundred pounds, for old times' sake.'

Stunned at the unexpected turn of events, Heather was rendered speechless. Then, as the full realisation that she had been beaten at her own game sank in, Heather's lips curled back over her teeth in fury, and with a loud scream she sprang from the settee, her arm raised ready to strike out at the grinning man, but Jimmy was too quick for her. Leisurely catching hold of her arm, he drawled, 'Now, now, Heather, we don't want any unpleasantness, do we? I could decide to take back my offer. It's up to you, but I want an answer now. I'm a busy man with a full day's work ahead of me. So, what's it to be?'

Heather glared at him with hate-filled eyes. 'You bastard,' she spat at him. 'You cold-hearted, miserable bastard. Well, you can stick your paltry hundred pounds. I'm taking James with me, and there's nothing you can do about it. Unless you want your son to witness the spectacle of his parents brawling over him.'

With a sharp twist of his wrist, Jimmy sent Heather spinning across the room. 'You're taking the boy nowhere, you mercenary bitch. You thought you were so clever, didn't you, but you made three big mistakes. First of all, no court in the land would give you custody of a child, not after hearing about all these so-called uncles you seem to acquire by the bucket load. And the fact that you were prepared to sell him for the right price wouldn't go down too well either. Not even the most sympathetic of judges would hand James over to you, not after

293

hearing all the evidence concerning your character. Furthermore, it just so happens I have a very good friend who happens to be a judge. We go back a long way, me and Bernard Forsythe. If you're stupid enough to try and take me to court, it'll be simple enough to ensure Bernard is on the bench at the trial. Your second mistake was in trying to palm off a forged birth certificate on me.' Jimmy gave vent to a low growl. 'You know, Heather, I gave you more credit than you're entitled to. Surely you must know that that piece of paper wouldn't stand up in a court of law? Oh, it may be my name that's written on it, but it isn't my signature, a fact that can be easily verified. Which is a shame on your part, because if the certificate had been valid, you might have had a chance of keeping James. But your third, and by far the worse mistake was thinking you could backmail me into keeping you in a life of luxury.'

Shaking his head in amusement, Jimmy added, 'You know Heather, I had you down as a lot of things, but I never thought of you as a stupid woman, but then greed often clouds the mind, and they don't come any greedier than you.' Standing with his back to the fireplace Jimmy arched his eyebrows. 'Well, Heather, what's it to be? Are you prepared to fight me in court for James, or take the money offered? But be assured that if you do decide to take the money, it'll be the last penny you'll ever get out of me. With that thought in mind, I'd advise you to invest it wisely – it's going to have to last you a long time. So make your mind up. Like I've already said, I haven't got all day.'

Rubbing her bruised wrist, Heather tried to control her breathing. That damned birth certificate! She had paid some virtual stranger five pounds to sign Jimmy's name on the document, not stopping to think Jimmy would query its origin. She should have known better. Jimmy had always been very thorough. An hour ago, she had been filled with the prospect of receiving monthly sums of money in exchange for allowing Jimmy to see his son on a regular basis. There had also been the hope that in due course the feelings Jimmy had once had for her would return. Now all those hopes and dreams had turned to dust. For a brief, rage-filled moment she considered calling Jimmy's bluff and fighting for custody of the child, but that idea was quickly squashed. Jimmy had been right in his assumption that no court would allow her to keep James, not with the damning evidence that could be dredged up. Jimmy thought he knew all about her, but there were some things he didn't know. Things that caused her, as hard as she was, sleepless nights of shame. But those secrets would soon come to light if the law was to get involved. She had no doubt that Jimmy would hire private investigators if necessary. After all, as he had pointed out, he was an important man now, with important friends – one of them a High Court judge.

Lifting her head up proudly, she said quietly, 'All right, Jimmy, you win. I don't have any choice now, do I?'

Jimmy's eyes flickered over his former lover. If he had seen just a glimmer of real emotion in her, he might have relented, but he could detect no remorse or grief at the thought of giving up her only child. Opening a drawer in the bureau, he took out a long, white envelope and handed it to Heather.

'It's all there. You can count it if you want. After all, I wouldn't want to be accused of cheating you out of your blood money.'

Silently Heather took the envelope and placed it in her bag, carefully keeping her face averted so that Jimmy couldn't see the bitterness on her face. She may have lost the war, but the battle wasn't over yet, not by a long chalk.

'Goodbye, Jimmy. I wish I could say it's been nice seeing you again, but under the circumstances it—'

'Just a minute, Heather. Aren't you forgetting something?'

Heather turned in surprise. 'I don't think so. Unless you want a receipt for the money.'

Jimmy uttered a derisory laugh. 'As a matter of fact I did intend to make you sign a document stating that you had accepted my offer as a one-off payment, but I don't think that will be necessary now. No. I was referring to James. Don't you even want to see him one last time, or are you so heartless you intend to walk out of his life without so much as a last embrace?'

Heather lifted her shoulders in resignation. 'What good would that do? I don't see any point in prolonging the situation. All things considered, I think it would be better all round if I just slipped away quietly. I'll leave it to you to explain why his mother can't take him home with her. I hope he'll be understanding when you tell him the truth. That you've threatened me with the law if I try to take him home with me. Somehow, I don't imagine James is going to be very happy with you, Jimmy. In fact he may come to hate you as much as I do. Goodbye, Jimmy.'

Her words cut through Jimmy like a knife, then he drew himself upright. Squaring his shoulders, he said gruffly, 'I'll manage, Heather. You see, I've grown to love the boy, and in time I hope he'll learn to love me. But there's one thing I have to know before you leave. It's something that's been gnawing at the back of my mind for weeks. Why on earth didn't you marry Sean Finnegan when you had the chance? From what James has told me, the man was obviously besotted with you. He was wealthy, had what James describes as a castle set in its own grounds, and I would imagine a healthy bank balance. It doesn't make sense that a woman like you would pass up the opportunity of marriage to such a man.'

Standing by the open doorway, Heather answered softly, 'I had my reasons, but you'd never believe me. Goodbye, Jimmy.'

In a flash, Jimmy was by her side. 'Hang on, I'll walk down with you, and, Heather . . .' Jimmy gripped her elbow tightly. 'If James appears you leave the talking to me, and agree with anything I say; d'yer understand?'

Heather flicked her gaze over him disdainfully. 'My, my, your newly acquired grammar nearly deserted you then, Jimmy, but all right, I'll go along

297

with whatever you say. In fact I'd be interested to hear how you're going to explain my departure.'

Keeping a tight grip on her arm, Jimmy led Heather down the stairs, hoping and praying James wouldn't hear them, but he hadn't counted on Heather's malicious nature, or the fact that she had given in to his demands too easily.

They were at the front door when Heather turned, smiled sweetly at Jimmy, then raising her voice she called out, 'Bye, Bessie. It was a pleasure seeing you again after all these years.'

Taken by surprise, Jimmy hadn't a chance to push her out of the door before James's high-pitched voice shattered the air. 'Mummy, Mummy. Where're you going? Wait for me, Mummy, wait for me.'

His features contorted with a murderous rage, Jimmy slammed Heather up against the wall. 'You spiteful bitch,' he hissed furiously. 'You say one more word to upset James and I swear, I'll break your fucking neck, you old slag.'

All her bravado vanishing, Heather swallowed nervously and nodded, for the look in Jimmy's eyes left her in no doubt he wouldn't hesitate to carry out his threat if pushed too far.

'Whoa, there, little fellow, don't panic, your mummy's just got to go out for a little while.' Jimmy scooped the small form up into his arms and swung him high in the air. 'Anyway, weren't you going to go Christmas shopping with Amy, or have you changed your mind about getting me and Bessie a present? And your mummy, of course.'

James's small face looked from one parent to the

other, his initial panic subsiding a little at Jimmy's genial tone and manner. 'I didn't forget, but I thought Mummy was going to wait here until I got back.' His wide eyes searched Heather's face for reassurance. 'I won't be long, Mummy. Amy and me are only going down the market, not up the West End like Jimmy took me yesterday, that would take too long.'

Heather forced a smile. 'You went up the West End? My, that must have been a treat for you. It's a wonderful place to visit at this time of year. Did you enjoy yourself?'

'Oh, yes, Mummy. It was smashing. Sure, and I've never seen anything like it before. The shops were so big, Jimmy had to hold my hand all the time in case I got lost, and when we were out in the street he lifted me on his shoulders so I could see over all the people's heads. And afterwards we had dinner in a big restaurant with proper waiters in posh uniforms. I wish you could have come with us, Mummy.' His little face lit up as he recalled his excursion of the previous afternoon. 'I know, Mummy,' he cried excitedly, 'we can all go next year.' Turning to Jimmy, he asked hopefully, 'Can we, Mister?'

Jimmy gazed into the trusting, pleading eyes, his heart beating hard against his ribcage. The child would know the reality of the situation soon enough, why spoil his Christmas by telling him the truth now?

'Of course we can, son. Now you give your mummy a kiss, then go and help Bessie until Amy arrives. She should be here soon . . . Ah, speak of the devil.' Jimmy let out a sigh of relief as he spotted Amy walking towards the house.

When Amy had turned the corner she had seen the woman standing in the doorway with Jimmy and had recognised her instantly. Her steps slowing, her heart filled with sadness, she reluctantly approached the house. It looked like Becky had been right after all, for the sight of the trio framed in the open doorway made a charming picture of the perfect family.

'Sorry I'm a bit late, Jimmy. I had to get some last-minute shopping. Hello, James, I see you're all dressed and ready to go down the market.' Deliberately ignoring the red-haired woman's presence, Amy wedged herself between Jimmy and Heather, her arms held out to James. 'Come on, love. We'd better get going before all the bargains are gone. See you later, Jimmy, I won't keep him out too long.'

'Bye, Mummy. I'll see you later,' James called out happily.

Heather and Jimmy stood side by side as they waved Amy and James off, but as soon as they had disappeared from view, they dropped their pretence of amiability.

'Well, I'll be off then,' Heather drawled casually. 'Though I wouldn't like to be in your shoes when you have to explain to James why his mother isn't coming back for him.' Shaking her head maliciously, she murmured, 'No, Jimmy, dear, I wouldn't like to be in your shoes at all. He's going to hate you for what you've done, and no amount of money or presents is going to make him love you like he loves me. You—'

A furious screech sounded behind them, causing Heather and Jimmy to jump in startled surprise. Then Bessie appeared, her face bearing the murderous look

300

that had recently been mirrored on Jimmy's own. Brandishing a large wooden rolling pin, she advanced on Heather.

'Get outta here, yer old trollop, before I bash yer brains in. And don't think I wouldn't, 'cos I'd gladly swing fer yer if it meant my Jimmy and the boy were rid of yer fer good. Now, piss off if yer know what's good fer yer, and don't show yer face round 'ere again, or yer won't 'ave any face left ter show.'

Staggering, backwards under the elderly woman's wrath, Heather shot one last venomous look at both of them.

'You'll be sorry for this, Jimmy, and you, you old bag . . .'

If there was one thing in life apart from money that Heather was proud of, it was her self-esteem, but that characteristic pride that she held so dear was shattered as Bessie, her arm raised high, brought down the rolling pin, narrowly missing Heather by a matter of inches. All thoughts of maintaining a dignified exit dissolved in a flash of fear and, without looking back, Heather ran for her life, conscious of the neighbours' curious stares at the sight of the well-dressed woman running pell mell down the street with Bessie's strident words of invective following her.

Stopping at the top of the street, Heather slowed down and flagged down a passing cab. Once safely inside the carriage, she began to breathe more easily, her mind seething with rage at the humiliation she had suffered in front of the common rabble who occupied the street where Jimmy lived in such sumptuous surroundings.

301

Calmer now, she thought back to Jimmy's query as to why she hadn't married Sean Finnegan. The answer was simple. She hadn't married Sean because she hadn't wanted to spend the rest of her days in that godforsaken rambling house in the back of beyond with the nearest neighbours over fifty miles away. Heather had always loved the bright lights and night life of London, and there had hardly been a day during those eight years when she hadn't wished she was back home in England.

When she had first realised she was pregnant it would have been the simplest thing in the world to have passed the child off as Sean's, but to have done that would have meant tying herself to him for life. She had made up a story about her landlord forcing himself on her the night before she had met Sean in the park, adding tearfully that she had been too ashamed to tell him the truth at the time. Sean had been deeply hurt to discover the child wasn't his, but had raised him as if he were his own, while constantly pressurising Heather to marry him and allow him to adopt the child he regarded as his own flesh and blood. Yet above all she had never stopped thinking about Jimmy, always hoping that one day she would be able to return to London and pick up where they had left off, especially as she would have had the advantage of presenting him with a son, a son he hadn't known existed. She had consoled herself with the notion that even if Jimmy hadn't wanted her back, he would have accepted her if only for the sake of his child. Of course, if she'd known Sean was going to drop dead at the relatively young age of fifty she would have married him years ago. If she had, she'd now be a rich woman, for the house and grounds alone had been worth thousands, and that was without the considerable sum of money Sean had accumulated over the years. Numbly she thought of how her life could have been if only she'd married him. For a start she'd have sold the house, cleared out his bank account and been on the first boat back to England before he was cold in his grave. Now, through her own stupidity, she was penniless, except for the measly hundred pounds Jimmy had so graciously given her. Such an amount would have been considered a fortune to most people, but Heather had become accustomed to the good life living with Sean, and she wasn't going to go back to the life of scrimping and saving she'd endured throughout her youth.

'Where to, darlin'?' The cabbie shouted through the hatch in the roof of the cab.

Where to indeed, Heather thought miserably. Then her face cleared, her eyes narrowing, as a germ of an idea entered her mind.

'Nowhere. Just wait here, please, until I tell you otherwise.'

The cabbie shrugged. 'All right, darlin'. You're paying.'

Heather smiled grimly. After today she wouldn't be the only one paying. And pay they would. Sitting back more comfortably on the padded seat, Heather prepared herself to bide her time, waiting patiently for the opportunity to strike.

CHAPTER TWENTY-ONE

The East End markets were always busy at week-ends, but this being Christmas Eve, Roman Road market was packed almost to the point of bursting, with everyone on the look-out for a last-minute bargain. Which was a delight for the stall holders, but not so pleasant for the customers, who were forced to move along the long, narrow road at a snail's pace, while fighting their way past the huge throngs of people crowding knee deep at most of the stalls. Normally Amy loved this time of year, and the hustle and bustle of last-minute Christmas shopping combined with the good-natured camaraderie and high spirits that could only be captured at this almost magical time in the season. But today she was in a hurry, as too was her small charge, though both of them for different reasons. The child was anxious to get back to see his mother, and Amy was equally anxious to get to Richard's factory and try and have a word with him concerning Phil's disastrous state of affairs.

The animosity she had first felt after discovering what her brother had done had quickly disappeared. It had never been in Amy's nature to hold a grudge, and while she couldn't condone his behaviour, she could understand he couldn't help himself. Gambling was like an illness. Phil couldn't help the way he was. Since the day Jimmy had sacked him, Phil hadn't left the house. In fact he'd hardly left his room, except to make himself a meal. Only yesterday, as she'd been about to go out, Phil had been on his way to his room carrying a breakfast tray when the milkman had knocked on the door. At the sound, Phil had turned white with fear, his hands trembling so badly Amy had had to take the tray off him before it crashed to the floor. Amy knew he owed money to someone called 'Big George', because Phil, having no one else to confide in, had told Amy all his troubles. And with each day that passed, the interest on the debt kept rising, and there was no way it could be paid off. Phil was too frightened to leave the house to look for work in case the bookie's thugs were lying in wait for him, Becky couldn't go out to work, not with Maude to look after, and Amy herself certainly couldn't earn that sort of money. Even if she took Jimmy up on his offer of working for him, the wages, though they amounted to three times what she earned in the teashop, still wouldn't be enough to cover Phil's debts. There was only one way Amy could think of to get Phil out of trouble, and that was to go and see Richard and ask for his help. She knew she was the only one with any hope of succeeding in getting Richard to lend her the money. Phil certainly wouldn't dare ask, not after the way Richard had treated him on their last meeting. And Becky wouldn't ask Richard for a favour even if she was starving to death. So it was up to Amy. Only she had to be quick, just in case Richard decided to leave work early today on account of it being Christmas Eve.

Finally shoving her way to the end of the market, Amy, still gripping James's hand tightly for fear of losing him in the crush, leant back against a wall and gave a big sigh of relief. 'Phew! That was a bit of a tight squeeze, wasn't it, love?' She grinned down at the boy who was still hanging onto her hand for dear life.

'I got squashed, Amy. And everyone kept stepping on my feet, and pushing me in the back. Sure, and I wish Jimmy had come with us, then he could have carried me on his shoulders, like he did when we went up the West End.'

Amy arched her eyebrows playfully. 'If that's a hint for me to give you a lift, then you're wasting your time, young man. I'm worn out myself. Anyway, it's only a ten-minute walk home from here, so come on, best foot forward, my little soldier.'

James giggled. 'You are funny, Amy, so you are. And I wasn't hinting, honest I wasn't.' He lowered his eyes, then glanced up impishly. 'Though I wouldn't say no, if you were offering.'

Amy's laughter joined his as hand in hand they

made their way back to the house with James chattering all the way.

'It was nice of Jimmy to give me the money to buy my presents, wasn't it, Amy?'

'Well, he is your dad, after all, James, and that's what dads do for their children.' A silence fell on them as they approached the top of the road leading to Jimmy's house. Then, picking her words carefully, Amy asked, 'What do you think of Jimmy being your dad, James? I mean, do you like him, even just a little?'

'Oh, yes, Amy. I like him a lot. I didn't at first, but that's only because I was scared. He's been very kind to me, and it's nice having a dad. It'd be even nicer if him and my mummy lived together, like other mummies and daddies do.' Lifting his large green eyes to Amy's he asked hopefully, 'D'ye think they will, Amy? I mean, live together some day?'

Amy averted her eyes. *God forbid!* she thought, horrified at the mere notion. There was only one woman Amy wanted to see installed in that house as Jimmy's wife, and it certainly wasn't that painted trollop she'd encountered earlier.

Quickly changing the subject, Amy let go of James's hand and shouted brightly, 'I know, let's play a game. I'll count to five, then we'll start to run. Last one home's a stinker.'

With a whoop of joy, James bounded off, his short, sturdy legs racing over the cobbled pavement.

Shifting the small bag of presents James had bought to her other hand, Amy was about to give chase when the door of a waiting Hackney cab was rudely thrust open, narrowly missing hitting Amy full in the face.

Startled, Amy was about to make some form of protest when she saw the red-haired woman jump from the carriage and run in James's direction. In a flash Amy knew what the woman's intentions were. Obviously Jimmy had been as good as his word when he had declared he would be keeping James. Now it seemed Heather Mills had other ideas. Well! Not if she could help it. Her face set in grim lines of determination, Amy raced after the running woman. Within three long strides, Amy caught up with Heather, and, without stopping to think, grabbed at the abundant hair and pulled as hard as she could. Caught by surprise, Heather let out a cry of pain, but before she could retaliate, Amy kicked her legs out from under her and, with a smothered shout of frustrated rage, Heather went down onto the cobbled pavement like a sack of coal.

James, still playing the game, was blissfully unaware of the drama unfolding behind him, his only thought being to beat Amy back to the house.

Without even pausing for breath, Amy was off like lightning, her long legs eating up the short distance that separated her from James. By this time, James was only a few yards from the house, and with a quick, fervent glance over her shoulder, Amy saw a bedraggled Heather, no longer looking so high and mighty, being helped back into the carriage by an amused cabbie. Knowing the danger to James was over, Amy slowed her footsteps, allowing the child to reach the house first.

'I won, Amy. I won,' he cried out in delight.

Panting for breath, Amy smiled weakly. 'Yes, you did, love. Now, let's get inside quick, otherwise everyone will be wondering where we've got to.'

Bessie answered the door, her lined face creased in worried frowns. 'Where on earth 'ave yer been? Jimmy's been going . . .' Roughly Amy pushed her way into the house, slamming the heavy door behind her. Bessie looked first at the sweating face of Amy, then down to the excited child, before returning her attention to the perspiring young girl.

Still breathing heavily, Amy mouthed over James's head, 'She tried to snatch him in the street. I only just got to him in time.'

Bessie stepped back, her hand flying to her mouth. 'Oh, me Gawd! Did the little 'un see anything?' she whispered back, her anxious eyes darting to the child, who was running towards the kitchen, eager to get his carefully chosen presents wrapped and delivered.

Amy shook her head tiredly. 'No, thank goodness. He was running on ahead at the time. But, oh, Bessie, I was that frightened. I didn't stop to think. I just grabbed her hair and knocked her to the ground, then chased after James. The last I saw, she was getting into a carriage at the top of the road.'

'Bessie, Bessie, quick. We've got to wrap up the presents, but you mustn't look at yours, else it won't be a surprise, a'tall.'

James had run back into the hall to find out what was keeping Bessie and Amy.

Tenderly lifting the child into her arms, Bessie buried her face into his neck. 'All right, me lad. I won't look, I promise.' Pulling her head back, she stared deep into the boy's eyes and summoned up a smile. 'Tell yer what, lad. Let's me and you go and wrap up the presents now, while Amy goes and has a word with yer dad, eh?'

James's eyes sought Amy's. 'Don't let my mummy come down until we've finished wrapping the presents, will you, Amy?'

Her lips quivering, Amy managed a smile. 'Of course I won't. Now you go with Bessie like a good boy, and don't come upstairs until I call you, understand?'

The dark head nodded. 'All right, Amy. But don't be long. Sure, and I can't wait to see my mummy's face when I give her her present.'

Amy had barely reached the top step when Jimmy appeared on the landing, his face, like Bessie's had been, etched with worry. And, like Bessie, he also exclaimed, 'Where on earth have you . . .'

Wearily Amy held up her hand to silence him. Sweeping past the towering figure, she walked unsteadily into the room and flopped down heavily onto the nearest chair and repeated what she had just told Bessie, her breathless words hitting Jimmy in the stomach like a physical blow. What a fool he'd been to think that Heather would give up her meal ticket so easily. If Amy hadn't acted so promptly . . . A shudder rippled through his lean body. The thought didn't bear thinking about.

Clenching his teeth, his mind swiftly clicking into

gear, Jimmy growled, 'Well, she's not going to get another chance, I can promise you that.'

Amy shook her head. 'What can you do, Jimmy? With the best will in the world, you can't watch over him every minute of every day. And you can't keep him cooped up here like a prisoner either. He's got to go out sometime, even if only for a breath of fresh air. And what about his schooling? You can take him back and forth each day, but what's to stop Heather trying to take him out during school hours, or at play time. She is his mother, after all, and I can't imagine any teacher trying to stop a mother taking her child out of school; especially a woman like Heather. You don't argue with someone like her.'

Jimmy stopped his pacing and stared down fondly at the pretty girl. 'It didn't stop you though, did it, Amy.' Then he threw his head back and let out a roar of laughter.

'Lord! But I'd have given anything to have seen Heather sprawled in the dust. She must have thought it would be an easy matter to take James from you, but she underestimated you, didn't she, love?' Remembering the incident when he had tried to see Rebecca, Jimmy grinned, adding wryly, 'Like a lot of people do, myself included.' Lowering himself down beside her, Jimmy took hold of her hand and said softly, 'How can I ever thank you enough, love? I already owe you so much, and now this. I don't know what to say, except that if you ever need anything, you only have to ask.'

Amy wet her lips nervously. Could she? Could she possibly dare ask Jimmy for the money Phil

needed? He would give it to her, she had no doubt
on that score, but if she asked him now, it might
seem as if she was capitalising on the part she had
played in preventing Heather from abducting James.
No, Richard was her best hope.

Now the unpleasant incident was over, Amy was
suddenly aware of how fast the time was flying by.
Getting to her feet she mumbled, 'Don't be silly,
Jimmy. Did you think I would stand by and let
that odious woman take James from you without
a fight?' A shy smile touched her lips. 'Though I
can't believe I attacked her so viciously. I just saw
red. I've never hit anyone before in my life. And I
didn't just hit her, I really hurt her, and . . . and, you
know what's worse, Jimmy?' She raised her eyes to
his, and the glimmer of amusement she felt on her
face was reflected in Jimmy's as she added proudly,
'I really enjoyed it. Isn't that an awful thing to admit?
But when I grabbed her hair, I pulled so hard, some
of it came away in my hands, and when I knocked her
legs out from under her and saw her fall, it was all I
could do not to give her a good kicking as well.'

As she spoke, Jimmy could visualise the scene,
and wished once again he could have been there to
witness Heather's humiliation, her precious dignity
shattered, with all the neighbours hanging out of
their windows looking on. Then his amusement
vanished as quickly as it had come. That woman
wouldn't stop, not now. If she had been determined
to snatch James before, she would redouble her
efforts after her humiliating experience. Always one
for quick thinking, Jimmy's mind sprang into action.

He had to get the boy away from here, away from
Heather's clutches. And the only way he could be
sure his son was safe was to take him as far away
from this house as possible. He was so wrapped up
in his thoughts that he forgot Amy's presence until
she spoke.

'Look, Jimmy, I've got to got out for a while. I
won't be too long, but . . .'

Jimmy whirled on her, his face aghast. 'What! You
can't leave now, Amy. I need you here. James will
be up at any minute looking for his mother. I don't
know what I'm going to tell him, but whatever I say
isn't going to make his pain any less when he finds
she's left him again.'

Amy, her face set, answered reluctantly, 'I'm
sorry, Jimmy, but, like I said, I've got to go out. It's
. . . it's urgent, or else I wouldn't leave, you know
I wouldn't. You'll just have to manage without me.
And you won't be on your own. Bessie will help.'
She got to her feet. 'I'll be as quick as I can, but I
really must go now.'

In an instant Jimmy was barring her way, his
eyes pleading. 'Please, Amy. Whatever it is, can't it
wait? Can't I help with whatever this urgent matter is?'

Amy's gaze faltered, her heart beating rapidly.
Could she ask Jimmy? After all, he knew her better
than to think she would take advantage of him,
and it would save her the ordeal of facing Richard
and begging for money on Phil's behalf. Her mind
struggled with her conscience, and she was on the
verge of confiding in Jimmy when the door burst

open and James ran into the room clutching a gaily wrapped present.

Smiling broadly, he looked at Jimmy and Amy, then, his eyes darting around the large room, his smile faltered. 'Where's Mummy? I've got her present. Bessie helped me wrap it up. Where is she, Mister?' The child's voice rose higher, betraying his growing fear. 'Has she gone shopping again? She will be back soon, won't she, Mister?'

Jimmy and Amy exchanged anguished glances, their sorrowful expressions not lost on the boy, who immediately let out a loud wail and began to rush around the room as if expecting to find his mother hiding behind the furniture.

His throat dry, Jimmy said kindly, 'Come here, mate. I want to talk to you.'

James backed away, his eyes accusing. 'What have you done with my mummy? She said she'd wait for me. She promised . . . She promised! What have you done with her?'

Frantic now, he looked to Amy for reassurance, but saw only a deep sadness reflected in the girl's lovely features, and he knew. Knew that once again his mother had deserted him. Before Jimmy and Amy's eyes, the boy seemed to age. His head dropped onto his chin, and his small shoulders slumped in despair as he whispered, 'She's gone again, hasn't she?'

His heart wrenched with sadness, Jimmy swept the forlorn figure up into his arms. 'I'm sorry, James. I'm so very sorry.'

For a few brief moments the boy remained still

against Jimmy's chest, then, like a wild animal, he began to scream and hit out at the man holding him.

'Let me go. Let me go, Mister. I've got to find my mummy. I want my mummy. I want my mummy.'

Jimmy held on tighter to the squirming body, his heart almost bursting in torment at his son's anguish.

Unable to witness the poignant scene any longer, Amy backed from the room, her throat thick with tears. There was nothing she could do to help Jimmy now, he would have to deal with the situation himself. Before letting herself out of the house, she told Bessie that Jimmy needed her, then quietly, her eyes blinded by tears, she took a deep breath to fortify herself for the meeting with her uncle.

When Bessie entered the room she stopped dead in her tracks, her hand clutching at her throat as she saw her Jimmy sitting on the settee holding the boy tight in his arms. The only sound in the room was the child's quiet sobs. Jimmy sensed her presence and made a motion with his head for her to leave, and Bessie, for once unable to help her beloved Jimmy, dumbly left the man and boy alone.

Stroking the soft hair, Jimmy murmured words of comfort, until the child, his tiny body quivering with emotion, pulled away from Jimmy's grasp and asked haltingly, 'She's not coming back, is she, Mister? My mummy's not coming back. She's left me for good, hasn't she?'

Swallowing hard, Jimmy held the quietly sobbing

boy at arm's length and said tenderly, 'No, son, she's not coming back.' For the child's sake, Jimmy attempted to justify Heather's desertion. 'She wanted to stay, but she couldn't. You see, she wants what's best for you, and . . . Well, she thinks I can look after you better than she can. That's why she left. It doesn't mean she doesn't love you, she does, she loves you very much . . .'

The boy squirmed in Jimmy's arms, then, his voice low and resigned, he answered sorrowfully, 'No, she doesn't, Mister. My mummy doesn't love me. I tried to make . . . make her love me, I . . . I tried so hard, but . . . but I just couldn't.' Lifting his gaze to Jimmy's, he asked fearfully, 'Can I stay here till after Christmas, Mister? I'll be good, honest I will.'

Jimmy's eyes flew open in amazement. 'Of course you can stay here. You're going to stay with me for ever. Haven't you been listening to me, son? Your mummy left you with me so that I could take care of you. And that's what I want to do, if you'll let me.'

Like an old man, James shook his head. 'Thanks, Mister, but you'll get fed up with me after a while. All my uncles did, except for my Uncle Sean. But . . . but, if I can just stay here for Christmas, you can put me in the orphanage afterwards.'

Jimmy almost leapt in the air at the child's mournful words. Grabbing James's arms, he looked deep into the frightened green eyes and said firmly, 'Now you listen to me, James. You're not going to any orphanage. Good God! Whatever put that idea into your head?'

The boy's shoulders lifted dispiritedly. 'My mummy

said she'd have to put me into an orphanage one day, because she couldn't afford to keep me.'

With a loud groan of despair, Jimmy cried, 'Oh, son, you poor little sod. Orphanages are only for children who haven't any parents. And you have. At least, you have me. I'm your dad, James, and nothing or no one is ever going to take you away from me again.'

The child stared back into Jimmy's eyes, searching for some sign that maybe this man was telling the truth. But he had been let down so many times during his relatively short time in England, he didn't trust anyone any more. All of his new-found uncles had started off being kind to him, but they had soon grown tired of having him around, even though he had tried his very best to be a good boy. But in this man's eyes, James could see only love and tenderness, and for the first time since Sean Finnegan's death, James felt the first stirring of hope that maybe, just maybe, he had found a real home at last. A place where he could stay for ever without living with the constant fear of rejection.

Placing his small hands either side of Jimmy's face, he asked timidly, 'You're not just saying that, are you, Mister? You really won't get fed up with me and put me into an orphanage.'

His entire body swelling with love, Jimmy gulped loudly and, keeping the boy's gaze steady, he said thickly, 'I'll never get fed up with you, James. Your place is with me now . . . That is, if you want me.'

Fresh tears spurted from the child's eyes, and with a cry of relief he threw his arms around Jimmy's neck and hung on for dear life.

'I . . . I want you. I want to stay with you and Bessie . . . and Amy.'

Jimmy felt the child's tears wet against his neck and gave up the struggle to hold back his own. He thought in this quiet, precious moment he couldn't feel any more emotional, until the boy, his arms still clinging to Jimmy's neck, whispered, 'I love you, Mister. Can . . . Can I call you Dad, please, Mister? I've always wanted a daddy. Can I call you Dad, Mister, please?'

For an answer, Jimmy held fast to his son and, his voice thick with tears, murmured, 'I'd like that, son. I'd like that very much.'

CHAPTER TWENTY-TWO

'Well! Well! This is a pleasant surprise. And to what do I owe the honour of this unexpected visit, my love?'

Richard Fisher, his fleshy face alight with pleasure at the sight of his lovely young cousin, came from around his desk and took her in his arms.

'You were lucky to find me here. I was just about to leave. There's still a lot to do for the party tonight, and seeing as Rebecca is still unwell, I've decided to take the worry off of her and deal with the preparations myself.'

Squirming uncomfortably, Amy released herself from Richard's embrace, her stomach churning at what she had to say next. Gathering all of her courage, she asked quietly, 'Uncle Richard, I've come to ask you a favour . . . Not for me,' she added hurriedly. 'It's for Phil.'

Richard stepped back, his beady eyes narrowing

suspiciously, his mind already knowing where this conversation was heading. 'Phil, eh? Well, it doesn't take a genius to work out why you've come to me, if it concerns that no-good brother of yours. I suppose you want me to bail him out of the mess he's got himself into, eh! Is that it, Amy? Is that why you've come to me?'

Deeply embarrassed, Amy lowered her head and whispered, 'Yes. I know he's done wrong, Uncle Richard, but he's truly sorry for the trouble he's got himself into. And . . . and I'm not asking you to give me the money he owes, it'll only be a loan. I'll pay it back somehow. And once Phil's paid back his debts, he won't be afraid to leave the house, and . . . and he'll soon find work, then together we'll repay you as soon as possible.'

Moving away from Amy's tempting body, Richard strutted around the small office, his hands clasped tightly behind his back in the manner of a man of importance. 'I must say I'm surprised you would want to help Phil after the despicable way he treated you and Rebecca. I knew he was never the most reliable of men, but I never had him down as a man who would steal from his own sisters.'

Amy's jaw dropped in stunned surprise. Neither she nor Rebecca had mentioned Phil's betrayal to anyone, so how . . . !

Richard saw the look etched on her face and gave a triumphant laugh. 'Oh, don't look so surprised, Amy, love. There's not much I don't know. Word gets around, especially in a place like this.' Waving towards the window that overlooked the shop floor,

320

he said slyly, 'I employ over fifty people in this warehouse, all of whom live in the East End. And like I said, word soon gets around. Still, I admire your loyalty, though I can't say Phil deserves it. I doubt Rebecca would be so forgiving.'

Amy was beginning to feel the strain of the day creeping up on her, and in an uncharacteristic mood, she said stiffly, 'I don't have a lot of time, Uncle Richard. Jimmy is expecting me back at the house. If you won't help me, then just say so, and I won't take up any more of your valuable time.'

His eyebrows rising in surprise at the steely tone in the usually pliable young girl's voice, Richard instantly changed tack. 'Now, now, Amy, love. I didn't say I wouldn't help . . . Here, take your coat off. Make yourself comfortable, while I pull down the blinds so we can have a bit of privacy. We don't want that rabble below gawping in on us, and starting more rumours, now do we, eh?'

'I'm not stopping, Uncle Richard. Like I said, I have to get back to Jimmy.'

Pulling down the blind, Richard came over to where Amy was standing by the desk. Clucking and making a fuss as one might do with an errant child, he began to unbutton her coat. 'Don't worry about getting back to Jimmy's, love. I'll be leaving soon myself, I'll give you a lift. So you might as well take your coat off and have a hot drink before we go, or else you won't feel the benefit of it when we get out into the cold.'

Somewhat more relaxed at the genial tone in Richard's voice, Amy took off her coat and sat

down while Richard called down to the shop floor
for a tray of hot tea and biscuits to be sent up.

When the refreshments had been delivered and
consumed, Amy stirred restlessly on her chair while
Richard busied himself in making smalltalk, especially about the forthcoming party, which was the
last thing on Amy's mind. Just as she was beginning
to think he would never get to the matter in hand,
Richard rose and walked over to a small safe in the
corner of the room. Spinning the dial, he opened
the steel door, took out the contents and reseated
himself behind the desk.

'This must be your lucky day, love. I had planned
to leave an hour ago, but some problem came up that
I had to deal with. If I'd left when I meant to, you'd
not only have missed me, I wouldn't have had the
money to give you. This lot' – he pointed at the pile
of notes and coins spread across the desk – 'would
have been safely deposited in the bank by now. Well
now, just how much does that reprobate brother of
yours need to dig himself out of the hole he's landed
himself in?'

Amy felt her entire body slump with relief. So
Richard was going to help after all. Thank you,
God! She sent up a silent fervent prayer. At least
with Phil's problems resolved for the time being, it
would be one less thing for her to worry about.

Smiling gratefully, Amy answered shyly, 'I'm not
quite sure, Uncle Richard. He said he owes some
bookie over sixty pounds, but that there'll be some
interest on top of that by now.' Her trusting eyes
looking to the man she called uncle for advice, she

asked, 'How much do you think that interest will be, Uncle Richard?'

Savouring his moment of power, Richard sat back in the leather chair, his fingers held against pursed lips. 'Sixty pounds, you say. Well now, by my reckoning, and I'm no authority on these matters, you understand, not like your Jimmy Jackson . . .' He paused before carrying on. 'I'm surprised you didn't ask Mr Jackson for the money. After all, he does seem remarkably fond of you and Rebecca. Seeing as how he's just paid a small fortune for her nursing, I'm sure he wouldn't have hesitated to give you the money if you'd asked.'

Amy fidgeted awkwardly on the hard chair. 'I'm sure he wouldn't have, Uncle Richard. But this is a family matter, and seeing as you're family, I thought it would be better if I came to you.'

Richard gave a satisfied smile. 'Quite right too, love. Mr Jackson may be a big man around these parts, and he has shown a good deal of interest in our affairs. But like you say, he isn't family. You did the right thing in coming to me.' He gave a benevolent smile. 'After all, that's what families are all about, aren't they? Helping one another in times of trouble.' Turning his attention back to the pile of money on the desk, he began counting out a bundle of notes. 'I think eighty pounds should cover Phil's debt, and any outstanding interest he might have incurred . . . Oh, what the hell! Let's make it a hundred, just to be on the safe side.'

Amy sat speechless as she watched Richard count out the notes, and felt a lurch of fear. One hundred pounds! How on earth were she and Phil ever going to be able to pay back that huge amount of money? For a wild, reckless moment she was tempted to call the whole thing off. It would take years to pay back a sum of that magnitude. And when Rebecca found out, and find out she would, because she, Amy, would have to tell her . . . Amy shivered nervously. Becky would go mad when she told her, but what else could she do in the circumstances but to take Richard's kind offer and hope and pray Phil would get himself a decent job and stay away from the bookies in future? He must do, he must. Especially after the fright he'd had, surely he wouldn't be so stupid as to risk the same thing happening again. Her mind made up, Amy drew back her slim shoulders and took the money, albeit reluctantly, and placed it carefully in her bag.

'Thank you, Uncle Richard, you don't know what a relief it is to have this worry lifted from my mind. And I'll . . . I mean, we'll, me and Phil, we'll pay back every penny. It will take a long while, I'm afraid, but you'll get it all back in time.' She smiled gratefully, and added impishly, 'With interest, of course.'

Glancing at the clock on the office wall, she cried in alarm, 'Goodness, I had no idea I'd been here that long. Are you ready to leave yet, Uncle Richard? Jimmy will be wondering what's happened to me.'

Scooping up the remainder of the money, Richard quickly stuffed it into a large briefcase and rose to his feet. 'Here, let me help you on with your coat, then we'll get going. I didn't realise the time either. I have to get to the bank before going to the house to make sure everything's in order for the party preparations.'

Feeling as if a load had been lifted from her shoulders, Amy happily let Richard help her on with her coat. She was about to do up the buttons when Richard's hands closed over hers.

'I know I've said it before, but I'll say it again. Phil's a very lucky man to have someone like you to care about him. You're a lovely young woman, Amy, and I'm very fond of you, you know that, don't you?'

Amy laughed. 'Of course I do, Uncle Richard. You've always been very kind to me, and now this.' She pointed to her handbag where the money rested. 'I don't know how I'll ever be able to thank you enough.'

Impulsively she leant forward and kissed Richard's cheek, and the feel of her soft lips against his face finally broke the control Richard had been holding in check for years.

Grabbing her to him, he held her slim body against his, his arms circling her waist. 'You don't have to pay back the money, you know, Amy, love. We could come to some arrangement . . . if you know what I mean. It'd be our little secret.'

Richard had held Amy in his arms many times over the years, but this time, she began to feel uncomfortable. And what did he mean about coming to some arrangement? Because of her trusting nature and innocent character, she didn't immediately understand what Richard meant. Then she felt his hand begin to wander over her body, and in that moment she knew. Knew, but still refused to believe what was happening. This was a man she'd known and trusted

325

since she was a small child not much older than James. But when Richard's wet, slobbering lips nuzzled against her neck, and his hand moved down to stroke her buttocks, Amy could deny what was happening no longer. Disgusted and frightened, she began to struggle, while pleading, 'Please, Uncle Richard, don't . . . Please, don't,' but his hands continued to wander over parts of her body that had never been touched before.

'Oh, Amy, my own darling Amy. You must know how I feel about you. How I've always felt about you. Be nice to me, Amy. Be nice to me, and you need never have to worry about money ever again.'

Sobbing wildly, her heart beating so fast she could feel it knocking against her ribcage, Amy continued to struggle and plead for Richard to let her go. But Richard was past reasoning with. Pulling at the top buttons of her dress, he slipped a fat, clammy hand inside her chemise. It was then that Amy, terrified beyond reason, let out a loud scream that shattered the stillness of the office.

The piercing sound brought Richard sharply back to his senses. Frightened that someone would come to see what was happening he quickly stepped back, his hands held out in abject apology. 'Oh, my God! Amy, Amy, love, I'm sorry. I don't know what came over me. Look . . . Look, Amy, please. You won't tell anyone, will you? I swear it'll never happen again. Please, Amy, tell me you'll keep quiet and I promise I'll . . .'

'Dear me, have I come at an inconvenient time, Richard? I can always come back later, if you wish.'

Richard spun round to see Ivy framed in the

doorway, but before he could utter a word, Amy, her face streaming with tears, her innocence finally and irretrievably shattered for ever, ran from the room, nearly knocking over Ivy in her desperate need to get away from the man who had not merely betrayed her trust, as Phil had done, but had also stripped her of the last precious vestige of childhood.

Closing the door behind the fleeing young girl, Ivy strolled into the office, her face betraying none of the contempt she was feeling towards this man who was soon to become her husband.

Behind her, Richard was babbling wildly, 'Now, look, Ivy. It's not what you think. The girl came to me for money to get that worthless brother of hers out of debt. She was in a terrible state when she arrived, and when I tried to comfort her, she . . . she just went hysterical.'

Flickering her eyes over the red, sweating fat face, Ivy felt the gorge rise in her stomach. She knew what she had seen, and her heart went out to the pretty young girl for the nauseous ordeal she must have suffered at the grubby hands of the man she looked on as her uncle.

If Ivy wasn't in such dire straits, she would call off the wedding here and now. Unfortunately she was in no position to do that. Pulling up the blind that Richard had lowered to keep his employees from looking in, Ivy fixed her eyes unseeingly on the shop floor, unaware of the curious gazes being levelled up at her from below, her mind preoccupied with her financial problems. Only ten days ago she had been a wealthy woman, all of her money left to her by her two previous husbands securely tied up in stocks and shares. Now those same stocks and shares that had kept her comfortably off for years had gone, her carefully invested money wiped out after a disastrous day's trading on the Stock Market.

Before the catastrophic event that had left her virtually penniless, she had already been having second thoughts about marrying Richard, especially when he'd told her he planned to move back into his old home until he could sell it and move to somewhere more salubrious. The idea of sharing a house with that obnoxious old cow Maude had sent Ivy's hackles rising, but Richard had been adamant. It was then the first doubts had begun to creep in. She was comfortably off, she still had her looks, and she loved her house where she'd lived for many happy years, and had no intention of selling it. Now everything had changed. The house was the only possession she had left, but the house was no good to her without the means to run it. She could sell it and move to a smaller place and still have a tidy bit of money left over, but how long would that last her? No! Her only hope of remaining in the luxury she had enjoyed for over twenty years was to marry Richard. But by God, the instant that ring was on her finger, he would never know another minute's peace. She still wanted a child, but that child needn't be fathered by her husband. There were plenty of men who would be only too willing to help her in that department. Then, if and when she found herself pregnant, she would allow Richard access to her body, just the once, so that the child, if there was one, would have a legitimate name.

Composing her face into a loving smile, she turned and said sweetly, 'Don't be silly, Richard. I never imagined for a moment that anything untoward was going on. After all, you may not be the girl's uncle in the eyes of the law, but you've always behaved like one towards her. And what sort of man would be so despicable as to take advantage of his own niece, especially one as young and innocent as your Amy?'

Richard peered anxiously into Ivy's face, searching for some sign of ridicule or contempt, and found only a genuine smile of complete amusement that she could ever think such a thing of him. Wiping his perspiring face with a damp linen handkerchief he muttered, 'Of course. Naturally, I wouldn't dream of doing such a thing. I'm glad you understand, my dear. Some women might have got the wrong idea.'

Ivy smiled back sweetly, 'Oh, you don't have to worry about that, Richard, darling. I never get the wrong idea about anything – or anyone for that matter. I'm a very astute woman.'

Again Richard's eyes darted to Ivy's face, his guilty conscience tormenting him, then he relaxed. Ivy didn't suspect a thing, and Amy wouldn't say anything, he was sure of that. She would be too ashamed to tell anyone what had transpired between them. Even if she did, it would be her word against his, and Amy had never been one to cause trouble.

It had been a close shave, but he had got away with it. Providing Amy kept her mouth shut.

329

CHAPTER TWENTY-THREE

The skies had already begun to darken, the keen December air turning to a biting coldness, but still the streets were humming with crowds of people, rushing to and fro in a mad dash to get their last bits and pieces before heading back to the warmth of their homes. Hordes of children ran alongside their harassed mothers; their faces, although stinging from the icy wind, were bright and excited at the prospect of the forthcoming visit from Father Christmas and what he might leave in the stockings or pillowcases they planned to hang at the foot of their beds.

Amy sat on a street bench, her mind oblivious to her surroundings or the coldness that was beginning to seep through her heavy coat into her bones. All she could think of was what had happened in Richard's office, and every now and then she shuddered at the memory of his hands on her body

330

and his wet mouth on her neck. It was like a nightmare, but unlike any other bad dream she'd ever had. She still couldn't believe it had happened, and cursed herself for being a naive fool. All these years Becky had tried to warn her not to be alone with Richard, and Amy had laughed her sister's warnings off, thinking Becky was overreacting simply because she didn't like Richard, and never had. But Becky had been right all along. Thumping her knee with a mittened hand, Amy groaned silently. Oh, why hadn't she listened to Becky? But she'd never had any reason to distrust Richard. He had always been so kind and loving towards her, spoiling her at times with little treats, and telling her not to tell Becky, else he'd get into trouble. Closing her eyes, Amy looked back at those times. She could see her and Richard, their heads close together, herself only a child willing to play along with the game. And all the time he had been thinking of her in that way. Again she shuddered. Every inch of her skin seemed to be crawling with unseen insects, the deeply unpleasant sensation reminding her once again of Richard's hands on her body, but still she was unable to move from the hard, cold bench. Even if she could rouse herself, where would she go? Not home, no, definitely not home. Richard would be there organising the party for tonight, and she knew that if he were so much as to lay a finger on her, she would start screaming. And once the pain and humiliation that was racking both her mind and body was allowed free rein, Amy was afraid she might not be able to stop. Then there was Becky. Becky would know at once there was something wrong. Amy had never been any good at hiding her feelings, and she couldn't take the chance of Becky finding out what Richard had done, or attempted to do. For such was her sister's hatred of the man that Becky would go for him with murder in her heart.

For the same reason, she couldn't go back to Jimmy's house either, for Bessie's keen eyes didn't miss a trick, and Amy was afraid that if questioned too closely she might break down and tell the truth. If that happened, then Richard would be either dead or seriously injured before the night was out. If not by Jimmy then certainly by her Charlie. As she thought of the young man she regarded as her sweetheart, Amy choked back a sob. Dear Charlie. Dear, sweet, funny, kind Charlie, who always gave the impression of a happy-go-lucky lad who wouldn't harm a fly. But Amy knew him better than most people. Beneath his cheery, nonchalant manner there lurked a man of strength, a man who wouldn't hesitate to kill or maim for someone he cared about. And he cared very much about Amy. He had already hinted at their future together, making a joke about buying her a ring for her sixteenth birthday. A sudden thought struck her, chilling her to the bone more forcefully than the freezing winter temperature. What if Charlie didn't want her if he found out? Men could be very funny about things like this. He might even think she had encouraged Richard in some way. The idea was so appalling that it brought Amy to her feet. But she had been sitting in the cold for so long that her feet had gone numb, and she stumbled, only saving herself from falling by clutching wildly at the side of the wooden bench.

'Yer all right, love?'

A woman, laden down with shopping baskets, accompanied by five excited children, stopped by Amy's side.

Startled, Amy looked up, then smiled weakly. 'Oh, yes, I'm fine, really. I just lost my balance for a minute, I'm all right now, but thank you for asking.'

The woman peered at the young girl in concern. 'Yer'd best get yerself off 'ome, love. Yer look 'alf froze ter death.'

Stamping her feet to get the circulation going, Amy replied over-brightly, 'Yes, you're right. I was just on my way.' Her mouth fixed in a frozen smile, Amy nodded at the woman. 'Thank you for stopping, goodbye.'

'Yeah, all right, love. You take care now, yer 'ear me?'

Amy continued to smile as she walked away.

'Merry Christmas, lady,' one of the children shouted after her.

Turning her head over her shoulder, Amy waved back. 'And a very Merry Christmas to you all.'

Pulling up the collar of her coat, Amy gripped it tightly around her neck and began to walk in the direction of Roman Road.

Bypassing the top end of the market that was still doing a roaring trade, Amy began to drag her feet. One part of her wanted to carry on walking forever, the sensible side of her knowing she had to get in out of the cold before she ended up like Becky had been the past week. Though that prospect at this minute seemed very tempting. There was nothing she would like better than to go to bed and sleep. Just sleep and sleep without dreams. To be able to forget, if only for a short while, the awful thing that had happened to her.

Like a riderless horse driven by instinct, Amy found herself standing outside the large house she had come to think of as her second home. Too cold and numb to walk any further, she knocked loudly on the door.

'Bleeding 'ell, girl. Where've yer been? It's nearly five o'clock. Yer've been gone hours . . . 'Ere, what's up? What's 'appened ter yer?'

Bessie's keen eyes raked Amy's face, and Amy, knowing she was going to have to lie to save herself from further questioning, said through chattering teeth, 'Let me in, Bessie. I'm freezing.'

Fussing like a mother hen, Bessie pulled Amy into the warmth and began divesting her of her coat, only to be thrust aside roughly. 'No, it's all right, Bessie. I'd rather wait until I warm up a bit before taking my coat off.' Just in time Amy had remembered the torn buttons on her dress. If Bessie had seen the state of her attire there would be no getting let off lightly. 'Sorry, Bessie, I didn't mean to push you. And I'm sorry if I've worried you, especially as it's the second time today I've been late back. I had to go out to get Becky a Christmas present. With all that's been going on here, and at home, I completely forgot about it. Then I couldn't find anything I liked, so I

334

went up Mare Street to see if I could find something in one of the shops.' Aware she was babbling, but unable to stop herself, Amy rushed on. 'I was lucky in the end. I managed to get a lovely writing set in Woolworth's. The assistant even wrapped it up for me, so I thought, seeing as I was near home anyway, I might as well drop it in and see how Becky was feeling before coming back here. I didn't realise it was so late.'

Amy was amazed at the ease with which the lies rolled off her tongue. She comforted herself with the knowledge that Bessie was unlikely to catch her out unless she spoke to Becky, and that possibility wasn't likely to happen. Becky had often teased her about her vivid imagination, but now Amy was glad of it, though this was the first time she had ever used her gift to tell blatant lies. She was so wrapped up in her anxiety to keep up a normal façade that at first Amy didn't notice the pile of suitcases and valises lying in the hallway.

'What's going on, Bessie?' she asked in surprise when she finally caught sight of the luggage. 'Are you planning a holiday?'

Impatiently tutting, Bessie pulled at Amy's arm. 'Well, if yer'd 'ave let me get a word in edgewise, I'd've told yer.' Guiding Amy through to the kitchen, Bessie pulled up a chair by the iron range and within minutes Amy had her hands clasped around a mug of steaming tea. Taking a few sips gratefully, Amy glanced up to see Bessie busily packing up food into large boxes and realised Bessie had been talking all the while. '. . . then outta the blue, Jimmy comes down an' tells me we're going away. Tonight, of all nights, I said ter him, where we gonna find somewhere ter stay on Christmas Eve at this short notice? But it's no good arguing with my Jimmy when his mind's made up. Out he went, about an hour ago, Gawd knows where, then comes back and tells me he's telephoned some hotel and got us all reservations. He's determined ter get the boy away from 'ere in case that one comes back fer him.'

Amy stared at the pile of food in amazement. 'But why are you packing all that food, Bessie? Surely Jimmy doesn't plan to set up a tent somewhere . . .'

Bessie gave a short laugh. 'He'd better not, else I wouldn't be going. I like a bit of comfort at my age. No! This lot's fer the neighbours. Jimmy reckons he'd rather they had it than let it go off stuck in the cupboards while we're away.'

Her ordeal with Richard temporarily put to one side, Amy asked, 'He must be planning to stay away for some time then, Bessie. Judging by the amount of luggage in the hall, and you parcelling up all the perishable food in the house . . . I mean, how long are you going to be away for?' A sense of dread swept over Amy. If Jimmy and Bessie were taking James away for who knows how long, then this house, which was her only refuge from Richard now, would be denied her. A feeling of panic rose in her chest. If she couldn't come here . . .

Bessie paused in her task, her eyes staring down at the table strewn with food. 'Well now, love. That's why I was so anxious fer yer to get back early. Yer see, Jimmy wants yer ter come with us. He thinks it would make it easier on the lad if yer was with us. Sort of give 'im a bit more security, like. 'Cos he's very fond of yer, is James. The first thing he asked when Jimmy told him we was going away fer Christmas was if yer was coming with us. Now, I told Jimmy . . .' She held up her hand as Amy stirred restlessly in the chair. 'I said ter 'im, there's no way that girl's gonna come with us and leave her sister at 'ome on her own. Especially as yer sister ain't been too well, and it being Christmas an' all, but you know Jimmy. When he gets a bee in his bonnet, there's no shifting him. And . . . and, well, ter be honest, love, I'd feel better if yer was coming with us, but I know yer can't, so that's that.' Heaving a great sigh, Bessie shook her head. 'Yer'd best get upstairs and tell him yerself. But don't let him try and charm or blackmail yer into coming with us, 'cos you'd only be miserable away from yer sister, and quite right too. But you'd better get a move on, 'cos Charlie's gonna be here any minute with the carriage.'

At the mention of Charlie's name, Amy's heart lifted. 'You mean Charlie's going with you?'

Bessie's eyebrows rose in surprise. 'Course he is. Jimmy don't go anywhere without the lad. And who'd drive us anyway, except Charlie?'

Her mind racing, Amy climbed the stairs. If such a proposition had been put to her a few hours ago, she would have turned it down without a second thought. She had never spent a Christmas without Becky. In fact she'd never spent a night away from her sister. Even during the time she

337

had been working here, she'd always insisted on going home at night. But now things had changed. Hanging onto the banister, Amy squeezed her eyes shut. What was she thinking of? Of course she couldn't leave Becky alone. She would just have to make sure she was never alone with Richard again. But, oh, how wonderful it would be to just get up and go. Anywhere, she didn't care if she ended up in the back of beyond, as long as she was safely away from Richard. Her body slumping, she lifted her foot and was about to continue up the stairs when, in a startling reconstruction of the morning, Jimmy appeared, his face creased with worry.

'Thank God! I thought you'd never get here.'

Wetting her dry lips, Amy began to speak. 'I'm sorry, Jim—'

'Never mind. Never mind. Here, come up, quickly, I've got something to ask you.'

Once again Amy found herself being deposited into a chair, though this time she had no sooner sat down than James was nestling in her lap. Grateful for the tiny figure's presence, Amy cuddled him to her.

'We're going away on holiday, Amy. But it's all right, Dad's going to leave a message for Father Christmas to tell him where we're going, so I'll still get my presents in the morning. And Dad said you can come too, if you want. You will come with us, won't you, Amy? Please come with us. It won't be the same without you, so it won't.'

Amy's eyes shot over James's head to where

338

Jimmy was standing nearby, looking extremely guilty. Instantly he threw up his hands.

'Hang on, Amy, I didn't put him up to it, I swear. Though I must admit it would be very nice if you could come with us, but, as I've already explained to James, you have a home of your own, and a sister that needs you, so . . .' He raised his shoulders in resignation.

James sat upright on Amy's lap. 'But, Daddy, you said that if I asked, Amy would . . .'

Jimmy coughed, a little too loudly, and a little too quickly. Plucking the boy from Amy's hold, he said firmly, 'Now then, James, I didn't say any such thing. I merely said it wouldn't do any harm to ask, but like I've just explained, Amy has her own home to go to.'

James opened his mouth to protest further, But Jimmy, striding out onto the landing, shouted down, 'Bessie, Bessie, get up here, will you.'

Puffing and panting, Bessie arrived and took the child from Jimmy's arms. Glaring at him, she snapped brusquely, 'I ain't a bleedin' magician, yer know, mate. You've already got me doing half a dozen things at once. I'll 'ave an 'art attack if I carry on like this.'

Jimmy laughed. 'Get off. You're as tough as old boots, and you know it.' Then, in a softer tone, he added, 'Just look after the boy while I have a quick word with Amy, will you, Bessie?'

With a great deal of muttering, Bessie departed with the child under her arm.

'Sorry about that, love. I didn't mean to put you

on the spot. Everything's happened so fast, I don't know whether I'm coming or going.' Picking up the brandy decanter, Jimmy poured himself a drink before continuing. 'The thing is, love, I won't feel safe until I get James away somewhere his mother can't find us. I know I can't keep him away for ever, but I want to be able to enjoy Christmas with him without constantly worrying that Heather might show up and spoil it for him. She's spiteful enough to do it, just to get her own back at me. I thought by giving her the money, it would satisfy her, but I should have known better. A hundred pounds would have been enough for anyone else, but I could have given her a thousand, and she still wouldn't have been satisfied.'

Amy dropped her gaze to her lap. The mention of the money brought back the memories of the afternoon. And she still had the money in her bag. With all that had happened, she'd forgotten all about it. It seemed a hundred pounds was the going rate for buying the rights to another human being. Jimmy had paid that amount to get James, and Richard had imagined the same amount would entitle him to use her as he wished.

She didn't realise she had made any sound until Jimmy asked, 'What? Did you say something, Amy?'

Shaking her head, Amy replied. 'No. Nothing important, Jimmy. Look, I'd better go. You're busy, and I want to get off home.' She stopped, then raised her eyes to Jimmy, and in that moment she dropped her guard, and Jimmy experienced a jolt to his system at the mute appeal mirrored in the lovely blue eyes.

'Amy! What's wrong. Tell me, please. And don't bother lying. Something's upset you, I can see it in your face. Who was . . .'

Instantly Amy's guard was back in place. She had done well so far, much better than she had expected of herself, she mustn't lose control now, for to do so would be fatal. And not only for Richard, but for the sake of all those dear to her.

'Nothing's wrong, Jimmy. Except that I'm tired and missing Becky, and not looking forward to this wretched party that's been forced on us. If Becky was well, we'd go out for the night, but Dr Barker's told her she has to stay indoors for at least another week, unless she wants to risk another bout of influenza.'

Jimmy clapped a hand to his forehead. 'Good Lord! I'd forgotten all about that.'

At the look of puzzlement on Amy's face, Jimmy explained, 'Tom came round while you were out and asked me if I'd like to attend this party. Normally I'd be only too pleased to come, especially as Rebecca issued the invitation.' A warm smile touched his lips. 'At least, not in so many words, she didn't. But Tom gave me the distinct impression that I'd be very welcome.' The smile vanished as Jimmy realised the opportunity he was being forced to miss. Hell! This was the first real sign that Rebecca had some feelings for him, and he was going to have to let her down again. But that didn't mean he couldn't see her and explain the reason why before they left.

341

A loud knocking from downstairs was followed by equally loud laughter.

'That's Charlie at long last. He's been looking after the punters since your brother's hasty departure. He had to wait until the last race was over in case he had any winnings to pay out. Still, he's here now, so we might as well be off. I'll give you a lift home, and drop in to say hello to Rebecca, and explain why I can't attend the party.'

Twenty minutes later, with the parcels of food delivered to grateful neighbours, the cases loaded onto the top of the carriage and the occupants settled inside, Charlie directed the horses towards what was becoming a familiar journey to Hackney.

CHAPTER TWENTY-FOUR

All afternoon Rebecca had sat in her room, refusing to go downstairs where a small army of caterers was busily setting up tables and preparing food. She had also ignored Maude's calls for assistance, until, goaded beyond endurance, Phil had finally left his room to see what Maude wanted.

Staring down onto the gas-lit road, Rebecca waited patiently for Amy to arrive home; they had a lot to talk about. Amy wasn't going to be pleased when Rebecca told her they were leaving just as soon as she felt strong enough, but leave they would. After witnessing Maude's miraculous recovery, and the hoard of money secreted beneath the bed she'd spent the best part of her life in, there was no way Rebecca would ever lift a finger to help her again. What with Maude's deceit, and nursing a deep suspicion that Richard was up to something, and that something wouldn't be to their advantage,

343

Rebecca was determined to leave as soon as humanly possible. Amy might protest at first, but after she had heard what Rebecca now knew, she'd do as she was told. As for Phil . . . Rebecca sighed. He was a grown man, and she'd looked after him for far too long. It was about time he learnt to stand on his own two feet, instead of expecting other people to look after him and sort out his problems. Even so, Rebecca felt guilty about leaving her brother. She was still angry with him, but having had time to mull things over, she had decided to let the matter drop. What was done was done, there was nothing to be gained by holding onto a grudge. Not now, when she wouldn't be here for much longer. And despite her anger, she still loved Phil. He was her brother after all, despite his many faults. And he wasn't bad, just very weak, selfish and immature. She had done all she could over the years to make him into a strong man, but his character was too weak, and always would be. Phil's best chance in life was to marry a strong woman who would look after him, because he'd never be able to manage on his own. The matter of the money he owed played heavily on Rebecca's mind, for she knew that until that debt was paid off, Phil would be too scared to leave the house. And once she and Amy had gone, what would Phil do? He had no one he could call a real friend, no other real family except her and Amy. She couldn't just walk out and forget about him. But if he could pay off his debt and find a decent job, then she wouldn't have him on her conscience.

Up until last night, Rebecca had thought there was

344

no way out of Phil's mess – that was until she had
unwittingly stumbled upon Maude's secret hoard,
the memory of which still rankled. If Rebecca was
the kind of woman to call in her dues, then she
would certainly think that money was owed her for
her years of servitude, and being an unpaid skivvy.
But Rebecca wasn't that sort of woman. More's the
pity, she rebuked herself silently. It was good to
have a conscience, but it could be a real nuisance
at times. But once Phil learnt about the cash Maude
had hidden, Rebecca doubted he would have any
such scruples about helping himself to the money
he so desperately needed. That decision, though,
would be up to Phil. As long as she didn't know
if he had taken enough to pay off his debt, then she
would have no cause to feel guilty.

Hearing a carriage pull up outside the house,
Rebecca looked down again. She had been expecting
Amy, and wasn't surprised to see Charlie helping her
down from the vehicle. She was surprised, however,
to see Jimmy and the child follow her sister into the
house. Her hand flew to her mouth in alarm. Good
Lord! She had been hoping Jimmy would arrive some
time this evening with Dr Barker, but she hadn't
expected to see him here as early as this. She wasn't
properly dressed, nor had she had time to arrange
her hair. The nurse had kindly washed and dried it
for Rebecca before leaving a few hours ago, and had
offered to dress the long tresses into the style Rebecca
normally wore, but this further kind offer Rebecca
had refused, preferring to do her hair herself. The
nurse had been reluctant to leave until Amy arrived,

but Rebecca had convinced her to go. Now she was wishing she hadn't been so hasty. She had attempted to do her hair, but after only five minutes her arms had felt like lead and she'd had to give up the effort, thinking she would let Amy do it when she got home. Then she drew herself upright. There was nothing for it but to greet her visitors as she was. Smoothing down her red workdress, she peered into her dressing-table mirror and groaned. Goodness, her hair was all over the place. She looked like a wild woman. But it couldn't be helped. She had neither the time nor the energy to make herself presentable.

'Becky, Becky, I'm home.' Amy's voice filled the house, bringing a smile to Rebecca's lips. Even though the house was teeming with catering staff, it had still felt empty without Amy's presence. Now she was home at last. But Rebecca wasn't the only one to have heard her arrival. Within seconds Maude let out a shout for assistance, but for once Amy ignored her elderly cousin and came straight in to Rebecca.

'Hello, Becky. I gather by Maude's screeching that the nurse has already left. Well, she'll just have to wait a while, because I've brought home some company. I hope you don't mind, Becky, but I couldn't really stop him.'

Rebecca grinned. 'No, I don't suppose you could, love. Though I wish I'd had more notice. I'm hardly dressed for visitors.' She grimaced down at her appearance, but Amy's mind was clearly elsewhere. 'Oh, Jimmy won't mind. He's not exactly one to stand on ceremony, is he? Anyway, he's off on

346

holiday and he wanted to say goodbye before he went.'

The happiness Rebecca had experienced at knowing Jimmy was downstairs waiting for her vanished in a puff of smoke. 'Going away,' she whispered in disappointment. 'But Dr Barker never mentioned them going away when he visited me this morning, and he's a close friend of Jimmy's.'

'Dr Barker doesn't know . . . Look, Becky, let's sit down a minute while I tell you what's been happening today.'

When Amy had finished recounting the events of the day, carefully glossing over her visit to Richard, Rebecca's eyes clouded.

'I see. In the circumstances I can't say as I blame him. The woman sounds a thoroughly nasty piece of goods.' A glint of humour broke through Rebecca's sorrowful mood. 'You mean you actually pulled her hair then knocked her down? That doesn't sound like the Amy I know. You must have . . .'

But Amy seemed a million miles away. Looking closer at her sister, Rebecca noted the flushed cheeks and glittering eyes, and for an awful moment thought Amy had caught influenza.

'Amy, love, what's wrong? Are you ill? You look dreadful.'

Amy's eyes darted around the room, refusing to meet Rebecca's, because she knew, knew without doubt, that this awful strain she was under wouldn't withstand Rebecca's penetrating gaze.

'No, I'm fine. Just a bit off colour. I mean, it's not every day you have a brawl in the street, is it? It upset me a bit, then there's Charlie going away and not knowing when I'll see him again. I was looking forward to spending time with him over Christmas, but it can't be helped.' *Keep on talking*, she told herself, *just keep rambling on. Don't say anything that might make Rebecca suspicious.* 'I'll miss James too. I've grown very fond of him, and he's very upset I can't go with them. But like I explained to Jimmy, I—'

'Hang on!' Rebecca held up her hand. 'What do you mean, the child was upset you weren't going with them? Did Jimmy ask you to?'

Still refusing to look at her sister, Amy dropped her head and nodded. 'Yes, but I told him I couldn't leave you, especially not at Christmas, and you not being well. Jimmy was very understanding, but the boy, I mean, James, well . . . children don't understand, do they? Anyway, I'd better go and see what Maude wants, before she shouts the house down.'

Rebecca stared hard at her sister. So that was the reason for Amy's distress. She obviously wanted to go with Jimmy and the child, and Charlie of course; instead she was tied here because of her. Her conscience tugging at her, Rebecca thought furiously. Christmas without Amy. It didn't bear thinking about. Neither did the idea of spending the festive season stuck here with Maude and Phil. It certainly wasn't going to be a merry Christmas for her if Amy wasn't here. Amy was the only thing in her life that kept Rebecca sane. At the same time, it would be selfish of her to deny Amy the chance of a

holiday away from the gloom and despondency of
the house, when she could be with her sweetheart. If
Amy went, then she, Rebecca, would be miserable.
If Amy stayed with her out of loyalty, then they
would both be miserable. There was nothing else
to do but to let Amy go. But, oh, she would miss
her, she would miss her dreadfully.

Swallowing hard Rebecca asked, 'Do you want to
go, Amy? The truth now. If I wasn't still recovering
from the influenza, and had somewhere else to go
myself, would you go with Jimmy and the child?'

Tears sprang to Amy's eyes. Of course she wanted
to go. Wanted it more than anything else in the
world right now. But not just for Charlie's sake,
or anyone else's, just her own. She was so afraid.
Afraid that if she were to come face to face with
Richard, and that must happen sooner or later, then
she wasn't sure she would be able to keep quiet,
and then all hell would be let loose. That, and that
only, was the real reason she wanted to get as far
away from this house as possible. If this afternoon's
incident hadn't taken place, then she wouldn't even
have considered leaving Becky. The notion wouldn't
have entered her mind. But her world had been
turned upside down, and things weren't the same
any more, nor would they ever be. When she felt
Rebecca's arms encircle her shoulders, it took all of
Amy's willpower not to break down and spill the
awful truth. But she must keep quiet, she must.
For everyone's sake, no one must ever know what
Richard had tried to do.

'If you want to go, love, then go. I doubt I'll be

much company anyway, not the way I'm feeling. In fact Dr Barker suggested I stay in bed over the holiday, and the nurse is only too willing to come back and stay with me. So you see, love, there's nothing to stop you going. And you do want to go, don't you?'

'Oh, yes, Becky, yes.' The words tumbled from Amy's lips. 'But I can't leave you alone at Christmas. I'd feel so guilty, I wouldn't be able to enjoy myself anyway.'

Rebecca held her close. Ignoring her own pain, she murmured soothingly, 'Don't be silly. It would be different if I was well and we'd made plans, but as I'll probably spend the holidays in bed, then you might as well go off and have a good time. There's no sense in both of us having a miserable Christmas, is there?'

Holding a tear-stained face up to Rebecca's, a ray of hope sprang into Amy's reddened eyes. 'Do you really mean it, Becky? You're not just saying it to make me feel better, are you? Because you know I'd never leave you if you needed me.'

Forcing a laugh, Rebecca chuckled, 'I know you wouldn't, silly. Now why don't you pack a few things while I go down and greet our guests? I'm sure Jimmy won't mind waiting while you pack. And I'm sure a certain young man will be delighted you're going with them.' Giving Amy a gentle squeeze she added playfully, 'And I'm not talking about James either.'

The look of relief on Amy's face was painful to see, and suddenly Rebecca was suspicious. She knew how fond Amy had become of Jimmy and Bessie, then the child, and especially Charlie. Yet even with all that taken into consideration, Amy still wouldn't leave her – unless there was some other reason she seemed so desperate to leave the house. Her eyes alert, she tilted Amy's chin upwards and demanded, 'Is there something you're not telling me, Amy? Has something happened I should know about? Come on, Amy. We've never had any secrets, have we? And if there's something troubling you, then I want to know about it.' She could feel the trembling of Amy's body and hugged her tighter, her mind racing, as she imagined all sorts of terrible things that Amy might be keeping from her.

'AMY! AMY!'

Maude's voice yelled across the landing, and in a tone that belied her physical state, Rebecca yelled back, 'Shut up, you old cow. If you want something, then get it yourself, you're not helpless.'

The anger in Rebecca's voice jerked Amy back to her senses. Good Lord. Another minute and she would have crumbled. If Becky could get that angry because Maude wanted her to fetch and carry, then what would she do if she found out about Richard? A new strength entered Amy's body. She knew that Rebecca would give her life for her if need be, and Amy wasn't prepared to take the risk of Rebecca hanging over that fat, old swine of a man. Her mind clearing, she knew what she must do.

'No, Becky, there's nothing I haven't told you. It's just like I said. That fight this morning really upset me, and then finding out I wouldn't be seeing

351

Charlie over Christmas.' She shrugged and tried to smile gamely. 'It just got to me a bit, I suppose. But if you're absolutely sure you'll be all right, then I will go with them. If you were all right, Jimmy would ask you along too, I know he would.'

Rebecca gave a shaky laugh. 'I'm not so sure about that, love. Phew! You had me worried for a minute. I thought you were hiding some terrible secret from me. Now, go and pack, or else we'll both be stuck here for Christmas, and like I said, there's no point in both of us being miserable,' she added jokingly.

Leaving Amy to her packing, Rebecca took a deep breath and prepared to greet her guests.

As soon as Rebecca had left the room, Amy darted across the landing and knocked on Phil's door.

'Phil! Phil! Open the door, quickly.'

Phil, who had been staring morosely at the ceiling, nearly fell off his bed in startled amazement at the tone in his sister's voice. If it had been Becky, that would be one thing, but for Amy to call out to him like that . . . !

Opening the door cautiously he said, 'What's up, Amy? You don't sound like—'

'Get out of my way, you.' Her slight frame pushed past him, and with an anxious stare down the empty corridor, Phil closed the door behind him.

'Now see here, Amy. I won't be spoken to like that.'

'Oh, shut up, Phil. Just . . . Just shut up!' Phil's eyebrows nearly disappeared under his hair. This couldn't be his little sister talking to and looking at him in this manner. But it was. Her next words, however, struck him dumb.

'Here! Here's your money. Now you can pay your gambling debt and find yourself a job. There's a hundred pounds there, courtesy of dear Richard. I did offer to help you pay it back, but all things considered, I think I've already paid my share. Though given the choice I'd much rather have paid it back in coinage.'

As the implication of her words sank in, Phil's mouth dropped open. Then, his nostrils flaring, his cheeks turning red in indignation, he spluttered, 'Did he touch you, Amy? Did that overblown bastard touch you, because if he has, so help me, I'll . . .'

Amy spun on him like a wild animal. 'You'll do nothing, Phil. Just like you always do. Oh, you'll shout and bluster, and tell everyone who'll listen exactly what you plan to do, but you won't do anything, you never have. You're all mouth and no trousers. That's an expression I picked up from Bessie. I've never heard it before, but the minute I did, I knew it fitted you to a tee.' She glared at him, and under her accusing gaze Phil's eyes dropped. 'I knew it. I knew you wouldn't do anything, that's why I told you how I got the money, because I had to tell someone or burst. And you were the only one I could think of to share my little secret with, without being afraid of the consequences. Because if ever Becky found out, then, ill or not, she'd probably kill him – or have a bloody good try. So would Jimmy and Charlie, and even Bessie, as old as she is. But not you, Phil. Not my big, protective brother. The so-called man of the house. Huh! That's a laugh. Becky's been looking after you since our parents died. Now I'm off. I don't really want to go, but I'm afraid if I stay I'll blurt it all out. Jimmy's taking us all on holiday for a while. Normally I wouldn't have even considered leaving Becky alone with you and Maude for company, but like I said, I've got no choice. Not unless I want to see Becky in prison, or worse. And Richard isn't worth hanging for.'

Phil sat dumbly on the edge of the bed, Amy's words raining down on him like hammer blows, but still he did nothing. The decent part of him wanted to take the money and shove it in Richard's face the moment he walked in the door, then give him a good thrashing. But he knew he wouldn't. The money lying on the bed was his only salvation. Without it, he was doomed. A wave of self-loathing, so strong it left him breathless, swept over him as he took a long hard look at himself. Everything that Becky had said to him over the years was true. And now here was Amy, his only champion, turning on him as well. What hurt the most was that he knew it was all true. He was weak, and selfish, and gutless – and God help him, but he'd always be the same. He just didn't have what it took to change. Dropping his head in his hands, he let out a soft groan, but Amy was unmoved.

'Don't bother with the old head in the hands bit, Phil. I've seen it all before, but this time I'm not falling for it.'

Bleary-eyed, Phil peered cautiously up at his sister before running a shaking hand over his unshaven chin. 'Amy . . . Please, please don't look at me like that. I know I deserve it, but please . . . won't you give me one last chance?'

Amy was already halfway out of the room. Pausing, she bit at her bottom lip, her face now sorrowful. All her temper evaporated as she gazed on the pathetic figure she had looked up to for years, and she shook her head. Ignoring Phil's plea she said softly, 'You didn't even bother to ask what Richard did. Oh, I know you made a feeble effort at playing the outraged big brother, but that didn't last long. I could have been raped for that hundred pounds. It was only my screams that stopped him – that, and an unexpected visitor. You forgot all about me the moment you saw the money, and realised what it could do for you.' She shot him a pitying glance. 'I'm going now, Phil. I won't wish you a Merry Christmas. It would be hypocritical under the circumstances.'

Phil heard Amy go into Maude's room, then, like someone drunk, he staggered over and shut the door. Leaning his back against it, he whispered anguishly, 'I do love you, Amy. You don't know how much.' But not enough to give up the money that had cost his little sister so dearly. Oh, no, he didn't love her enough to do that. His inner voice mocking him, Phil picked up the money from where Amy had thrown it onto the bed and, clutching it tightly, he began to cry.

*   *   *

'Good Evening. I'm sorry I'm not dressed for visitors. I wasn't expecting any guests until much later. Please, take a seat and make yourselves comfortable.'

Rebecca smiled at the small band of people standing in front of the cheerful blaze of the fire. She recognised Bessie at once and was heartened when her smile of greeting was returned, as the elderly woman thankfully took a chair by the fire. A young boy, muffled up to the eyes in a thick coat and scarf, sat on Bessie's lap. Rebecca couldn't see much of his face, but she could sense his unease at being in this strange house. On either side of them stood the men. Charlie, warming his legs before the fire, his normally cheerful face solemn, and Jimmy standing behind Bessie's chair, one hand resting reassuringly on the child's shoulder.

'Can I offer you some refreshments?'

Giving the boy an affectionate squeeze, Jimmy shook his head. 'No thanks, Rebecca. We haven't time . . . Unless any of you would like something before we leave.' He looked towards the small group.

Bessie sniffed loudly. 'Thanks, ever so. It's nice of yer ter think of the rest of us.' Looking towards Rebecca she said, 'I wouldn't mind a nice hot cuppa, if there's one going, love. Though I can see you've got yer 'ands full.' She directed her glance at the heavily laden table and the three men and two women who kept darting in and out of the room.

'I'm sure I can manage some tea, Bessie.' Flicking her eyes to Charlie, she added, 'What about you,

Charlie? Wouldn't you like something while you're waiting for Amy? She's upstairs getting packed. She shouldn't be too long.'

At Rebecca's words, Charlie's face lit up like a beacon. The child too seemed to come alive. 'Amy's coming with us, miss?' James pulled down his scarf and peeped up at Rebecca hopefully. 'She said she couldn't come, because she had to look after her sister. Are you her sister, miss?'

Bessie's voice rose. 'There, there, young fella. Enough of yer questions. 'Course it's Amy's sister. Who'd yer think she was, her blooming granny?' The boy giggled, his small form relaxing against Bessie's chest.

Jimmy followed Rebecca into the kitchen. Avoiding the bustle around them, Rebecca managed to get to the stove. 'There, the kettle will soon be boiling. Won't you sit down, Jimmy? Like I said, Amy won't be long.'

Looking around for a spare chair, Jimmy shrugged then laughed. 'I think I'll stand. Bleeding hell! Who's Richard got coming to this party, the King himself?'

Smiling broadly Rebecca answered, 'You'd think so, judging by the amount of effort he's making. Though I think he's up to something. Richard never spends money if he can help it. Anyway, let's not waste time talking about my odious cousin . . . Oh, the kettle's boiled. I'll make the tea, then we can talk. Only, not here.' Pouring out the piping hot beverage, she looked in dismay around the crowded room and the curious glances being directed at them. 'Let me take this to Bessie, then we can go upstairs. It will be more private,' she added, sending a wry look at a hovering young waitress who immediately returned to her duties.

With Jimmy following close behind, Rebecca led him to her room, passing Amy on the way down.

When the door closed behind them, cocooning them into a little world of their own, Rebecca had to sit down quickly. The influenza had already left her limbs weakened, and finding herself in her bedroom with this charismatic man she suddenly felt as weak as a day-old kitten.

If Jimmy was aware of the effect he was having on her he didn't show it. Sitting opposite on Amy's bed, he began to talk, but Rebecca was only half listening. Most of what he was saying Rebecca had already heard from Amy, and she was content to just sit and listen while savouring the intimacy of the moment without having to concentrate on Jimmy's words.

'. . . So you see, I must get the boy away for a while, though it couldn't have come at a worse time. I had a devil of a job getting through to the hotel. The telephone cables aren't working properly because of the bad weather, and I had to go all the way to my solicitor's to find a telephone because he's the only one I knew who had one. I wanted to get a telephone installed in the house when they first appeared on the market, but Bessie made such a fuss, I decided to let the matter rest . . . For the time being.' He grinned devilishly. 'And Charlie's been on at me to get one of the new automobiles. He can't wait to get behind the wheel. I'm tempted myself to be truthful.

The horse and carriage will soon be a thing of the past, though when I broached the subject . . .'

'Bessie nearly had a fit,' Rebecca interjected playfully.

Laughing loudly, Jimmy nodded. 'You're absolutely right. If the people of the East End knew how hen-pecked I was, they'd have a good laugh at my expense.'

'You wouldn't change her though, would you, Jimmy?'

'No, I wouldn't.' His eyes sombre now, he continued. 'She's been like a mother to me. If it wasn't for Bessie, I doubt if I'd be alive today. My own mother was a drunken slattern who didn't know I was around half the time, and when she did remember she had a child she beat me black and blue. Now, all these years later, I find I have a son with a similar mother. Oh, Heather may not be a drunk, nor does she beat him physically. But there are many ways to destroy the human spirit, and I'm not going to allow my son to endure the same fate I did as a child. I want him to feel loved and secure. After what happened this morning, my initial reaction was to take him away from London for good, but that idea soon passed. The East End is my home, and I'm damned if I'm going to let Heather Mills drive me away. No, that's not the answer. What I have to do, if possible, is to spend time with James. Let him see I really love and want him, and I'm not going to get fed up with him and throw him out the minute he puts a foot out of line. Also I want him to come to think of me as his father.

359

Oh, he already knows I am, but a name isn't enough. I want him to truly think of me as his dad, and trust me. That's the most important part of all. Because once I've gained his trust, and hopefully his love, then I won't have to fear Heather any more. The only power she has over me is the child, but once James gets used to being with me, and wants to stay by my side, then that power will be taken from her. When that day comes I'll finally be able to relax.'

Leaning forward, he took Rebecca's hands. 'It's very good of you to let Amy come with us, I know how you'll miss her while she's away, but I'll take good care of her. I've grown very fond of Amy, just like I've grown very fond of her big sister. In fact I could say I love Amy's sister, though I'm not quite sure how she feels.' His dark eyes bored into Rebecca's as if he could see into her very soul. 'Do you happen to know? Is there any chance for me, Rebecca? If not, just say, and I'll never mention the subject again.'

Rebecca blinked furiously, her entire body churning with emotion. Her throat felt constricted and she had to gulp in a very unladylike fashion before she could answer, 'I think both the Bradford sisters are very fond of you, Jimmy, especially the elder, stuck-up one, as Bessie once called her.'

Blowing out his cheeks in profound relief, Jimmy tightened his grip on Rebecca's hands while leaning nearer. 'So you'll wait for me, Rebecca? I don't know how long I'll be gone. Hopefully I'll be back before you know it, but like I've said, I have to gain my son's trust and be content in my own mind that even if Heather reappears, he'll want to stay with me.'

A surge of alarm swept through Rebecca's body. 'I . . . I thought you were only going away for a few days, but . . . but the way you're talking it sounds as if you plan to be away for some time. What about your bus . . . business,' she fumbled over the word and Jimmy, knowing how she felt about the way he earned his money, grinned.

'I haven't had time to think about that part of my life, but now that I have responsibilities, it may be time to start thinking about going into another line of work. After all, I can't take the chance of being arrested for illegal activities now I have a son – and hopefully a wife in the not too distant future.' He cocked his eyebrows roguishly, his humour disappearing when he saw the distress on Rebecca's face.

Jimmy closed his eyes in confusion, not knowing if his light-hearted remark about acquiring a wife or his imminent departure was causing Rebecca's obvious misery. Thinking quickly, he said urgently, 'Come with us, Rebecca. I know you're still recuperating, but if you dress up warmly, I'm sure it'll be all right.'

Rebecca gently loosened her hands from Jimmy's and shook her head. 'There's nothing I'd like better, Jimmy. But I'm still very weak, and Dr Barker has warned me that if I so much as put my nose out of the window, he won't be responsible for the consequences. Besides, I'd only be in the way . . . Yes, yes, I would,' she added quickly as Jimmy

361

started to protest. 'The whole reason you're going away is to be with your son. To spend time with him and gain his trust. You can't do that if you have an invalid to care for as well. And the child might see me as a threat. If what Amy tells me is correct, and the child has had numerous "uncles", what's to stop him from thinking his father is the kind of man who's going to provide him with numerous "aunts".' Her head moving from side to side, she whispered, 'It wouldn't be fair on James. He needs your undivided attention, and you won't be able to provide that if I'm around to distract you.'

Jimmy knew she was right, but it pained him to leave her. Especially here, in this house with her motley assortment of relations. Then he had an idea.

'I know, I'll ask Tom . . . Dr Barker if you can stay with him until I return. I know he'd like the company, he's been very lonely since his wife died. You'd be doing each other a good turn, and it would set my mind at ease if I knew you were with Tom instead of stuck here being at everyone's beck and call.' As if the decision had already been made, Jimmy added eagerly. 'He'll be here tonight, unless some emergency crops up. You tell him what I've suggested. I know he'll be overjoyed.'

Rebecca smiled weakly. She had no intention of doing any such thing, but she wasn't going to argue. Let Jimmy and Amy think she was with Dr Barker. It would ease both their minds.

Then she jumped as Jimmy moved from Amy's bed to sit beside her. Stroking her long, luxurious

362

hair, Jimmy pressed his lips against the freshly washed tresses. 'When we're married, you must wear your hair like that for me every night. Until then, there's some unfinished business we have. You remember, the last time we were together. I was just about to kiss you when you mentioned Heather's name and, fool that I was, I made a very hasty departure. But she's not here to distract me now, and I need something to remember you by while I'm away.'

When his lips came down on hers, Rebecca's body crumbled. It was only Jimmy's strong arms that kept her from sliding off the bed into an undignified heap onto the floor. The world to Rebecca seemed another planet away as the man she loved held her in his arms, locked together, his warm, firm lips on hers. Then the idyllic moment was shattered by the fretful sound of the child's voice.

'Daddy, Daddy. Where are you? Daddy, Daddy.'

Reluctantly Jimmy ended the embrace, but kept a tight lock on Rebecca's waist and leant his forehead against hers. 'I thought he'd never call me by that name, but since this afternoon, when he knew Heather wasn't coming back, he hasn't stopped calling me Daddy. He even told me he loved me, poor little sod. It's as if he's trying to reassure himself somehow, and to his young mind he probably thinks he does. He's so desperate for someone to love him . . . But look, before I go, I have something for you.' Fumbling in his coat pocket, he brought out a red velvet box. 'I'm afraid I haven't had time to wrap it. Here open it . . .'

With trembling fingers, Rebecca opened the box. There, nestled on a red satin cushion, was a gold locket. 'It's beautiful, Jimmy,' she breathed, her voice filled with emotion. 'I've never had anything like it in my entire life.'

Taking the locket from her shaking fingers, Jimmy tenderly fastened it around her neck, and was about to kiss her again when the romantic mood was once again interrupted by the sound of James calling for his father.

'You'd better go, Jimmy,' Rebecca said, a tremor in her voice. 'It sounds as if your son is becoming fretful.'

Delving once again into his pockets, Jimmy brought out a bunch of keys and an envelope.

'Look, take these, darling. They're the keys to my house. You never know if you might need them. Just in case you forget to ask Tom what we spoke about.' There was an unmistakable glint of humour in Jimmy's eyes. 'There's also the name of the hotel at which we'll be staying, and the combination of my safe, and where to find it . . . Just in case you need any money.' He held up a warning hand. 'I know you'll never use it, but humour me, will you. If I know you've a place to stay and money to live on while I'm gone, then I'll be able to give all my attention to James knowing you're well provided for. It'll be up to you whether you take advantage of my offer, an offer that's made out of love and concern for you. The point is it's all there if you need it.' Placing a tender kiss on her lips, he said huskily, 'I'll see you soon, darling, I promise. And

I'll send Amy back just as soon as James is more settled.'

Not daring to answer in case she burst into tears, Rebecca nodded, her thoughts whirling. Jimmy loved her. That declaration would have been enough to set her heart soaring, but she had never expected him to broach the subject of marriage. It didn't matter that he hadn't actually asked her in so many words; he hadn't needed to. The reference to his future wife, and asking her to wear her hair loose when they were married was as good as any formal proposal.

The next ten minutes were spent in a flurry of tearful goodbyes as Rebecca waved the carriage carrying the two people she loved most away from the house.

Alone in her room, she sat staring at the gold locket lying just inches above her breasts, her mind repeating over and over every word Jimmy had said until, her eyelids drooping, she drifted off into a satisfying sleep, her fingers still clasped around the locket, and with a smile on her lips.

She might not have rested so easily if she had known that Phil had been outside her door and overheard the conversation she'd had with Jimmy.

Phil's eavesdropping hadn't been intentional. He had been on the way to spruce himself up for the party when he'd heard Jimmy's voice. Out of curiosity, and a guilty conscience, he had stopped to listen, just to see if his name was mentioned. When he'd realised the intimacy of the conversation, he had quickly become embarrassed and was about to move on when his ears had pricked up at the mention of the safe, and the fact that Rebecca was now in possession of the keys to Jimmy's house and the combination and location of the said safe.

Once he had finished his ablutions, Phil lay down for a rest before the party was due to start. Now that he had the money Amy had managed to get from Richard – his mind swiftly glossed over how his sister had come by the solely needed cash – his money problems were over. Still, it didn't hurt to know there was more to be had if he should need it. Not that he would of course. Oh, no. After this scare, he would never get himself into such a predicament again. He'd learnt his lesson. But one never knew what the future held. His mind at peace for the first time in weeks, Phil closed his eyes and, like Rebecca, he fell asleep with a smile on his lips.

CHAPTER TWENTY-FIVE

'May I have your attention, ladies and gentlemen?' Richard stood in the middle of the room, obviously in his element. By his side stood an elegantly dressed woman whom Rebecca judged to be in her late thirties. She seemed familiar somehow, but the only place Rebecca could imagine having seen her before was that night in the restaurant. It must be the same one, Rebecca thought wryly. For Richard to have one lady friend was astonishing, for him to have two was, to Rebecca's mind, beyond the realms of possibility.

Through the small crowd that had crammed into the modest-sized sitting room, Rebecca could see Maude, dressed for once, filling up the entire breadth of the cloth-covered armchair that normally resided by the fireplace. She had insisted she be brought downstairs, saying that if she was to be denied her much-needed rest, she might as well join the guests Richard had invited. Her appearance had come as no surprise to Rebecca. There was no way Maude would be content to lie in her room while there was a party in progress, she would be too afraid she might miss something. Rebecca had watched in amusement as Phil and Richard had struggled to carry the obese woman down the relatively short flight of stairs, all the time knowing her cousin could have easily managed them on her own.

Now Maude's gimlet eyes were fixed with a cold ferocity on her brother and the woman by his side, and it took all of Rebecca's willpower not to laugh aloud. It was so obvious now why Richard had gone to all this trouble. He was going to announce his engagement. It was the only possible reason for the build-up to tonight's event. It was a pity Dr Barker had to cry off at the last minute, due to some emergency. Rebecca didn't know any of the people gathered for the occasion, and she would have enjoyed having someone to talk to, particularly about Jimmy, and his unorthodox proposal. She was positively bursting to share her news with someone, and Tom Barker was the only one she could think of to confide in. Now it seemed there was another wedding about to be announced. It was also equally obvious that Maude knew what Richard was up to, judging by the vindictive look etched into the folds of her fat face. But Rebecca must put her own thoughts to one side and pay attention to what Richard was saying, if only out of curiosity. It didn't matter what he did now, it was no longer of any consequence to her. With the feel of the locket Jimmy had given her resting against her skin, and the knowledge that he loved her, Rebecca felt a warmth of contentment she had never experienced before.

'. . . proud to announce that Ivy here has done me the honour of agreeing to marry me. The wedding will take place at Saint Stephen's church on the twenty-eighth of December. I'm sorry it's such short notice, but at our age, we don't feel a long engagement is necessary. No formal invitations have been sent out, but you are all welcome to attend the ceremony, and the wedding reception that will be held here afterwards.'

Richard, his rotund body looking fit to burst, so proud of himself did he feel, looked to the young woman who had always treated him with open disdain, to gauge her reaction to his news. In this he was vastly disappointed. For, far from looking put out, Rebecca seemed positively delighted. His feeling of triumph momentarily slipped away, then anger took over.

Well! He'd soon wipe that infuriating, superior look from her face. Now that her fancy man had left London she would have nowhere to go when he, Richard, threw her and that worthless brother of hers out onto the streets. Then see how smug she would look then. Mind you, it had been a stroke of luck Amy going with Jimmy Jackson and his lot. Yes indeed, a great stroke of luck. She was a good girl, was his Amy. He had known she wouldn't say anything about that unfortunate incident, but still, one never knew with women . . . !

369

Denied the response he had hoped for from Rebecca, he cast his eyes to his sister, and instantly his body regained its former importance. The murderous glare Maude was levelling at him had been worth all the expense and aggravation he had endured over the past few weeks. Smiling sweetly, he raised his glass of champagne in her face. 'I'm sure my dear sister will be the first to congratulate me on my good news, won't you, Maude, dear?' he added sneeringly.

Maude, her body wedged tight in the chair, felt all eyes on her. Using the only part of her body she could move, she raised her head defiantly and smiled back at Richard. 'Of course, Richard. I'm delighted. If you're happy, then so am I.' Raising her own glass, she called loudly, 'A toast everyone. To my dear brother Richard, and his lovely fiancée Ivy. Good health and happiness to you both.'

For a brief, wild moment, Rebecca was tempted to stand up and applaud, so great was the performance Maude was putting on. But even Maude's sterling accomplishment was nearly destroyed when Richard, his face still smug, said, 'Thank you, my dear, loving sister. We haven't seen much of each other over the years, what with my business commitments taking up so much of my time, but as soon as we get back from our honeymoon, you'll be delighted to know that we plan to move in here. For my part, it'll be like coming back home, and Ivy is just as enthusiastic as I am to start our married life in the house I was born and raised in.'

The colour blanched from Maude's ruddy cheeks as the import of Richard's words sunk in. And if she

370

had any lingering doubts, she had only to look into his gloating eyes to see that her days in this house were numbered.

Smiling inside and out, Rebecca let her eyes wander over the room. There would be another person who wouldn't be too happy at the news of the impending arrival of Richard and his new bride. Then she spotted Phil lounging by the kitchen door, a drink in one hand, a plate of food in the other. Sensing he was being observed, Phil glanced in Rebecca's direction and arched his eyebrows in amusement. This act alone brought a surge of suspicion to Rebecca's mind. She had expected Phil to have a similar reaction to Maude's. Because once Richard moved in with his new bride, there would be no room for Phil. Yet her brother didn't seem at all concerned. Now that was very puzzling. Very puzzling indeed!

Her eyes fixed on her brother's, Rebecca inclined her head towards the stairway then got to her feet. Responding to the silent message, Phil followed his sister to her room.

'Well, well, that's a turn-up for the books, isn't it, Becks? Who'd have thought he had it in him, eh? I tell you what, Becks. If Richard can get himself a wife, then there's hope for me yet.'

Perplexed by Phil's apparent lack of concern at his imminent homelessness, she asked, 'You do realise that once Richard's married, there'll be no room here for you. There's no way Richard will support you, and I have no intention of staying once the new Mrs Fisher is installed here. My days of being an unpaid servant are well and truly over. So, why aren't you panicking like you normally do?'

Phil shrugged. 'There's no point, is there, Becks. I'm not as stupid as you think I am. It was obvious Richard was up to something the minute he started chucking his money around on a Christmas party, and insisting it was held here. Looks like you and me'll have to start looking for somewhere else to live, and seeing as neither of us has any money, and no job, it's going to be a bit difficult. Mind you, it's Maude I feel sorry for. She's for the chop and no mistake. Richard's always resented supporting her. I wouldn't be surprised if he chucked her into one of those old people's homes and left her there to rot, poor old cow . . . Oh, hang on, Becks . . .' He sneezed loudly, then again.

Fumbling in his pocket, he searched for a handker-chief while Rebecca watched him, her mind sud-denly attacked by guilt. She had been so sure Phil would go to pieces and expect her to look after them both; instead he was acting like a responsible adult for once and intending to take charge of his own life. Maybe the shock of having the security of his home taken away from him had finally forced him to grow up. Yet he was powerless to start a new life until that blasted gambling debt was repaid. Thanks to Jimmy, her life was now secure, but she couldn't see Jimmy being so charitable to Phil. The idea that had occurred to her earlier came flooding back. In her mind's eye she could see once again the pile of money heaped on top of Maude's bed. Rebecca had been thinking a lot as to how Maude had managed to acquire such a huge amount. The only possible explanation Rebecca could think of was that Richard had been giving Maude a weekly allowance for her keep. But instead of handing it over to Rebecca, the greedy old cow had kept it all for herself. If that was indeed the case, then Phil, having supported them all for years, before he had become addicted to gambling, was entitled to some of that money Maude had so deceitfully withheld from them. Her mind made up, Rebecca was about to tell Phil about the money when the wad of notes that Amy had given Phil earlier fell from his pocket onto the floor.

Her eyes stretched wide, Rebecca could only stare in disbelief at the small fortune lying at her feet. Still caught up in a bout of sneezing, Phil didn't realise the money had fallen from his pocket, nor did he notice Rebecca's transfixed gaze as if she was witnessing an apparition.

Sniffing, he wiped his nose and smiled sheepishly. 'Sorry about that, Becks. It looks like I've caught . . . What! What are you looking at me like that for?' A feeling of alarm trickled along his spine. Then he followed her gaze and swiftly picked up the incriminating evidence.

'Now, wait a minute, Becks. I was just about to explain.' He was afraid to look at her, afraid of what he would see in her face. Instead he turned on his heel and began to pace the room, his fingers running through his thick hair in agitation. 'I only got that money a few hours ago. I was going to tell you, but you were asleep, and I didn't want to disturb you. The thing is—'

'Where did you get it, Phil?' Rebecca's voice was low and harsh. 'You've got some explaining to do, so you'd better make it good . . . I'm waiting.'

Distracted and scared, Phil looked around the room as if searching for some form of escape, but Rebecca was barring the door, and unless Phil was willing to physically tackle his sister there was nothing else to do but try and bluff his way out.

'Now, listen here, Becks, I haven't been out robbing banks, if that's what you're thinking. I admit I put off telling you about the money, but only because I didn't think you'd believe me. I can hardly believe it myself. The fact is that Richard loaned it to me, and that's the truth, so help me, God! He's been in a good mood lately, and now we know why. I can only think his current state of mind has mellowed him.' Phil tried to laugh, but the feeble effort came out merely as a choking sound. And all the time he was painfully aware of Rebecca's eyes, brimming with accusation, boring into him. Clearing his throat, he stuttered anxiously, 'Honestly, Becks, you can ask him if you like, he—'

'*Liar,*' Rebecca spat at him. 'Richard wouldn't give you a farthing if you were starving in the gutter, not unless there was something in it for him. Now I'm warning you, Phil, no more lies. If Richard gave you that money, then he must have had a good reason, and I want to know what it was. You'd better tell me, because I'm not leaving this room until I hear the whole truth, and neither are you.'

Knowing he was defeated, Phil sank onto Amy's

bed, his body slumped in despair. 'All right, you win, you always do, don't you, Becks,' he muttered bitterly. 'I wasn't lying when I said the money came from Richard, but he didn't give it to me, he gave it to Amy. She was worried about me, so she went and asked Richard for help, and he gave—' Phil's body jerked violently as Rebecca let out a piercing shout.

'Amy! You mean to say that Amy got that money for you . . . Oh, my God. No! No!' Like a bolt of lightning striking her, Rebecca knew instantly why Amy had been in such a hurry to leave the house. Her hasty departure had nothing to do with wanting to be with Charlie, or the child, but because something had happened with Richard. A bout of nausea swept over her as the real cause of Amy's distress sank in. She no longer doubted Phil when he said the money had come from Richard, but what price had her sweet, innocent Amy had to pay for the generous offer? Squeezing her eyes tightly shut, Rebecca groaned. Please, God, not that. Anything but that.

'Becks, please. She was only trying to help me, and . . . and, she's the only one who could get Richard to part with his money. I didn't ask her though, you've got to believe me, Becks. I never asked her. She did it on her own. I would never put her in that position, I swear.' Yet even to his own ears his words sounded false. When Rebecca remained silent, Phil cautiously lifted his head, and that was his biggest mistake. For Rebecca saw at once the guilt and shame that ravaged Phil's face, and knew with sickening certainty that her fears were correct. What was worse was that Phil also knew – knew and had done nothing about it.

'You bastard!' The words were dragged out with such loathing that Phil, knowing he couldn't stay in the same room with Rebecca for a second longer, sprang to his feet and, pushing Rebecca aside, ran to his own room. He grabbed his hat and coat and, taking the stairs three at a time, ran through the startled throng of people enjoying the free food and drink and out of the house into the dark night. And as he ran, his face streaming with tears of shame, he knew it would be a long time before he would see his sisters again.

It was a good half an hour before Rebecca left her room, and when she did she was carrying a battered suitcase, her lovely features resembling a face carved in stone. Her conscience no longer bothering her, she stopped only long enough to take a handful of coins from beneath Maude's bed. She would need some money to tide her over until she was well enough to get a job and somewhere to live, and she didn't see why Jimmy's money should support her when there was enough hidden under that fat old cow's bed to aid her financially. Particularly as that same money was, if not legally but morally, hers to take.

Once again the assembled guests were treated to an unexpected form of entertainment as Rebecca, stopping to stand directly in front of Richard, said loudly, so that all present could hear, 'I know all about the money, Richard. What I'm not sure of is just what my Amy had to do to procure it from you. But rest assured I'll find out.' Rebecca was aware the room had fallen silent as each guest strained to hear her every word, but her attention was fixed firmly on the red-faced man, whose eyes were frantically darting from one guest to another, fearful of what she might say next. Rebecca didn't move, nor did her gaze waver. 'If your conscience is clear, then you've nothing to worry about; if not, then you'd better learn to sleep with one eye open. Because if I find out that you've harmed my Amy in any way, then I'll kill you, you have my word on that.'

She didn't remember leaving the house, nor did she hear the babble of noise that erupted before the front door had closed behind her. Her mind, so full of hatred, didn't notice at first the freezing temperature. But if her mind was oblivious to the biting cold, her weakened body immediately reacted to the sudden, dramatic change of climate. A wave of dizziness swept over her and she had to fight to keep her body upright.

The keys to Jimmy's house were in her coat pocket, but there was no way she could make that journey in her condition. Even if she could, she didn't relish the idea of going to the large, unfamiliar house on her own. What if she had a relapse? No one would know she was there. There would be no one to look after her, or send for help if her condition worsened; and she didn't intend to die alone. She didn't intend to die at all, not now, when she had so much to live for. Furthermore there was still the matter of Richard to contend with. She had meant every word she'd said.

377

Once Amy was back home, she would get the truth out of her – and if Richard had molested Amy in any way, then he would pay dearly for it. Another blast of icy wind hit her full in the face. Knowing she had to get in out of the freezing night air, she stumbled next door.

Billy Gates opened the front door, his large, homely features dropping in amazement when he saw who his late-night visitor was. Rebecca tried to say something, but her fragile body had other ideas. Her last memory was of Billy Gates calling for his mother, then being carried into the warmth of their home.

CHAPTER TWENTY-SIX

Rebecca's stay at the Gateses' house turned into two weeks, by the end of which she was nearly climbing the walls with boredom and frustration. Overnight she had gone from being a skivvy, nursemaid and general dogsbody into an exulted guest who was waited on hand and foot. Which was very nice, at first, and made a pleasant change from her previous existence. Ada Gates fussed over her new lodger like a mother hen. Rebecca only had to cough and Ada was there with a cup of tea, or the bottle of medicine Dr Barker had left when he had visited her on Christmas Day.

At first he had gone next door and been told, rather tersely, by the new master of the house, that none of the Bradford family resided there any longer. Luckily, Ada, a kindly but inquisitive soul, had seen his carriage pull up and no sooner had the door of number 17 slammed in his face than she had opened hers wide and invited him into her home.

That had been a happy day, for Ada, proud to have such a distinguished gentleman in her modest house, had invited Tom to stay for Christmas dinner. It had come as a huge relief to Rebecca when he had accepted the invitation, for she had become very fond of the kindly, gruff-spoken man. Their Christmas entertainment had been heightened by the loud shouting from next door, as Maude and Richard fought like cat and dog over his impromptu wedding arrangements. Then Ivy Harris had arrived, and the arguments had ceased for the time being, only to resume some two hours later. Through the thin walls, the occupants of the Gates household could hear every word. And from what they heard it was obvious that Richard's fiancée wasn't prepared to take up Rebecca's duties. The four people eavesdropping next door strained their ears, their faces alight with glee as they heard Ivy's strident voice issue Maude an ultimatum. Either to get her lazy backside out of bed and run the house or to be carted off to a home. It had come as a great source of amusement to the listeners to hear Richard make numerous attempts to have his say, only to be shouted down by the womenfolk. Only Ada had shown any sign of concern for Maude's future, until Rebecca had informed her that the so-called invalid had been living a lie for nearly twenty years, and was just as capable of looking after herself as any other woman of her age.

Rebecca's news had come as no surprise to Tom,

who had suspected all along that the irritating, unpleasant woman's claims of suffering from a debilitating illness were all a sham simply to get attention, and avoid work. Before he left that evening, Tom advised Rebecca to make the most of being cosseted, adding kindly that if anyone deserved looking after, she did; and Ada Gates was only too willing to help the young woman who had always shown her respect and kindness.

With such loving care and attention, Rebecca was soon back on her feet, and such was the concern of Ada and Billy Gates for her well-being, she didn't have the heart to leave them. But by the end of the first week of January, Rebecca had had enough. What with Ada hovering around her like a shadow, afraid the young woman might fall dead at her feet at any moment, and Billy following her around like a puppy, his soulful eyes pleading for some sign of affection from the woman he adored, Rebecca decided it was time she moved out.

It had been an emotional farewell, particularly on her part. They had been very good to her and she felt guilty and ungrateful about leaving them, but once she was fully recovered she could no longer ignore the strong urge to be on her way.

Before she left, she had found herself a small flat above a shop in Mare Street and immediately sent a letter to Jimmy and Amy at the hotel where they were staying, informing them of her new address. She had played down the reason for her hurried departure from her home on Christmas Eve, simply stating the plain facts, that Richard was planning to marry and move his new bride into the house, and that she, Rebecca, had fallen out with the future Mrs Fisher, and was staying with the Gateses for the time being. If she had even hinted that something was seriously wrong, she knew Jimmy and Amy would have been back on the first train, and she hadn't wanted to ruin their Christmas. She had given the matter considerable thought before putting pen to paper, and decided that, in the circumstances, it would be better for all concerned to keep her suspicions to herself until they returned from their holiday – however long that might be.

She knew Jimmy would be disappointed that she hadn't taken up residence in his own home, but Rebecca hadn't felt comfortable at the thought of living by herself in such a huge house. She had also experienced an urgent desire to prove, if only to herself, that she was capable of standing on her own two feet. Her independent streak was too strong to allow her to sponge off others, even the man she intended to marry. For years she had longed for a place of her own, and her independence. Now she had the chance, she wasn't going to let the opportunity slip away. Once she was married, she would become an ordinary housewife, supported by a man who was financially well off, leaving her no excuse to find a job of her own, and she desperately needed to know if she was capable of making something of her life – even if it was for only a short period of time.

Her next task was to find employment, and that wasn't as easy as she had imagined. With no skills, the only jobs on offer were for menial labour, and she'd had enough of that sort of work. But by the 1st of February, with her money running low, she'd had to swallow her pride and take a job as a machinist in a small dressmaker's establishment, where she toiled away in a back room with three other women from eight in the morning until six at night. All in all, it wasn't a bad job. The shop was only five minutes' walk from her flat, and her employers, two middle-aged sisters, were kindly enough.

Then a letter from Jimmy had arrived, telling her he intended to take James to France for the remainder of the winter months. The letter had been lovingly written, asking her to understand his need to strengthen his bond with his son, and begging her to be patient a little while longer. The disappointment was double-edged, as Amy had also written a pleading letter, asking if she could go with them. Rebecca had been devastated. She had braced herself for the knowledge that it might be several months before she saw Jimmy again, but she had imagined Amy would be back with her by the New Year. She had been sorely tempted to write back, demanding that Amy return home, but at the last minute she had changed her mind. As desperate as she was to learn the truth as to what had happened between her sister and Richard, it was obvious that Amy had her heart set on going abroad. Taking into consideration that the opportunity might well be the last one Amy would ever have to travel, Rebecca had put her own hurt and disappointment aside and given her permission for her sister to go.

The only comfort she had over the following

months were the weekly letters from Jimmy and Amy, which she would read over and over again to pass away the lonely evenings. And at those times, which were many, when she returned to her solitary flat and experienced a sense of loneliness wash over her, she reminded herself that this was what she had wanted. What she had dreamt of for years. To have her own home and a paying job, to feel a sense of pride that she was at last supporting herself. Yet such is human nature, that dreams, when they do come true, never quite manage to live up to expectations.

To break the monotony of her life, she often went to Jimmy's house at the weekend, familiarising herself with the layout of the home she hoped she would soon be the mistress of. But without the presence of Jimmy and the irrepressible Bessie, the house seemed desolate and unwelcoming.

Then her fortune changed.

The first piece of luck she had occurred one day in the first week in March. She had been working on a dress for herself. Having no sewing machine, she'd had to make it by hand, as she had always done. It had been a long, tedious process. With the hours she put in at work during the day, she had little enthusiasm to pick up her needle and thread when she arrived home. Yet some evenings, she had found her hobby soothing; it had also helped while away the lonely evenings. Eventually the dress was finished and, without thinking of her accomplishment, she wore it to work the following day, and was immediately asked by the proprietors of the shop where she had purchased it. When she told them she'd made and designed it herself, they became very excited, bombarding her with questions as to how long she had been engaged in such work. Rebecca was astounded by the fuss. She had never seen her sewing skills as anything more than a necessity, and was content with the sense of satisfaction she'd always felt when a particular garment was finished.

Within a week, she was promoted from the dreary day-to-day work of routine machining and given the task of making a costume or dress to her own specifications, with the view to becoming a designer in the shop, depending on if her creation, when completed, was good enough to sell. Unfortunately Rebecca had never been any good at drawing, her ideas coming from her creative mind and nimble fingers. That fact didn't deter the sisters, who were delighted they had found such a unique talent. An unused boxroom became Rebecca's office, and from there she made her first dress for the shop.

When the final stitch had been sewn, Rebecca examined the garment over and over, searching for any fault she might have overlooked, before showing it to the owners. Finally, when she could stall no longer, she took a deep breath and presented the soft green silk costume to the eagerly waiting sisters.

For what seemed like hours, Rebecca held her breath while the two middle-aged women examined the two-piece costume, turning it this way and that, peering at the intricate white lace trimming the collar and cuffs of the jacket, and the tiny red buttons that ran in a zigzag pattern across the bodice. Then they turned their attention to the skirt, which Rebecca had left unadorned and fashioned into a straight line with a two-inch flute at the hem. Then they looked at each other, their thoughts unspoken but understood. They had indeed found a treasure in this young woman – a treasure that was doubled by the fact that the young woman in question clearly had no idea of the talent she possessed.

Rebecca wasn't aware she had stopped breathing until her employers, their faces beaming with delight, asked her to display the costume in the window straight away. Within two hours it had been sold, and from that moment Rebecca's life changed.

Every waking hour was now filled with her work. As soon as she had completed a garment, it would be placed instantly in the shop window, and be sold by the end of the day. Word of the unusual designs soon spread, and the small, modest shop soon became the focus for the well-to-do woman, all of whom were anxious to possess a dress or costume that no one else had.

To meet the demand, Rebecca began working at home as well as at the shop. Though now she had the use of a sewing machine, provided for her by her employers, who still couldn't believe their luck at finding such a talented seamstress – until they realised that Rebecca could now easily set up on her own, and take the majority of their customers with her. By this time, Rebecca had become aware of their anxiety, and assured them she had no ideas about setting up on her own, as she was due to be married as soon as her fiancé returned from abroad. But her employers weren't so easily reassured. They immediately doubled her wages, and allowed her to work her own hours. This Rebecca did, often working into the small hours of the morning. It was hard work, but it took her mind off her loneliness and sadness.

The winter months had long gone, as had spring, and Rebecca was beginning to wonder if she would ever see Jimmy or Amy again. They both wrote each week without fail, and in every letter Jimmy sent he promised it wouldn't be much longer before they were together, but still there was no definite word as to when they would be returning to England.

She was re-reading Jimmy and Amy's letters one Sunday in June, when there was a knock on her door. Thinking it might be Dr Barker, who was her only visitor these days – and those visits were rare as he was a very busy man – Rebecca eagerly ran to the door.

'Hello, Becky.' Amy, her face filled with appre-hension, as if not sure of the welcome she would receive, stood nervously on the threadbare-carpeted hallway.

She needn't have worried. With a yell of pure joy that resounded throughout the building, Rebecca pulled Amy into her arms, then they both burst into tears. Tears of relief, but mostly tears of joy that they were finally reunited.

387

When the paroxysm of tears abated, they both
started to talk at once.

'Oh, Becky, I've missed you . . .'

'Amy, love, I was beginning to think I'd never
see you again. How have . . .' Then they started
laughing, then crying again, as they hugged and
kissed and babbled incoherently.

Much later, after they had calmed down, they sat
talking, never taking their eyes off each other, as if
frightened that if they did one of them might vanish. Even though they had been exchanging letters
regularly, telling each other all their news and what
was happening in their lives, they still had a lot to
talk about, but Rebecca, just grateful to have her
sister back with her again, let Amy do most of the
talking. Yet even in her joy, Rebecca couldn't help
noticing how much her little sister had changed. She
had left a young girl, now she had the appearance
and confidence of a woman much older than her
sixteen years.

Also Rebecca couldn't help but feel a twinge of
jealousy as Amy recounted her experiences over the
past six months. Up until now, Rebecca had been
feeling very proud of her achievements, but her small
claim to fame seemed to pale into insignificance
compared to the wonders of staying in posh hotels
and lying on sun-drenched beaches in the South of
France. Then she rebuked herself for her pettiness.
If anyone deserved a taste of luxury, it was Amy,
particularly in light of what might have happened
to her.

Rebecca was bursting to ask Amy about that

afternoon when she had gone cap in hand to Richard in order to get Phil out of trouble, but, seeing the glow in Amy's cheeks, which was apparent even under her tanned skin, and the happiness radiating from her eyes, Rebecca hadn't the heart to broach the subject. Not that she was going to let the matter rest. Oh, no! Not until she knew the truth. For now though, she must bide her time and wait for the right opportunity to bring up the subject.

Then, her silent thoughts were nearly wrenched from her mind into speech as Amy, looking around the small but tidy room, asked, 'Have you seen Phil lately?'

At the mention of her brother's name, Rebecca felt the old anger returning, but just as quickly curbed her temper.

Shrugging, she answered, 'No, I haven't seen him since Christmas Eve. I would have mentioned him in my letters if I had. The last time I saw Phil, he was leaving the house without so much as a "Merry Christmas". As soon as he heard Richard was getting married and moving back in, Phil knew his time there was limited. I suppose he wanted to move out on his own accord before he was thrown out. Still! He's a grown man. I dare say he's managed to find some kind of employment and a roof over his head. If he hadn't, he'd soon have taken the trouble to find out where I was and moved in here . . . Oh!' She shook her head impatiently. 'You already know most of this from my letters; I haven't seen anyone from that house since Christmas Eve. Though I still see Ada Gates from time to time, usually when I'm out shopping.' A smile spread over her face. 'There I go again, telling you things you already know.'

Leaning back in her chair, Rebecca's eyes became thoughtful. 'Now then, what did I write in my last letter? I've told you Richard and his new wife aren't getting along too well, and that Ada says they're always fighting. You know how thin those walls are between the houses, especially if you put your ear up against them.' She laughed gaily, but inside she was hoping that the mention of Richard would prompt some reaction from Amy, but her sister showed no signs of distress. Maybe nothing had happened. Maybe it was just her hatred of the man in question that made her think the worst of him. But if that were true, then why had Phil looked so ashamed when she had tackled him? And why had he left the house in such a hurry and, to this day, made no effort to contact her?

But Amy was talking again. 'Never mind them. I still can't get over the fact that Maude was never a cripple. When I read your letter telling me about her, I just couldn't take it in. I mean, what sort of person would lie in bed for twenty years and let their life just pass by? I still can't understand it. And when I think of how you had to wash and clean up after her . . . Ooh, it makes my blood boil.' The anger in Amy's voice caused Rebecca to flinch. It was as if she was listening to a different person. Then the moment was gone, and the old Amy was back. 'Let's not talk about them any more, Becky. I want to hear about you. Oh, Becky, I'm so proud of you. I always knew you were good at dressmaking, but I never dreamt you could make such a good living from it. Why, it sounds like you'll soon have your own shop.' Her face alight with enthusiasm, she laughed gaily. 'I can just see the sign now: "Rebecca's Fashions", hung over one of those posh shops up the West End.'

Now Rebecca laughed. 'Whoa! I don't think that's very likely. I've only been doing it for a few months. I hardly think the big stores up the West End are about to lose any sleep over me stealing their trade.'

'Don't put yourself down, Becky. I think you've done brilliantly. I couldn't have done it. I'd be quite happy waiting on tables for the rest of my life if I had to, although Charlie says . . .' Her cheeks turned red under the sun-tanned skin.

'Oh, yes. Charlie says what exactly?' Rebecca teased.

The colour in Amy's cheeks deepened as she plucked at the skirt of her dress nervously. 'Nothing, really. You know what Charlie's like. Always muck-ing about. He just said that . . . Well, that when we were married, the only waiting I'd be doing was for him . . . But . . . but, he was only joking. I mean, I'm only sixteen. That's much too young to be thinking about getting married . . . Isn't it, Becky?'

Rebecca's heart melted at the wistful note of hope that had sprung into Amy's voice. 'It all depends, love. I don't think age matters when you love some-one, as long as you're sure it's the real thing and not just infatuation.'

'Oh, no, Becky. It's not infatuation,' Amy replied earnestly. 'I love Charlie. I thought I did before, but I wasn't sure. After all, he's the first man I've ever been out with. But after all the past months being with him every day, I know for sure . . . I love him, Becky, and . . . and he loves me.' Looking Rebecca straight in the eyes, she asked, 'Would you mind, Becky? I mean, would you mind me marrying Charlie one day? You do like him, don't you, Becky?'

Rebecca felt the back of her eyes begin to sting. It looked like she and Amy wouldn't be together for very long after all. If Amy had been possessed of a frivolous character then Rebecca would have firmly vetoed the idea of her marrying so young. But she had always known that her sister was the type of woman who wanted nothing more out of life than a loving husband, and a home and family of her own.

Anyway! She sat up straighter. Wasn't she planning to get married herself in the near future? So what was she fretting about? Yet Amy was still so young, but there was no mistaking the love shining from her eyes when she spoke Charlie's name.

'Has he actually asked you to marry him, love?'

Amy shook her head, a smile on her lips. 'Not in so many words. I mean, he hasn't gone down on one knee and asked for my hand in marriage . . .' she giggled infectiously. 'You know, like they do in the books and magazines I like to read. But he keeps making comments about what it'll be like once we're married, or making jokes about making an honest woman of me one day.'

Remembering Jimmy's words to her on Christmas Eve, Rebecca thought wryly that it appeared they had both fallen in love with men who hadn't an ounce of romance in their souls. But what did that matter? A sudden thought struck Rebecca.

'Where is Charlie, by the way?'

At Rebecca's question, Amy jumped in the air, her hand flying to her mouth. 'Oh, my goodness. I told him to wait downstairs. I wanted to see you first on my own. I completely forgot all about him.'

Rebecca roared. 'So much for you being madly in love with the man. You've been here for nearly two hours, the poor lad must be wondering if I've tied you to a chair to prevent you escaping from me again.'

Dashing across the room, Amy asked breathlessly, 'Is it all right if he comes up, Becky?'

Still laughing, Rebecca nodded. 'If he's still there, he can. I wouldn't have waited around all this time. I suppose Jimmy's already back at the house. Oh, I nearly forgot to ask. How's the child? Did Jimmy taking him away work out all right?'

Amy halted her rapid dash in mid-flight. 'Oh, Jimmy didn't come back with us . . .' Seeing the shocked hurt that suddenly covered Rebecca's face, Amy ran to her side, adding quickly, 'I'm sorry, Becky. Oh, trust me to open my mouth without thinking. What I meant to say was that Jimmy, Bessie and James will be back home in a few days. He did try to get us all on the same boat, but he left it too late and there were only two spare tickets, so he let me and Charlie have them. We were going to write and let you know we were coming home, but Jimmy said it would be a surprise for you if we just all showed up. Only it didn't turn out that

393

way.' Suddenly Amy let out a loud laugh. 'I still can't believe we managed to get Bessie on the boat to France in the first place. I know I've already told you about it in my letters, but, oh, you should have heard her when Jimmy said he wanted to take us all to France. She went stark, raving mad, saying there was no way she was getting on any boat, not after what happened to the *Titanic*. I must admit, I was a bit frightened too. I mean, all those poor people drowning, and on a big ship that was supposed to be unsinkable, but Jimmy kept saying that lightning doesn't strike twice, and that kind of thing. In the end he wore her down . . . Well! I knew he would eventually. But she didn't stop complaining all the way there, and she was beginning to frighten some of the other passengers with her talk of the *Titanic*, she wouldn't stop going on about it – and that was before we even got on the boat. Jimmy got so fed up with it, he gave her a bottle of brandy, and half an hour later she was dead to the world. Luckily Charlie managed to distract James, so that was all right. Mind you . . .' She leant forward and winked at Rebecca. 'I think Charlie was as scared as Bessie and me, but he'd never admit it. Still, we're home safe and sound, and so will Jimmy be in a few days. Though I wouldn't like to be in his shoes when he tries to get Bessie back on the boat. She'll make his life hell – bless her! Right then, I'll go and fetch Charlie. Won't be long; get the kettle on, will you, Becky? Charlie hasn't had a proper cup of tea since Christmas.'

The moment Amy left the room, Rebecca's body

slumped with relief. For one awful moment back then she had imagined . . . ! As Amy's footsteps sounded on the stairs, Rebecca dropped her head into her hands. She felt sick with relief; her hands were clammy and her heart was pounding rapidly, and she didn't know whether to laugh or cry. If she'd harboured any lingering doubts about the love she felt for the man whose company she'd been in fewer than a half-dozen times, that heart-stopping moment when she thought he wasn't coming back for her had dispelled all further doubts.

She remembered Tom Barker's recollection of how he had fallen in love with his wife at first sight, and her lips trembled into a smile. There was someone else who would be glad to see his old friend back in the country again. He hadn't said much on his visits, but it had been plain that Tom had missed his old sparring partner very much.

Now the waiting was nearly over, and by the time an unusually bashful-looking Charlie entered the room with Amy prodding him from behind, Rebecca had fully composed herself. In an uncharacteristic gesture, for she wasn't one to display her feelings – that was Amy's province – Rebecca threw her arms around the startled Charlie's neck and gave her future brother-in-law a fierce hug.

CHAPTER TWENTY-SEVEN

Later that same night, Phil Bradford was weaving his way drunkenly down Walthamstow High Street. He was in a very good mood, in fact he'd had a good night all round. First he had managed to get himself into a lucrative game of cards held at the back of the Flying Horse, and had come out ten pounds better off. Then the barmaid he'd had his eye on for weeks had invited him back to her place, where he had spent a very pleasurable few hours. Now he was on his way home to his room in a local boarding house with a good few brandies warming his system and ten pounds richer than he had been on leaving his lodgings.

He was passing an alleyway when, from out of nowhere, three men appeared blocking his path. Peering up through bleary eyes, Phil became suddenly stone cold sober. For the man in the middle was none other than Big George himself.

'Well! Well! If it isn't me old mate, Phil. How've yer been? We ain't seen yer for a while. Found yerself a new bookie, 'ave yer?' Big George hadn't come about his name by chance. He was a giant of a man, both in height and breadth, and even with an amiable smile on his face he oozed menace.

Stumbling back a pace, Phil pasted a sickly smile to his face. 'Hello, George. I've been meaning to come by and see you . . .'

The towering man stepped closer. 'Well, now I've saved yer the trouble, ain't I.' Putting a heavy arm around Phil's shaking shoulders, he added, 'You was looking very pleased with yerself just then, though yer ain't looking so good now. I wonder what could've caused that. Maybe a guilty conscience, like the matter of the twenty pounds yer still owe me, eh?'

Phil gulped, a feeling of dread sweeping through him. 'Now look, George. I paid back that sixty pounds, and another fifteen on top of that. I don't owe you anything . . .'

The friendly hug suddenly turned into a fierce grip. 'Now that's where yer wrong, mate. Yer see, that new bookie yer've been dealing with 'as suddenly gorn outta business. The competition was too strong. You know how it works, Phil. One bookie sells his business to another, and the debts go with the deal. And, you, me old mate, 'ave been up ter yer old tricks again, ain't yer. Some people never learn, do they?' The man's huge head shook from side to side in mock admonishment. ''Cos according ter Smilie's books yer owe 'im twenty pounds.

397

Only now he's sold his stake, guess who's bought him out? Though he wasn't that keen ter sell, I 'ad ter use a bit of persuasion. Yer know what I mean, mate? Mind you, he was never cut out for the game. The stupid bastard let 'is punters walk all over 'im. Letting them run up debts, then not 'aving the bottle ter collect what was owing 'im. There's nearly a thousand pounds unpaid debts on old Smilie's books. The difference is, I ain't the sorta bloke who lets people take the piss, know what I mean, Phil? Things 'ave been looking up fer me lately. Now that Jimmy Jackson's gorn off somewhere and closed down his business, there's only me left, apart from the losers like old Smilie, an' I expect they'll be happy enough to sell ter me, given the right incentive. And I can be very persuasive when I want ter be . . . Can't I, boys?' He looked over to where the other two men were waiting in the shadows.

Then, without warning, in a sudden, terrifying turn of mood, Big George slammed Phil up against the wall. Placing an iron arm across Phil's throat, he growled menacingly, 'I want me money, Bradford, an' I want it soon. But I'm a reasonable man, an' I'm prepared ter do a deal with yer. The thing is, Phil, I've never liked that Jackson bastard. Always came across as the sorta bloke who thought he was better than the rest of us bookies, an' he nicked a lot of me punters over the years, an' I don't like people treading on me toes. It's been nice an' quiet while he's been away, but word on the street is he's on 'is way back 'ome. Now I can't stop 'im coming back, but I can make 'im think twice about setting up in business again – wiv a bit a help, of course.'

The sweat was pouring down Phil's forehead into his eyes. Blinking furiously he spluttered, 'Why are you telling me? I can't do anything, I . . .' His words were silenced by the heavy arm leaning harder across his windpipe.

'Let me finish, Bradford, I don't like being interrupted. Now, where was I? Oh, yeah. Jimmy Jackson, an' the surprise I've got lined up fer 'im when he gets 'ome.' The soft glow from the lamppost further down the road was bright enough for Phil to see the vicious expression on the face of the man holding him in a vice-like grip and he felt his knees buckle. The unpleasant smell of stale beer and cigars wafted in Phil's face as Big George continued in a softer, but no less menacing tone. 'I know fer a fact that Jackson's got something going on wiv yer sister, she's been seen going in and outta 'is 'ouse while he's been away, an' Jackson ain't the type of bloke ter give 'is 'ouse keys to any old tart, so she must be something special ter him – yer sister I mean. And that's where you come in, Bradford. I did send me boys round a few times, ter Jackson's place, but it's locked up tighter than the Bank of England. Well, it's only ter be expected, ain't it. I mean, a man like Jimmy Jackson ain't gonna go away an' leave his gaffe open ter every thief in the East End, is he? Nah! He's too clever fer that. Then there's 'is neighbours. Very popular man, is our Mr Jackson, so I'm told. And yer know what it's like round these parts, everyone knows everyone else's business, an' a couple of strangers 'anging around Jackson's 'ouse would be spotted straight away. Now, here's the deal. You get those keys from yer sister, an' hand 'em over ter me. I won't need 'em fer long. Just long enough ter make an impression of 'em. Why! Yer'll be able ter put 'em back before she even knows they're missing. My boys will get in without no trouble, turn the place over and be back out without anyone being any the wiser. I'll settle past scores with Jackson, an' yer slate'll be wiped clean.'

A ferocious grin spread over the thick lips. 'I even know where he keeps 'is safe. One of me boys used ter go out with some tart that worked there fer a while, before that old hag, Bessie Wilks, gave the girl 'er marching orders. Yer know what women are like, Phil; love ter 'ave a nose round, an' this tart 'ad a very good look around the 'ouse before she was sacked, an' like most women, she couldn't keep 'er gob shut. Like I said, Jackson's very popular round these parts, an' the silly cow thought she was someone important, just 'cos she was working fer him. My boy's ears pricked up when he 'eard 'er mouthing off about the lovely, big 'ouse. A couple more drinks down her neck, an' she was telling him all about the safe, hidden behind a wall in the upstairs dining room. I tell yer, Phil, I thought me luck was in. 'Course, once my boy had the information outta 'er, he dropped her like a stone; didn't want no connection coming back ter me. So, yer see me problem, Phil? I practically know the layout of the place, even where the safe's hidden, only up till now, I ain't had no way of getting into the place. It was a bit a luck fer me finding out Jackson's piece of stuff was yer sister, an' then finding yer name on old Smilie's books – well! . . . It sort of looks like it was meant ter 'appen, don't it? Sort of like having it handed ter me on a plate, an' I'd be a fool ter let the chance of doing Jackson's place over pass by.'

Vainly, Phil tried one last time to reason with the man holding him. 'Look, George. I'll get the money, I swear. I can't go to Becks . . . I mean, my sister. I haven't seen her since Christmas. We're not even on speaking terms any more. I—'

A heavy fist collided with the side of his head, and for a few seconds Phil blacked out. Then he heard the low voice, thick with rage, whispering in his ear. 'I ain't fucking interested in yer family quarrels, Bradford. You just get those keys ter me before Jackson gets back, or else yer won't 'ave a leg ter stand on . . . And that ain't just a figure of speech. Yer get me meaning . . . MATE!'

Unable to move, Phil stared into the hard, cold eyes, his insides turning to water. Then the three men vanished as quickly as they had appeared. Phil remained leaning against the rough wall, his whole body petrified with terror. Then the drink he had consumed earlier, combined with his fear, brought his body double as he was violently sick onto the pavement.

'I'll get it, Becky,' Amy called out when the knock sounded on the door. Expecting to see Charlie, Amy's eyes stretched wide in surprise at the

401

unexpected visitor. 'Phil! Blooming hell, I didn't expect to see you. Come in, come in,' she pulled her brother into the room, calling out, 'Becky, Becky, come and see who's here.'

Coming out from the bedroom, the only other room in the small flat, Rebecca stopped dead in her tracks. The last time she had seen Phil she had wished never to set eyes on him again, but the pull of the family bond that had kept them together for so many years was too strong to sever that easily. She was now beginning to think that maybe her suspicions about Richard were wrong, and that Phil had looked so shame-faced because his little sister had had to get him out of trouble. Even though Amy had only been with her since Sunday, just two days, she had shown no sign that anything was troubling her, so maybe Becky had been mistaken after all. Knowing her temper as she did, she now felt ashamed that she could have thought such a dreadful thing of her only brother. He might be a lot of things, but even Phil, as desperate as he had been for the money to pay off his debts, wouldn't have stood by and done nothing if he'd had the slightest inkling that Richard had laid his grubby hands on the sister he loved.

Besides, all their lives had changed during the past six months. She and Amy had never been happier. Amy had her Charlie, and Jimmy was due back tomorrow, providing his travel arrangements hadn't altered. And once he was home, she would make sure she never lost sight of him again. Without speaking, Rebecca stepped closer to Phil, her eyes

raking over his anxious face. And when he gave that
wry grin, and lifted his shoulders in the manner she
knew so well, her heart went out to him. It was
time to heal the rift between them and become a
family once more. Besides, with both her and Amy
planning to marry, they would need someone to give
them away.

'Don't just stand there like a stranger. Come in,
you silly devil.'

Phil's body sagged with relief. He hadn't known
what to expect when he'd decided to track Rebecca
down. It had been simple enough. All he'd had to
do was go and see old Mrs Gates; she had told him
where to find his sister.

He hadn't expected to find Amy as well.

Half an hour later he was sitting in a shabby
armchair drinking a cup of tea and talking and
laughing with his sisters as if they had never been
apart. And that fact alone tore at his very soul. For
his only purpose for being here was to get himself
out of trouble, and he was going to do it in the
only way he knew how – by using his sisters. He
had hardly slept since his run-in with Big George
on Sunday night. Up until then, life had been very
good to him. He'd had enough money left over after
settling his debt to live on while he looked for work.
It was true he hadn't tried very hard, but he had
managed to get a few days' labouring work now
and then when his money was running low. He
still gambled of course, it was in his blood, and for
the first time in years, his luck had held good – for
a few months. Then, as with all gamblers, his luck

had started to run out, and before he knew it, he was running up yet another debt. But he hadn't worried about owing money to old Smilie. Everyone owed Smilie money, the old bookie knew he would get paid back eventually, and he usually did. Though Smilie wasn't a fool. He never let his punters run up debts over thirty pounds, that was his limit; and Phil had been within that limit, until two nights ago!

'What's the matter, Phil? You've gone very quiet all of a sudden.'

Rebecca's voice cut into Phil's troubled thoughts. Glancing up, he stared into the blue eyes he knew so well and felt his stomach turn in self-loathing at what he was planning. He knew from the conversation he had overheard on Christmas Eve that Rebecca had the keys to Jimmy's house, and also knew the whereabouts of the safe. What he had never imagined was that Big George would find out about Rebecca's involvement with Jimmy Jackson. It seemed the only thing Big George didn't know was the combination to the safe – but Becky did!

He tried to ease his conscience by telling himself that Jimmy Jackson could afford to lose whatever money he had left lying in his safe, and also that no one would be hurt in the burglary. Amy had already told him that Jimmy wasn't due back from France until tomorrow, so the house would be empty until then. All he had to do was somehow get the keys from Rebecca without her knowledge, and put them back once Big George had taken an impression of them. It had sounded so easy as he had lain awake thinking about it, but nothing in life is ever as easy in reality. He couldn't very well just ask her for them, or the combination to the safe either. He groaned silently. Now, looking into his sister's trusting eyes, he knew he couldn't go through with it. He couldn't betray her and Amy again. He still had some money. He could buy a train ticket out of London and start a new life somewhere Big George would never find him.

Phil sat up straighter, his mind suddenly clear. Yes! That's what he'd do; in the circumstances, it was the only solution left open to him. It would be hard for him, but at least he would be able to sleep at night, and maybe regain some self-respect; but most of all, he would keep the girls out of the mess he had made of his life.

Then fate stepped in and took a hand, and by doing so changed Phil's life for ever.

Clearing his throat he replied, 'Nothing's the matter. Sorry, Becks. I didn't get much sleep last night; besides, I'd much rather listen to you two talk.'

'Well, that makes a change,' Amy laughed, waving a hand merrily in Phil's face.

Then, Rebecca, her face alive with pleasure, cried happily, 'Who fancies some fish and chips? It'll be like old times, except this time there's no lamb stew simmering away on the stove.' She laughed at Phil. 'And no Maude screeching for her piece of haddock.'

As memories flooded over the three sibblings, they all laughed, yet the laughter was tinged with sadness. They all knew that their time spent together, like this, just the three of them, was painfully short.

Phil was about to offer to go and get their supper when Rebecca said, 'Me and Amy were going out anyway. We've got to buy some milk and a few odds and ends to take to the house tomorrow; we might as well pick up our supper on the way back.' She was already on her feet. Picking up her bag, she rummaged around before taking out a set of keys, saying, 'I'll be glad to hand these back. I've felt like I've been carrying around the Crown Jewels in my bag since Jimmy left.'

Phil eyed the keys nervously. 'I'm surprised you didn't move in when you had the chance, Becks. After all, Jimmy's place would've been much more comfortable than this.' He waved his arm around the shabbily furnished room.

Rebecca grinned wryly. 'That's what Amy's been telling me, but like I told her, I wouldn't have felt comfortable there by myself. Besides, I haven't done too badly on my own. Now then, what about our supper? Come on, Amy, the shops will be shutting soon. Phil can make the tea and lay the table while we're out. Oh, you'd better lay an extra place for Charlie.' An impish grin touched Rebecca's lips as she playfully nudged Amy in the side. 'He'll be here soon.' Rebecca took her purse from her bag and they left, their girlish laughter echoing down the hall. But Phil could only focus on Rebecca's handbag, which was lying on the worn sideboard by the door. His limbs shaking, Phil licked his lips nervously, his mind screaming at him to stop, but the temptation was too great for his weak character to resist. He had been so close to leaving, so close to doing the right thing for a change, and now this had to happen. Before he knew it, the keys to Jimmy's house were in his jacket pocket. He also found a neatly written number on a piece of paper tucked into the lining of Rebecca's handbag. The sweat pouring from his body, Phil looked at the numbers, committing them to memory before placing the scrap of paper back where he'd found it.

He was setting the table when the girls arrived back, accompanied by a grinning Charlie. Phil wasn't fooled by Charlie's easy-going manner, though that in itself was genuine enough. It was what was underneath that counted. And in Charlie, Amy had found herself a strong man, as had Rebecca with Jimmy, and for that Phil was truly grateful. They'd both had enough of unreliable men in their lives; it was comforting to know his sisters would be cared for by men who would never let them down.

Shortly before eight, Phil rose and said, 'Well, I'm off back to my lodgings. Thanks for the supper, Becks, and the company.' His eyes swept round the trio. 'I really enjoyed it.'

'Oh, you don't have to go so soon, do you, Phil?' Rebecca had also risen, her hand lying on Phil's arm. 'I was hoping you'd stay a bit longer. We've got a lot of catching up to do.'

Swallowing loudly, Phil thought swiftly. It seemed as if fate had once more stepped in to lay a helping hand. He had intended to drop the keys back early tomorrow, but what if instead he . . . ! As his thoughts trundled furiously round his head, Phil quickly made up his mind. It might work. If he was quick enough, it just might work. Looking at his watch he exclaimed, 'Well, look, I've got to meet a friend; we'd arranged to go for a drink, but I could go tell him I'm busy tonight.'

'Oh, yes, do that, Phil.' Amy was nodding up at him.

'I might be about an hour, if that's not too late.'

Rebecca and Amy both smiled.

'No, that's not too late,' Rebecca replied. 'I work my own hours now, and Lady Muck here doesn't have a job to get up for.'

An hour later Phil was back at the flat, his heart hammering against his ribcage. Instead of his original plan he had been to Jimmy's house and unlocked the back door, then gone to Big George and told him what he had done. He had also told the bookie the combination of the safe, thinking that the sooner Big George's men were out of Jimmy's house the better. This piece of information had earned Phil an extra five pounds. He had been loath to take the offered money, but had decided it would be wiser for him to keep on good terms with the sinister bookmaker. He had also told the menacing figure that tonight was the only opportunity he was going to get, because Jimmy Jackson would be back the following day.

It was close on eleven o'clock before Charlie announced he was going home, and Phil offered to walk with him.

Leaving Amy and Charlie a moment's privacy to say goodnight, Rebecca took the tray of dirty cups over to the sink, and while her back was turned, Phil, with trembling fingers, quickly took the opportunity to slip the keys back into Rebecca's open handbag. Then he turned and smiled at her.

'I'm glad things have worked out for you and Amy, Becks. After all you've told me, I'm not surprised you walked out. I only wish we'd all gone long ago, it would have saved a lot of hardship. But that was my fault. I should have looked after you better; both of you, especially Amy. And . . . and, I want you to know, Becks, that even after the things I've done, I've never stopped loving you and Amy. Will you remember that, Becks . . . Please? Always remember what I've just said, no matter what happens? Promise me, Becks!'

Rebecca stepped nearer, her anxious eyes boring into his. 'You sound like you're going to do another disappearing act. Are you in trouble again, Phil? Is that why you came round?'

Phil heard the deep pain in Rebecca's voice and felt his shame and guilt rising once more. Now he knew what Judas must have felt like. Yet even Judas had had the decency to take his own life rather than live with his betrayal. Not like him. Oh, no. He, Phil Bradford, would always look after his own skin. But maybe he could start again, only not some place miles away, but here, with his family. He would have to see how things went tonight. Besides which, it would seem very suspicious if he were to vanish the very day after Jimmy's house was burgled. Feeling a little more confident, he shook Rebecca's hands in a playful gesture.

'No, I'm not planning to disappear again, and I'm not in any trouble either. It's just that I can't see your future husband welcoming me with open arms, can you? I just feel a bit awkward, that's all.'

Rebecca's face cleared. 'Don't you worry about Jimmy, Phil. I'm not saying you two will ever be the best of friends, but I don't see why you can't be civil to each other.'

Bending down, Phil kissed her forehead. 'Thanks, Becks. It would mean a lot to me. Now then, where's that little sister of mine? We'd better not leave her too long alone with her young man. It wouldn't be proper, now would it?' He winked playfully.

When he parted company from Charlie some fifteen minutes later, Phil turned the corner and leant up against the wall, his breathing coming hard. He had done it. His gambling debts were once again erased, and there was nothing to link him with the break-in. But, oh, dear God! What a nightmare the last few hours had been. Now it was over, and when, for the umpteenth time, he vowed never to get into debt again, his mind sneered back at him, *Yeah, of course you won't. Until the next time!*

Pulling himself from the security of the wall, Phil straightened his shoulders and, feeling a little easier in his mind, he walked on.

He wouldn't have felt so confident if he could have read Charlie's thoughts.

*   *   *

410

Watching the broad figure of Phil Bradford walk away, Charlie's eyes were wary. There was something about the bloke that troubled him. For a start he had been on edge all night long, then when he'd come back from meeting his so-called friend, he had been distinctly agitated. Neither of the girls had noticed anything amiss, but then they hadn't been looking. Charlie, like Jimmy, had been brought up rough on the East End streets, and was used to observing the signs to a man's character or behaviour. The instinct to know who you were dealing with wasn't born into a person, it was something you learnt at an early age, particularly if you had been bred in an environment where your life could hang in the balance if you didn't have your wits about you.

Shrugging off his mood, Charlie strolled on, his thoughts returning to Amy, and the imminent arrival of his governor. Walking faster, Charlie passed his lodgings, making for Jimmy's house a few streets further on. The girls were bringing round some milk and a few bits of food in the morning, just in case the boat and trains arrived a bit earlier than expected. Bessie would be in a bad enough mood after being forced onto a boat again, without her coming home to a house with no welcoming cup of strong tea waiting for her. Whistling softly, Charlie turned the corner and let himself into the large, darkened house. Jimmy had asked him to open all the doors and windows to let in some fresh air before Bessie got home. Charlie had planned to come here first thing in the morning, but knowing how bad he was for oversleeping, had decided at the last

411

moment to spend the night at the house. Then if he did sleep in, at least the girls would be around early, and their arrival would surely waken him. For though he might sleep soundly, the slightest noise would wake him up – yet another legacy of his early upbringing.

Charlie was halfway up the stairs when he was hit forcefully from behind. The attack came so quickly, Charlie never heard a sound, nor felt the impact as his body hit the stairs one by one, as he rolled down the steep staircase. When he hit the last step, his body jerked in the air before landing with a sickening thud in the middle of the dark, spacious hallway.

Charlie didn't hear the urgent whispers and arguments coming from the disturbed intruders, nor did he hear them leave; he never heard a sound.

'Never again. I'm telling yer now, lad. Never again. Me insides feel like they've been pulled through the mangle.'

Standing by the Hansom cab with James asleep on his shoulder, and their luggage piled high on the pavement, Jimmy growled back, 'Yeah, and so do my nerves. You ain't stopped moaning since we left France, you miserable cow. Now, do you think you could get the door open while I pay the cab – if it's not too much trouble, of course.'

Bessie bridled at his tone, though deep down she knew herself to be at fault. Nevertheless she shot back sarcastically, 'Well I would, if I had me keys, but yer told me ter give 'em ter Charlie, didn't yer, so he could come round early and give the place an airing. Huh! That was a waste of time, wasn't it! Seeing as how we've arrived back in the middle of the night.'

Shifting James's weight a little further up his shoulder, Jimmy groaned silently before replying in a clipped voice, 'It's broad daylight, you daft . . .'

'Only 'cos it's summer. If it was winter, it'd be pitch black at this time of the morning. Bleeding hell! It ain't even five o'clock yet. And ter me, mate, that's the middle of the night.'

Giving up the argument, Jimmy rummaged in his pocket for his keys. 'Here, take mine. Just get the door open, and give it a rest, please, Bessie. Just give it a rest.'

Still indignant, but knowing she was pushing her luck, Bessie took the keys, while Jimmy paid off the grinning cabbie.

'Cheers Guv'nor!' The man's eyebrows rose in pleasant surprise at the generous tip. 'D'yer want me ter carry the cases in fer yer? Yer seem ter 'ave yer hands full . . . Wiv the little 'un, I mean.'

'Thanks, that would be a help. As you say, I've already got my hands full.'

Instantly the cabbie jumped to the ground, and was just about to pick up the heaviest looking case when Bessie's screams almost lifted him off his feet.

Jimmy, too, jumped in fright. Without stopping to think, he thrust the sleeping boy into the startled cabbie's arms and raced into the house. He hadn't had time to think what he might find, but he never expected to see the crumpled body of young Charlie lying in the hallway.

Bessie had the dark head cradled in her lap, her face, streaming with tears, looked up at Jimmy as she cried piteously, 'I can't wake 'im up, Jimmy. I can't wake the lad up, an' his head's bleeding. Get some help, lad. Quickly, get some help.'

Jimmy hesitated for a few seconds, his instinct urging him to go to his friend's side, but Bessie was right. Spinning on his heel, he turned and found the cabbie staring in at the front door, his eyes stretched wide at the scene he was witnessing. Then the child was taken from his arms as Jimmy, his face and voice urgent, said, 'I want you to go to eleven Chapman Place, and fetch a Dr Barker back here with you. Quickly, man, it could be a matter of life or death.'

The cabbie's big frame seemed to swell as he took on the mantle of a man on a mission. With an air of importance that was unfamiliar to him, the cabbie said tersely, 'Yer can rely on me, Guv'nor,' then he was back up in the driving seat, urging the horses towards the address he'd been given.

'What's the matter, Dad?' James, his voice sleepy, sat up in Jimmy's arms and rubbed his eyes. 'What's wrong, Dad?'

Swiftly gathering his son to his chest, Jimmy averted the boy's eyes from the distressing scene. 'Nothing, son. Nothing for you to worry about. Look, let's get you up to bed, eh. Then you can have a proper sleep, all right?'

Talking rapidly, Jimmy pressed James's face into his shoulder as he negotiated a pathway around the weeping Bessie and the silent form of Charlie. Anxious to get James safely tucked up in bed before Tom and the police arrived, Jimmy held his breath as he lowered the small figure onto his bed. He needn't have worried. The moment the child's head hit the pillow, he went instantly back to sleep. Jimmy waited a few moments to make sure James wouldn't awaken, then, confident that the boy would sleep for a good few hours, he closed the bedroom door.

Out on the landing Jimmy could hear Bessie's heart-wrenching sobs as she rocked the young man's body in her arms, and felt his eyes prickle with unshed tears. Slowly he descended the staircase, his mind filled with dread at what he might find at the bottom.

But whatever the outcome, the men responsible would pay – and pay dearly.

CHAPTER TWENTY-EIGHT

Jimmy Jackson was on the warpath!

Word was out on the street that a big reward was waiting for anyone who could give a lead into the burglary at the Jackson house, and the subsequent attempted murder of young Charlie Bull. With his money and influence, Jimmy cast his net wide, calling in all favours owed, from high-ranking officials to the lowest street runner, yet the perpetrators remained at liberty.

Now, a week on, neither the police nor Jimmy were any closer to finding the men responsible. The only consolation was that Charlie was going to be all right. He had taken a bad knock to the back of his head, and the fall down the stairs hadn't helped. The only reason he'd survived was because he had been found quickly. As Tom Barker had told Jimmy, another few hours and it could have been a very different story. Even so, to all intents and purposes, the men who had attacked Charlie had left him for dead and, to Jimmy's mind, that was as good as murder.

He was still thinking along the same lines as he stood waiting outside the dress shop for Rebecca to finish work, his foot tapping impatiently as the minutes ticked slowly by. Tutting beneath his breath, Jimmy peered into the shop window, hoping to catch a glimpse of Rebecca, and instead caught the attention of a middle-aged woman whom he assumed was one of the ladies who owned the shop. This was another state of affairs he hadn't bargained on. He had been slightly miffed when Rebecca hadn't taken the opportunity to move into his home, opting instead to take up residence in a small, shabby flat. And while he had admired her independent nature for refusing to take the easy option, he nevertheless had imagined that once he was home, Rebecca would give up her job and devote her time to him and James. It was a selfish wish on his part, he admitted to himself, and he was beginning to realise that Rebecca's new-found employment was more than just a job to her. It wasn't going to be easy to persuade her to give it up. Pursing his lips, Jimmy let his thoughts wander. Once they were married and the first child was on its way, she would probably be only too eager to stay at home. No sooner had the thought crossed his mind than he felt an uncomfortable twinge of shame and guilt, for even by thinking such a thing, he had subconsciously lumped her with the majority of women he had encountered over the years; and Rebecca was

417

worth far more than any of her predecessors. In an effort to counteract his disparaging thoughts, Jimmy concentrated on the reason he was here.

Charlie was due to come out of hospital today, and Jimmy wanted Rebecca with him when he picked up his friend. Amy was already with Charlie; indeed, that poor girl had hardly left the young man's bed-side since the vicious attack that had almost cost him his life.

'Come on, love. What are you doing in there? The shop was shut over ten minutes ago,' he muttered beneath his breath. Glancing up, he saw with some dismay that the woman was smiling at him, while beckoning him to enter the shop. Putting up his hands in a gesture of refusal, Jimmy smiled as he shook his head, but the woman was already striding towards the front of the shop. The bell over the door tinkled.

'Won't you come in and wait, Mr Jackson? Rebecca won't be much longer. A few last-minute hiccups, I'm afraid.' She smiled timidly, as if expecting a rebuff.

Jimmy saw the awkward hesitation and grinned, 'Thank you, I think I will. I don't want to get arrested for loitering, do I?'

The woman tittered, her cheeks colouring as she moved aside to let him enter. 'Oh, Mr Jackson, you are a caution. Loitering indeed, whatever next?'

Jimmy's eyebrows rose in amusement at the response to his feeble joke. Obviously the woman didn't get out much, poor soul.

'Would you like some refreshment, Mr Jackson?

418

Lemonade, perhaps, or maybe you'd prefer a cup of tea? Oh, please, do have a seat.' She gestured to three plush red velvet armchairs arranged in a triangle in the middle of the shop floor.

Sitting down, Jimmy made himself comfortable, while at the same time trying to push down his irritation at the delay in getting to the hospital. Poor Charlie must be counting the minutes after a week's stay in that dismal environment.

'No, thank you, Mrs . . . ?'

Her hand flying to her throat, Stella Barnsley felt her heart racing as she stared down into the enigmatic face. Lucky Rebecca, the middle-aged woman reflected enviously.

'It's miss, sir. Miss Stella Barnsley. My sister and I never married.'

'Well, if that's the case, I can only say there must be many men who've missed out on a wonderful opportunity.' Jimmy winced inwardly as the words left his mouth. Strewth! This was what came of mixing with the so-called upper-class society. Well, he wasn't in France any more, but back home where he belonged, thank God! Conscious of the woman's anxious eyes, and knowing that when a woman said ten minutes she usually meant about half an hour, Jimmy resigned himself to a long wait and said cheerfully, 'As a matter of fact, I would like a cup of tea, if you'll join me.'

Immediately flustered, the woman twittered, 'Of course, Mr Jackson. If you'll just bear with me a moment.' Hurrying, as if afraid the stylish gentleman might vanish if left alone too long, Miss Stella

Barnsley lifted the flap in the counter and went through a door leading off to the back of the shop.

Left alone, Jimmy let his eyes roam around the shop. So this was where Rebecca spent her days. It wasn't an overly large room. The area where he was sitting was carpeted in a thick, blue pile, and on two of the walls there hung long, gilt-edged mirrors, their reflections causing Jimmy some disconcertment. Pulling the chair to a different angle, he continued to study the room. Turning his head, he saw two curtained-off areas which he surmised were the changing rooms, and to his right ran a long mahogany counter. The door that Miss Barnsley had disappeared through remained closed, though Jimmy could hear the sound of sewing machines in operation. Obviously Rebecca wasn't the only one working late.

He shifted his gaze as the door opened and Miss Barnsley came towards him carrying a silver tray upon which rested a silver teapot, a small milk jug, and two tiny porcelain cups, the sight of which caused Jimmy some amusement. At least he needn't worry about having to leave his tea half drunk if Rebecca made a sudden appearance. Why, there couldn't be room enough for two small gulps out of those delicately made cups.

'I'm sorry to have to keep you waiting, Mr Jackson, but really, Rebecca is to blame, you know.' Taking the chair opposite Jimmy, Stella Barnsley handed Jimmy his tea.

Jimmy raised his eyebrows in query. 'Really, how so?'

420

Smoothing down the front of her black skirt, Stella Barnsley looked into the rugged, tanned face and swallowed nervously. She and Doreen, her elder sister by three years, had been afraid that once Rebecca's young man returned from overseas, she would leave them. In fact, she had told them months ago that she would be leaving to get married, but both she and Doreen had hoped she might be persuaded to change her mind. Now she had met Rebecca's future husband, Stella Barnsley's hopes sank. What chance had she or Doreen to keep the young woman here, when she could be with this charismatic man. She knew what choice she would make given half the chance.

Sighing loudly she answered truthfully, 'I'll be perfectly frank with you, Mr Jackson. Before Rebecca came along, we, that is, my sister and I, were just barely keeping our heads above water. The fashions over the past few years have altered so dramatically, we were unable to attract any new customers, and the ones we did have were slowly drifting away. Even our machinists, women who've worked for us for years, were becoming disgruntled. We couldn't afford to pay them higher wages, you see, not like the big stores. The advert we placed in the *Gazette* was there for weeks before Rebecca applied for the job, in fact we were beginning to despair. Then she came into work one day wearing one of her own creations, and we couldn't believe our luck.' She smiled whimsically. 'Rebecca couldn't understand why we were so excited. She is one of those rare people who doesn't recognise their own talent. But we did. Since then the business has picked up at a remarkable rate. Women come in off the street asking for Rebecca. Of course, it is a lot of work, too much really for one person, and Rebecca won't be rushed. We've been fortunate enough to continue selling our old stock to those of our clients who aren't that concerned about the new fashions, but those women are, I'm sorry to say, pitifully few.' The thin shoulders rose in resignation. 'Doreen and I had hoped for an early retirement, but that is out of the question now.' The worried face softened suddenly. 'At least we experienced the start of a thriving business, we're both grateful for that . . . Oh, here, speak of the devil . . .' Stella Barnsley's gaze moved towards a large-built woman who had come from the room behind the counter, with Rebecca following close behind. 'I was just telling Mr Jackson here how grateful we were to find Rebecca.'

The older woman smiled pleasantly at Jimmy. 'Indeed we were. I do hope you're not planning to take our treasure away too soon, Mr Jackson.'

Jimmy got to his feet, his alert eyes noting the hidden anxiety behind the woman's words, and felt a pang of sympathy for both women's plight. He also experienced a sense of guilt, a feeling that intensified as both women continued to hold him in their gaze. Then Rebecca came to his rescue.

'Well, he won't be taking me away just yet, Miss Barnsley.' Linking her arm through Jimmy's, Rebecca added, 'I should have that dress for Mrs Curron finished tonight. Goodnight to you both.'

'Goodnight, dear. See you in the morning.'

'Goodnight, Rebecca.'

Jimmy held the door open for Rebecca to pass. Inclining his head towards the sisters, he grinned engagingly, 'Goodnight, ladies.'

Strolling along the pavement, Rebecca sniffed at the summer air and sighed.

'Sorry about keeping you waiting. I was going over the order book with Miss Doreen. I think I might have bitten off more than I can chew. I've a dozen orders waiting to get started, and I've told Miss Doreen not to take any more until I catch up.'

'They seem very fond of you,' he winked down at her. 'Can't say as I blame them. I'm very fond of you myself.'

Rebecca smiled tiredly. She hadn't slept very well last night, in fact she hadn't had a proper night's sleep since . . .

Jimmy was talking. '. . . they'll be wondering what's keeping us. I told Charlie and Amy we'd be at the hospital before six, and it's nearly that now. I'll be glad to see the back of that place, so goodness' knows how Charlie must be feeling. Every time I think of why he's in there . . .' He glanced down at the figure by his side. 'I know I keep on going over and over what happened, love, but I can't help it. My blood boils every time I think of Charlie lying in an empty house, left for dead . . . And there's the other business. The house wasn't broken into, someone had unlocked the back door for the thieving bastards . . . Oh, I'm sorry, sweetheart, I know you've heard it all a dozen times before, and I suppose the main thing is that Charlie's going to be all right.'

Rebecca smiled weakly, but all she could see in her mind's eye was the look on Phil's face that morning when the three of them had learnt of the incident. She had thought it odd when Phil had turned up that morning, especially when he didn't normally get out of bed until noon if he could help it. He had said he was on his way to an interview at a local factory where an assistant manager's position was advertised, and as it was near Roman Road, the destination she and Amy were heading for, he had decided to drop by and make the journey with them.

The news of the burglary and the vicious attack on young Charlie Bull, who was a very popular young man in the area, reached them before they had even alighted from the tram. Gossip, especially when it involved drama, travelled faster than any form of normal communication in the East End.

Amy's lightly tanned face had turned pale, then she had been off and running down the street before Rebecca could stop her. Starting to run after her sister, Rebecca had turned to Phil, and the stunned look of sheer horror on his face told her more than words could ever have done.

He had never been any good at hiding his feelings, and Rebecca had felt as if she'd been punched in the stomach when she'd witnessed the damning evidence of her brother's reaction to the news. She had known instantly that once again, despite all his brave words, Phil had used her and Amy to get himself out of trouble. But this time he had gone too far. The most sickening part was him vanishing before he knew if Charlie was going to live. If he had owned up to his part in the robbery, she would still have been terribly hurt, but at least he would have taken his punishment like a man, instead of scurrying away like a frightened rat. Ever since that awful morning when she and Amy had arrived at the house to find the whole street out and Bessie sobbing her heart out in the kitchen, neither of them had mentioned Phil. It was as if he had never appeared that night. It was as if he had never accompanied them on their journey that Wednesday morning; it was as if he had never existed.

Peeping up at the profile of Jimmy's set face, Rebecca's heart lurched. Jimmy knew, of that she was certain. That was why he kept dredging the affair up, in order to give her the chance to speak out. But, oh, it was hard, so very, very hard to turn on your own. Even though Rebecca knew Phil deserved everything he had coming to him, still, she didn't want to be the one to turn him over to the police; no more did Amy.

'Hang on, love, you look dead on your feet . . . Hey, Cabbie!' His piercing whistle seemed to go right through Rebecca's head, sending her already frayed nerves further on edge. It was a relief to get out of the sun into the Hansom cab. Laying her head against Jimmy's chest, Rebecca closed her eyes. She should have spoken out immediately instead of letting it drag out this long, but now it was even harder. Oh, damn it! It wasn't fair. It wasn't bloody fair. In all those lonely six months she had visualised countless variations of the longed-for reunion with

Jimmy, some of them causing her to blush at her own thoughts. But, never, not once, had she imagined anything like the reality, and the circumstances surrounding their much-anticipated reunion. That day seemed like a distant memory, even though it was only a week ago. She had gone to the hospital with Amy, holding on to her sister for fear Amy would suddenly faint with the shock she had received. But her sister was a lot tougher than she was given credit for.

As for her reunion with Jimmy . . . ! It hadn't been romantic, it hadn't even been ordinary. They had met up in a long, dark corridor of the hospital, surrounded by dreadful sounds and smells, yet they had fallen into each other's arms as if they'd never been parted. The three of them had waited in frightened silence outside a hospital ward, with Jimmy supporting them both, each one of them drawing comfort from the other. Looking back it had seemed like hours before Tom had emerged from the ward to tell them Charlie would be all right. It was then, as Amy had risen to her feet, that her knees had buckled and Jimmy had swept the unconscious girl up into his arms and rocked her like a baby while Rebecca had sobbed with relief.

Her eyes flew open as the carriage drew to a halt.

'Here you are,' Jimmy handed up a half a crown to the cabbie.

'Cheers, Guv'nor.'

Helping her down, Jimmy folded her arm through his as they made their way through the hospital grounds. They were passing the fountain in the forecourt when Rebecca knew she could keep silent no longer. Pulling Jimmy to a standstill, she blurted out, 'It was Phil, Jimmy. It had to be him . . . I'm so . . . so sorry. I . . . I should have kno . . . known.' The torrent of tears burst forth as the words spilt from her trembling lips. 'How . . . how could he do some . . . something like this? I'll . . . I'll never forgive him ne . . . never.'

Jimmy pulled her tight, his hand running tenderly over her hair, his voice soothing, yet his eyes were as cold as ice.

So! He had been right. As soon as Charlie had told him about Phil Bradford putting in a surprise visit, added to the fact that the back door had been left wide open, and only Rebecca was in possession of the keys to gain entry, it hadn't taken a genius to work it out. Yet as much as he disliked Phil Bradford, Jimmy had wished from the bottom of his heart that he was wrong; for the girls' sake. To what extent Bradford had been involved in the robbery Jimmy hadn't been certain. It was more likely he unlocked the door and gave the combination of the safe to someone else. He doubted if Bradford would have carried it out on his own. Besides, Charlie had said he'd walked part of the way home with Bradford, and whoever was responsible for attacking Charlie was already in the house at that time. Then, last night, he had been informed that Big George had gone into hiding following the hue and cry that had ensued from that night's work.

It all fitted into place like a jigsaw puzzle. Phil

427

Bradford and Big George. It wasn't hard to make the connection.

Rebecca's body trembled from head to foot as she continued to sob, stomping her feet like a child, her heart and mind filled with anguish at her brother's betrayal.

When at last the tears ceased, Rebecca pulled back from Jimmy's embrace and, staring up at him through blurred vision, she asked, 'Do . . . do you still want to ma . . . marry me, Jimmy?'

Jimmy's eyed widened. 'What! Well, of course I do, you daft mare.'

At the sound of his gruff tone, Rebecca hiccuped, then smiled weakly. 'You're so romantic.'

Knowing the trauma she was going through, Jimmy attempted to lighten the atmosphere. 'Romantic! I'll give you romantic – here!' Sweeping her off of her feet, he twirled her up in the air, then, propping her up against the side of the fountain, he dropped to one knee. Taking out a small blue velvet box from his inside pocket, he grinned up at her.

'I was gong to wait until this evening, when we were on our own, but since you've insisted . . . Miss Rebecca Bradford, will you marry me?'

Embarrassed now, Rebecca was aware of a small group gathering. Her cheeks burning, she tried to walk away, but Jimmy had tight hold of her hands.

'Jimmy! Get off . . . Look, there's people watching us.' She squirmed, but Jimmy wasn't letting go.

'I don't care who's watching, darling. I'm not letting go until you say yes.'

The small crowd was growing larger by the minute.

428

'All right, all right,' she muttered.

'What's that you say?' Jimmy mimicked, now playing to the audience, who were loving every minute of the spectacle.

'I said, all right,' she shouted, a sudden recklessness seizing her. A loud cheer went up as Jimmy placed the ring on her finger, then smothered her face in warm kisses.

Her arms wrapped tightly around his neck, Rebecca whispered lovingly, 'Oh, Jimmy. I love you, Jimmy.'

Yet even in her joy, her tortured mind cried, *Oh, Phil . . . Oh, Phil!*

CHAPTER TWENTY-NINE

As Rebecca walked down Welbeck Road she felt her stomach churn as memories flooded back to the time she had lived here. She had approached the road from the top end so that she wouldn't have to pass her former home. If she hadn't felt obliged to personally invite Ada and Billy Gates to her forthcoming wedding, she would never have returned to the area that held so many unhappy memories. In truth she wouldn't be here now if Amy hadn't pricked her conscience.

Amy now did the weekly shopping for Bessie, although the older woman often accompanied her, and every week Amy met up with Ada Gates down the market. And Amy, being the kind person she was, always made time for her former neighbour, keeping her up to date with all the news, while Bessie wandered off with James, allowing the child extra time to peruse the various stalls selling toys and games. Every week, Amy would tell Rebecca how Ada had asked after her, but last Saturday Amy had openly reproached Rebecca for ignoring their old friend. Rebecca had fully intended to write and invite Ada and Billy to her wedding, but with Amy's accusing looks and admonishments weighing heavy on her mind, Rebecca had decided to pay Ada a visit.

Feeling suddenly shy she knocked on Ada's door. She needn't have worried.

'Why, Rebecca, love. Come in, come in.' Ada Gates, her lined face beaming with genuine pleasure, ushered Rebecca into her home.

'Oh, this is a surprise, love. I always ask after yer whenever I see Amy down the market, but I never thought I'd see you around these parts again.' Ada had made the obligatory pot of tea and was in the act of pouring out the inky liquid while she chattered on happily. 'Not that I blame yer, love. Gawd 'elp us. After what that old cow next door did ter yer . . . Well! It beggars belief, it does that. Every time I think of the times she 'ad me running round like a blue arse fly, an' all the time she was as fit as me, well, it makes me want ter spit. I tell yer, love, you're well outta it.' Handing over a plate of home-made scones, she carried on. 'I see 'er down the market. Maude, I mean. Waddling along, huffing an' puffing, wiv a load of shopping, looking like she's about ter drop any minute. The first time I saw 'er, she tried ter do 'er 'elpless act, yer know, pretending she wasn't well, hoping I'd carry the shopping fer 'er. Now I ain't a spiteful kind of person – yer know me,

431

Rebecca, 'elp anyone out I would – but I ain't a fool neither. So I just said, "Morning, Miss Fisher," all polite, like, an' left 'er to it. Gawd! If looks could kill, I'd've popped me clogs on the spot.' Throwing her head back, Ada let out a roar of laughter at the memory. 'The next time I saw 'er, she cut me dead. And I can tell yer, love, that suits me fine, 'cos the less I 'ave ter do wiv that lot next door, the better I like it . . . Yer tea all right, is it, love?'

Rebecca looked down at her tea in some dismay. She preferred her tea weak, with plenty of milk, but she wouldn't hurt Ada's feelings for the world. Taking a deep breath she bravely sipped at the piping hot beverage, steeling herself not to shudder as the bitter liquid attacked her taste buds.

'It's fine, Ada, lovely.'

Satisfied her guest was enjoying her hospitality, Ada carried on talking, delighted at the unexpected company and eager to tell Rebecca all the news regarding the house next door. 'Things ain't changed much since the last time I saw yer. All I ever hear through the wall is arguing and shouting. If it ain't Ivy and Maude gong fer each other, it's Richard and the pair of 'em going at it hammer and tongs.' Leaning over the table, Ada winked gleefully. 'It ain't exactly been love's young dream between them two. An' I'll tell yer something else an' all. I wouldn't be at all surprised if Ivy upped an' left 'im. She ain't a bad sort, Ivy, I mean. At least she stops an' talks ter me when we meet in the street, not like the other two.' Pausing for breath, she beamed at Rebecca. 'Hark at me. Ain't let yer get a word in since yer crossed the doorstep, but I'm that pleased ter see yer, love. It ain't been the same round 'ere since you and young Amy went. But, like I said, yer better off outta it, an' good luck ter yer both. Now then, love,' she said briskly. 'Yer ain't come round 'ere just ter 'ear all the gossip. What can I do fer yer?'

Glad for the opportunity to speak, Rebecca laid down her cup and smiled fondly at her former neighbour. 'First of all, I'm sorry I haven't been around sooner, Ada. No, no, I should have made the effort,' she added guiltily as Ada waved her apologies aside. 'Actually I came to ask you and Billy to my wedding. It's on the third of September at Saint Dominic's Church at four o'clock and—'

Ada let out a loud scream of delight. 'Oh, Rebecca, love. Oh, I'm so pleased. I was dying ter ask how things were getting on wiv you and yer young man, but I didn't want yer ter think I was being nosy. I know all about Amy and her young man, but she never gossips about yer business. She's a good girl, is your Amy. And that young man of hers seems a good sort an' all. But, 'ere, now, let's get back ter your bit of news.' Clapping her hands Ada raised her voice. 'Getting married, yer say, Rebecca. And ter that gorgeous man Jimmy Jackson. Well, yer'll be set up fer life now, won't yer, love, 'cos he ain't short of a few bob, is he?' She smiled and nodded towards the far wall, and Rebecca, knowing that Ada was deliberately raising her voice for the benefit of anyone listening next door, smiled broadly. Keeping her voice loud, Ada continued. 'I bet yer'll 'ave a proper wedding an' all. No expense spared if I'm any judge. Not like some I could mention wiv their tuppenny halfpenny affairs an' acting like it was a royal do. Huh! All that palaver, an' what did some folks 'ave. A quiet ceremony wasn't in it. There wasn't more than half a dozen people in the church, so I 'eard, then back 'ome fer a few mangy sandwiches, and shop-bought cakes. Not that I was invited, like. But I wouldn't 'ave gorn if I had been. I had something special on that day. I 'ad ter clean out me range. An' I'll tell yer something else. I 'ad a sight more fun doing that than I would've 'ad going ter that so-called wedding.'

Looking across the table at the tiny woman, Rebecca couldn't believe it was the same shy, timid person she'd known for so many years. Conscious of the wide grin spreading over her face, Rebecca reflected that you never really knew someone, no matter how long you'd been acquainted with them.

Changing the subject, Rebecca asked warily, 'How's Billy, Ada?'

Ada, wiping the tears of joy from her eyes, answered cheerfully, 'Oh, he's fine, love. And he's got 'imself a lady friend.' At the look of surprise that suddenly covered Rebecca's face, Ada nodded sagely, saying, 'Yer remember old Mrs Blackburn from number twenty-five?'

Rebecca furrowed her eyebrows trying to recall the neighbour Ada was talking about. 'Oh, yes, I remember. She had her daughter come to live with her after the daughter's husband died last year. I didn't have much to do with them, just a good morning or afternoon when we met in passing. She seemed like a nice enough woman from what I could gather. Her name's Norma, isn't it?'

Ada's head bobbed in agreement. 'Yeah, that's her. Anyway, old Mrs Blackburn died a couple of months back, an' Billy offered ter 'elp wiv the funeral arrangements, 'cos Norma, poor little thing, went ter pieces when the old girl died. And yer know my Billy, always wanting ter 'elp people out when he can.'

Rebecca lowered her head, remembering how Billy had felt about her. Ada noticed the gesture and smiled kindly. 'Now, don't go feeling guilty, love. It wasn't yer fault yer didn't feel the same as my Billy did. And ter tell yer the truth, love, I always knew yer was way outta my Billy's league, bless him. And deep down he knew it too, but yer can't help but 'ope when yer in love, can yer; even when yer know nothing can ever come of it. Now, Norma, she's much better suited ter my Billy. She's a bit of a scatterbrain, yer know the type, always needing someone ter lean on, an' that's just the sorta woman my Billy needs. He's me own flesh an' blood, an' I love 'im ter death, but a mother knows 'er own child, and my Billy's not the sorta man who'll set the world on fire, now is he? And a woman like Norma will make 'im feel important, yer know, more manly, though I don't suppose he'll ever forget you, love.'

Relieved that Billy was courting at long last, Rebecca rose to leave.

'I'll have to go, Ada. I want to get home and finish a costume I've been working on, so that I'll have the weekend free to spend with Jimmy and James.'

'That's another thing I wanted ter ask yer, love. How yer getting on wiv the little 'un?'

An image of James's small face, so like Jimmy's, floated across Rebecca's vision, bringing a tender smile to her lips. 'He's lovely, Ada. A really nice little boy, and thankfully he seems to like me too. I was worried he might not take to me, but so far we've been getting on fine.'

'And what about that Bessie Wilks. I've 'eard tell she's a right old tartar. Mind you, speak as yer find, I always say, and she's always civil enough ter me whenever I see her with Amy. How does she feel about 'er precious Jimmy getting married?' Ada glanced at Rebecca worriedly.

'Oh, Bessie's all right once you get to know her,' Rebecca replied happily. 'Mind you, she frightened the life out of me when we first met, but that was only because I got on the wrong side of her.' Inclining her head towards Ada, Rebecca grinned. 'I'm still not entirely sure she wants Jimmy to marry me because I'd make him a good wife or because she's desperate to stop any chance of him getting back with James's mother. I think she sees me as the lesser of two evils. Anyway, Ada, I must get going. The sooner I get home the sooner I'll finish the costume I'm working on . . . Oh, I nearly forgot to tell you my other news.'

Resuming her seat, Rebecca grinned widely. 'Jimmy's bought me a part ownership in the shop where I work. The ladies that own it are keen to take an early retirement, though I doubt that will be for another few years yet, it all depends on how well the shop does. But hopefully in the not too distant future, I'll be the owner of my very own business; what do you think of that, Ada?'

Ada's eyes stretched wide in disbelief. 'Yer mean ter say, yer'll be carrying on working after yer married. Don't Jimmy mind, love? I mean ter say, it's different fer the likes of me, I always had ter work, I didn't 'ave any choice, but yer could stay at home an' put yer feet up after yer married, if yer wanted to.'

Rebecca laughed softly. 'But that's just it, Ada. I don't want to simply stay at home. For the first time in my life, I've found something I'm good at. Not only that, I can make a living out of it, and after the life I've had, you can't imagine how it makes me feel to know I'm worth more than just fetching and carrying. As for Jimmy, he's delighted . . . Well! He wasn't at first. Like you, he imagined I'd be only to happy to live life without having to work again, but I love what I do. Anyway . . .' She winked mischievously. 'Now that Jimmy's given up the bookmaking racket, he says he might as well invest in a respectable business.'

Yet Ada didn't seem convinced. 'That's all very well, love. But what about when the children start arriving? Yer won't be able ter go out ter work wiv a couple of kids hanging round yer skirts, will yer?'

Pulling a face, Rebecca said lightly, 'Hang on, Ada, I'm not even married yet. But we have talked about it, and as I said to Jimmy, we'll cross that bridge when it comes. Though I can't see it being a problem. I can always work from home, like I do most of the time now. Still, that's in the future. Now then, will you and Billy . . . and his lady friend, of course, be able to come to the wedding?'

A wide devilish grin spread over Ada's lips. 'Yer can count on it, love. Why, I can just see it now. Me, my Billy and Norma, all dressed up and telling the street where we're off to . . . Oh, I can't wait, love . . . Bleeding 'ell, 'ere we go again.'

Ada raised her eyebrows as furious shouting came thundering through the walls. Then their eyes widened as they heard Maude's unmistakable voice screeching, 'Go on then, you trollop, clear off. We'll be better off without you. You only married my Richard for his money, and you ain't even got the guts to wait until he gets home to tell him to his face. Well, you won't be getting another penny out of him, I can tell you that for nothing.'

A low voice answered, but try as they might, Rebecca and Ada couldn't make out what Ivy's retort was. Then they heard the sound of a carriage coming down the street and, as if of one mind, both women dashed to the front of the house, just as Ivy, carrying two heavy suitcases, came out of the house next door.

They watched open-mouthed as the cabbie jumped down from his perch and lifted the suitcases on top of the carriage, before helping Ivy inside, while Maude continued to levy insults at the silent woman from the safety of her front doorstep.

Anxious to be on her way, and not wanting to let an opportunity to see Maude bested slip by without comment, Rebecca hastily kissed Ada on the cheek, saying breathlessly, 'Bye, Ada. I've really got to go. Not that I'm being nosy, of course. But I wouldn't miss this for the world.'

Ada grinned gleefully. 'Me neither, love. I'll just stand on the doorstep and wave you off, like.'

Stepping out onto the pavement, Rebecca walked slowly towards her old home. Maude still stood in the doorway, her face almost purple with rage as she watched her hated sister-in-law about to drive off.

Not able to resist a parting shot of her own, Rebecca stopped. 'Hello, Maude. My, you do look well. I must write to the Pope and tell him about your miraculous recovery. It must rate alongside the rising of Lazarus.'

Taken by surprise, Maude staggered back into the doorway, but she quickly recovered her composure. Poking her finger in Rebecca's direction, she screamed, 'You can clear off and all. In fact why don't you ask Ivy for a lift back to your fancy man? You'll be in good company. A couple of slags together.' With that she slammed the door in Rebecca's face. Resisting the impulse to bang on the door, Rebecca decided it wasn't worth it. Besides, she didn't want to take the risk of bringing herself down to Maude's level, and that's what would happen if she got the chance to confront her hated cousin face to face.

'Rebecca. Can I offer you a lift?' Ivy was leaning out of the carriage, her painted face pensive, and after a moment's hesitation, Rebecca waved goodbye to the hovering Ada and climbed into the cab.

In the confines of the carriage, an awkward silence

descended on the two women, with Rebecca wishing she hadn't acted so impulsively. After all, she hardly knew the woman. She'd only seen her twice. Once in the restaurant, and once on Christmas Eve, and neither time had they exchanged any words; then Ivy spoke.

'How on earth did you stick it all those years? I admire you, Rebecca, I honestly do. But then, I suppose our circumstances were different. You had no choice at the time, but Good Lord! How you resisted the temptation to put a pillow over that old bat's face while she was sleeping, I'll never know. You must have extraordinary willpower.'

Rebecca felt herself relaxing. 'Believe me, the thought crossed my mind on more than one occasion, then I'd remind myself that Maude wasn't worth swinging for.'

Ivy nodded thoughtfully. 'Even so, there are times when one doesn't stop to think of the consequences. I've been expecting you to turn up at the door with a loaded shotgun since Christmas Eve. Still, as you say, no one's worth swinging for, not even Richard or his sister. I must have been mad to marry him, but at the time I didn't seem to have much choice. You see, I suddenly found myself virtually penniless, otherwise I'd never have gone through with the wedding. Also I thought Richard was my last chance to have a child. I've been married twice, as you probably already know, but I never became pregnant, and I'm at the age when a woman becomes desperate. Now I know nothing is worth the price of being saddled with Richard.

'The only good thing to come out of the whole sorry affair is that I've ruined him. He doesn't know it yet, but he soon will. You see, he made the mistake of letting me oversee his accounts. You know how mean he is, and the idea of not having to pay a qualified accountant appealed to his avaricious nature. I may not have the papers to prove my accountancy skills, but I managed both my previous husbands' books for years. It was simple enough to gradually transfer Richard's money into another account, my account. Now he is in the same position I was when I married him – penniless. The funny thing is that he still thinks I've pots of money lying in a bank vault somewhere. His greedy little mind has been working overtime wondering how to get his hands on it. Well, he's finished now. And the reason for my impromptu departure is that he's gone to see his bank manager today, to discuss investing his assets into stocks and shares. Only when he gets there, he'll find his account has been wiped out. Oh, I've left him and Maude enough to live on – barely. But if he wants to survive, he's going to have to sell the warehouse and live on the proceeds until they run out.' Ivy fell quiet.

Rebecca's initial elation at hearing how her hated cousin had been destroyed was marred by something nagging at her mind. Something Ivy had said . . . Before Rebecca could delve further into what was worrying her, Ivy resumed the one-sided conversation.

'The reason I wanted to have this little talk is because my conscience has been bothering me for

441

quite some time now. I've tried to get the image of Richard with your poor sister out of my mind since I walked in on them on Christmas Eve, but bad memories don't disappear that easily. I'd been having second thoughts even before then, about marrying Richard, and after witnessing that disgusting scene, I very nearly decided to call the whole thing off, and report him to the police. But as I said, I was in desperate straits at the time. Even so, my conscience has been bothering me ever since.'

Putting Rebecca's silence down to the fact that the sordid affair had been dragged up again, Ivy leant forward and tapped her gently on the knees. 'I know I haven't come out of this affair in a good light, and for that I feel deeply ashamed, but at least you have the comfort of knowing that Richard is ruined. This time next week, God willing, I'll be at the other end of the world, somewhere Richard will never find me. I don't suppose I'll ever return to England, but then, one never knows what life has in store for us. Please give my regards to your sister, and tell her how sorry I am that she had to go through such a dreadful ordeal. I can still see her little face in my dreams. The image haunts me to this day. She looked so scared, so bewildered and frightened, I . . . '

Ivy stopped, her heart beginning to race as she looked at the young woman sitting opposite. Rebecca was staring at a point somewhere above Ivy's head, the lovely blue eyes filled with such venom that Ivy recoiled in her seat, and in that brief moment she knew with a sickening certainty that Rebecca, up to this point in time, hadn't known about Richard and Amy; and, deeply shocked, she voiced her thoughts.

'Dear God! You didn't know, did you?' she whispered. 'After what you said to Richard on Christmas Eve, I knew you had your suspicions, and I thought it was only a matter of time before you found out for sure. That's why I was so surprised when you didn't do anything about it. Oh, my dear, dear girl. I'm so sorry. I was so sure Amy would have told you by now. If there's anything . . .'

Rebecca felt strange. She couldn't explain her emotions, except that the sudden surge of rage had evaporated, and the red mist that had descended over her eyes had suddenly lifted, leaving her curiously numb.

'Could you stop the cab, please, Ivy? I think I'll walk from here.'

Ivy stared hard into the calm face opposite and felt her heart lurch in fear. Not for herself, but for the young woman, whose face appeared carved in marble, ice cold marble. 'Rebecca, dear. Please, don't do anything stupid. Richard isn't worth going to prison for, and like I've told you, he's already ruined, I've seen to that. And to my mind, knowing Richard as I do, that's the worst punishment he could possibly receive.'

Rebecca stared back as if she hadn't heard a word Ivy had said. 'I'll get out here. Thank you for the lift, Ivy. And I wish you a happy new life, wherever you decide to go. Goodbye.'

Helpless to stop her leaving the carriage, Ivy bit

hard on her bottom lip as she watched the slim figure walk away.

A good five minutes passed before Ivy instructed the cabbie to drive on. There was nothing more she could do, and she had her own life to live. A bright future was beckoning her, but as she drove off, instead of the heady feeling she had expected to experience at having finally escaped from Richard's clutches, Ivy had only a bitter taste in her mouth, and one that would stay with her for a very long time.

Rebecca walked on, her eyes unseeing as she negotiated the familiar journey by instinct. She was feeling very strange. She had imagined that after hearing what Richard had tried to do to Amy she would have been burning up with hatred, but she felt so calm it was as if she had been transported outside of her own body and was watching herself from above.

The front door to Jimmy's house was open, allowing Rebecca to slip inside without announcing her arrival. The first sound she heard was the now all too familiar strident tones of Bessie. 'I don't care what yer say, lad. I ain't 'aving that thing in the house. What if the child got 'is 'ands on it? Nah! I ain't changing me mind, Jimmy, so yer can take it back from wherever yer got the blasted thing from.'

Climbing the stairs, Rebecca felt a smile tug at her lips. Dear Bessie. She had become very fond of the irrepressible woman, who would soon become her surrogate mother-in-law.

'Now look here, woman, I'm not taking it back, so

444

you can stop going on about it. Bloody hell's bell's. I'd've thought you'd be pleased to have some kind of protection in the house after what happened. I can't be here all the time, and until they catch the men responsible for what happened to Charlie, I ain't gonna be happy leaving you on your own; especially with James to worry about as well.'

'Yer can talk till yer blue in the face, lad. It's been over a month now. Those men ain't coming back an' yer know it. Yer told me yerself it was Big George that organised the whole thing, an' he's gorn missing, ain't he? We ain't gonna see him around these parts for a good time, if ever. And after the palaver yer made, no one in their right mind's gonna risk breaking in 'ere again.'

Pushing the living-room door ajar, Rebecca saw Bessie and Jimmy glaring at each other, neither one of them willing to back down.

Looking over Jimmy's shoulder, Bessie exclaimed loudly, 'Ah, hello, love, maybe you can talk some sense into that thick head of this obstinate bugger, 'cos he ain't taking any notice of what I say, not that he ever did.'

Distracted, Jimmy turned, running his hands through his thick hair in a rare display of agitation. Throwing out his arms, he cried in relief, 'Hello, sweetheart.' Striding forwards, he put his arm around Rebecca's waist and kissed her lightly on the lips. 'Would you please talk some sense into the old trout, before I bleeding well strangle her?'

Rebecca laughed, but it wasn't a merry laugh.

Instead the sound was tinged with hysteria.

'What's the matter, love? Yer look as white as a sheet.'

Bessie was examining Rebecca closely, her keen eyes missing nothing.

A warning light came on inside Rebecca's mind. Careful. Careful, you don't want to get them suspicious, now do you?

At Bessie's words, Jimmy became all contrition. 'Are you all right, sweetheart?'

A serene smile on her face, Rebecca answered calmly, 'Of course I am. I've just been to see Ada Gates to invite her and Billy to the wedding and I bumped into Maude.' She tried to laugh, but the sound caught in her throat. Still maintaining a calm exterior, she added, 'I also saw Ivy. She's left Richard, only he doesn't know it yet. We had a little chat, and it seems she's not only left him, but taken all his money as well.'

Bessie gave a loud grunt. 'Well, it's no more than the bugger deserves. Slimy little git.'

Jimmy shook his head. 'You've never even met him.'

Bessie snorted. 'That's as may be, but I've heard enough about the fellow ter make up me mind about him. Anyway, it looks like he's gonna get a surprise when he gets home, don't it?'

Rebecca's lips twitched. 'Oh, yes, Bessie. I'd say Richard has a few surprises coming to him today.'

Grabbing his coat, Jimmy said, 'Look! I've got to go and see Charlie. We've got some unfinished business to sort out. There's still a lot of loose ends need tying up before I can concentrate on setting up any new ventures. Stay and talk to Bessie, will you, sweetheart? Try and make her see sense.'

Darting an exasperated look at the grim-faced woman, Jimmy shook his head in bemusement and left.

'Well, don't yer come crying ter me when yer come home and find James with his little 'ead blown off . . . Oh, sod it!'

Rebecca had walked over to the bureau and was looking down at the cause of the heated argument. Bessie noticed the focus of her attention and said bitterly, 'Gawd knows what he's thinking of. We've lived in the East End all our lives, and we've never had any reason ter get a gun before now, but there's no arguing with Jimmy when he gets a notion into his head – bloody stubborn git. Here, let me lock it away before James gets in 'ere.' Bessie slammed the drawer shut and locked it, placing the key on a high shelf overhead. 'There, at least I ain't gotta worry about the little 'un getting his 'ands on it.'

Rebecca's eyes seemed riveted on the locked drawer. 'I wouldn't mind a cup of tea, Bessie. If it's not too much trouble.'

Bessie snorted loudly. 'Get away with yer, yer daft mare. 'Course it's no trouble. I'll be glad ter be doing something ter take me mind off that bloody thing.'

Left alone, Rebecca quickly took the key down from the shelf and opened the bureau drawer. Without stopping to think, she placed the small, pearl-handled pistol into her bag. As if in a dream, she

447

turned and left the room, walking quietly down the stairway so as not to alert Bessie of her departure.

She was at the front door when Amy and James appeared.

'Hello, Becky. I didn't expect to see you until later. I thought you were going home to finish that costume you've been working on.'

'Becky, Becky. We've been over the park. Look, Becky, my dad bought me a new ball.'

Rebecca glanced down at the smiling boy and absently patted his head before turning to Amy. Staring lovingly into her sister's heart-shaped face, Rebecca lifted her hand to stroke the soft cheek, murmuring softly, 'You should have told me, love. You should have told me. I knew something was wrong at the time. You poor love. Don't worry, he's not going to get away with it.' Patting her handbag, she added mysteriously, 'I said he'd pay if he ever laid a finger on you, and now I'm going to carry out my promise. It's lucky I've still got my key. I can surprise him; and what a surprise I've got lined up for him.' Shaking her head in quiet amusement, Rebecca gently pushed Amy to one side and walked on.

Amy stood rooted to the spot, her heart racing as the full horror of Rebecca's ominous words sank in.

'Where's Becky going?' James was looking up at Amy, his small face troubled. 'She didn't even say hello to me. Is she upset with me, Amy? Did I do something wrong?'

Shaken out of her reverie, Amy said quickly,

'No, love. You haven't done anything wrong. Look, let's go and find Bessie and see if there's anything to eat.'

Brightening up at the thought of food, James bounded into the house, his high voice calling out for Bessie.

Amy's head was whirling. Rebecca knew. Somehow she must have found out, but how? And she had looked and sounded so strange. If her elder sister had been shouting and filled with anger, Amy wouldn't have felt so scared, but Rebecca had been so calm – unnaturally calm, almost as if she had become devoid of all emotion. And in that state, her sister was capable of anything.

Running into the kitchen, while James went up to the bathroom to wash his hands, Amy cried to a startled Bessie, 'Where's Jimmy, Bessie?'

'He's gone out ter see Charlie, love. Why, what's the matter?'

Knowing that it was useless to continue the pretence, Amy blurted out what had happened with Richard, and her fear that Rebecca was going to do something terrible.

Bessie's face stretched in disbelief, her expression swiftly turning to one of deep rage as she listened to Amy's tearful, heart-rending confession.

'Why, the dirty bastard. And you've keep quiet all this time. In the name of God, why, love?'

Babbling now, Amy sobbed fearfully, 'Because I was frightened of what Becky would do if she found out. She's always hated Richard, and . . . and even though nothing happened . . . Oh, Bessie, I'm scared,

449

I'm really scared. And . . . and she said he was going to pay, then she patted her bag . . . I don't know what to do, Bessie. What if she's got a knife in her bag? Oh, Bessie . . .'

Bessie clutched at her throat, her eyes gazing upwards, a sudden thought entering her stricken mind. 'Oh, my Gawd!'

Dashing past Amy, she ran up the stairs as fast as her aged legs would carry her, with Amy close behind. Running to the bureau she saw at once that the drawer was open – open and empty.

'She's taken the gun. Oh, I thought there was something wrong with her the minute she walked in, but I was so busy arguing with Jimmy, I didn't take much notice.' Pushing Amy from the room, she shouted wildly, 'Go after Jimmy, quickly. You'll be able to catch up with him if you run . . . Go on, then, love . . . Run . . . Run, like you've never run before.'

Needing no extra bidding, Amy sped down the stairs and out into the street, all the while her mind pleading, *Please God, don't let her do anything. Please God, don't let her use the gun on Richard, because if she does then she'll hang, and it'll be all my fault.*

Billy Gates had just got in from work when he happened to glance up and see Rebecca walking past his window. Smiling, he hung his coat up and opened the front door.

'Hello, Becky. Twice in one day. Mum said you'd been round earlier. Did you forget something?'

Momentarily distracted, Rebecca turned to Billy,

and the dead look reflected in her eyes caused Billy's stomach to twist in alarm.

'What's up, Becky? What . . .'

But Rebecca seemed not to have heard him. Walking past the startled man, she calmly took out a key and opened the door of her former home, just as Billy had seen her do a hundred times before.

His blunt face puzzled, Billy quietly closed his own door, but he remained standing. Deep in thought, Billy called through to the scullery, 'Mum! Mum, Becky's just gone in next door. She didn't look right ter me. D'yer think I should go and see if she's OK?'

Ada Gates appeared, wiping her hands on her apron. 'Becky's gorn in next door! What would she be doing in there? You sure, lad?'

Impatiently Billy clicked his tongue. ''Course I'm sure, I . . .' He broke off as Richard's voice, high with rage, could be heard clearly through the wall. Then both Billy and Ada jumped in fright as they heard Maude scream. Rushing out into the street, Billy pressed his face up against next door's window, and what he saw brought his eyes out on stalks. Without pausing to think, he lifted his heavy-booted foot and kicked in the door.

'You stupid bitch. You mean to say you just stood by and let her walk out without trying to stop her?' Richard was pacing the room like a man demented. 'She's cleaned me out, d'you hear me, you fat old cow, Ivy's taken every penny I have. The vicious bitch has left me without a penny to my name. Well! Don't just sit there like a stuffed pig, you

451

stupid cow. Don't you realise what this means. I'm ruined . . . ruined. Didn't she say where she was going? Think, woman, for fuck's sake try and think if she said anything . . .'

Maude stiffened in her chair, her fat face dissolving into lines of anger. 'Don't you use that sort of language to me, Richard, I won't stand for it. It's not my fault you married that trollop. I warned you not to go through with it, but oh, no, you wouldn't listen to me, would you, and now you're paying for it.' She squinted up at the distraught face, her nose curling with distaste at the pitiful figure her brother presented. Any other man, a real man, in his position would be out doing something, but not her dear brother. Oh, no! Instead he was doing what he'd always done. Blustering and posturing, not resourceful enough to try and sort his own mess out by himself. He was a lot like Phil in that respect. Neither of them had ever had any gumption.

Settling herself more comfortably in her armchair, Maude's furtive mind began making plans. Now that Richard's money was gone, she wasn't going to hang around. She had her secret hoard under her bed, minus what that deceitful cow Rebecca had stolen from her. Fortunately her cousin hadn't taken much, and she still had some of the money her parents had left in trust for her safely put by in the bank; with interest, it must be worth a tidy sum by now. Oh, yes, she was going to be all right. The first chance she got, she was going to follow in Ivy's footsteps and leave. She would easily find a place to stay, and in due course she would advertise for a companion. There were plenty of women in dire straits who'd be only too pleased to look after her in return for a roof over their heads and food in their stomachs, together with a small allowance – a very small allowance. She wasn't going to throw her money away. With careful handling it would last her her lifetime. She wasn't going to waste any sleep over her brother; he could fend for himself.

When the front door opened and Rebecca appeared, both Maude and Richard were stunned into silence. Then Richard, glad of the opportunity to vent his spleen onto somebody else, pulled himself upright and spat out viciously, 'I don't know why you've come round here, madam, but you can sling your hook. You're not welcome in this house, and that goes for the rest of your good-for-nothing family. And I'll have your key back too, you little guttersnipe.' Richard swayed on his feet pompously, his haughty demeanour turning to stark fear as Rebecca produced the gun.

Her pale face betraying no trace of anger, Rebecca said calmly, 'Remember what I said to you on Christmas Eve, *Dick*? Well, now I know what happened. You tried to rape my Amy, didn't you, you disgusting little man. Maybe you thought I'd never find out, or maybe you imagined my threat was an empty one. If that's the case, then you're very much mistaken. I said I'd kill you if I found out you'd laid a finger on Amy, and now that I know for sure, I intend to carry out my promise.' Lifting the gun, she aimed it directly at Richard's chest.

453

Terrified, his eyes bulging, Richard staggered back, his hands held out in a defensive gesture. 'No! No, you've got it all wrong, Becky. I never harmed Amy . . . Oh, please, don't hurt me . . . Please . . . don't hurt me . . . I'm sorry . . . I'm sorry . . .'

Rebecca watched Richard dispassionately. She didn't feel anything towards him any more. No hate, no anger, just a determination to avenge Amy and the horror she'd endured. She sensed Maude's presence, but ignored her. She no longer had any quarrel with Maude. It was Richard she'd come for. Steadying her arm, she locked her finger around the trigger. Maude screamed in terror, but Rebecca didn't even flinch. Looking into the pale, sweating face only a few feet away from her, she squeezed the trigger just as Richard dived to the floor.

Then two things happened at once. The sound of the gun going off seemed to snap Rebecca out of her trance-like state, just as Billy Gates kicked in the front door. Then she was being held firmly, a strong hand trying to prise the gun from her fingers. With a soft groan, she dropped the small pistol, her body collapsing against the safety of Billy's comfortable, broad chest. She was vaguely aware of Richard screaming, his voice, high-pitched with fear, sounding like an old woman. Then more people entered the house, and she found herself being transferred from Billy's grasp into the protective arms of Jimmy.

Dimly, as if from a long way off, she heard Jimmy say gruffly, 'Thanks, mate. Thank God you were here. I owe you one for this, Billy. Thanks again.'

'No need ter thank me, Mr Jackson. I'd do anything fer Rebecca, anything. Yer a lucky man, Mr Jackson. Take good care of her, won't yer?'

The two men clasped hands before Billy, his entire body filled with well-deserved importance, ushered his anxious mother back into the privacy of their home.

Rebecca was crying freely, the salty tears running into her open mouth as she wept and clung to Jimmy, shocked back into reality at last.

'I'll have the law on her, you see if I don't. Bursting into my house and threatening me . . .'

Jimmy whirled menacingly on the sweating Richard. 'You do that, Fisher. I'm sure the police would be very interested to know the reason why Rebecca came here. In fact I'll save you the trouble. I'm going there myself, right now, and I'm going to tell them how you tried to rape a fifteen-year-old girl – a girl who trusted you, a girl who looked on you as an uncle. You filthy bastard. I hope they lock you up and throw away the key.' With one last murderous look in Richard's direction, Jimmy carried the weeping Rebecca from the house and into a waiting carriage.

Word of the unfolding drama had quickly spread through the small street and as Richard walked unsteadily over to close the door he saw small groups of people out on the pavement, their heads nodding towards the house, their faces alive with ghoulish curiosity. With a vile oath, he slammed the door shut.

Badly shaken, he staggered to the sideboard and poured himself a large brandy. During all this time Maude hadn't said a word. She was too busy thinking how this latest incident would benefit her. Until Rebecca had shown up, all Richard's troubles had been down to lack of funds. Now, not only was he ruined financially, but his entire life was destroyed beyond repair. No money could help him now, even if he had any.

Richard was himself thinking the same thing. Throwing back the drink, he quickly replenished his glass, his mind turning this way and that, trying to find some way out of his predicament. But this time there was no way out. He was utterly ruined, in every sense of the word. If it had only been the loss of his money that was the root of his problems, he could have possibly found a way to recoup his wealth, given time. But there was no way he was going to escape from the charge of attempted rape. Once that news hit the papers, he would be ostracised. Even if he got off the charge, and that he very much doubted, he was finished. He had no money, he was going to prison, and, depending on the length of the prison term, by the time he came out he would be an old man with nothing to live for.

Like a drowning man, Richard cast his mind back over the years, trying to find out where his life had gone so badly wrong. And the answer came flashing in front of his eyes. Maude! If she hadn't put the kibosh on his wedding to Ivy the first time around, he would by now be a happily married man surrounded by his own children. Then he would have had no need to bring those blasted Bradfords back with him to London, and would have been spared the temptation of the delightful Amy, a temptation that had proved to be his final downfall. All that had happened could have been avoided, if it hadn't been for Maude. His eyes red, his heart and soul filled with loathing, he looked across at the woman he blamed for all his misfortunes.

'*You!*' The word was spat out between clenched teeth, and such was the bitterness and hatred echoed in that one word that Maude felt the first twinge of fear. She had been startled into a scream when Rebecca had appeared brandishing that gun, but she hadn't been afraid for her own safety. It had been obvious it was Richard Rebecca had come looking for. Now, looking into the murderous gaze of her brother, Maude felt the trickle of fear begin to gather momentum. Pulling her cumbersome frame forward, she was about to rise when Richard's low, thick voice stopped her.

'It's all your fault, you revolting fat bitch from hell. You couldn't stand to see me happy, could you? All those years ago, when I had a chance of happiness with Ivy, you couldn't stand it, could you? So you suddenly became a cripple overnight, and like the young fool I was, I believed you, and look where it got me. Ivy saw through you, even the doctors I brought in knew you were faking it, but I stood by you, and gave up my chance of happiness to look after you. And this is where it's got me.'

Recovering her composure Maude shot back

bitterly, 'Don't give me all that malarkey. If it had
been down to you, you'd have shoved me into a
home and not thought twice about it. The only
reason you stayed with me was because you were
worried about what people might think if you sent
me away. That's always been your trouble, Richard.
Always worried about what other people thought
of you, and do you want to know something funny?
Despite all your efforts to convince people you're
such a nice man, you never fooled anyone. People
aren't fools, they can sum up a man's character
by themselves, but you were convinced that if you
acted the part, people would like you and respect
you. Huh! That's a laugh. Nobody's ever had the
slightest respect for you, Richard, that's a com-
modity that has to be earned, and you, my dear,
pitiful brother, just don't have that quality, and
never will have. Now, if you'll excuse me, I don't
want to be present when the police come for you.'
Heaving herself out of the chair she said mockingly,
'You want to know something else that's funny,
Richard? Before Rebecca turned up, I was making
plans for my future. You see, I've got a tidy sum
put away under my bed, and a good bit gathering
interest in the bank. You thought I'd spent all my
inheritance, didn't you? But I must have known I'd
be left on my own one day, so I took the precaution
of investing in a nest egg. I was going to find myself
somewhere else to live, but now you've saved me
the trouble. I can stay here now, 'cos you won't be
here much longer.' She let out a grating laugh of
triumph. 'I'll be upstairs counting my money. When

the police come, go quietly, won't you, Richard? After all, we don't want the neighbours seeing you in your true light, do we? Because I know how much appearances mean to you. Though once word gets round that you tried to rape your own cousin, and her only fifteen . . . Well! Even I didn't think you'd stoop that low. Maybe Rebecca might have done you a good turn if she had shot you. At least she would have spared you the humiliation and ordeal of a public trial.'

Giggling quietly, she had one foot on the bottom stair when Richard's voice, low and menacing, halted her in her tracks. 'You spiteful, deceiving bitch. Do you really think I'm going to let you live in comfort while I'm rotting in jail? Oh, no, Maude, my dear, loyal sister. We've been together all my life, more's the pity, and I'd hate to be parted from you now.'

A chill ran up Maude's back. Turning slowly, she saw Richard holding the gun Rebecca had brought to the house. Her eyes blinking furiously, she stared at the small, silver pistol, her mouth suddenly dry. She'd forgotten all about the gun. Swallowing hard, she attempted to reason with Richard. A conciliatory note in her voice now, she wheedled, 'Don't be silly, Richard. Look, I didn't mean what I said. There's enough money for both of us. I'll get you a good lawyer, the best, I promise you. I mean, this business with Amy . . .' She laughed nervously. 'It's only her word against yours after all.'

Her lips parted in a startled scream as the first bullet tore into her thigh. 'Richard . . . don't . . .' She fell heavily on the bottom stair, her eyes beseeching as she gazed up at the man standing over her. 'I'm your sister, Richard . . . I'm your own flesh and blood . . .' Her body jumped as another bullet entered her shoulder.

Richard stood looking down at the mountainous form of the woman now lying helpless at the foot of the stairs, his gaze merciless. 'That's right, Maude. You're my own flesh and blood, God help us both. And now you're going to get what you've always wanted. We're going to be together for ever. Good-bye, Maude.'

Keeping the gun steady, Richard fired two more bullets into her huge frame, then, without giving himself time to think, he held the gun under his chin, took one last look around the house he had been born in, closed his eyes tightly and squeezed the trigger.

CHAPTER THIRTY

The wedding of Rebecca Bradford to Jimmy Jackson hit the front pages of both the local paper and the dailies. Not because of Jimmy's relatively minor fame, but due to the fact that the bride was the cousin of the couple involved in the murder and suicide scandal that had rocked the East End. Mercifully, Amy's name had been left out of the sordid affair. Those who knew what had triggered Rebecca's visit to Richard Fisher's home were keeping quiet; and the only other two who knew were now dead. There had been much speculation as to the whys and wherefores of the case, but as only Billy Gates had witnessed the actual event, and that loyal man was keeping his mouth tightly closed, no one ever knew what had really happened the day Richard Fisher had murdered his sister before turning the gun on himself. Gradually interest died away as new headlines took over the front pages.

So it was that by the time Amy, on her seventeenth birthday in February 1914, married Charles Bull, the quiet ceremony went virtually unnoticed. Rebecca, as matron of honour, looking beautiful in a pale blue gown, stood behind her sister as Amy made her vows in the cold church.

Dr Tom Barker, who had given Rebecca away, now proudly repeated his duty as he stood in for Amy's late father.

Neither young woman would ever forget the awful tragedy that had occurred, but with the passing of time, and with their husbands beside them, Rebecca and Amy looked forward to a happy life; their only regret was that Phil, because of his own actions, was no longer a part of their lives.

For Rebecca, there was another person to worry about. Even though she was safely married to Jimmy, she still thought about Heather Mills. James was settled now. He looked upon Jimmy as his father, and adored and hero-worshipped the strong, handsome man he so proudly called Dad. He had taken the news of Jimmy's forthcoming marriage to Rebecca with ill-concealed fear, until they had sat down with him and reassured the child that nothing had changed regarding his position in Jimmy's life.

Now, on a warm Sunday morning in April, James was walking happily between his father and Rebecca, his small hands clasping the protective ones either side of him. Every now and then, he was swung into the air, his high-pitched childish cries of glee filling the spring air.

Stopping for a rest on a park bench, Jimmy and Rebecca watched fondly as James ran around the park, kicking his favourite ball.

There was someone else watching the family scene. From the pavilion, Heather Mills sipped at her tea, her green eyes following her son's every move.

It had been over a year since she had last clapped eyes on either Jimmy or James. During that time she had seethed and plotted at ways to get her son back, and in the process have Jimmy beholden to her until James grew to adulthood. When Jimmy had disappeared with the child, Heather had been furious, but unable to do anything about it. So she had bided her time and waited as patiently as she knew how.

During that time Heather hadn't been idle. She had soon met someone else, and allowed herself to be supported by the besotted man until his wife had found out what her esteemed husband was up to. Still, she'd come out of the short-lived affair with a nice fat cheque in exchange for her silence. That cheque had made Jimmy's hundred pounds seem paltry, yet still she wasn't satisfied.

But she had made one big mistake. She had dismissed Rebecca as being just another novelty to Jimmy, and had been dumbfounded when, after only knowing the girl a relatively short time, he had married her. Yet even that hadn't deterred Heather. In her mind she still thought of Jimmy as being her private property. Even now he was married, Heather still imagined she could get him back, if only through the child. That was the only hold she had over Jimmy now, and she wasn't going to relinquish it easily. She would never have Jimmy's name, but she was still the mother of his son, and nothing would ever alter that fact.

Throwing down two florins on the tray, she left the pavilion and strolled casually towards where James was happily playing by himself. She passed within feet of the couple on the bench, her lips curling triumphantly as she witnessed their startled surprise. Satisfied that they had seen her, Heather approached her son.

'Jimmy! It's her; it's Heather. Oh, Jimmy . . . !'

Rebecca made to rise, only to find her arm held in a firm but gentle grip.

'Leave it, sweetheart.'

Bewildered, Rebecca looked down at Jimmy's impassive face. 'But, Jimmy. Remember what she tried to do the last time? What if she tries to take James away again.'

Pulling her gently down beside him, Jimmy said quietly, 'I can't live the next ten years looking over my shoulder, always afraid that one day she'll appear and take James away from me. Don't you see, sweetheart, that's why I left you to take James away, so that he would have the chance to get to know me, and trust me. So that he would look on me as his real dad, not just another so-called uncle who would walk out of his life without warning. I knew this day would come eventually. Now I can only hope and pray that James will never leave me voluntarily. I need to know he wants to stay with me out of love, and not just because his mother isn't around. Sit down, love. The day of reckoning is finally here. I only hope all my efforts haven't been for nothing.'

Her heart thudding, Rebecca did as Jimmy bid, but she couldn't relax. In the short time she'd spent with James, she had come to love the young boy. Yet even if she hadn't taken to the child, she knew that to lose his son would destroy Jimmy. Even if eventually they had children of their own, Rebecca knew no child she gave him would ever replace his first-born son. She knew that and understood it. Glancing at Jimmy, she saw the anxiety mirrored in his eyes, belying his outwardly calm exterior, and her heart went out to him. Reaching out, she took hold of his hand, and Jimmy, his attention focused on his son and the red-haired woman approaching the small figure, clung onto Rebecca's hand like a drowning man.

'Hello, darling. Aren't you going to say hello to your mummy?'

James looked up, his small body jerking in surprise as he saw his mother bending over him.

'He . . . Hello, Mummy. I didn't see you. How are you, Mummy?'

Heather threw her head back and laughed gaily. 'My! How formal you are, son. Anyone would think I was a stranger. Don't I get a kiss from my favourite little boy?'

James's eyes darted anxiously towards the park bench, his small body relaxing somewhat as he saw

Jimmy and Rebecca were still there. For a moment he had been afraid they had left him. His lips trembling slightly, James waved towards the bench, and was reassured when both Jimmy and Rebecca waved back. More importantly, they showed no sign of leaving.

Heather's sharp eyes noted James's relief and she felt a surge of anger. This wasn't what she had expected. She had thought James would be all over her the moment she appeared. Keeping a smile pasted to her lips, she bent down and scooped the confused child up into her arms.

'How about we go for a walk, James, eh? Just the two of us. Then you can tell me all your news, and . . .' Heather stumbled as the child began to struggle in her arms.

'Don't, Mummy, don't. I can't go with you, not without Dad. Please, Mummy . . . You're hurting me, Mummy. Let me go, Mummy. I want my dad . . . Dad . . . Dad . . . !' His plaintive wail split the air.

In that instant, Jimmy was off the bench and striding towards the struggling figures. 'I'll have my son back, if you don't mind, Heather. You seem to be frightening him.' Reaching out, Jimmy took hold of James's arm, but Heather clung on grimly.

'Don't be stupid, woman,' Jimmy hissed beneath his breath. 'Don't you see you've lost. If you've any real feelings for the boy, then let him go, or lose him for ever.'

Heather glared into the handsome face, her eyes blazing. Then she heard the child's quiet sobs and her arms loosened their hold on her son. The moment she relinquished her grip, James flew into Jimmy's arms, his small frame hanging onto the broad figure as if his life depended on it. And the feel of his son's arms gripping him so fiercely washed away any lingering doubt Jimmy might have had. An overwhelming surge of relief flooded Jimmy's body, causing him a momentary weakness in his limbs. His son loved him, truly loved him and wanted to be with him. He need never worry about Heather again.

'You'd better go, Heather. Your presence is upsetting the child.'

Heather drew back, a look of defeat showing in her eyes, then she shrugged. 'All right, Jimmy, you win. You can't say I didn't try, but then, I was never one to give in easily, was I?'

Jimmy looked hard into the face of the woman he had once loved with a young man's passion and smiled ruefully. 'No, you never were, Heather. But you always knew when to call it a day too; and that day is here.'

'Can't I at least kiss my son goodbye?'

Jimmy nipped at his bottom lip. Then, gently pulling James's arms loose from his neck, he smiled into the tremulous face and said, 'Your mummy's going now, James. Give her a kiss goodbye, there's a good boy.'

James peeped at the beautiful woman who was his mother, his small lips quivering, his young mind torn between both parents. Then he lifted his face to Heather and, his voice tinged with nervous anxiety, he said, 'Bye, Mummy. Will you come and see me at Dad's house?'

Kissing the smooth cheek, Heather stepped back. 'I'll try, James, but I can't promise. Mummy has to go away again, but you be a good boy for your dad, and I'll see you when I can. Goodbye, love.'

Snuggling against Jimmy's chest, James smiled shyly. 'Bye, Mummy. I'll see you soon.'

With one last look into the green eyes, Jimmy nodded curtly and strode away.

If he had waited another moment, Jimmy would have seen those same eyes suddenly fill with tears. Heather watched the trio leave the park and swallowed hard over the lump that had formed in her throat. For the first time in her life she was experiencing real emotions. Never in her wildest dreams had she imagined she would feel the loss of her only child so acutely, but as she watched her son walking out of her life for good, the welling in her eyes intensified.

'Miss Mills. Good afternoon, how nice to meet you like this.'

Shaken out of her reverie, Heather spun around to face the plump, eager-faced man. Immediately a smile attached itself to her full lips.

'Mr Cooksly, how lovely to see you. Are you by yourself?'

Jeremy Cooksly, the manager of the bank where Heather had an account, smiled broadly. 'Alas, madam, I am always by myself. And you?' he added hopefully.

Heather gave a tinkling laugh. 'It seems we find ourselves in a similar position, sir. I wonder . . . Would you be so kind as to escort me to the high street? There are so many undesirables roaming the streets, a woman doesn't feel safe without a man by her side.'

'Of course, of course, Miss Mills. I'd be delighted.' The man's face lit up in delight, as he extended his arm. Heather put her arm through his. It seemed she had found another mug; he wasn't much, but he would do for now.

As she left the park, she glanced over her shoulder for one last look at her son, and once again felt her throat tighten and tears prick the back of her eyes. It came as a shock to Heather to discover, too late, that she really loved her son, inasmuch as she was capable of loving anyone. Blinking rapidly, she sent a silent message after her child.

Goodbye, darling. Have a long and happy life. I was never a good mother, but I did love you. In my own way, I did love you.

Then she tightened her hold on the man's arm and walked out of her son's life for ever.

'I'll get it, Bessie,' Rebecca called out as she went to answer the door.

'Hello, Becks. Long time, no see.'

Rebecca gaped in amazement at the figure standing on the doorstep, then quickly stepped out into the street.

'What the hell are you doing here?' she hissed angrily. 'If Jimmy sees you, there'll be hell to pay.'

469

Phil's eyes flickered, his shoulders going up in that same old characteristic shrug.

'I know, Becks, I know. And I don't blame him, but I had to see you before I left.'

'Left! What are you talking about . . . ? Oh, I see. You're in trouble again. Well, you've used up every favour you ever had owing you, Phil. There's nothing left for you here, not any more. Now, go away before Jimmy hears you.'

'I'm going, Becks, but I'm not in trouble, in fact quite the opposite. Look!' With a flourish he threw his coat open to reveal a khaki uniform. 'I've joined up, Becks.'

Rebecca's mouth opened and closed with no sound being uttered.

Phil laughed. 'I thought you'd be surprised, but the way I see it, I'm always going to be in and out of trouble. I've got no willpower. But that last escapade . . . Well! It really shook me up, made me take a good look at myself, and I didn't like what I saw. I also know I'm never going to change, so I thought the best thing to do was to put temptation out of harm's way. I was talking to a fellow in the pub a few weeks ago, and he said he was thinking of enlisting because he couldn't find any decent work, and as he said, at least he'd have a roof over his head and three square meals a day, plus a wage packet. And I thought, why not? It'd get me out of the East End. You never know, Becks.' He raised an eyebrow in derision. 'It might even make a man of me.'

Rebecca leant back against the door. 'Oh, Phil. You stupid sod. Talk about going from one extreme to another. You'll never survive army life, you've had it too soft.'

For an instant Phil's face fell. 'Cheers, Becks. It's always nice to get a bit of encouragement,' he said bleakly. 'Anyway, like I said, I just wanted to see you one last time. Give my love to Amy, won't you . . . And tell her . . . Well, tell her I love her, and I'm truly sorry about what happened. I'm glad Charlie came out of it all right, he'll be a good husband . . . Bye, Becks . . . Love you.'

He turned to go, and Rebecca, with a soft cry, threw her arms around his neck. 'Look after yourself, you daft beggar. And . . . and I love you too, so does Amy – not that you deserve it. Write to me, Phil . . . Promise.'

Phil grinned. ''Course I will. You never know, if there's a war, I might even come back a hero. Wouldn't that be a turn-up for the books. Me, Phil Bradford, a hero. Huh! You wouldn't have got me within ten miles of any recruitment office if I thought there might really be a war. All the gossip – the headlines in the papers – is just scaremongering, to sell more newspapers. There's been loads of talk about us going to war since last year, and nothing's come of it yet. Nah! I'll be back, just like a bad penny. See you, Becks.'

Rebecca watched until the tall figure had disappeared from view, then she quietly went back indoors, her expression thoughtful. Phil hadn't even mentioned what had happened to Richard and Maude. But then, why should he? That part of their lives was over and done with. And Phil, being Phil, had probably pushed

471

that deeply unpleasant affair to the back of his mind.

'Who was it, sweetheart?' Jimmy was crossing the hall with James perched high on his shoulders.

Rebecca looked lovingly into the rugged face of her husband and put her brother from her thoughts. He would be all right. Phil always landed on his feet, though the men in his regiment might find themselves a little short in their pockets come payday. A warm smile touched her lips.

'No one important, Jimmy. Just some man selling his wares. I told him I already had all I needed.'